MEGAN HART

Stranger

Spice

Spice

STRANGER

ISBN-13: 978-0-373-60527-9
ISBN-10:   0-373-60527-7

PLEASE RECYCLE
THIS PRODUCT IS RECYCLABLE

Recycling programs
for this product may
not exist in your area.

www.Spice-Books.com

Printed in U.S.A.

Stranger

Chapter 01

I was looking for a stranger.

The Fishtank wasn't my usual hangout, though I'd been inside it once or twice. Recently redecorated, it sought to compete with a bunch of brand-new bars and restaurants that had opened in downtown Harrisburg, but though the tropical theme and aquariums were pretty and the drinks cheap enough, the Fishtank was too far away from restaurant row to really compete. What it did have that the other, newer bars didn't, was the attached hotel. The Fishtank, "where you hook 'em," was sort of a joke with the young and single crowd of central Pennsylvania. Or at least with me, and I was young. And blessedly, purposefully, single.

Scanning the crowd, I wove my way through the closely set tables toward the bar. The Fishtank was filled, literally, with people I didn't know. One would be the perfect stranger, emphasis on perfect.

So far, I hadn't seen him, but there was still time. I took a seat at the bar. My black skirt rode up a little and my stockings, held up by a garter belt of wispy lace, slipped on the leather stool. The sensation whispered up my thighs, bare above the tops of my stockings. My panties, of even wispier lace, rubbed me as I shifted.

"Tröegs Pale Ale," I told the bartender, who passed me a bottle with a nod.

Compared to many of the women in the Fishtank, I was dressed conservatively. My black skirt was cut fashionably just above the knee, my blouse silky and formfitting, but in the sea of low-riding jeans and navel-baring T-shirts, spaghetti straps and hooker heels, I stood out. Just the way I wanted.

I sipped my beer and looked around. Who would it be? Who would take me upstairs tonight? How long would I have to wait?

Apparently, not long. The seat next to mine had been empty when I sat, but now a man took it. Unfortunately, it was the wrong man. A stranger, yes, but not the one I was waiting for. The guy had blond hair and a gap between his two front teeth. Cute, but definitely not what I wanted. Also unfortunately, he didn't seem to take a hint.

"No, thanks," I said when he offered to buy me a drink. "I'm waiting for my boyfriend."

"You're not waiting for your boyfriend." He said this with unshakable confidence. "You're just saying that. Let me buy you a drink."

"I have one already." I gave him points for persistence, but I wasn't here to go home with a frat boy who thought "not" jokes were the height of humor.

"Okay, I'll leave you alone." Pause. "NOT!"

He laughed, slapping a thigh. "C'mon. Let me buy you a drink."

"I–"

"Are you hitting on my date?"

Frat Boy and I turned, and both our jaws dropped. I'm pretty sure we each had different reasons. His was probably surprise at being wrong. Mine was in delight.

The man standing next to me had the dark hair and blue eyes I'd been looking for. The earring. The jeans, deliciously worn in all the right places and the white T-shirt with a leather jacket over it. I was seated on a high bar stool and he still towered over me. I guessed him to be at least four inches over six feet, if not more.

Very, very nice.

My stranger flicked his hand like he was brushing away Frat Boy. "G'wan, now. Go."

Frat Boy, to give him credit, didn't try to make excuses. He just grinned and got off the stool. "Sorry, man. You can't blame me for trying, can you?"

My stranger turned to look at me, and his blue-eyed gaze roamed over my every inch before he answered. "No." He sounded considering. "I don't guess I can."

My stranger took the vacated seat. He held out the hand not gripping the glass of dark beer. "Hi. I'm Sam. Don't say *Sam I am,* or I'll toss you back to that doofus."

Sam. The name suited him. Before he gave it I might've imagined him as anyone, but once he did I could think of him as nobody else.

"Grace." I shook his proffered hand. "Nice to meet you."

"What are you drinking, Grace?"

I lifted my bottle. "Tröegs Pale Ale."

"How is that?"

I sipped. "Pale."

Sam held up his glass. "I've got Guinness. It's not pale. Let me buy you one."

"I haven't finished the one I have," I said, but with the smile I hadn't given Frat Boy.

Sam leaned in. "C'mon, Grace. It'll put hair on your chest."

"Uh-huh. Do I look like I want hair on my chest?"

Sam blatantly eyed the front of my blouse. "Without seeing the chest in question, I'm afraid I can't say."

I laughed. "Riiiight. Try again."

Sam gestured to the bartender and asked for two more bottles of the pale ale. "For when you're done with that one."

I didn't take the second bottle. "I can't, really. I'm on call."

"Are you a doctor?" Sam tipped back the last of his beer from his glass and pulled a bottle toward him.

"No."

He paused, waiting for me to say more, but I didn't. He drank, swallowed. He gave the sort of manly grunt and lip-smack guys make when they drink beer from bottles and are trying to impress women. I watched him without speaking and sipped from my own bottle, wondering how he meant to do this. I really hoped he'd make it convincing enough for me to go upstairs with him.

"So. You're not here to drink, then?" Sam eyed me, then turned on his stool so our knees touched.

I smiled at the touch of challenge in his tone. "Not really. No."

"So…" He paused, as if thinking. He was very good. "So what you're saying is, let's say a guy, oh, bought you a drink."

"Okay."

"Before he knew you weren't here to drink."

I smiled again, holding back a laugh. "Sure. Let's say that."

Sam swiveled on his stool to fix me with an intense gaze. "Would he already have fucked up too bad, or would you give him a chance to make it up to you?"

I pushed the bottle he'd bought me toward him. "I guess that would depend."

Sam's slow grin was a heat-seeking missile sent straight between my thighs. "On what?"

"On if he was cute or not."

Slowly he turned to show off his profile, then to the other side until he finally looked at me head-on. "How's this?"

I looked him over. His hair, the color of expensive black licorice and spiked on the crown, feathered a bit over his ears and against the back of his neck. His jeans had rubbed to white in interesting places. He wore black, scuffed boots I hadn't noticed before. I looked back up to his face and the quirking mouth, the nose saved from being too sharp only by the way the rest of his features came together. He had brows like dark wings, arched high over the center of his eyes and tapering to nothing at the outside corners.

"Yes." I leaned closer. "You're cute enough."

Sam rapped the top of the bar with his knuckles and *wahooed*. The noise turned heads, but he didn't notice. Or he pretended not to. "Damn. My mama was right. I am purty."

He wasn't, really. Attractive, but not pretty. Still, I couldn't help laughing. He wasn't what I'd been expecting, but…wasn't that the point of meeting a stranger?

He didn't waste any time.

"You're very pretty," Sam, beer finished in record time, leaned to murmur in the vicinity of my ear.

His lips tickled the sensitive skin of my neck just below my lobe. Already primed by the fantasy, my body reacted at once. My nipples pushed against the lace of my bra and outlined themselves in the silk of my shirt. My clit pulsed, and I squeezed my thighs together.

I leaned close to him, too. He smelled a little like beer, a little like soap. A whole lot like yum. I wanted to lick him. "Thanks."

We each sat back on our stools. Smiling. I crossed my legs and watched his gaze follow the hem of my skirt as it rose to give him a glimpse of bare thigh. His eyes widened in satisfactory appreciation. His tongue slid along his bottom lip, leaving it glistening.

He looked into my eyes. "I don't suppose you're the type of girl to go upstairs with a guy she just met, even if he is cute as all hell?"

"Actually," I told him, matching his low, breathy tone, "I think I might be."

Sam paid the bill and left a tip big enough to make the bartender grin. Then he took my hand to help me down from the stool, holding me steady when my foot came down wrong as though he'd known all along I'd stumble. Even in four-inch heels I had to tilt my head way back to look into his face.

"Thank you," I said.

"What can I say?" Sam replied. "I'm a gentleman."

He stood head and shoulders over most of the crowd, which had grown considerably since I came in, and he led me without faltering through the maze of tables and bodies toward the door to the lobby.

Nobody could have known we'd just met. That we were strangers. I was going upstairs to a stranger's room. Nobody could know that, but I did, and my heart thumped hard and harder the closer we got to the elevator.

The walls inside reflected us both, our faces blurred by the dim lighting and the abstract pattern of gold in the mirrors. His T-shirt had rucked up out of his jeans. I couldn't look away from his belt buckle or the hint of bare skin just above it. When I looked up again to meet his gaze in the mirror, Sam's smile had shifted.

I saw him put his hand on the back of my neck before I felt his touch. The mirror had created that distance, that second of delay. Like watching a movie or TV, but somehow that small disconnect made this seem all the more real.

At the door to his room Sam took his hand away from the back of my neck to dig in his pockets for the key card. He tried both front pockets and came up with nothing but a few coins. He fumbled. His nervousness charmed me even as it prompted my own. He found the key inside his wallet, tucked into a back pocket.

I liked his laugh when he pulled it out and fit it into the door. The lock blinked red, and he muttered a curse I deciphered by tone, not by word. He tried again, his hands so big they engulfed the slim plastic card. I couldn't stop staring at his hands.

"Fuck," Sam said clearly, and handed me the card. "I can't get the door open."

I reached for the card. Our hands touched. Then somehow his hand had encircled my wrist and my back pressed against the still-closed door. Sam pressed against my front. His mouth found mine already open for him. His hand discovered my leg already cocked to fit his grasp just behind my knee. He fit between my legs like the key ought to have fit in the lock, without hesitation, opening my door. His fingers slid higher beneath my skirt above the edge of my stockings and found bare skin.

He hissed into my open mouth and his fingers tightened on my wrist. He lifted an arm above my head, pinning me with his hands and body and mouth to the door. There in the hall he kissed me for the first time, and there was nothing slow or easy about it. Nothing soft or hesitant.

Sam stroked my tongue with his. His belt buckle pushed my belly through my silky shirt. Lower, his cock nudged me, too, through the barrier of his jeans. He let go of my wrist.

"Unlock the door." He stopped the kiss just long enough to speak into my mouth.

His hand hit the door handle as I rammed the key, without looking, into the lock. Behind me the door flew open with the pressure of our bodies, but neither of us stumbled. Sam was holding me too tightly for that.

He moved me, mouth still glued to mine, two steps into the room and kicked the door shut behind us. The slam of it echoed between my legs. Sam, breathing hard, pulled away to look into my eyes.

"This is what you want?"

I found the voice to rasp, "Yes."

He nodded, just once, and took my mouth again. His kiss might have bruised me, had he not pulled back just enough to keep it from hurting. Without the door holding me up, I had to rely on Sam's arms around me. One slid behind my shoulders. The other left the secret treasure of my thigh to go around my lower back. He pulled me along with him even as he step-by-stepped me back toward the bed. It hit the back of my legs. He broke the kiss again.

"Hold on a second." Sam reached around me to tug down the comforter, tossing it unceremoniously into a pile on the floor.

He grinned at me. His cheeks looked a bit flushed, his eyes a trifle sleepy-lidded. He reached for me again, and I stepped again into his arms. Mine went around his neck. His went around my waist.

We made it to the bed in a tangle of limbs and laughter. Sam was as long lying down as he was standing, but on the bed I could move up to kiss him without having to tilt my head so far. I found his throat, the jut of his Adam's apple. His skin tasted of salt. I rubbed the first poking bristles of his beard with my lips.

My skirt had ridden up, helped by Sam's hands. He pushed the material higher. One large hand cupped my thigh. The edge of his fingers brushed my panties, and my breath caught.

I looked up to see him looking down with an expression of mingled amusement and something else I couldn't quite decipher. I took my mouth from his skin and sat up a little, pushing back but not pulling away.

"What?"

His hand on my thigh shifted higher while his other went to prop his head. Stretched out that way, his clothes askew and our limbs tangled, he looked enviably comfortable in his own skin. Men often did. Sometimes they had to put it on, that confidence, the way they put on cologne. Sam's seemed more innate, an awareness of himself as much a part of him as the color of his eyes or those long, long legs.

He shook his head. "Nothing."

"It can't be nothing," I said. "You're looking at me funny."

"Am I?" He sat up a little but didn't take his hand from my thigh. He crossed his eyes and stuck out his tongue. "Was it like this?"

I burst into laugher. "Not quite."

"Ah, good." Sam nodded and leaned to catch my mouth in another kiss, speaking without taking his lips from mine. "That would have been embarrassing."

Then he laid me back onto that big, soft bed and proceeded to kiss me breathless. His hand stayed on my thigh, sometimes slipping down closer to my knee and moving up again, but though his fingers occasionally brushed the lace of my panties, he never actually touched me there. He didn't lie on top of me, either, squooshing, but kept his weight to the side. Nothing was going quite as I'd expected…but wasn't that what I wanted? To be surprised?

He kissed me fast. He kissed me slow. He nibbled and nuzzled and licked, and all the while his hand stayed in its maddening position so close to where I wanted it, but never quite making it there.

"Sam," I whispered finally, hoarsely, unable to take it any longer.

He paused in kissing me to look into my eyes. "Yes, Grace?"

"You're killing me."

He smiled. "Am I?"

I nodded and slid a hand between us to tug on his belt buckle. "You are."

His hand inched higher. "Can I make it up to you?"

I unhooked the buckle. "I think so. Maybe."

He turned his hand as he moved it. When he touched me, finally, the heel of his palm pressed flat to my cunt, and my mouth parted in a gasp I didn't bother to try to keep silent.

"How'm I doing so far?" he asked, his head bent so his mouth brushed my cheek.

"Good. Very…good." Speaking took the effort of concentration I found difficult with his hand on me. So far he'd done no more than press against me. Hadn't even rubbed. But primed by the long, slow minutes of kissing and the hours of mental foreplay I'd gone through already, my body was more than ready for him.

His lips slipped down my neck to center over the pulse in my throat. Sam sucked, gently, then took the skin between his teeth. The bite didn't hurt, but it did send sensation ripping through me. I arched beneath him. My hands found the back of his head, the smooth silk of his hair, and I wound my fingers in it. Pressing him to me, keeping his mouth there while he sucked my skin. I would bruise. I couldn't, just then, care.

"I like the way you say my name," he murmured. His tongue slid along the place where he'd left his mark. "Say it again."

"Sam." I breathed it.

I heard the smile in his voice when he spoke again. "I am."

Then we were laughing again, until he took his hand from between my legs and used it to tug open the buttons on my blouse, one at a time. Then I stopped laughing, too breathless to do more than sigh. He eased open my shirt. He pushed himself up on one elbow and folded back the material to show my bra. His fingers traced the lacy edges over the tops of my breasts.

My nipples had gone tight, hard, aching. When Sam's thumb passed over one, I sucked in a breath. I watched his face as he looked down at me. When he bent to kiss my exposed skin, I bit my lower lip. My body moved beneath him.

Sam sat up. He shrugged out of his leather jacket and pulled his shirt off over his head, leaving his hair standing up all over the place. His body was as long and lean as his legs. He knelt beside me, one hand rubbing his chest almost absently. His other hand toyed with the open belt buckle, then the button beneath. He undid it, but left the zipper alone.

I watched him, enjoying the show. "Are you going to take those off?"

Sam nodded, solemn. "Absolutely."

I lifted an eyebrow. "Tonight?"

Sam laughed. "Yes."

I slid one stocking-clad foot up over his thigh and rubbed the front of his jeans. "Are you shy?"

Sam's hips pushed forward at the touch of my foot, and his mouth parted. His hand paused in its rubbing, fingers going flat over his heart. "Maybe. A little."

Holy hell, that was hot. I didn't believe him, really. He hadn't acted shy anytime tonight. "Want me to go first?"

Sam's grin melted me. "Okay."

I got off the bed to make it easier for myself. Without my shoes on, I was face-to-chest with him—not a bad view at all. Sam's bare chest was smooth and muscled, with a hint of six-pack abs but nothing overdefined. I took a couple steps back. My shirt hung open, courtesy of his unbuttoning. I took my time sliding the fabric from one arm, then the other. I tossed the shirt onto the chair. Sam's eyes didn't even follow it. They stayed on me.

I'd chosen my skirt for the ease of getting it off, but though it would have taken me but a second to unhook and unzip it, I took much longer than that. Never taking my eyes from his, I slipped open the button at my hip. A second later I unzipped, inch by slow inch. Then I slid the fabric over my hips and let the skirt fall to the floor in a puddle at my feet. I stepped out of it and hooked it out of the way with my foot. I stood before Sam in my white lace bra and matching panties, in the wispy garter belt and nude, seamed stockings.

The look on his face had made every second worth it.

I would never win any beauty contests. Too many bulges in places I wanted to be flat, too little curve in places I wanted to be round. I also knew that really didn't matter. Not really, not to most men.

Sam didn't appear to have any shields on his expression. His pupils had gone large and dark, nearly swallowing the green-blue. His lips glistened from where he'd swiped his tongue. "…Wow."

The compliment was all the nicer because it sounded so sincere. "Thank you."

He didn't move. One hand still pressed over his heart, the other hooked into the front of his jeans. He looked at me, his mouth pulling up on one side. "My turn, huh?"

"Your turn, Sam."

"God," Sam said. "I love the way that sounds."

"Sam," I whispered, stepping toward him. "Sam, Sam, Sam."

I'd heard of kinkier fetishes, but he said he liked it, and…hell, I liked it, too. There was something sweet and sexy about the name. About him. The way each time the word purred from my tongue his smile twitched broader.

I reached for the front of his jeans. The metal button and zipper were cool compared to the heat coming through the denim. My heart skipped a little when my fingers traced the outline of his erection. He groaned. I wanted to get on my knees at that sound, but I didn't.

I looked up at him, instead. Way, way up. I tugged open the button. Click-clicked down the zipper. Always watching his face, not his crotch. Sam hadn't moved his hand from his chest, though his fingers tightened a bit on his skin. The pulse leaped in his throat, and a muscle in his cheek twitched. His smile had thinned. He reached to push the hair off my face.

I hooked my fingers in the denim at his hips and pushed. It didn't snag. He'd worn a belt for more than just fashion, and the jeans were loose enough I had no trouble sliding them down. He moved a little, helping me. Our gazes never left each other's as I bent to push his jeans all the way to his ankles and waited while he lifted one foot, then the other, to pull them off. I stood then, swiftly, running my hands along his endlessly long legs as I did.

I couldn't look at his crotch.

I didn't know why I had suddenly become shy. I wasn't a stranger to bulging boxers. Something in his face stopped me.

There is always a moment when the final barrier has to come down.

"Sam?"

He nodded. He stopped holding his heart and reached for me, instead. He bent, I stretched, and we met somehow in the middle with our mouths.

This time he covered me completely when he laid me on the bed, but I didn't feel crushed. I felt…embraced. Enfolded. There was so much of Sam he surrounded me.

I should've panicked, maybe. Felt trapped. But too busy with his mouth and his hands helping me off with my underwear, too busy reaching to free him from the cotton boxers, I didn't have time. I couldn't think of anything but the silky heat of his cock in my hands when at last I found it.

Sam made a small, helpless noise when I touched him there. I slid my hand along his erection. Sam's prick, like the rest of him, was long. His fingers closed over mine. There was no room to stroke him, not with him on top of me that way.

He buried his face in my neck. The rise and fall of his breath pushed our bodies together. The seconds ticked out between us, only a few. He moved down my body to kiss my breasts. His tongue stroked my skin and teased my nipples. He moved lower, over my ribs and the curve of my belly. He mouthed my hip, then down a little farther to my thigh.

I let the pleasure sweep over me, but at the odd motion of his head I had to look down. "What are you doing?"

"Writing my name," he said without apology, and demonstrated with his tongue on my skin. "S-A-M-S-T—"

It tickled, and I squirmed. He grinned up at me briefly before dipping his head lower. His breath gusted over my trimmed pubic curls, and I tensed. I always did at that moment, waiting for the first touch of tongue on sensitive flesh.

Sam, perhaps reading the tension of my muscles as distaste, moved back up my body. He looked up past my face, stretched and hooked open the nightstand drawer with a finger. The movement brought his chest within licking distance, and I didn't pass up my opportunity. He shivered. He pulled back to me and held open his hand.

"You pick," he said.

I looked over the selection of condoms in his hand, thinking how sweet it was not to need to wonder if there was going to be an issue about using protection. "Wow. Ribbed for my pleasure, extra-lubricated…glow in the dark?" I laughed at the last one.

He did, too, and tossed it to the floor. He held up one of the ribbed condoms. "This one, then?"

"Looks good to me."

He handed me the package, warm from his palm. Sam rolled onto his back, arms behind his head on the pillow. No more shyness, not for either of us. No point in it now.

His body was put together like someone had taken extra care to make sure everything fit just right. Legs and thighs and belly, hips and ribs and neck, shoulders, arms and hands. Each of Sam's pieces fit. Clothed he'd looked a little gangly, but naked he was pretty near perfect.

He watched me looking, and his mouth tilted again. I couldn't quite get a handle on Sam's smile. It wasn't a smirk, or smug. It was almost a little bemused.

Naked, I knelt next to his thigh. I stroked his erection, and he pushed his hips upward when I did. He untucked a hand from beneath his head and slipped it between my legs. His thumb pressed my clit, and it was my turn to shiver.

I stroked. He rubbed. In a minute we were both panting. He moved a finger along my folds. I knew he felt how wet I was. How ready. He slid a finger inside me and my grip on him faltered as I gasped.

"Grace," Sam whispered, voice gone guttural and low. "I hope you're ready, because I can't wait much longer."

Neither could I. "I'm ready." I paused, then added, "Sam."

I had no trouble figuring out what his smile meant that time. I shifted on his hand so he could slide free. I put the condom on him, and a moment after that, myself. His hands gripped my hips. I leaned forward, my hands on his shoulders.

We looked into each other's eyes.

He moved me, at first, with slow, steady strokes. We found our rhythm almost at once. My clit rubbed him with every thrust, the pressure tantalizing but not quite enough. Sam solved that problem in another minute when he put his thumb against me again.

I didn't care what came from my mouth just then. A string of words that made no sense, maybe. Something halfway between a prayer and a curse. But one thing I do know I said was his name.

Orgasms are like waves, no two alike. They ebb, flow, rise and crest. And crash. Mine crashed over me so fast it took me by surprise. Hard, almost sharp, the pleasure peaked as I moved on Sam's cock. His thumb ceased its pressure, easing off just when I needed it to, but in the next moment he'd started doing this little jiggling motion that sent me up and up again. The second climax followed the first without time for me to catch my breath, but when it was over, that was it. Warmth rippled through me and languor crept along my limbs. I put my hand over Sam's to keep him from moving it.

I didn't know how close he was, but when I opened my eyes, his were closed. His hands gripped my hips again. His thrusts got harder. Sweat had broken out along his hairline. I wanted to lick it, and the sudden stab of fresh desire surprised me as much as the intensity of my orgasm had.

"Sam," I whispered. I watched his face contort. "Sam…"

And he came. His face twisted and his fingers clutched, giving me more bruises. He arched and fell back onto the pillow, and let out one last, long and heavy breath.

He opened his eyes a moment later and smiled at me. His hand came up to twine in my hair. He tugged it, pulling me close to kiss my mouth tenderly. His pupils were still wide and dark, with nothing to reflect me.

We disengaged and took care of the things that needed to be done, but I hadn't yet managed to rouse myself enough to climb out of bed and go to the bathroom when the distinctive jangle of my phone came from my purse.

"Is that 'Smoke on the Water'?" Sam lifted his head to look at me.

"Yes." I ignored it, too sated to think about getting up for a phone call, even though I knew I should.

Sam's broad and hearty laugh shook the bed, and I looked over at him. "Awesome." He made rock horns with his fingers.

I had to laugh, too. He seemed younger with postsex sleepiness lodged in his eyes and his hair all rumpled. Not that it mattered.

He yawned and of course, unable to help myself, so did I. He kissed my bare shoulder and rolled onto his back again, hands tucked under the pillow, to stare at the ceiling.

"I knew that fortune cookie was right," he said without looking at me. "It said you will meet someone new."

"My last fortune cookie told me I was going to find money," I said. "So far, nothing."

Sam turned his gaze to me, though his head stayed still. "You've got time. I don't think there's a statute of limitations on fortunes."

I rolled my eyes. "I wish it would hurry up, though. I could use some money."

Sam's expression shifted, subtly, as we stared at each other. My phone rang again, this time with the less awesome ring tone that meant I had a message. I couldn't ignore that, since it was probably from my answering service. Someone must've died.

"I have to get that," I said without moving.

"Okay." Sam smiled.

I leaned over to kiss him quickly, on the cheek. I felt his

gaze on me as I gathered my fallen clothes and my purse and went to the bathroom. I punched in the number of the answering service as I slipped into my panties and juggled the phone while I hooked my bra. The garter belt and stockings I tucked into my bag, not wanting to bother with them when I was going home.

I took care of the call and finished dressing, then patted some cold water on my face. Sam's bathroom looked used, a rumpled towel on the floor by the toilet and a small toiletries bag on the sink. He used an electric razor and favored a different toothpaste than I did, but this peek into his private life seemed intrusive and personal and I stopped looking. I took an extra few minutes to freshen my makeup and tie back my hair.

When I came out of the bathroom, Sam had pulled his boxers back on. The remote lay next to him on the bed, but he hadn't turned on the television. He sat up when I came out.

"Hey," he said.

My phone beeped again with another message. Someone had called while I was on the phone. I pulled it from my purse but didn't flip it open. "It's been great, but I have to go."

He got up, towering over me even after I put on my heels. "I'll walk you to your car."

I shook my head. "No. You don't have to. I'm fine."

"But I really should."

I looked up at him. "Sam, it's okay."

We smiled at each other. He walked me to the door, where he bent to kiss me far more awkwardly than he had before.

"Good night," I said on the other side of the door. "Thank you."

He blinked and didn't smile. "You're...welcome?"

So cute.

I reached up to pat his cheek. "It was great."

Sam blinked again, those dark brows knitting. "Okay."

I waved and moved toward the elevator. He closed the door behind me, and I heard the blare of the television almost at once.

At my car I remembered to check my voice mail. Sitting behind the wheel, buckling my belt, I punched in my password and listened, expecting to hear my sister's voice. Maybe my best friend Mo's.

"Yeah, hi," said a voice I didn't recognize. "This is Jack. I'm calling for, um...Miss Underfire. We were supposed to meet tonight?"

He sounded uncertain; I felt suddenly sick. Miss Underfire was the name I used with the agency, the name I used to keep everything discreet.

"But I'm here at the Fishtank, and...well...you're not. Um...call me back if you want to reschedule."

I listened to a very long pause while I waited for the call to disconnect, but it didn't.

"Anyway, I'm sorry," said Jack. "Something got messed up, I guess."

A click, and he was gone, and the pseudofeminine robotic voice-mail message was instructing me how to delete the message.

I closed my phone and put it carefully into my purse. I gripped the steering wheel tight, with both hands. I waited to scream, or laugh, or cry, but in the end I only turned the key in the ignition and drove home.

I'd wanted to sleep with a stranger, and that's exactly what I'd done.

Chapter 02

"Earth to Grace." Jared snapped his fingers in front of my face. "Gloves?"

I blinked and shook my head a little, laughing off my lack of concentration. Jared Shanholtz, my intern, held up the box of latex gloves that had seen better days. "Sorry. They're in the laundry room, I think. On the rack of shelves by the wall."

He tossed the battered cardboard box into the trash. He nodded toward the body on the table in front of us. "Need me to bring anything else?"

I looked over Mr. Dennison's still form. "No. I think he's just about done."

I leaned forward to brush the hair back from his forehead. His skin, cool under my fingers, had a faint dusting of powder. It didn't quite match his natural skin tone. "On second thought, grab me the box of foundation, okay? I want to redo this."

Jared nodded and said nothing, though I'd already spent an hour on Mr. Dennison. I stared down at him. He couldn't care if he looked like he was wearing makeup, but I did. Even if his family didn't care, I still did.

Pride didn't do diddly for my fingers, though, that kept fumbling with the small pots and brushes I used on the corpses. I'd nearly made a mess of the embalming, too, but turned it around by giving Jared the "opportunity" to do most of it himself while I supervised. Jared was the first intern I'd ever hired and though it was hard for me to give up control of what went on in my business to give him the chance to learn, I was glad he was there then. Thank God he was good. If he'd been a bumbling disaster, we'd have been screwed.

Screwed.

I turned away from Mr. Dennison's placid face. I had to take small sips of air to keep from bursting into a flurry of giggles I would've been hard-pressed to explain to Jared. The stifled laughter twisted in my gut and made it hurt. Coffee would help. Maybe.

Shit, nothing would help. I'd fucked a stranger the night before, but the wrong one. Not the stranger I'd paid to play with. Dammit, not only had I taken a huge personal risk, I'd wasted a hefty chunk of change, too.

"Grace?"

I turned, again caught up in my own thoughts. I took the box of miscellaneous pots and jars from Jared, and set them on the table. "Sorry. My mind's wandering."

"If you wanted me to take over," Jared offered with a gesture at Mr. Dennison, "I could. Give you a break."

I looked at the man on the table, and at Jared. "No, thanks."

"Want to talk about it?"

I looked up. Jared gave me a look that told me I hadn't been as nonchalant as I'd thought. But...huh? Talk? To Jared? "About what?"

"Whatever it is that's bothering you."

"Who says anything is?" I stroked my cosmetic sponge down Mr. Dennison's cheek.

Jared didn't say anything until I looked up at him. "I've been here for six months, Grace. I can tell."

I stopped what I was doing to give him my full attention. "Do you want to take over with this? I mean, if you really want me to give you something to do, Jared, I can tell you the hearse needs to be washed, and I'm sure Shelly could use a hand with vacuuming the chapel."

Jared liked washing the hearse. I hated it. It worked out perfectly, and if he thought I was being nice by letting him do that instead of the hundred other tasks of running the funeral home, I was happy to let him think so.

He grinned, taking a bit of the wind out of my sails. "Sure, boss. If that's what you want. I just thought I'd offer."

He tipped me a salute. I smiled. "You could make sure there's some fresh coffee, too. You know Shelly doesn't have a clue how to brew it."

He nodded. "Late night, huh?"

"The usual." I shrugged.

"You know, Grace, I'd be happy to take more call time."

I concentrated on putting away my pots and jars and washing my hands as I answered. "I know. I appreciate it."

"Just thought I'd offer," Jared repeated, and left.

Quick and eager to learn, Jared was excellent with the clients and unafraid to take on new tasks. I was seriously considering offering him a position after he graduated. The problem was, though Frawley and Sons had grown every year since I'd taken over from my dad three years before, I still couldn't afford to hire another full-time funeral director. Not if I wanted to eat, anyway. I could make him take more call, but I'd have to pay him more and trust him to provide my clients with the same level of service I could give them myself.

Nobody could give them the same level of service I could. After all, I had very big shoes to fill. My dad and his brother, Chuck, both retired now, had taken over the business from their father. Frawley and Sons had been the only funeral home in Annville for fifty years. People could and did go to funeral homes in the adjoining towns, but that didn't mean I couldn't keep trying to be the best.

I busied myself with cleaning up the supplies I'd used on Mr. Dennison, glad for the chance to work in silence. I couldn't stop thinking about the stranger. Sam. The hair, the eyes, the smile. Those long damn legs. The way he'd gotten harder when I said his name. I hadn't even asked for his number.

Hell. He hadn't asked for mine, either. I don't blush easily, but I blushed just then, thinking what he must have thought. No wonder he'd looked so strange when I thanked him. He hadn't known it was an accident.

The first time I'd paid for sex had been an accident, too, though the date was on purpose. For years my parents had supported a local preschool's dinner-dance fund-raiser, but since taking over Frawley and Sons, I'd also taken on the social obligations that went along with the position.

With no boyfriend in the picture and no desire to get one, I'd done what any organized woman would do. I'd hired a man to take me.

I could have gone alone. I wasn't afraid of being without a man. Hell, the last boyfriend I'd had was in college and when that relationship ended, I'd been more relieved than upset. But dinner and dancing at the country club was always more fun with someone to dance with. It had been a no-brainer. I hired people to service my car and pull my weeds. Paying someone to pull back my chair and bring me drinks didn't seem any different. In fact, paying someone to treat me like a goddess without having to deal with any corresponding male-ego crap had seemed like the best idea I'd ever had.

It was ridiculously easy to find a place where men could hire female "companions," but it had taken a little bit of searching to find an agency offering similar services to women. As director of the funeral home I had to be discreet, but I also had a lot of contacts. People consumed by grief didn't always censor their commentary. I'd learned about a lot of crazy things while offering the tissue box to mourners, most of which was useless. Places to buy drugs, who was sleeping with whom, where Mr. Jones had gone to buy the garter belt and stockings he'd been wearing when he died. The mourning widow, Mrs. Andrews, had slipped me a card just before launching into full-on mourning-widow mode.

Mrs. Smith's Services for Ladies. Massage, conversation and other. I'd called the number on the card, made the arrangements and paid in advance. Mark had shown up at my door on time, perfectly groomed and handsome in a tuxedo that looked as if it had been cut to fit every line of his perfect, gorgeous body. It had been a little heady, being on his arm and entering the room filled mostly with people I'd known my entire life. Heads had turned and gossip had started, but the good kind.

It was, hands down, the best date I'd ever had. Mark was considerate, charming, a good conversationalist. If his responses were a wee bit slick and practiced sounding, that was all right, because the intensity of his deep blue gaze more than made up for any hint of role playing. I hadn't, even then, been fooled into thinking the promises in Mark's eyes were real. I didn't believe it from men who tried to pick me up in bars or the grocery store, much less from a man whose time and interest I'd used a credit card to secure.

Yet I couldn't help being flattered by the way his hand never strayed far from my shoulder, the small of my back, my elbow. By the end of the night, I had a pretty good idea what the "other" listed on the card meant. For safety reasons, and upon the advice of the anonymous Mrs. Smith, I'd met Mark in the parking lot of a nearby strip mall, then driven to the country club together in my car. On the way back to Mark's car the tension had been as thick as honey and just as sweet.

"The night doesn't have to be over," he'd said when I pulled up next to his road-worn Saturn. "Not if you don't want it to be."

We'd gone to a shabby motel in the next town. My college boyfriend, Ben, had been good looking but nothing like Mark, who was truly so handsome it sort of made my eyes hurt to look at him for too long. My hands had been shaking when I undid the bow tie at his throat and the buttons on his shirt. He hadn't rushed me. I'd unwrapped him inch by inch, revealing a body as delicious unclothed as it had been in the tux. I'd touched him all over, from the tight hard muscles of his belly to the thick branch of his cock, which swelled nicely in my hand. At his low noise, I'd looked up, startled out of my mesmerization. His gaze had gone dark. He'd reached out to touch my hair, softly, his fingers tugging it out of its loose coil.

I'd paid him to act like he thought I was sexy. I'd hired Mark to treat me like a queen—and in doing so learned I deserved to be treated that way. That I was lovely, and sexy. That I could get a man hard with a cocked hip and a slide of tongue on lips. Money can buy a lot of things, but a hard cock doesn't care about a bank account. I might have paid him to spend time with me, but when it came right down to it, he'd wanted to fuck me just as much as I wanted him to.

It wasn't the best sex I'd ever had; I was too nervous and uncertain to be adventurous. But Mark had made it easy for me. He was an expert lover, using his hands and mouth until we both lay panting in the tangle of sheets.

It was a hundred-dollar orgasm, when it finally happened, and worth every cent.

He didn't stay. He shook my hand somewhat formally at the door, then lifted it to his mouth and kissed it, shooting me a grin that no longer had any hint of plastic about it. "Ask for me anytime," he murmured against my skin, his eyes never leaving mine.

Right then, I'd understood exactly why the price had been so high.

Mrs. Smith had perfected an expert matching system to suit her clients. In the three years I'd been using the service, I'd never had a bad date. Whether I wanted to go to a concert or a museum, or spend a night having orgasm after orgasm while tied up with a red velvet ribbon, Mrs. Smith provided it all.

Contrary to my girlfriends, who either bemoaned the lack of a boyfriend or bitched about the men they did have, I was the most fulfilled woman I knew. I never had to go anyplace alone unless I wanted to. I never had to worry about what the sex "meant" and if my lover cared about me, because it was already prenegotiated and prepaid. Hiring escorts had given me the freedom to explore parts of my sexuality I'd never known existed, and without risking my safety or emotions.

More importantly, for their sake as well as mine, my gentlemen friends were utterly discreet. My business was open to constant scrutiny. It had been hard enough not being the son of Frawley and Sons. The funeral-home business was still mostly male dominated, and though I'd spent my entire life in Annville and had been a part of the family business for just that long, there were still those who thought a woman couldn't do the job a man could. There was far more to the work than sending death announcements to the newspaper and embalming corpses; a good funeral director offered grief support and helped each and every family through what was often the most difficult time of their lives. I love my work. I'm good at it. I like helping people say goodbye to their loved ones and making the process as easy and bearable as possible. Even so, I never forget that people won't bring their loved ones to someone they don't trust, or whose morals they felt were questionable—and in a small town, morals are easily questioned.

"Grace?"

Again, I'd been caught in contemplation. I looked up to see Shelly Winber, my office manager. She looked apologetic, though she didn't need to be. I'd been off in la-la land. "Hmm?"

"Phone for you." She pointed upward. "Upstairs. It's your dad."

Obviously upstairs, since my ever-present cell phone hadn't done so much as peep from its place on my hip. "Great, thanks."

My dad called me at least once a day if he didn't stop in. For someone who was supposed to have retired, my dad sure didn't take much of a break. I took the call at my desk while I listened with one ear and made the appropriate "Mmm, hmms" and scrolled through the columns of my advertising budget.

"Grace, are you listening to me?"

"Yes, Dad."

He snorted. "What did I just say?"

I took a stab. "You told me to come over for dinner on Sunday and bring the ledger so you can help me balance the books."

Stone silence meant I'd messed up. "How do you expect to succeed if you don't listen?"

"Dad, I'm sorry, but I'm a little busy here going over some things." I held the phone next to my computer mouse and click-clicked. "Hear that?"

My dad huffed. "You spend too much time on the computer."

"I spend time on this computer doing work to help the business grow."

"We never had e-mail or a Web site, and we did just fine. The business is more than marketing, Grace. It's more than just numbers."

His intimation stung. "Then why are you always on my case about the budget?"

Aha. I'd caught him. I waited for him to answer, but what he said didn't make me happy.

"Running the funeral home is more than just a job. It's got to be your life."

I thought of the recitals and graduations and birthday parties my dad had missed over the years. "You think I don't know that?"

"I don't know. Do you?"

"I have to go, Dad. I'll see you at dinner on Sunday. Unless I have to work."

I hung up and sat back in my chair. I knew it was more than a job. Didn't I spend nearly all my time here? Giving it my best? Giving it my all? But try to tell my dad that. All he saw was the new gadgets and logo and the commercials on the radio and ads in the paper. What he didn't understand was that just because I had nobody to sacrifice but myself didn't make my efforts any less noble.

* * *

"You're looking sparkly today." My sister, Hannah, raised an eyebrow.

I flicked one of my chandelier earrings until the tiny bells chimed. They matched the Indian-style tunic top I'd bought from an online auction. The deep turquoise fabric and intricate beading could be described as sparkly. "Thanks—eBay."

"I don't mean the earrings. They're cute, though. The shirt's a little..." Hannah shrugged.

"What?" I looked down at it. The fabric was sheer, so I'd worn a tank top beneath to keep it from being too revealing. Paired with the simple pair of boot-cut black slacks, I hadn't thought the outfit was too outrageous, especially with the black fitted jacket overtop.

"Different," Hannah amended. "Cute, though."

I checked out Hannah's demure scoop-necked shirt and matching cardigan. She was missing only a strand of pearls and a hat with a veil to be the epitome of a 1950s matron. The outfit was better than the cartoon-character sweatshirt she'd been wearing the last time we had lunch, but not by much.

"I like this shirt." I hated the defensiveness that rose up, hardwired to the buttons my sister knew just how to push. "It's...sassy."

"It sure is." Hannah cut her salad into precise, astoundingly symmetrical bites. "I said it was cute, didn't I?"

"You did." She'd said "cute" the way some people would say "unfortunate."

"Anyway. That's not what I meant." Hannah never

spoke with her mouth full. She gave me a dissecting stare. "Did you have a…date? Last night?"

At the memory of Sam's hand between my legs a few days before, I couldn't hold back the smile. "Not last night, no."

Hannah shook her head. "Gracie…"

I held up a hand. "Don't."

"I'm your big sister. I'm allowed to give advice."

It was my turn to raise an eyebrow. "Um…is that in the handbook someone forgot to give me, or what?"

Hannah didn't laugh. "Seriously, Grace. When are we going to meet this guy? Mom and Dad don't believe he exists."

"Maybe Mom and Dad spend too much time worrying about my romantic life, Hannah."

The more I denied having a boyfriend, the more convinced my family seemed to be that I was hiding one away. I thought it was funny, most of the time. Today for some reason, I wasn't as amused.

I got up to refill my mug of coffee, hoping by the time I got back to the table my sister would have decided to abandon the topic. I should've known better. Hannah with a lecture was like a terrier with a rat. Probably the only thing holding her back from full-on rant mode was the fact we were in a public place.

"I just want to know what the secret is. That's all." Hannah fixed me with the glare that used to be able to yank any secret from me.

It was still pretty effective, but I had years of practice at resisting. "There's no secret. I've told you before, I'm not seeing anyone seriously."

"If it's serious enough for you to look like that," Hannah said with a sniff, "it should be serious enough to bring him to meet your family."

This veiled reference to sex so stunned me, I could only stare. My sister, older and prone to lectures as she might be, had never been free with advice on lovemaking. Other girls had gone to their big sisters for advice on boys and bras, but Hannah, seven years older, had never made our relationship comfortable enough to discuss sex. I wasn't about to start now.

"I don't know what you mean."

"I think you do." Hannah picked me apart with another look.

"No, really, Hannah." I grinned, defusing her the best way I knew how. "I don't."

Hannah's mouth thinned. "Fine. Whatever. Be like that. We're just all wondering, that's all."

I sighed and warmed my hands on my mug. "Wondering about what?"

Hannah shrugged and looked away. "Well. You always make an excuse for why you won't bring him around. We're just wondering if…"

"If what?" I demanded. It wasn't like Hannah to hold back on anything.

"If he's a…he," Hannah muttered. She stabbed her salad as if it had done her wrong.

Stunned again, I sat back in my chair. "Oh, for God's sake!"

Hannah's mouth set in a stubborn line. "Is he?"

"A man? You want to know if I'm dating a man? Instead

of what…a woman?" I wanted to laugh, not because this was funny, but because somehow laughter might make this less strange. "You have to be kidding me."

Hannah looked up, lower lip pushed out in the familiar way. "Mom and Dad won't say it, but I will."

In a moment of insanity I considered telling her everything. Which would be worse, admitting I paid for sex or that I dated women? Maybe paying women for sex would've been worse, and the thought of my sister's face if I told her that curved my mouth into a smile. I resisted, though. Hannah wouldn't find it as funny as I did.

If it had been anyone else asking the question, I really would have laughed, but because it was my sister I just shook my head. "Hannah. No. It's not a woman. I promise."

Hannah nodded stiffly. "Because, you know, you could tell me. I'd be okay with it."

I doubted that. Hannah had a pretty narrow worldview. There wasn't much room in it for sisters who liked girls or who hired dates. Not that it was any of her business.

"I just go out. Have a good time. That's all. I'm not dating anyone regularly enough to bring him around the family, that's all. If I ever do, you'll be the first to know."

Probably the easiest way to figure out if you're doing something you shouldn't is if you can tell your family about it. There was no question about me telling my family anything about my dates. Hell, I'd never even told my closest friends. I wasn't sure they'd understand the appeal. The satisfaction of it. No worries. No hassles. Nothing to lose.

"Boyfriends take a lot of work, Hannah."

She rolled her eyes. "Try having a husband."

"I don't want one of those, either."

"Of course you don't."

I couldn't win for trying. Her sniff told me what she thought of that—it might be fine for her to complain about her spouse, but for me to say I didn't want one was like saying she was wrong to be married.

"I like my life."

"Of course you do. *Your* life," she said like an insult. "Your simple, personal, *single* life."

We stared each other down. After another long moment in which we battled with our eyes, she let hers go pointedly to my neck. I kept myself from touching the small bruise I knew Sam had left.

Much unspoken hung between us in the way it does with families. Hannah changed the subject finally and I let her, relieved to be past the awkwardness. By the time we parted, the regular balance of our sisterhood had almost been restored.

I say almost because the conversation clung to me for the rest of the day. It left a sour taste on my tongue. It made me clumsy and forgetful, too, refusing to be put aside even though I had a meeting.

"What can I do for you, Mr. Stewart?" I folded my hands on top of the desk my father had used, and his father before him. At my left, I had a pad of lined paper. At my right, a pen. For now I kept my hands folded between them.

"It's about my father."

I nodded, waiting.

Dan Stewart had regular features and sandy hair. He wore

a suit and tie too nice for the meeting, and probably was what he wore to work. It was too nice for an office job, which meant he was either a corporate bigwig or an attorney.

"He's had another stroke. He's…dying."

"I'm sorry to hear that." I might not believe in a chorus of heavenly hosts, but I understood grief.

Mr. Stewart nodded. "Thanks."

Sometimes they needed prompting, those who sat across from me, but after a second Mr. Stewart spoke again.

"My mom doesn't want to deal with it. She's convinced he's going to pull through again."

"But you want to prepare?" I kept my hands folded, not picking up the pen.

"Yeah. My dad, he was always the sort of guy who knew what he wanted. My mom…" Stewart laughed and shrugged. "She does what my dad wants. I'm afraid that if this isn't prepared in advance, he's going to die and she'll have no clue what to do. It will be a real mess."

"Did you want to begin the planning now, yourself?" It could be awkward, planning a service without the spouse.

He shook his head. "I just want to get started. Thought I'd take some stuff home, talk about options with my mom. Talk to my brother. I just want…" He paused, his voice dipping low for a moment and I understood this was for him more than anyone else. "I just want to be prepared."

I slid open my file drawer and pulled out the standard preplanning packet. I'd revised it myself, one of my first tasks when I'd taken over. Printed on ivory paper and tucked inside a demure navy blue folder, the packet contained checklists, suggestions and options designed to make the process as easy as possible on the mourners.

"I understand, Mr. Stewart. Being prepared can be quite a comfort."

His smile transformed his face from plain to stunning in seconds. "My brother would say I'm being anal. And please. Call me Dan."

I smiled in return. "I wouldn't. Planning a funeral can be stressful and exhausting. The more you take care of beforehand the more time you have to devote to your own needs when you're dealing with a loss."

Dan's smile quirked higher on one side. "Do you have a lot of people preplanning funerals?"

"You'd be surprised." I gestured at my wall of file cabinets. "Lots of my clients have planned at least something, even if it's just the type of religious service."

"Ah." He looked past me at the row of file cabinets, then met my eyes again. The intensity of his stare would have been disconcerting if his smile wasn't so nice. "Do you handle a lot of Jewish funerals, Ms. Frawley?"

"You can call me Grace. A few. But we certainly can accommodate your service. I know Rabbi Levine from the Lebanon synagogue quite well."

"And the *chevra kadisha?*" He eyed me, his mouth stumbling a bit on words he'd probably never had to say before.

I knew what the *chevra kadisha* did, though I'd never been present while they prepared the bodies for burial according to Jewish custom. Traditionally, Jews weren't embalmed, nor laid to rest in anything but the simplest of pine coffins.

"We don't have many Jewish services," I admitted. "Most of the local congregation goes to Rohrbach's."

Dan shrugged. "I don't like that guy."

I didn't much like him, either, but wouldn't have ever admitted it. "I'm sure we'll be able to provide your family with whatever they need."

He looked at the folder in his hands, his smile fading. Funny, though, how it left its imprint on his face, which I no longer would ever have considered plain. His fingers tightened on the blue paper, but it wouldn't crease.

"Yeah," he said. "I'm sure you can."

His hand, when he offered it, was warm and the shake firm. I stood as he did, and walked him to the door.

"Is it hard?" he asked, turning. "Dealing with so much sorrow all the time?"

It wasn't a question I'd never been asked, and I answered it the way I always did. "No. Death is a part of life, and I'm glad to be able to help people deal with it."

"It doesn't get depressing?"

I studied him. "No. It's sad, sometimes, but that's not the same thing, is it?"

"No. I guess not." Another smile tweaked his mouth and made him handsome again.

It invited me to smile, too. "Call me if you need anything. I'll be happy to talk to you and your family about how to take care of your father."

He nodded. "Thanks."

I closed the door behind him and went back to my desk. The unmarked pad of paper, the still-capped pen. I had paperwork to fill out and phone calls to return, but I simply sat for a moment.

There's a fine line between sympathy and empathy. This was my work. I dealt with grief, and this job might also be my life, but it wasn't also my grief.

The e-mail from Mrs. Smith had an innocuous subject line. "Account information." It could have said "Information about your fuck buddies," and it wouldn't have mattered. I had correspondence from Mrs. Smith and her gentlemen sent to a private e-mail address I accessed only from my laptop.

My account information showed a credit. Normally, missing the appointment wouldn't have meant anything. Clients paid whether or not they showed. There were no refunds, unless the escort had to cancel. But Jack hadn't canceled. He'd been unable to find me. I'd figured that three hundred bucks to be lost.

Mrs. Smith didn't seem to agree. Her polite tone and careful phrases were always the same. I pictured Judi Dench in red lipstick every time I read one of Mrs. Smith's messages. This time, she was offering to reschedule the "missed appointment" at my convenience.

I looked around my dark apartment. The only light came from my laptop screen, balanced now on my lap as I curled up on the couch. My iTunes shuffled through old favorites. Did I want to reschedule? Really?

It had been a week since I'd met Sam the stranger. An entire week in which I'd tried to forget him. I hadn't been too successful.

I set my laptop on the coffee table and went to the bathroom, where I climbed into the shower before the water had time to get hot. I hissed when the needles of cold spray stung my skin, but contrary to popular belief the cold water did nothing to quench my libido.

Fuck.

It was all I could think about. Sam's hands. His mouth. Oh, God, his legs, going all the way up to the fucking moon. The noises he'd made.

Was he thinking of me? Did he pick up women all the time in bars, take them to his room? Fuck them breathless the way he'd done to me?

If I went back there, would I find him again?

No longer a stranger, then. What would I do if I saw him again? More importantly, what would he do?

By the time the water was hot enough to make steam, my hand was between my legs. Shower gel slicked my skin, but I didn't need any extra lubrication. I'd been wet for a week, thinking about Sam. Thinking about strange.

I touched my clit with two fingers. The other hand went up against the glass brick of my shower wall. I closed my eyes, picturing Sam's face. Remembering the feeling of him inside me. How he'd smelled. Tasted. The length of his prick.

I wanted to feel it again in my fist and my cunt. My mouth. I wanted to take him down the back of my throat... Oh, God. Muscles in my thighs jerked and quivered as the tension built higher and higher.

I could get myself off in a minute or two this way, with the shower pounding down all around me. I could come in the steam, with the rush of the water pounding in my ears. I wanted to, certainly. And I was going to, in a few seconds more.

My hand slipped on the glass, old bricks from a half-hearted renovation that had never been fully completed. My clit pulsed. I was coming…and pain shot through my palm as I stared, made stupid by pleasure, at the blood welling up from the cut just below my right pinkie. Water washed away the blood, but it came right back. Pain and pleasure tangled together as my body tipped over into orgasm.

I held my hand under the spray as I caught my breath. The wound didn't look deep, but it stung under the water and the edges separated to reveal more red beneath. Looking at it churned my stomach. I got out of the shower and wrapped my hand in a towel, but by then the bleeding had slowed enough I needed only a bandage to cover it.

The shower off, I searched the glass brick but could find no sign of a chip or crack. I didn't want to find it with my fingers, either, so I didn't run my hands over the glass. I'd have to be more careful, I thought as I dried the rest of my body and slipped an oversize T-shirt over my head. It wasn't the first time I'd made myself come or bleed in the shower, though I wasn't sure how I would explain exactly how it had happened to anyone who cared to ask.

In my living room, the laptop had gone to sleep. It took only the touch of a fingertip to the keyboard to wake it. Mrs. Smith's e-mail hadn't disappeared. The offer still stood.

"Hello. You have reached Mrs. Smith's Services for Ladies." Mrs. Smith really did sound like Judi Dench. "If you are calling to make an appointment, please leave your name and telephone number, and one of our representatives will return your call shortly."

"Hello," I said briskly into the mouthpiece of my phone.

"This is Miss Underfire. I'd like to reschedule the appointment that was inadvertently canceled last Thursday, but I'd like to change the services. Please have someone call me for the details."

Then, the dirty deed done, I sat back and waited.

I didn't wait long. Mrs. Smith's gentlemen were used to being called on short notice. Jack returned my call within half an hour. I knew he'd been paged, but not what he'd been told.

"Hi, is this Miss Underfire?"

"It is."

"This is Jack."

"Hi, Jack." I studied the bandage on my hand. It had crinkled at the sides, and I could see a hint of pink beneath the beige adhesive. "What happened last week?"

"I'm sorry," he said at once, properly apologetic though I'd been the one to mess up the meeting. "I was running late, and then..."

I wasn't going to tell him I'd been an idiot and mistaken a real stranger for the faux. "It was a mistake. No need to be sorry. Can we reschedule?"

"Yes! Sure, sure. Great." He sounded eager, and I thought of Mrs. Smith's description. Dark hair. Earring. Slim build. Damn. I was thinking of Sam again. "Um...do you want the same...?"

"I don't, actually. I think I'm kind of soured on strangers."

He laughed, just a little, as if he wasn't sure I was joking. "All right. So what would you like, then?"

I'd paid quite a bit of money for the use of his time and conversation, and since I couldn't get it back, I might as well use it up. "Do you like dancing, Jack?"

A pause. I heard an intake of breath. Not a hiss or a gasp. Something deeper. A peculiar huff-breath-hold and a subtle sigh. He was smoking. "Yeah. I like to dance."

Mrs. Smith had assigned a smoker to me? Interesting. Well, I had requested someone different than my usual. I didn't like smoking, as a rule, though it did look sexy.

"Great. I want to go dancing. Does Friday night work for you?"

Another pause. I heard the shuffle of papers. "Yes."

"I'll meet you just outside the parking garage on Second Street at nine o'clock." I didn't have to check my calendar. "Listen, Jack. Since the arrangements have changed, can you tell me what you look like?"

Jack's deep voice became a low chuckle. "Sure. I have black hair and blue eyes. I've got two earrings in my right ear and one in my left, and a ring in my left brow."

I must have made some sort of noise, because he laughed again. "Is that okay?"

"It's fine." If I'd known all that, I'd never have mistaken Sam for the gentleman I'd contracted. Then again…yeah. A stranger.

"Let me ask you something else, Jack."

I heard the distinctive huff-breath-hold again. "Yeah?"

"How tall are you?"

"I'm almost six feet. Is that okay, too?"

"Perfect," I said, since any other answer would have sounded rude, and we both hung up.

He was definitely not going to be Sam.

Chapter 03

"*W*here's your head, Grace? Up your rear?" As usual, my dad didn't pull any punches. He waved the folder stuffed with bank statements in my direction. "C'mon, talk to the old man."

Somehow I couldn't imagine confiding in my dad that I'd picked up some guy in a bar and spent a few hours fucking him in a hotel room, and that my concentration was for shit since all I could think about was doing it again with somebody else.

"Sorry, Dad."

"Sorry?" My dad shook the folder again. "You think I don't have better things to do than spend my time balancing your checkbook?"

I managed a genuine smile for my dad at that. "What else would you be doing?"

"Fishing." He peered at me over the rim of his half specs. "That's what I'd like to be doing."

"Since when do you fish?" I leaned across the desk to yank back my folder, but my dad grabbed it out of the way.

"Since I retired and your mother told me I'd better find something to do to keep me out of the house."

I sat back in my chair with a laugh. "Uh-huh."

Even nearly three years later, it still felt wrong to be on the other side of this desk while he sat in the chair meant for clients. I don't think he liked it much, either, if the way he waved that folder was any indication. I didn't need my dad to go over the books for me, just like I didn't need him to ask me if I had enough gas in my car or if I needed someone to come in and fix my sink. I didn't like feeling second-guessed. He didn't entirely want to let go. It was half on the verge of ugly.

My dad grunted and pushed his glasses back up on his nose. He spread out the statements and stabbed one with his finger. "See, there? What's this for?"

Two clicks of the mouse brought up my accounting program, a system my dad had never used. "Office supplies."

"I know it's office supplies. The charge is from the office-supply store. I want to know why you spent a hundred bucks!"

"Dad." I tried to keep calm. "It was for printer ink, computer paper and stuff like that. Look for yourself."

He didn't do more than glance at the monitor before he dived back into the pile of papers. "And why are we getting a cable bill?"

"*We* aren't." I plucked it from his hand. "That's mine."

My dad wouldn't ever come out and accuse me of trying to slip my personal bills into the funeral home's accounting. He'd hammered hard the idea that the home's expenses had to be kept separate from family bills enough times that I had no trouble remembering it. Considering the fact I'd be expected to cut my salary should the business require it, I didn't see any issue with paying for my cable bill out of the same bank account, especially when it was ridiculous to have two separate cable Internet accounts to serve one location. I lived just upstairs. I could share the home's wireless.

"I'll have a talk with Shelly. Tell her to make sure the bills don't get all jumbled up like that." My dad harrumphed a little. "Maybe give Bob a mention, too, next time I'm at the post office. Make sure he's putting them in the right slots."

"Dad. It doesn't matter."

He gave me a look guaranteed to make me quake. "Sure it does, Grace. You know that."

Maybe it had when he was running the business while raising a family, but now it was just me, and I didn't agree. "I'll talk to Shelly. You'll just make her cry."

Fresh from two years of business college, Shelly'd never worked anywhere else before I'd hired her for the office manager position. She was young, but a hard worker and good with people. My dad huffed again, sitting back in the chair I could tell he still thought of as the wrong one.

"I wouldn't make her cry."

It wasn't too hard to make Shelly cry, but I didn't argue with him. I tucked the cable bill into the drawer where I kept my private things and looked back at him. "Anything else you have a question about?"

He looked over the bills and statements again, but perfunctorily. "No. I'll take these home. Get it all worked out."

I hadn't had a problem, but it was almost guaranteed

he'd come back with a list of questions about expenses I needed to justify. You'd have thought I was running the place into the ground, sometimes, the way he talked. I shrugged and he closed the folder.

"That still doesn't answer my question," my dad said. "About where your head is."

"I thought it was up my rear."

My attempt at humor didn't make him smile. "Don't be smart, Gracie."

I raised a brow in a perfect imitation of him. "You want me to be dumb?"

He didn't smile this time, either. He was really mad. Or upset, I couldn't tell. "Your sister says you're seeing somebody. Says you don't want to bring him around the house. Meet the family."

I held back the groan. "Hannah talks too much."

He snorted. "I won't argue with that, but is she right? You have some fella you don't want to bring around? You're ashamed of us, or what?"

"Oh, Dad. No."

"No, you're not ashamed," he said, "or no, you don't have a fella?"

I should've known better than to try to get around my dad by twisting words. "No to both."

"Huh." He gave me an eye. "Is it Jared?"

I wanted to laugh, but the sound that came out didn't quite make it. "What?"

My dad jerked a thumb toward my office door. "Jared."

"Oh, God. No, Dad." My head tried to fall into my hands, but I kept it up. "He's my intern."

My dad huffed a little more. "People talk, that's all."

"People like you?" I folded my hands together on my desk.

My dad didn't look ashamed. "I'm just saying. You're a lovely young woman. He's a young guy."

I sighed, heavily and on purpose. "And he's my intern. That's it. Drop it, okay?"

My dad just looked at me, up and down. He didn't say he was sorry, the way my mom would've, and he didn't bug me for answers the way my sister would have. He just shook his head slowly from side to side and left me to wonder what that meant.

"What's that sign out there say?"

Whatever I'd imagined he might say, it wasn't that. "Frawley and Sons."

My dad nodded. He put his glasses away into his breast pocket. He stood, the folder of bills in one hand. "Think about that."

He turned to go, apparently not planning to say anything else, and I got up. "Dad!"

My dad stopped in the doorway, but didn't look at me.

"What's that supposed to mean?" I cried.

He looked at me then, the same look he'd given when I'd sneaked in after curfew, or brought home a bad grade. The look said he knew I could do better. More than could. Should. Must. Would.

"I'm sure your sister won't let her kids come within an arm's length of this place. Your brother…" He paused, but only for a second. "Craig, if he ever has any, won't either."

"So it's up to me, is that what you're saying?" I blinked, hard, thinking the sting in my eyes would go away.

"You're getting older, too, Gracie, that's all I'm saying."

If I was getting older, why was he still so good at making me feel like a kid? "Dad! Are you kidding me? You are not actually suggesting I need to get married, are you? Have some sons? Just for a stupid sign?"

He bristled. "There's nothing stupid about that sign!"

"Right, nothing stupid except for the fact I'm not a son!" My shout shot around the room and hung there for a moment until silence defeated it.

Everyone had assumed my brother would take over from my dad. Everyone but Craig. The news had finally been delivered one Thanksgiving when the inevitable argument erupted between him and our dad about Craig stepping into the shoes of the son in Frawley and Sons. Craig, eighteen at the time, planned to go to NYU film school instead. Craig had left the table and not come back for a long time. He lived in New York with a series of increasingly younger actresses and made commercials and music videos. One of his documentaries had been nominated for an Emmy.

"I'll get these back to you in a few days," he said.

My dad pushed through the door and I watched him go, then sank back into the seat behind the desk. My chair. My place. My fucking desk, if you wanted to get right down to it. This was my office, and my business now.

Even if I wasn't a son.

I'd never thought of Jared as anything other than an intern, but knowing that other people were making romantic assumptions about us, I couldn't stop thinking about him like that. It pissed me off. Until now, we'd had the perfect working relationship. It was as uncomplicated as my dates with Mrs. Smith's gentlemen.

It wasn't as if I'd never noticed Jared was attractive or anything. He had a nice face, kept in shape, had an affable personality that made him easy to get along with. We joked a lot, but I'd never had even a hint that he was flirting with me, and I know I never did with him. Why couldn't men and women just be friends without someone, somewhere, shoehorning sex into it? On the other hand, why did everyone assume that having sex with someone meant you had to fall in love?

"Hey, Grace. Want me to give Betty a bath while I'm out there?"

"You know, I have noticed you have a serious hearse fetish, Jared." I took the last pile of brochures from the printer and stacked them neatly on Shelly's desk for her to fold. "But sure. If you want to."

"Sweet." Jared grinned and headed out through the back doors into the parking lot and the fresh April air.

Black Betty was my car. A 1981 Camaro, it had been Craig's first, purchased with his after-school newspaper-delivery money in honor of his obsession with the punk band The Dead Milkmen. I'd inherited it when he'd moved to New York. I only drove it when I didn't want to use the funeral home's minivan emblazoned with the Frawley and Sons logo. It was my sex car. She didn't quite run like lightning, but she sure sounded like thunder. Jared lusted after her. I noticed boys did that a lot. Ben had, too.

I followed him to the garage, a converted carriage house barely big enough to fit our hearse, the minivan we used to transport bodies and Betty. Bigger funeral homes had more cars, and someday I hoped to add a flower car or a vehicle mourners could ride in. One thing at a time.

"You coming to help me?" Jared filled a bucket with water from the spigot and grabbed up a big sponge from one of the neatly kept shelves. He'd already pulled the hearse out into the driveway. "I thought you hated washing the hearse."

"Yeah. My dad used to make me and Craig do it every Saturday." I didn't take a sponge and stayed well away from the splash zone. I was still dressed for work and had an appointment in an hour.

Jared gave me a curious look. "You worried I'm going to hurt Betty or something?"

"No." I looked fondly at the car that had seen me through two proms, college and numerous other escapades. "She's a big girl. She can take care of herself."

Jared snorted and dipped his sponge into the soapy water, then knelt next to the hearse and started working on the wheels. "Just as long as she doesn't come to life and start killing people. Hey. That would be a good twist, huh? The car goes around knocking people off to bring more business."

"Ha, ha." I shook my head. "Don't ever say anything like that to my dad."

"I won't. Your dad's scary enough." Jared scrubbed, then gave me a glance over his shoulder. "Boss, you've got something to talk to me about?"

I didn't, really. I couldn't exactly tell him my dad and

maybe half the town thought we were schtupping. "I just wanted to tell you that you're doing good work. That's all."

Jared stopped washing the tires and stood, his hands covered in foam. "Thanks, Grace."

His smile was nice enough but didn't send sparkles through me, and the fact I was even trying to see if it did pissed me off. "You're welcome."

He was still looking at me curiously. "Anything else?"

"No. Carry on." I shooed him with my hands and went back inside, where Shelly was busy folding brochures and answering the phone.

I went to my office, where I sat in my chair and surveyed my realm without the satisfaction it usually brought me. No matter how hard I worked, there were always going to be people, my dad and sister among them, who measured my success by their standards. I didn't want to let their view of what my life should be affect me.

Unfortunately, it did.

Jack's self-description had not been incorrect. He waited for me where I'd told him to, and though I knew he was a smoker I couldn't smell it on him. God, he was young. He looked no older than twenty-two or twenty-three, and that was being generous. Young but pretty, even with the metal in his face. More than pretty. Jack was downright gorgeous.

He'd said his hair was dark, but it was impossible to see that under the ball cap he wore pulled low over his eyes. I didn't recognize the name of the punk-rock band on the black T-shirt he wore over a long-sleeved white Henley pushed up on his elbows to show off an intricate design of tattoos beginning at his left wrist and covering all the skin I could see on his arm. He wore faded jeans low on his hips and held in place with a black leather belt.

"Jack?" I held out my hand.

He shook it firmly and didn't squeeze too tight or hold it for too long. "Yes."

"I'm Miss Underfire. But you can call me Grace."

Jack smiled. "Pretty name."

If my name were Esther or Hepzibah he'd have said the same thing. As if a name matters. And again, I was thinking of Sam.

"Thanks. So's Jack."

Jack smiled, and I stared, dumbfounded at the transformation in his face. Without a smile he was gorgeous. With one…incandescent.

Either he didn't understand this or he'd long ago learned to deal with gape-mouthed women, because he didn't look taken aback. "Sure, if you don't mind the nicknames."

I burbled something incoherent, unable to manage much more than that, at least until the superpower of his smile released me.

"Nicknames?"

He hung back a little, letting me lead. I turned left out of the parking garage's small driveway. The street was crowded and would only get more so as the night went on. Listening to Jack laugh was like sipping premium hot chocolate. Warm and decadent. Delicious.

"Jackrabbit," he said. "Jackhammer. Jack of all trades. Jack Sprat. Jackass."

I joined his laughter. We headed toward the Pharmacy.

Someone had bought the original drugstore on the ground floor and turned it into a hot spot for up-and-coming bands. There was dancing upstairs, where the walls were painted silver and cages were set onto the dance floor.

"I won't call you Jackass. I promise."

Jack turned a half-wattage grin on me, for which I was grateful. I didn't want to be struck dumb again. "Thanks. I'll try not to act like one."

This early we didn't have to wait in much of a line. I thought of sneaking a peek at Jack's driver's license when he pulled it out to show the bouncer at the door, but I could only catch a glimpse of his photo. He was old enough to get into the club, at least.

"Jacko," said the bouncer, barely looking at the license as he slid it into the nifty little machine that scanned it for legality. "You still over at the Lamb?"

Jack took back his license and slipped it into the plain black wallet he'd pulled from a back pocket. "Yeah. Part-time."

"Yeah?" The bouncer took my card without even looking at me. He slid it through the scanner perfunctorily. I guess I didn't look underage. "What else you doing?"

Jack didn't even give me a glance. "Going to school."

"No shit?" The bouncer goggled. "What for?"

"Graphic design." Jack shrugged a little. He neatly nipped the conversation short with a grin and one of those specifically male gestures that probably originated as caveman sign language. Kind of a trigger-finger, club-swinging motion.

I let him lead the way inside. Jack was good at picking up my cues, but he wasn't quite good enough to make it seamless. He got an A for effort, though, when he asked me what I wanted to drink and got it for me, along with a beer for himself.

Downstairs, an odd mix of current hip-hop and old-school rock blared from the speakers as people mingled in front of the small stage where the night's band would perform. It was cooler and less crowded here than it would be upstairs, and for the moment I was content to sip my beer and watch the crowd.

"So," I said by way of conversation. "Graphic design? That's interesting."

He grinned around his beer and gave the same sort of shrug he'd given the bouncer. "Yeah. I guess so."

"You must think so," I said. "Or else you wouldn't be studying it."

Jack nodded after a second. "Yeah. It is. I think I'll be good at it. I like it, anyway. And it beats bartending."

It might beat fucking for money, too, but I didn't say that. "You're a bartender?"

"Yeah. At the Slaughtered Lamb. Just down the street."

"I haven't been there."

"You should come by," he said, but couldn't make me believe he meant it.

Two girls dressed in too-tight tops and too-short skirts sidled by, eyeing him. "Hey, Jack," said the taller one.

Jack nodded. "Hey."

The girls eyed me next. I smiled and lifted my bottle, waiting for a challenge. The shorter girl tugged the taller's elbow, pulling her away before there could be one.

"Sorry." Jack looked pained.

"Old girlfriend?"

He shrugged, nodded, shrugged again. "*She* thought so."

"Ah." I drank more beer, wanting to finish before it got warm. "She the one who called you Jackass?"

God, that fucking smile again. The real one. Brilliance. It totally slayed me and erased each unsmooth moment of this date so far.

"Probably," Jack said.

This wasn't the best date I'd ever been on, but it wasn't the worst, either. Jack seemed new to this, which was forgivable. I wasn't as demanding a client as I knew some women to be. Sometimes the gentlemen, though they weren't supposed to, spoke out of school.

"Jack, do me a favor, would you?"

"Yeah?"

I leaned closer to him. Tonight I wore stack-heeled boots that allowed me to reach his ear with my mouth without stretching. "Take off your hat."

He did at once, hooking it with one finger and shaking his hair when it came off. *Guh.* So. Fucking. Pretty.

I don't believe in love at first sight, but I do know firsthand the way my body can be triggered into full-on lust mode at the sight of something simple. Jack's black hair streamed like silk over one eye. Short in the back, longer in front, it invited my fingers to run through it. He pushed it off his face, fingers stuttering just slightly as if he wasn't sure what to do with his hand.

"Very nice," I said.

He was nervous, I realized suddenly. More nervous than I was. I felt tender. Also very turned on.

I finished my drink and put the bottle on the bar. I leaned in again. He turned his head when I did, so his breath sifted over my face. I smelled beer and cologne and still no smoke. Heat filled the minute space between our faces.

I took his hand. "C'mon. Let's go dance."

I pulled him upstairs, his hand in mine, and led him to the middle of the dance floor where strobe lights threatened to give the dancers seizures and the music was so loud the bass thumped like a drum in my stomach. There was no question of talking here, so neither of us had to feel like we had to speak. We only had to move.

I love to dance. Always have. I've never had lessons, not even the ballet/tap/jazz classes so many little girls take. I wasn't a performer. I just liked to move, to sweat. To work my body. Good dancing is like good sex. Fucking with clothes on.

Lots of the guys up there stood back and watched the girls writhing. A few shuffled back and forth, or did some grinding. Some, fueled by fifty-cent drafts, jerked around like fish on a line.

Jack had moves. Nothing fancy, just an innate sense of rhythm that kept him moving in time to the beat. He looked good, and I caught more than one group of girls checking him out. He kept his eyes on me, the hat now tucked into his back pocket and his hair still falling like silk. He kept brushing it back, like it annoyed him.

We danced hard, and he kept up with me. When a slower song came on, the floor filled at once with couples doing some sort of grinding, rubbing thing. Jack looked at me. I looked at him and waited for him to take me in his arms.

When he didn't, I gave an inward sigh and crooked my finger. That grin again, the one that made my thighs twitch, lit up his face. He molded himself to my body without another hesitation. If I'd thought he was a decent dancer before, I discovered he was frigging brilliant, now.

He'd been waiting for permission, and once he had it, he didn't stop. We danced fast, we danced slow. It was constant full-body contact after that, his hands on my hips and ass and keeping us connected in all the important places. And every now and again he'd give me that grin. He was having fun. So was I.

The best part of all of it was knowing that no matter what happened on the dance floor, it would go no further if I didn't want it to. Of course, it would go no further if he didn't want it to, also. Legally, I was paying Jack for his time and company, not for sex. Any monkeyshines we got up to later would be between two consenting adults, only. I'd never had a date turn me down, though, and I didn't expect Jack to.

If I wanted him, I'd have him, but even though he was lovely and a good dancer, I wasn't entirely sure I wanted to take him to bed. Sam's face still lingered on the edges of my mind, and though I figured Jack wouldn't give a damn if I fucked him while I thought of another man, *I* would.

For now it was enough to dance a lot, drink a little. Feel his hands on me and watch that smile. Sweat slicked us both and kept his hair back when he pushed it off his face. When I pressed my cheek to his, I resisted seeing if he tasted like salt.

I'd half expected to get paged, but the night spun on without so much as a beep from my phone. I did, however, have a limit to my budget. When I gestured toward the stairs, Jack nodded. To my amusement, he didn't wait for me to lead this time. He took my hand and wove us through the crowd with the same confidence he'd discovered on the dance floor.

My ears still rang from the music as we reached the street. Jack hadn't let go of my hand. All hell didn't quite break loose, but it sure as shit rattled the bars of its cage.

"You asshole!" The tall girl from earlier had quite a bit more liquor in her now. She stumbled out of the doorway, her eyeliner and lipstick smeared.

Jack turned away, face pained again. His fingers tightened in mine, but I let go of his hand. He shot me an apologetic look, which I returned with a half shrug as we started walking.

"Hey, Jack! Jackass! Don't you walk away from me!"

"C'mon, Kira, don't." This came from the marginally less drunk friend. "He's not worth it!"

Scenes like this were probably commonplace at 1:00 a.m. but I wasn't usually the one involved in them. In fact, part of what I paid for was the privilege to not be swept up in interpersonal dramas from drunk barsluts showing off their thongs.

"Fuck you, Jack!" Kira couldn't let it go, apparently.

Jack grimaced and pulled his cap from his back pocket. He put it on, but didn't look at her. We hadn't gone more than another few steps down the sidewalk when Kira launched herself at his back.

Jack stumbled forward as she pummeled him, her legs and arms whaling akimbo. She didn't actually manage to hit him more than once or twice, but the spectators leaped out of the way of her whirling-dervish performance. She was shrieking insults, mostly stupid and incoherent ones.

Jack pushed her off him firmly and grabbed her arm at the same time so she wouldn't fall on her drunk ass right there on the dirty pavement. She kept trying to hit him and missing, and though it shouldn't have been funny I had to cover my mouth over a laugh.

"Stop it," Jack told her and gave her arm a little shake before letting her go. When she flew at him again she managed to knock his cap off. Anger crossed his face and he held her off with one arm while she struggled to get at his face with her nails.

"I hope your Prince Albert fucking rips out and you have to piss through three holes!" she screamed.

"Kira, c'mon," her friend pleaded, reaching for her.

Kira allowed herself to be led away, still shouting insults. Jack picked up his hat and brushed it off, but didn't put it on his head. He won more points for that bit of common sense, even if he'd lost a few for dating an idiot like Kira.

"Fuck," he said after a minute. "I'm sorry."

His chest rose and fell rapidly, and his hands clenched at his sides. He was shaking, just a little. He reached to his pocket like a reflex, but then pulled it away.

"It's okay." It wasn't, quite, but I wasn't going to make him feel worse than he obviously already did.

He walked me back to the parking garage in increasingly uncomfortable silence. By the time we got to my car he wasn't visibly angry any longer, but that didn't really help. I unlocked Betty's door and turned to him.

"Well, Jack, it's been interesting."

He ran his hand through his hair. "I hope…you had fun."

Three hundred bucks' worth? Not so much. "Sure," I said anyway, because there was no point in being a bitch.

Jack straightened a little at that. "You didn't have fun."

"No, no—"

"Grace," he said. "I know you didn't. I'm really sorry. Shit. I'm oh-for-two, huh?"

I leaned against my car to watch him. Again his hand drifted to his pocket and pulled away. I thought of the huff-breath-hold. "If you need to smoke, you can go ahead. I don't care."

Not now, when I knew there was no way I'd have to taste smoke on his tongue.

His look of relief was so vast I laughed. He pulled out a pack of cigarettes and lit one with a lighter emblazoned with a picture of the biohazard symbol. He offered me one, which I declined.

We stood a few feet apart, me still leaning against my car and him leaning against the one parked next to it. He blew the smoke away from my face and visibly stopped twitching. We didn't say anything until he'd puffed a few times. Then he looked at me.

"Sweet car." His eyes roamed over Betty's lines, seeing her as she should be, maybe, instead of how she was.

"It's my bitchin' Camaro," I told him with a grin.

Guys dig cars almost as much as they dig pussy.

"Nice."

It wasn't, really—it had rust spots and dings and dents and was saved from being a junker solely because of its "cool" factor rather than any extra-special care I'd given it.

"It runs." I opened the door. "That's the best thing that I can say about it."

Jack drew in more smoke and let it out. "She wasn't my girlfriend. We hooked up once or twice."

"You don't have to explain things to me."

He shook his head. "Yeah, I know. But I am, okay?"

In the parking garage's harsh lighting he shouldn't have looked so pretty, his face all smooth lines and curves. With a cigarette in his mouth and smoke squinting his eyes, he should've looked harder. Or at least older.

"Look," he said when I didn't answer. "I'll give you your money back."

"Mrs. Smith doesn't offer refunds."

"I know." He finished the cigarette and dropped it to the floor to grind it out beneath the toe of his black boot. "But this date really sucked, and I'm sorry."

"It wasn't all that bad. You're a good dancer."

His mouth tipped up a tiny bit. "Thanks. So are you. But that business with Kira…shit. That was fucked. I'm sorry."

"You can't help it she's a stupid cunt," I told him, and Jack looked shocked for one second before he burst into laughter.

"Can I give you some advice?" I asked, watching him laugh.

He nodded. "Sure."

"Do you plan on doing this a lot?"

He didn't ask me what I meant by "this." "Um…well, yeah."

"And you want to be good at it, right?"

"Yes. For sure."

I studied him another moment. "First of all, don't make appointments where you can't smoke."

Surprise swirled around his mouth and eyes. "No?"

"No. Watching you suck on that butt was like watching a baby going for its bottle."

He laughed, chagrined. "Sorry."

"Don't be sorry. Just don't make dates where you're going to feel like you can't be yourself. Because I have to tell you, Jack, that's what's going to work for you. Not trying to be someone else."

He nodded, slowly, and gave me an assessing glance. "I sucked that bad, huh?"

"No. Not really. But…" I thought of how to get my point across. "Okay, think of it this way. What am I paying you for?"

"My time and company," he answered promptly as he pulled out another cigarette and lit it.

At least he got that right. "Exactly. But you have to act like these are real dates, Jack. You have to do your homework. Read the information Mrs. Smith sends you, and pay attention. Be a little more confident. Don't make it so much like you're waiting for permission to show me a good time. Just go for it."

"What if I'm guessing wrong?"

"If you're doing everything else right," I said, "you won't be."

He sighed. "Great."

I laughed and reached forward to push the hair out of his face. "And don't go on dates where you're likely to run into psycho barsluts."

"Well, that limits me."

We laughed together. I looked into my car but didn't slide behind the wheel. He moved toward me, one arm sliding around my waist to hold me against his body.

"Is this what you're talking about?"

Against his dark brows, his eyes looked very blue. Not a hint of green anywhere. His hair had stayed off his face this time.

"Yes."

He inched me closer. "So…are we saying good-night?"

"Yes, Jack." I tempered it with a smile.

He didn't let me go. His fingers splayed on my hip. "Is it because of the way things went tonight?"

I shook my head and answered honestly. "No."

"The cigarettes?"

"Oh. No." I meant that, too.

Jack paused, his eyes searching my face but finding what, I didn't know. "Do you think you might call me again?"

"Sure." I might. Or might not.

"Great!"

Then he let me go and stepped back to let me get in the car. The world shook a little and my body with it, because he gave me that smile again, that bright and shiny brilliant smile that made me want to dip him in butter and gobble him up.

He sauntered away and I watched him go, and I realized something. That smile had almost made me forget Sam the stranger.

I would definitely be calling Jack again.

also something that make me almost mardani'l ten
beautiful and sincere

I would a lovely. It might not grow of

Chapter
04

I didn't have time to think of smiles or strangers for a few days. I had services to oversee and families to soothe. I know many people think what I do is morbid. Maybe even creepy. Few understand the purpose of a funeral director is not to take care of the dead, though that's a part of it. My job is to care for those whose lives stutter in the face of their grief. To make the horrible task of saying goodbye as easy as it can never be.

I appreciated Jared more than ever as the week began with three funerals on the same day. My dad and uncle had always had assistants, but when I took over, the business had initially dipped and I'd had to let them go. I'd turned it around quickly enough, largely in part by doing most everything by myself. Running the home wasn't impossible to do on my own, but it was pretty damn difficult. Having Jared there to help me organize and arrange services was a luxury I hadn't wanted to get used to.

When a person dies in a hospital or nursing home, there are staff and gurneys available to make the transferal easy, but when a body needs to be picked up at a private residence, I never go alone. Most people don't die conveniently by the nearest exit, and it can be too difficult to lift or transport a corpse down flights of stairs by myself.

We got a death call early Tuesday morning. The woman, in her early thirties, had died at home but had been taken to the hospital. Her husband would be coming in to make the arrangements with me while Jared went to pick up the body.

It's easier with some than others. When the deceased passes after a long illness, or at an advanced age, for example. When it's not a surprise.

"It was such a shock." The man in the chair in front of me cradled an infant against his chest. He wasn't weeping, but he looked as if he had been. A little girl played quietly at his feet with the set of blocks I kept for kids. "Nobody knew this was coming."

"I'm sorry," I told him, and waited.

I've heard horror stories about families being pressured into buying the best caskets and vaults, or being forced to make decisions hastily. Some other funeral homes operated like revolving doors, shuffling people in and out as fast as possible. Mr. Davis deserved my time, though, and he could have as much of it as he needed.

"She hated that van," he said. The baby against him peeped and he shifted it. A boy. I could tell by the baseball bat on his outfit. "Why would she want to die in it?"

It wasn't a question that needed an answer, but he looked at me like he thought I should have one. I tried hard not to gaze at the little girl on the floor, or the baby in his arms. I tried hard to just look at his face. "I don't know, Mr. Davis."

Mr. Davis glanced down at his children, then back up to me. "I don't know, either."

Together we planned a simple service. He gave me the clothes he wanted her to wear, and her favorite colors of lipstick and eye shadow. His son fussed and he pulled a bottle from a small cooler bag to feed him while we talked. I had Shelly take the little girl to give her some cookies and juice.

It was only routine to me, but for him it was the end of life as he'd known it. I did the best I could for him, but Mr. Davis left with the same blank gaze he'd had when he came in. When he'd gone, I went down to the embalming room to see if Jared had returned with Mrs. Davis. He had. Since he wasn't yet licensed, he wasn't able to actually do anything until I was there to supervise, but he'd set up the table and our supplies, and turned on some music.

He was quiet, though, when we uncovered her. Usually Jared's full of humor and jokes. Nothing disrespectful toward the people we're taking care of or anything. Just a generalized goofiness. Today he wasn't joking, or even smiling.

He stared at her. "She's so young."

I looked at Mrs. Davis. Her eyes closed, her face serene, skin pale and no longer flushed with the rosy glow of carbon-monoxide poisoning she'd have had when they found her. "Yes. She's my sister's age."

Jared looked startled. "Shit. That means she's my sister's age, too."

He turned to the sink, where he washed his hands vigorously. His shoulders hunched for too long. I'd forgotten Jared hadn't yet had to deal with anyone like Mrs. Davis.

He'd been with me for six months, and though we'd had our share of deaths from disease and old age, and a few accidents, we hadn't had any suicides. We hadn't, in fact, had anyone younger than forty-five.

When he turned back to me, though, he looked under control. "Ready?"

"Are you?" I hadn't done anything to get started. We weren't in a hurry.

"Sure." He nodded. "Yes."

"Why don't you tell me what we need to do first." I offered this to remind him this was a job, no matter how disturbing it might be sometimes.

Jared did, rattling off the steps of the procedures we needed to follow. But his eyes lingered too long on Mrs. Davis's face, and he had to turn away a few too many times as we worked. I put a hand on his arm, finally.

"Do you need to take a break?"

Jared let out a long, slow breath, and nodded. "Yes. Want a soda?"

"Sure." I didn't need a break, but I took one anyway.

We both had cans of soda from the ancient machine I kept stocked in the lounge just down the hall. With its battered furniture and scarred flooring, it wasn't the lounge we used for clients. Just a place for staff to eat lunch or kick back for a bit.

Jared cracked open his can and stretched out on the worn sofa while I plopped onto a floral-print armchair with mismatched cushions. We drank in silence. From above I heard the faint pitter-pat of Shelly's heels on the uncarpeted floor.

"I guess we need some new insulation." I looked up at the drop ceiling, then at Jared.

He nodded, staring at his can. "Yeah."

"It's really bothering you, isn't it." I watched him study his can as if it was going to tell him something secret.

He looked at me. "Yeah. Damn. Grace, I know it shouldn't—"

"It's okay if it does, Jared. A big part of our job is compassion."

"It doesn't bother you," he said. "I mean…does it?"

"Her being so young, you mean?" The cold bubbles tickled my throat and made me cough. Coffee would've been better, but that was all the way upstairs.

"Yeah. And…the kids. I saw the little girl when she was with Shelly and you were still talking to the husband. I came upstairs after I brought Mrs. Davis in and she was there. She was what, maybe three?"

"Yes, I think so."

"It doesn't bother you," Jared repeated.

"It's part of the job, Jared. My job is to make this as easy as possible for her husband and family, and to make sure she's taken care of."

He rubbed at his eyes and tossed back some soda. "Yeah. I know. You're right. It's just hard, sometimes. Isn't it?"

I thought of the conversation I'd had so recently with Dan Stewart. "It's sad, sure."

Jared shook his head. "Not just sad."

"Do you want me to finish her by myself?" I asked, generously, I thought.

"No. I need the hours and it's not like I won't ever have

to face this again." He looked up at me. "But…how do you do it, Grace? How do you not let it bother you so much you can't do it, but keep that compassion?"

"I find a way to put it away at the end of the day," I told him.

"Like…?"

"Like it's a job," I said. "Which it is. You have to find a way to be able to put it away at the end of the day."

"Even if you get a death call two hours after the end of the day?" Jared grinned.

"Even then." I finished my soda and tossed the can into the recycling bin.

"So, what do you do?" he asked on the way back to the embalming room.

What did I do? I went out and paid men to fulfill my fantasies. "I read a lot."

Jared snorted under his breath. "Maybe I should take up knitting."

"You could do that." We worked together for a bit longer. He didn't need a lot of instruction. "You're going to make a really good funeral director, Jared. Did I tell you that?"

He looked up from what he was doing. "Thanks."

We finished without any more philosophical discussion, but when he left that night, I thought more about what I'd said. My tumultuous relationship with Ben had ended with spectacular horrendousness. He wanted to get married. I didn't, and not because I didn't love him. Ben had been very easy to love. In fact, I'd assumed, as he had, that someday we'd get married and have some kids. Do the family thing.

I believed in love. Believed marriages worked. My parents were still happily married after forty-three years, and in my work I saw many families bound together by the strength of their devotion to one another.

I'd been around the dead my entire life, but it had never hit so close to home until I started my internship with my dad. I arranged memorials and talked with priests, ministers and rabbis in order to help the grieving families who came to us send off their loved ones in whatever way they deemed fit. Funerals weren't for the dead, but the living, after all. I overheard arguments between warring family members who wanted different levels of religion in the service, and assisted with preparations for nondenominational services, too. I listened to the prayers of hundreds of mourners, and though the method in which they prayed might differ, or the specific deity they implored to care for the deceased, one thing was the same. People wanted to believe their loved one was heading off to someplace beyond this one.

But they were wrong. The dirt fell on the coffins the same way, every time, no matter if it was a plain pine box or a casket costing thousands of dollars. The body inside eventually became dust and even the memories of the person to whom it had belonged faded and became dust, too. I'd overseen hundreds of funerals and never once seen angels taking a soul to heaven, nor devils dragging it to hell.

You died, they put you in a box in the ground or burned you to bits to hasten the process, and that was it. Done. Fini. There was nothing after that.

No ever after, happily or otherwise.

Ben blamed me for breaking us up, but I pointed the finger at the summer I worked for my dad full-time for the first time. I blamed the women who came to us shattered by the loss of their spouses, women who'd spent their lives so enmeshed with their husbands they had no idea where their men left off and they began. I blamed the wives so battered by grief they couldn't function, and the children who cried over losing their parents.

With Ben I'd been so tied up in the beginning of things, I hadn't thought so much about the end. Dead was dead, there was nothing else. I wouldn't know I was dead, so why be afraid of it? Everyone died. Everyone went.

I wasn't afraid of going.

I was afraid of being left behind.

There was no question that the dates helped me put away my job. I could have a cop, a firefighter, a teacher. I could play naughty nurse, or secretary, or anything else I wanted, limited only by imagination and my budget.

I told Jack to meet me at the hotel I'd been using for months, a recently renovated strip motel on Harrisburg's city limits. It had cheap rates and clean sheets, and was a good forty minutes' drive from my home, which pretty much guaranteed I'd never accidentally bump into someone from town. Or someone's aunt or uncle or brother, or someone I went to high school with who was home for a holiday, or someone whose brother or sister I'd gone to school with.

I never worried about bumping into someone for whom I'd done a funeral. Not just because most families I serviced were also from the local area, and in my town the local area meant a radius of no more than ten miles. It was simpler even than that. People who met me for the first time at a service didn't see me. They saw a funeral director, if they saw anyone at all through their own haze of emotions. Out of the very limited element in which they'd met me, I was unrecognizable.

I'd been to that motel close to a dozen times in the past year, but the clerk behind the desk didn't recognize me, either. It was the sort of place where the staff was paid to recognize anonymity.

I secured the room and left the small office with the key dangling from my hand. Renovations aside, the Dukum Inn hadn't switched over to key cards. I liked the weight of the heavy black plastic key ring with the room number inscribed on it in faded white. I liked the way the key fit into the lock and turned. It was tactile in a way sliding a card into a slot wasn't.

Jack, looking scrumptious in a battered black leather jacket, met me at the door as I opened it. Inside, the room was nothing spectacular. I couldn't have said whether or not I'd ever been in that particular one, as a matter of fact, though after the visits I'd made you'd think I might have bothered to remember.

Jack looked around as he shrugged out of his coat and tossed it onto the chair. "Looks like they've done some upgrades."

I closed the door and set the key on the dresser before I turned to him. "You've been here before?"

He shot me a sideways grin. "Couple times. Not for a while."

"Is that so?" I stepped closer, reaching for the front of his shirt. "Don't tell me. You're used to classier accommodations?"

His low laugh tickled me in hidden places. He let me tug him closer by the shirtfront. He had to tilt his head only a little to look down at me. The wind had blown his hair back, but even the tangles looked soft.

"Nah." He was smart enough not to elaborate, and I gave him credit for that.

Jack fit his hands onto my hips. Our bodies nudged. I leaned closer to take a breath, half expecting the smell of cigarettes and motorcycle exhaust. He smelled like spring-night air, the sort that can't decide if it wants to be cold or not.

"Hey," he murmured until I looked up at his face.

"Hey," I replied.

Jack leaned in, slow to kiss me, giving me plenty of time to turn my face if I wanted. I didn't. I wanted his mouth on me, all over, including mine. I like kissing. Sometimes that's all I wanted to do. Kiss. Soft and slow, hard and fast. Long, lingering kisses or brief brushes of lip on lip.

I'd given him unspoken permission to kiss my mouth, and Jack took it without a second pause. His mouth slanted over mine as he pulled me closer with one smooth motion. Our mouths opened. I tasted mint. He didn't use his tongue right away, but when he did, the sensation of his warm and wet flesh sliding against mine made me draw in a short, sharp breath that wasn't quite a gasp.

He pulled away, just enough to ask, "Is this okay?"

I pulled him back to my mouth. "Less talking."

Jack's smile curved against my lips. "Yes, ma'am."

I slid my hands beneath the hem of his buttoned shirt and found the soft cotton of a T-shirt beneath. I pushed that up, too, to give my fingers room to play on his bare skin. I slid my palm flat along his stomach, just above the waistband of his jeans. He pushed against my touch and left my lips to slide his mouth to my ear.

"Thanks for going out with me tonight."

I turned my head so he could kiss my neck. "You're welcome."

"I don't have to be home until midnight."

I'd been specific about what I wanted, but I'll blame the way his lips and tongue were painting a picture on my skin for how long it took for his words to click. "Midnight? But...oh."

I got it. I fought my smile by biting down on my lower lip, hard, and heard Jack's smile in his voice when he answered.

"Yeah. Mom and Dad said I could stay out a whole hour later because I made the honor society."

I put a hand on his chest and twisted away from his mouth and hands. "Is that so?"

Jack nodded, glee glinting in his eyes but his face solemn. "Yes."

I turned my back, part of the game, but also to gather my composure. I'd told Jack to do his homework and he had.

Good boy.

"You must have studied hard." I made my voice casual and didn't turn around.

"Yeah, I did. Really hard."

This was a game I'd never had the chance to play before,

and my heart stepped up its thumping as I contemplated how it should happen, exactly.

I turned to face Jack. "So, I guess you think you deserve a reward."

He gave me a perfect, puppyish look. "I was hoping you'd say that."

"I don't know." I feigned skepticism. "I'm not so sure it's a good idea. Your parents—"

Jack looked indignant. "I'm a freshman in college! They can't tell me what to do forever!"

I fought back a giggle at his grand gesture. It was my game, and if I didn't hold it in, how could I expect him to?

"This is serious!" I shook my finger, as much a warning to myself as it was part of the role playing.

Jack crossed his arms over his chest. "I might not even be home by midnight, so there."

"Well, then," I answered. "You know what that would make you."

One corner of his mouth twitched. "Bad."

My hips swayed a bit more than usual when I moved closer to run a fingertip up the line of his buttons to stop just below his chin. "Is that what you want to be, Jack? A bad boy?"

He shook his head. "No." He put his hand over mine and pulled it away from his chin. "So don't make me be one."

He'd improvised, surprising me. I looked at his hand circling my wrist, and to the way his face had shaded from eager to intent. Yet unlike at the Pharmacy or even the first time he'd kissed me, Jack wasn't hesitating now. He was going for it the way I'd advised.

It was working.

There is always a part of me that can't get lost in the game. No matter how thoroughly I've imagined the scenario or how good the players, something inside me refuses to cooperate. Refuses to allow myself to be convinced, even for an hour, that I'm someone else. It was why I'd never played this game before, the older woman giving the younger man his First Time.

Except here and now, I was older. Jack was younger. And this was our first time.

I tugged my hand, but not hard enough to break free of his grip. "What makes you think I shouldn't?"

His fingers closed tighter. "Because you want to."

And I did, a fact the heat rising in my throat and cheeks couldn't hide, nor the way my nipples poked at the front of my shirt. Or the way my mouth parted to allow the swipe of my tongue along my bottom lip. Jack looked at all of these signs, so blatant, but he kept the role in which I'd cast him.

"Do you want to touch me?" The words came out scratchy and hoarse, but I didn't clear my throat.

He nodded. We stayed that way, him holding my wrist and staring into each other's eyes for as long as it took for my heart to stutter-thump a few times. Jack's fingers opened, freeing me. I put my hands out to my sides.

"Then go ahead."

His gaze fell to my body. For a minute I wished I'd worn something sexier, a short skirt and garters, maybe. Yet when he put his hands on my waist, pushing up my shirt to do so, I was glad I wore jeans and a long-sleeved T-shirt. It was less of a cliché…which made it feel more real.

Jack's thumbs pressed my belly while his fingers curled around to each side of my spine. He waited, taking a deep breath and staring hard at the place his hands disappeared beneath my shirt.

I was supposed to believe he'd never touched a woman before, at least not like this. Watching the set of his mouth and his steady stare and feeling the skid of his hands along my sides, it wasn't so hard for him to convince me.

We had no script. Nothing had been agreed upon. Only a few words checked off a list and a few scribbled sentences in the comments section of an almost-forgotten questionnaire from a while ago.

It was enough.

Jack pushed my shirt up and I raised my arms so he could pull it off over my head. He tossed it away and put his hands back on my waist at once. His gaze followed every curve before going to my face.

"Are you sure?" His already deep voice had gone even lower. "I can touch you?"

I took his right hand and slid it upward to just below my breast. We were both breathing hard by now. My nipples felt like iron pegs. Between my legs, my pulse throbbed and thrummed.

He touched me. I drew in a breath that had no trouble becoming a gasp. Jack cupped my breast in his hand and let out a slow hiss of his own breath. We stayed that way for a moment, until he slid his left hand up to do the same. Then he bent his head to brush his lips over the exposed curves. He straightened and looked into my eyes.

"Come to bed," I said. I turned and didn't watch to see if he would follow. There was no question that he wouldn't.

"Take off your shirt," I said when we got there.

He did. I stared for a second, then reached to touch the silver barbell through his left nipple. It wasn't exactly in keeping with the image of an honor-society nerd. It was also pretty hot.

Jack's skin humped into goose bumps at my touch, though I knew he couldn't be cold. I smiled. My finger traced his nipple, then the other one, and finally right down the center of his chest. I stopped just above his navel.

"Take off your pants."

His hands went at once to the button and zipper and in moments he'd pushed his pants down to step out of them. He kicked them to the side. Neither of us bothered to look where they landed.

Jack's black boxer briefs rode low on his hips, exposing a hint of dark hair. The front bulged impressively, but he wasn't quite hard. Not yet.

"Those, too." I watched his face.

He was good at this, much better than I, who had to think carefully about my reactions to make them authentic. Emotions drifted across Jack's face and got trapped in his eyes. Pride. Excitement. A hint of anxiety.

He hooked his thumbs into his waistband, but before he could push them down, I put my hands on his. Remembering, suddenly.

"Wait."

He gave me a curious look.

"Is there…anything I should know?"

His brow creased. "...No?"

I thought about what Kira had shouted in her drunken assault. I looked at the metal in his eyebrow and nipple. I looked down to the bulge in his briefs. I didn't want to lose the mood or destroy the illusion, but the thought of being suddenly faced with a cock ring had made my heart pitter-pat and not in a good way. A Prince Albert, the barslut had called it. I'd seen a few, but never on someone I was about to have sex with.

I let go of his hands. "Take them off."

I wasn't aware I was holding my breath until he stepped out of his briefs and showed me his entire body, nude. No Prince Albert to be found. I let out the air in my lungs with a little squeak. I looked at his face. Confusion had joined the other emotions.

I'd tell him later why I'd hesitated. For now I had some deflowering to do. I stepped back and let my gaze sweep over him.

His cock twitched when I looked there again. I glanced up at his face. "Tell me what you want, Jack."

"I want to...I want to take your clothes off." He swallowed and licked his mouth. His eyes gleamed. His cock grew longer and thicker.

"So do it." He reached for me at once, but I held up a hand to stop him. "Take your time."

His eager hands slowed at my command. He manipulated the button and zipper of my jeans and slid them over my hips, but didn't pull down my panties with them. I didn't warn him about my boots, but he figured it out when the denim slid past my knees and he realized he wouldn't be able to pull them all the way off without taking my boots off first.

It was perfect, really, the fumbling. Sweet and eager but controlled because I'd ordered it. Jack pulled my boots off one by one, then eased my jeans off, too. On his knees before me, he lifted my feet to peel away my socks. He looked up at me with a grin when I giggled at the tickling touch.

He straightened and his hands went to the mechanism on my bra that any woman can manipulate with one hand but often stumps even the most dexterous of men. He struggled a little more than I thought he had to, but I suffered it because it, too, was perfect in this scene.

When at last he'd unhooked the bra and stepped back to slide the straps down my arms, Jack paused before pulling the lace from my breasts. He took a few shallow breaths, ducking his head. I touched his cheek, turning his face until he looked up at me.

"Take it off."

He did, fingers trembling with eagerness or anxiety or good acting, I didn't care which. When the bra fell away, Jack cupped my breasts again. He moved so close I felt the flutter of his lashes on my skin just before he kissed each breast.

I put my hand on his silky hair. When he licked my nipples, I moaned softly. His hands moved down to my hips, hooking into the sides of my panties as he sucked gently on my nipples.

Jack wasn't the only one trembling with eagerness this time. Together we pushed my panties down as he stood and our mouths met. Our teeth clashed from the force of our kiss but we didn't stop.

"Sorry," Jack muttered between kisses.

I said nothing, just pressed against him as soon as I was as naked as he. His cock was hard now. Thicker than I'd expected. It rubbed my belly as he moved his hips.

"Put your hands on me, Jack."

He did, in as many places as he could manage. Passion glued us together in half a dozen places as we walked toward the bed, where we ended up in a tangle of limbs.

His erection pressed urgently against my hip as his hands roamed and his mouth tasted me. Jack nudged my head upward so he could feast on my throat, then lower. He sucked at my nipples, one then the other as his hands smoothed over my belly and thighs.

His hand slid between my legs, already parted. His thumb stroked the sensitive flesh of my upper inner thigh, and my body tensed in anticipation. I'd forgotten I was supposed to be teaching him.

Jack buried his face into my neck. His thumb pressed my clit and my hips moved, pushing my cunt against his hand. I closed my eyes and listened to the sound of our mingled breathing.

I know women who've fucked more men than I have, but who would think I'm a slut for paying what they give away for free. There are a lot of differences between their choices and mine, but one thing I feel certain is the same. There's always something unexpected about the first time you go to bed with someone new.

With Jack it was how readily and well he took on a different persona. How convincing he made his performance. How he picked up on my subtle cues and went with them—and how much faster and better he was at it when he was pretending to be someone else than the first time we'd met.

"Jack." I opened my eyes. The ceiling swam into focus, then the edges of his profile. He'd been kissing my shoulder.

He looked at me and murmured. I touched his hair, falling over one eye. "I don't feel like playing this game anymore."

When I was in high school, slap bracelets had been all the rage. Stiff, thin strips of flexible metal covered by fabric. The trick had been to slap them when they were straight onto your wrist, where they'd curl. Straightening them made them stiff and flat again.

Jack went rigid like a slap bracelet. Tension infused his arms, his legs, even his belly. He pushed up on his arms and tossed the hair from his eyes.

"Okay," he said, not moving. I gave him a moment, after which he said, "Why?"

I shifted a little. "Because I decided I don't really want to teach you how to fuck. I want to see if you know how to do it already."

And fuck, that smile again, this time made even brighter by the laugh accompanying it. My entire body went awash with heat. Jack rolled onto his side, one hand still on my belly. "You're sure?"

I got on my side, too, facing him. His hand slid to my hip. I slid my thigh between his. "I'm sure."

"Okay." He paused again, brow furrowed as if he was thinking. "But…I didn't guess wrong, did I?"

About the fantasy, I understood him to mean, and it

pleased me how he'd taken my advice to heart. "No. Definitely not."

"Good." He flashed a dimmer version of the thousand-watt grin. His hand slid back between my legs. "So I don't have to pretend I've never done this before?"

"Not today."

He pressed gently, in just the right spot. "Okay."

We didn't say anything for a minute. We didn't move. Jack's eyes were the color of an August sky without clouds, but thick black lashes cast shadows in them when he blinked.

He kissed me again, soft and sweet and slow. His fingers moved in small circles on my clit. When I sighed, he smiled.

He knew what he was doing, there was no question of that. He paid attention. He didn't rush. Was patient, even though it was taking me a long time. And what I liked best was that he didn't use my slow response as an excuse to trot out every sexual position or act in an attempt to get me off sooner. Jack kissed me and rubbed my clit in small, gentle circles without cease until I finally gripped his arm, my body tense, and whispered, "Now."

He moved faster, then, to slide on the condom and get between my legs. But slow again when he slid inside me. Slow, too, when he began to move. The few seconds' reprieve had faded my urgency, though not by much. Our bodies worked and moved together, each push and pull an experiment in timing.

Tension coiled, tighter and tighter. I made a wordless noise. He picked up the pace. My hands slid along the smoothness of his back, to the sharp curve of his shoulder blades and the shallow groove of his spine.

I came, finally, making no sound as my body tightened around him. Jack shuddered and lifted his head to look at me with heavy-lidded eyes. He closed them, hard, face tensing, and thrust once more with a low groan. He rolled off me after a minute.

I looked over at him as he sat on the edge of the bed, facing away. His shoulders had hunched as he took care of the condom. I yawned and stretched, letting the glow wash over me, but after another moment I sat up, too.

I got out of bed and used the bathroom, not hurrying. When I came out, Jack had pulled his jeans back on. Cool currents of air swirled in the room and I thought I smelled the faintest odor of smoke.

"Hey," Jack said with a small smile.

"Hey." I smiled, too, and gathered my clothes. I stepped into my panties and hooked my bra, well aware of Jack's gaze on me, but not turning again to look at him until I sat on the motel's rickety chair to pull on my socks and boots.

I hadn't felt awkward until it looked as if he might. I took an envelope from my purse and went to the bed and sat next to him. He looked at the envelope, then at me.

"This is for you." I pressed it into his hand.

He took it, staring down at the plain white paper. I'd sealed it. He turned it over and over in his fingers.

"It's a tip." I hadn't thought I needed to explain.

His brow furrowed for a second before he looked up at me again. "Okay."

"Don't your other ladies give you tips?"

His mouth quirked. "Not like this."

I raised an eyebrow. "How do they do it?"

He shrugged. "They usually just give me a twenty or something."

I had no idea how much training Mrs. Smith gave her gentlemen, only that each was an independent contractor. They set their own rates and negotiated their own dates, and gave Mrs. Smith a cut of the fees for the privilege of providing the scheduling and clients. Both times I'd called the service to arrange for Jack's company, I'd had to list exactly what I'd wanted for the date with the understanding that anything additional would be taken care of in cash between the two of us. That was the way it worked.

"Huh," I said. "Well…far be it from me to tell you how to do your job, Jack, but…"

He groaned and fell back on the bed, arms flopping out. "Wrong again?"

I laughed and rubbed his denim-clad thigh. "It's not wrong if it works for you."

He looked up at me through the fall of his hair. "This job didn't come with an employee manual, okay?"

"I guess not."

He groaned again, then sat up and tried to put the envelope back in my hand. "You don't have to give me this."

"Yes, I do!"

Laughing, we tussled for a minute until the envelope landed on the floor. We both looked at it. I nudged it with my toe.

"Don't you even want to know how much is in there?" I asked.

Jack shook his head. Then nodded. Then shook it. We laughed again. He was still half-naked and the warmth of his shoulder against mine felt good. I kissed it, tasting the clean salt flavor of sex-earned sweat, and got up. I picked up the envelope and put it in my pocket.

"Stand up."

He did, obedient.

"Okay," I said. "You read my file."

He grinned. "Yes."

"What sorts of things do I like to do, Jack?"

He thought for a spare second. "Movies. Dancing."

"What else?"

"You like to play games?" he said, less certain. "Role-play. Like what I tried to do with you tonight."

"Yes. I like to play games. So we're going to play the game right now, and it's called making a date."

Jack raised both brows. "Okay."

"I'm calling you." I demonstrated. "Hello, is this Jack?"

"Yes."

"Jack, I'd like to see you for a date. I'd like to go to the movies and then dinner."

"Okay."

We were both trying hard not to laugh. "And if things work out, I'd like to spend some time with you after the date."

"Okay!" Jack gave me a thumbs-up. "Awesome."

"Don't say awesome," I said.

"Why not?"

"Well…it doesn't sound professional."

"Right. Okay. Um…very well, miss, I think I can accommodate you."

We laughed again. "That's better. Okay. So, how should I compensate you for your company?"

"Gee, Grace," said Jack. "Nobody's ever said it that way before."

"Just go with it."

"Okay. Um…two hundred dollars."

"And what about the additional time?"

Jack scuffed the carpet with his foot. "All the other times it was more up front. You know. Meet them somewhere and screw. That was it."

"Huh." I looked him over. "So you don't ask for more?"

"Nope." The smile. "I just consider it a bonus."

Now I really started laughing, hard. "Jack!"

"What?" He shrugged. "What can I say? I'm twenty-four, I like girls."

I was all at once very fond of Jack. "It shows."

He laughed, too, and ran a hand through his hair again. "You want to know something?"

"Sure."

"I thought this would be easier."

I chuckled. "I'm sure you did."

He looked at me. "I'm not a total loser, Grace. I do know how to take a woman out on a date."

"I'm sure you do. You're very cute."

He made a little face. "It's just that this is different. I want to do a good job, you know?"

I nodded. "I know you do. And, Jack…you're not doing a bad job. Really."

Thumbs-up. "Awesome."

I kissed his shoulder again, then patted it. I pulled the envelope from my pocket and handed it to him. "This is for you. Don't look at it now. That's tacky."

He gave me a scornful look. "I know that."

"And next time, negotiate ahead of time," I told him as I headed for the door. "Get the money for additional time in advance. Excuse yourself to go to the bathroom to count it so you're not getting scammed."

He turned the envelope over and over in his hands. "Won't they think it's rude?"

"The ones who do this a lot will expect it. The ones who are new won't know any different. Watch out for yourself, Jack. Even women can be pricks."

He nodded. "Sure. Okay. Next time."

His voice stopped me at the door. "Grace?"

I turned. "Hmm?"

"Will there be a next time?"

I gave him a thumbs-up. Jack smiled.

Awesome.

Chapter 05

$\mathscr{T}$he call came as soon as I got home, patched through to my cell from the answering service. I returned the message at once.

"Hi. Miss Frawley. It's my dad. He's gone." I heard Dan Stewart swallow hard as if against tears. "I'm sorry to call after hours, but the message said to call at any time, and we need to make arrangements."

I never fail to be touched and amazed at the courtesy of those who have just lost someone they love. It's easy to be rude when you're being slain by grief. Dan Stewart wasn't rude. In fact, he was bending over himself to be polite.

"It's not a problem at all. It's what I'm here for. Where did your father pass away?"

"At the hospital. My mom was with him. I wasn't here, I was at home."

I recognized the tone of shock. The need to explain. It's my job to be smart for those whom grief has made temporarily stupid. I helped him through the order of things and made arrangements to meet the family first thing in the morning.

Since I was already home, I called Jared to have him pick up the body from the hospital while I stayed to let in the *chevra kadisha*. They'd be responsible for preparing the deceased for burial according to Jewish law, and their tasks included washing, praying over and dressing the body. At least one would stay to watch over the body, another Jewish custom.

An hour later Jared had come and gone and Syd Kadushin was knocking at the back door. He shook my hand and offered me a peppermint the way he always did, but when I let him into the dark hall, he was all business. He went right away to the embalming room.

The door locked automatically behind me as I watched the last arriving member go downstairs. The security precaution always made me feel better. Frawley and Sons had never had a problem with vandalism, though at Halloween we sometimes had more than our share of ring and runs at the door. Still, knowing that the downstairs would be locked up after the *chevra kadisha* left made me feel better about being so far away from the front door in my third-floor apartment.

I took the narrow back stairs that had once been for the servants. The large front staircase leading to the second floor was for clients and traffic to the offices upstairs. The back stairs led all the way to the third floor.

My parents had lived here with Craig and Hannah until just before I was born. Then, the third floor had been a series of rooms connecting to a narrow hallway down the center of the attic. Sloping ceilings had made some of the bedrooms small and cramped, and the kitchen was a galley-style space inadequate for a growing family, according to my mom. It had stayed empty for years after my parents moved out.

The summer of my internship, before Ben and I had ended in disaster, he'd worked in construction. With the help of our friends, a bunch of pizzas and some beer, we'd spent a few weeks remodeling. We'd knocked out the walls, creating an open space for the living and dining areas. The sloping ceilings toward the back of the house didn't matter with a bedroom large enough for a king-size bed and a love seat, and the bathroom had been expanded, too. Unfortunately, summer had ended, along with my relationship with Ben…and so had the remodeling.

The apartment was nice, but unfinished, and every time I thought about buying new appliances to replace the harvest-gold relics from the 1970s, or replacing moldings, I remembered all those things cost money better spent on improvements to the rest of the home or the business of my social life. It was a matter of priorities.

Despite its lack of luxury, the apartment was mine. If I wanted to have friends over, I had plenty of room for them, if not enough chairs. And it was quiet, of course. Nobody below me making noise, not even the whisper of voices floating up through the heating vents.

Lots of people are superstitious about places where the dead rest. I know a lot of my friends are creeped out by the fact that at any time I might have corpses in my basement. Inevitably when new acquaintances discover my profession, I'm asked about "weird" things happening, or if I've ever been scared to live above the dead.

What nobody thinks about is that people don't die in a funeral home. By the time they come to me, the circumstances of their passing have already occurred. All I get is the mortal remains. Nothing left of the soul, if there exists such a thing. There's no reason for a spirit to haunt a funeral home, or a cemetery, for that matter, because by the time the body reaches those places, whatever happened to the soul is already done.

Not that you can convince most people of that. The dead, who can do nothing, cause no harm, who don't breathe or eat or sleep, don't shit or screw, freak people right the fuck out.

After my date with Jack I was tired enough to take a long, hot shower. I deep conditioned my hair and shaved every stray, offensive hair I could. I loofahed, moisturized and steam-cleaned my pores and when I was done, I put on my favorite flannel sleep pants and my soft, faded Dead Milkmen T-shirt and curled up on my sofa with the TV remote, the latest doorstop-size novel I was reading and a pot of tea. I was by myself.

Dammit, I liked it that way.

Didn't I?

I clicked off the TV and went to the bathroom. Too much tea. I pondered my eyebrows in the mirror, decided they could use a tweeze and spent ten minutes wincing and sneezing as I plucked.

It was too late to call any of my friends. I was still alone. Nobody to answer to, that was me. That was an advantage to having a real boyfriend, but then again, that had its own price, and one more steep than what Jack charged to make me happy.

I was often alone, but tonight for the first time in as long as I could think, I was also lonely.

My book, a tome I'd picked up from the library, had promised action, adventure and romance. So far there'd been a lot of pining and a little bit of angst, and I was already nearly a hundred pages into it. Since my thought was that by a hundred pages in, someone ought to have already died or gotten laid, I closed the book and put it aside.

Which left nothing but the TV. I flipped channels. Nothing of interest by the time I hit the top limit of channels. I held my television viewing to the same standards as my book reading—if nobody was dying or fucking by the time I reached a hundred, I was done.

Just before I reached my limit, I paused on a popular ghost-hunting show I'd heard about but never watched. A mixed team of psychics and unbelievers visited locales supposed to be haunted, each team seeking proof of the supernatural or attempting to debunk it. They always went in at night, of course, as if spirits couldn't be arsed during daylight.

I don't believe in fate, but there's no denying serendipity. Though the show took place all over the country, tonight, the first episode I'd ever seen, had been filmed at the now-closed Harrisburg State Hospital. It was jarring to see familiar street signs and landscapes as they drove to their targeted spot. I'd never been inside the place myself, but I knew where it was and had driven past a few of the build-

Megan Hart

ings. The Angelina Jolie film *Girl, Interrupted* had been filmed there, and a bunch of my friends and I had tried to catch glimpses of the movie stars working on the project.

Maybe it was because I could too easily associate this location with my life, or maybe the episode was particularly scary, but as I watched, by myself in darkness, the creeps that usually left me alone sneaked up and down my spine.

I should've turned it off. This wasn't like watching cheesy horror movies in a packed theater. This was chilling, and downright disturbing, but like a child afraid to go to the bathroom in the middle of the night for fear the monster under the bed will reach out to grab her ankles, I pulled my knees up to my chest and hid my face behind the crocheted throw from the back of the couch. Of course, hiding behind a crocheted blanket didn't offer much protection, since it was a series of holes linked together to form a pattern, and I saw everything. Yet, though I told myself I was being absolutely ridiculous, I couldn't stop watching until the program was over. At the end of the show, in daylight, each team was supposed to present their evidence. Tonight's program ended in a definite decision of "paranormal" even the unbelievers couldn't disparage. Too much creepy shit had happened.

And now it was all in my head, in the dark, alone. Three floors above a room filled with corpses.

It had never bothered me before and I was determined not to let it bother me now. I turned off the television and turned on the lights. I picked up that book and tried to read. Curse my small bladder, though, and the effects of the tea, because no sooner had I turned a page or two than I had to get up and go to the bathroom again.

All I have to say is, if you're going to have the piss scared out of you, the bathroom's the place to be.

I'd just finished washing my hands when I heard it, the soft plink-tinkle of music. I froze while scalding water made pink gloves of my hands. I hissed and turned off the water. Listening.

I heard nothing for long enough to convince myself it had been my imagination, but a second after that I froze again as the faint but unmistakable sound of musical notes drifted to my ears. I leaned toward the tiny, stuck-shut window, thinking the noise could have come from traffic, but heard nothing. Not even a passing car. After all, it was past midnight on a residential street in a small town that pretty much rolled up the sidewalks at 9:00 or 10:00 p.m.

In the living room, my TV was turned off. In my bedroom the clock radio was my next target, but it, too, was off. I checked my laptop, my cell phone, anything electronic that might have decided to rebel and start playing music. All silent.

I listened, hard, straining. I didn't realize I'd clenched my hands so hard until my fingernails stung my palms. I forced myself to relax then. The show had spooked me, but faint phantom music wasn't anything to fear. I didn't fear the dead. The dead don't sing or play guitar, and as I listened with every muscle and nerve in my body, that's what I heard.

I'd seen too many horror movies to try to find the source of the noise. There was no way I was going to slip down the stairs in my pajamas with an inadequate weapon in my hands to confront what surely was a homicidal maniac with a hook for a hand and his mother's head on a platter. A maniac bent on desecrating corpses—and that was what got me moving, finally, an old golf club of my dad's clutched in one hand.

If there was some freak downstairs, getting ready to disrespect the dead, it was my duty to stop him. They couldn't do it for themselves.

The music started and stopped. As I reached the second floor I lost it. I stopped in the small, hidden doorway that closed off the stairs from the hall and listened. Nothing from my office or Shelly's. I put my ear toward the bottom of the stairs and heard another few notes and the hint of a voice. On the first floor I stopped again, but I already knew whoever was playing wasn't there. If someone was lurking, he'd be by the bodies.

My hand sweated and loosened my grip on the golf club. I paused to dry my palm and get a better grip. I thought of what I'd say and do. Too late, too stupid, I realized I'd been as much an idiot as the heroine of any slasher flick. I hadn't called the police.

The stairs at the bottom were even narrower, and darker. I came out into the hallway leading to the embalming room, the laundry room and the closed door to the small lounge. I listened again.

Music. The slow pluck of guitar strings and a low, male voice murmuring words I couldn't make out. I gripped my golf club tighter, in two hands.

Who the hell was singing and playing guitar over a corpse at one in the morning?

In a dozen steps I was in front of the door. With one foot

I kicked it open and leaped through it, club held at the ready. I made a noise, something meant to intimidate, that sounded extra loud in the small room.

Three things happened. First, I remembered, too late, that Mr. Stewart was in this room. Second, I remembered that Mr. Stewart was being watched over by members of his religious community in keeping with their customs. And third, the man sitting next to the coffin, the man with the guitar in his hand, jumped up at my entrance and turned, his face a twisted mask of terror.

It was a stranger.

It was Sam.

"Holy fucking shit!"

A string on his guitar twanged, protesting his tight grip, and snapped. Sam, whose face had gone as white as milk, staggered back and hit his knees on the back of the chair upon which he'd been sitting. He went over like a sack of rocks. The guitar hit the floor first with another protest, but though the sound of jangled strings was discordant it was not nearly as awful as the noise the back of Sam's head made when it cracked against the tiles.

I gasped. I might have said something else, something not in keeping with the image of a calm and compassionate funeral director. It might have been something related to intercourse and waterfowl, I'm not entirely sure, because at that moment all I could think of was the stranger from the Fishtank lying sprawled on the floor near the coffin and the way his arm had jostled the gurney as he fell. And the way the coffin was now looking as if it meant to tilt, and how quickly something like that could go over, once it decided the floor was really where it wanted to be.

I dropped the golf club and sprang over Sam's discarded guitar. And Sam. I pushed against the coffin just in time. It only needed a tiny shift to get the balance back onto the gurney just right and prevent disaster, but though I hadn't had to do much, my arms and legs trembled like I'd had to lift the entire thing by myself. My heart filled my ears with the sound of its pounding. I gripped the back of the chair, certain I was going to keel over as dramatically as the man on the floor.

I got my breathing under control and sat, unable to do anything else with my knees as limp as noodles. I blinked back the sick, faint feeling and the red haze tingeing the edges of my vision. I drew in another slow breath and pressed my thumb between my closed eyes, hard. When I opened them, Sam was still sprawled at my feet. His eyes were open, and though I half expected to see a spreading pool of blood from beneath his head, the floor remained bare. He looked stunned.

I knelt beside him and lifted his hand. His pulse throbbed beneath my inexperienced fingers. I had no idea if it was strong or thready or if he was even conscious, because though his eyes were open, he didn't blink.

"Are you all right?" My voice sounded hoarse. How loudly had I shouted when I came through that door like a berserker?

Sam moaned. His fingers in mine were cold, but the room was pretty chilly, out of necessity. He had calluses on his hands I hadn't noticed the first time.

His eyelids fluttered, sending dark, thick lashes over eyes electric blue under the fluorescent lighting. He groaned, a sound distinct from a moan but no less disturbing.

I chafed his hand. "Sam? Are you all right?"

"Am I drunk?" His thick voice did sound slurred.

"I don't think so. You hit your head pretty hard."

"Shit." Sam sat up with a wince, his other hand going to the back of his head. His fingers probed, and he hissed in a breath. "Damn, that hurts. And I am drunk. A little."

I let go of his hand and sat back on my heels. "God. I'm so sorry. I heard music, and…"

He was staring at my breasts, unbound beneath my thin T-shirt. The chill in the room had tightened my nipples prominently, and I hunched forward to ineffectively loosen my shirt. Sam's gaze roamed over my whole body, taking in not just the tight T-shirt but my flannel pants, now riding lower than normal, and my bare toes. He leaned forward without a second's hesitation and took my shoulders in his big, callused hands to hold me still.

He kissed me, hard and well.

Stunned at the sudden assault, I did nothing for as long as it took him to nudge open my mouth with his and slip his tongue inside. I gasped. He mumbled. I jerked back, out of his grasp, and slapped him across the face.

Sam sprawled again onto the floor, one hand on his cheek. "Well, I guess that answers the question about whether or not I'm dreaming."

I scrambled to my feet, my chest heaving in breath after breath but my lungs still empty. "What the hell?"

Sam got up, too, his hands held out in supplication, but

didn't approach me. "I was just checking. I mean, c'mon, can you blame me for wondering?"

With fingers trembling only a little with affront and a whole lot with an entirely different emotion, I wiped my mouth. "This is not the place!"

"I'd tend to agree." Sam's gaze took in my clothes again, then moved to my face. He touched his jaw with a wince and probed the inside of his mouth with his tongue. He bled now, a tiny drop at the corner of his lips. "But honestly, what do you expect? I'm watching my father's corpse and the woman who I met in a bar a couple weeks ago shows up dressed like she's ready for a slumber party. Am I supposed to assume this isn't a dream? I mean, maybe I got that whack on the head and I'm still out cold."

I crossed my arms over my chest. "You're not dreaming."

"Well…then what are you doing here?" Sam pointed upward. "I'm all about having my prayers answered, but I didn't think it was going to happen quite this way."

"I work here." I looked at his father's coffin. "I think we should move this conversation outside."

Sam looked, too, at the plain pine box. "The old man can't hear us."

I lifted my chin. "It's disrespectful!"

Sam shrugged. "Fine. Okay. Outside."

I tried not to think of his eyes on my rear as he followed me, but when I turned around to face him out in the hallway, that's exactly where I found them. "Can you…leave him?"

"Technically? No. But considering the circumstances, I think God might understand."

"What about your father?"

Sam's tongue slipped out to lick away the blood in the corner of his mouth. "He'll have to deal with it, too."

I took him upstairs, where we kept the coffeemaker. I didn't think of much beyond keeping my hands steady as I poured coffee grounds into the filter and added water from a gallon jug. When I pulled out mugs from the cupboard and set sugar packets and dried creamer on the counter, I tried not to think about what sort of serendipity had brought Sam here. To me.

"Thanks." Sam pulled a mug toward him when I'd filled it with coffee. He drank it black without a wince.

I added sugar and creamer to mine until the black brew turned golden brown, then blew on it to cool it, but I didn't drink. The first sip would fill my mouth with the taste of coffee and chemicals, and wash away the taste of Sam.

"Soooo," Sam said after a moment in which we stared at each other over our mugs. "That's my dad in there. And you work here."

"Yes. I'm the funeral director."

Sam lifted an eyebrow. "Wow."

Another few moments of silence while we stared.

"What are you doing here?" I said finally.

"Watching my father."

"And playing guitar? What…I mean, I didn't think that was allowed."

Sam shrugged. "I'm not the praying sort."

I shook my head a little. My heart had finally stopped trying to burst out through my chest. "You nearly killed me."

"Me, kill you?" Sam's eyes went wide. "When you burst through that door with the golf club—"

He demonstrated, waving his arms above his head and making a guttural, horrible battle cry, his face wild. "I nearly crapped myself. Hell, I'm not sure I didn't."

I didn't mean to laugh, really, but laughter often strikes me when it's not supposed to. I covered it by drinking, at last, the coffee I'd made too strong for my taste. "Sorry."

He shrugged. "I was just surprised. They didn't tell me there was going to be anyone here."

"I knew there was going to be someone here, and I still was surprised."

Sam sipped. "You live here?"

I nodded. He nodded, too. His smile tilted the side of his mouth I hadn't made bleed. His lip was already puffing a little.

"Convenient."

"Most people usually say creepy."

He grinned. "Nah. Dead's dead."

"Yes." I wrapped my hands around the mug. "I'm sorry about your dad."

Sam's crooked smile faded into nothing. "Yeah. So's everybody else."

I offer a lot of sympathy. Part of my job is knowing when to stop. I didn't say it again.

Sam cleared his throat. "Anyway. Sorry I freaked you out."

"I'm sorry I hit you. And about your head. Oh, God, you need some ice, don't you?"

Sam put a hand to the back of his head and winced again. "That might be nice. And some aspirin, if you have it. Hell, a bottle of Smirnov might work better."

"I can get you the ice and the aspirin, but I don't have

any vodka." And the ice and aspirin weren't here, they were upstairs. "Are you going to go back to your dad, or should I bring it here?"

Sam shook his head. "If you don't tell my mom or brother I left him, I'll come get it. I've had my fill of singing tonight."

I hesitated, not sure I wanted to take him to my apartment but unable to think of a reason why. "Are you sure?"

Sam nodded with a grimace. "Yes. To tell you the truth, my dad hadn't stepped foot in a shul for the past fifteen years. His favorite appetizer was shrimp wrapped in bacon. Somehow I doubt the old man would give a rat's ass about someone sitting with him until he's in the ground."

I understood Sam's reference to Jewish dietary laws, just barely, but I nodded as if I knew what he meant. "Okay. If you're sure."

"Dead sure."

I've heard jokes like that before, but it didn't seem like Sam was making one, because an instant after he said it, he winced.

"Sorry. Bad choice of words."

"It's okay. I'm used to it." I gestured. "C'mon upstairs with me."

Sam followed me upstairs, and again I pretended I didn't feel the heat of his gaze on my ass. I also ignored the fact I never, never took men here. Not ever. Yet here I was, taking a man upstairs not just to my office, which was a private space, but to my apartment. To my home.

It was only slightly less foolish than not calling the police had been, but I was glad now I hadn't dialed. I'd have been thoroughly embarrassed had they shown up.

I hadn't even closed my door. Sam followed me inside. He was looking around when I turned to face him.

"Nice place," he said.

"Thanks. Have a seat."

Like we were at a cocktail party. Ridiculous, particularly when I remembered that within twenty minutes of meeting him for the very first time I'd been following him up to his hotel room. My mind might wish to block out the memory, but my body wasn't so willing. My heart kept up its insistent pitter-pat and every movement seemed made through butter, slick and sweet.

I grabbed a sweatshirt quickly from the back of my bathroom door and slung it over my head, then grabbed out a bag of frozen brussels sprouts from my freezer, found the economy-size bottle of ibuprofen, along with a glass of water, and took them to Sam who'd made himself comfortable on my couch.

"Here."

He looked up and took what I offered, swigging down the pills and setting the impromptu ice pack on the back of his head. He handed me back the glass and settled against the cushions, those million-mile legs stretched out like he belonged there.

And, heaven help me, he looked as if he did. Like my couch had been made to cradle him. Like my brussels sprouts had been grown for his comfort.

Shaking myself, I took the glass to the kitchen. His mouth had left a smudge on the rim, and I touched it with my finger before putting it in my ancient dishwasher. When I turned to look at him, he'd stretched out with his head propped on the frozen sprouts on the arm of the couch. His legs hung all the way down to the other end.

When I came around to look at him, his eyes had closed. He looked paler than I remembered, with grayish blue circles under his eyes. Even his lips looked pale beneath the puffiness. A definite hazy bruise was forming on his jaw.

"Sam."

His eyes fluttered open, half-lidded. My guts clenched. Weren't people with head injuries supposed to stay awake?

"I don't think you should go to sleep."

"No?" He gave me a lazy, tilting smile.

"You hit your head pretty hard. Aren't you supposed to stay awake? How many fingers am I holding up?"

"Both of you are holding up two."

My guts clenched again, until I saw his smile twisting and realized he was teasing. "Not funny."

"Sorry." He didn't sound sorry. He blinked again, slowly. "I'm okay. Really. Just tired."

"Sam!"

His eyes flew open. "Grace, I promise you, I'm fine!"

I crossed my arms over my chest. "Then you can be fine downstairs. You don't have to be fine on my couch."

Sam sighed and shifted his weight a little, but didn't get up. "So I'll stay awake." Pause. Beat. Breathe. Smile. "Any ideas on how we might do that?"

I was not in the mood for flirtation. Not here, not even with him. "I think you need to leave."

At that, he sat up. "Hey, I'm sorry. Really. I just thought—"

"What?"

He shrugged and set the bag of frozen vegetables on the coffee table. "Hey, it's not like we're strangers."

"I'm sorry, Sam, but we are."

Strangers. My heart, dammit, skipped in my chest and my throat, dammit, dried up faster than beef jerky in a dehydrator. I kept my expression as neutral as I could, but my face must still have given something away, because Sam's gaze flared with interest.

"Are we?" His voice, husky and low, tempted me.

A lot.

I nodded. "Yes. We are."

Sam stood, all gazillion feet of him. I should've felt intimidated with him looming over me, but I only felt…intimate.

"You need to leave, Sam. Now."

He reached to touch one fingertip to my fleece-covered shoulder. The contact was instant, electric, burning. He traced my arm all the way to my elbow and made a right turn to continue until he'd ended at my wrist, where he could go no farther with my hand tucked beneath my opposite arm. Sam's blue eyes caught mine and held them tight.

"Don't you think it means something?" he whispered. "You being here?"

"I don't believe in 'something,'" I said.

"Too bad."

I gave as pointed a glance as I could toward the door. Inside, I shook and quaked. Inside, I got on my knees and took him down my throat and fucked him until we both came ten times. Inside. But outside I managed to unhook my hand from beneath my arm and point with a semi-steady finger.

"Go downstairs and sit with your father. Or leave. Go home."

"Can't. I'm not close to home. I've been staying in a hotel for the past month, waiting for the old man to die. But…you already know that, don't you?"

I blushed fiercely at the memory of that hotel and what we'd done there. "Go!"

"Do you treat all your customers so coldly?" He touched the back of his head, then the corner of his mouth. "Or am I just the lucky one?"

"I don't ever invite my clients to my personal apartment," I told him through taut jaws.

Sam nodded. He hadn't moved away and the heat from his body was making me sweat inside my heavy sweatshirt. His eyes never left mine, and I didn't look away from his, either.

"So I'm not just lucky. I'm special, too."

My mouth tried so hard to stay stern, but I lost against the smile. "You have a funeral to go to in the morning. You're supposed to be sitting with your father. This is a difficult and entirely emotional time in your life—"

Sam kissed me again. Soft, light, the barest brush of his lips on mine. And like a schoolgirl in one of my role-playing fantasies, I closed my eyes when he did it. It couldn't have lasted more than a second, but like his legs, that kiss went on forever.

"What were you saying?"

This was not a fantasy, and this was not the time nor the place for this. Eyes still closed, I licked my lips and tasted him. "You need to go."

"Say it."

I knew what he meant, and I smiled without opening my eyes. "You need to go...Sam."

His sigh drifted over my skin and I waited for another kiss, but all I got was a chill when his heat pulled away. I opened my eyes and saw him in my doorway. His head nearly reached the top.

"See?" he said, just before ducking out. "We're not strangers, after all."

And then he was gone.

Chapter 06

When I was a kid, Christmas morning always took too long to arrive. I'd wake in darkness and strain my ears for the hint of reindeer on the roof, or the thud of Santa's boots hitting the floor as he slid down our chimney. I'd creep to my sister's bed and shake her, though she was nearly always awake, too, and we'd whisper together to urge the sun to rise faster, faster! It never did then, and it didn't now, either.

I didn't know if or how Sam had managed to sleep during his vigil over his father. I knew he wasn't supposed to, but then he hadn't been supposed to play the guitar or leave the room, either. Whatever he did was in silence, though, for I didn't hear even a single note for the rest of the night.

With three full floors between us, I still felt Sam's presence beside me in my suddenly too-empty bed. I knew just how he'd feel stretched out beside me, his head on one end, feet at the other. How his body would bump the blankets and ooze warmth all around me.

It was a very long night.

By the time I could finally convince myself it was all right to get up, I'd dozed off. Prying my eyelids open I stumbled to a steamy shower, then dressed in my favorite black suit, the one fitted at the hips to give me a silhouette. I paired the outfit with a silky white blouse with wide lapels that layered over the suit's jacket. The suit was professional but also pretty and feminine. I was dressing to represent my business, but I was also dressing for Sam, and I wasn't about to pretend otherwise.

I met the Stewart family first thing Monday morning. Though I'd met Dan previously, this was the first time I'd met his mother. He ushered her into my office and seated her in the middle chair, while he took the one to her right.

"My brother's not coming," he said, revealing a lot more with his expression than with his actual words.

My heart sank.

"He'll be here." Mrs. Stewart clutched a handkerchief and dabbed her eyes occasionally with it but didn't sob.

Dan didn't sob, either, though his eyes had the red-rimmed look of a man who's been fighting tears for hours and barely winning. His face had grown a hint of beard and his sandy hair looked rumpled, but he wore the same sort of natty suit he'd worn at our first meeting. He pulled the folder I'd given him from his black leather briefcase, but didn't open it.

"Sam's not going to be here, Ma."

Mrs. Stewart shook her head and answered in a quivery voice, "He will. Of course he will."

Dan slid a look to me, then shook his head. "I told him not to come."

Most families have hot spots that can usually be ignored, but even those who manage to keep everything shiny most of the time can stir up drama when faced with the pressure of dealing with a death. I'd seen just about everything from stuttered accusations to a fistfight over an open coffin.

There was a moment of awkward silence while Mrs. Stewart turned in her seat to stare at her son. "Why would you do that?"

Dan scrubbed his face with his hand, but then looked at her. "We don't need to talk about this now."

"Fine." She faced forward, hands clutched tight in her lap, and now her lower lip trembled with the threat of tears. "Fine, Daniel, fine. You've decided it all, haven't you?"

Dan shot me an apologetic look, and I gave him what I hoped was an appropriately sympathetic look of my own. "Yeah. Ma, whatever. Let's do this."

I waited a beat to see if she'd reply, but she only sniffed and refused to look at him. I held out my hand for the navy blue folder he still held. He passed it to me. Since we'd already preplanned the arrangements and talked with the rabbi who'd perform the service, there wasn't much to talk about. In keeping with Jewish tradition, the service would be held as soon as possible, later this morning.

Mrs. Stewart made a strangled noise, and I looked up. She dabbed her eyes again. "So much to think about! So much to do!"

Dan looked as if he might reach for her shoulder, but drew back his hand at the last second. "Ma, that's why I arranged all this ahead of time. There's nothing to worry about. Dad's going to be taken care of." He looked at me. "Right?"

"Absolutely, Mrs. Stewart." With Jewish funerals I really didn't have to do much other than provide the place for the body to rest until burial and get the deceased to the cemetery. "I'll be happy to help you take care of everything."

Mrs. Stewart sighed and gave me a shaky smile and looked at Dan. "I'm sure you will. I just wish your brother was here."

"He'll come to the service." Dan's face was stony. "At least, he said he would. He doesn't have to be here now."

"But maybe he'd have some ideas–"

"Ma," interrupted Dan in a tone that said he'd gone over all of this before. "Everything is under control. What would he do, anyway? Play guitar?"

Another moment of heavy silence surrounded us. Dan looked back at me, but Mrs. Stewart looked at her hands twisted in her lap. "My brother," Dan said, "isn't very responsible."

Mrs. Stewart let out another long, shuddering hiss into her hankie. This time when Dan reached to pat her shoulder, he actually did instead of pulling away. Then he leaned across the desk to shake my hand.

"Thanks, Ms. Frawley."

Again, his politeness touched me. "You're welcome."

"We'll be back in a couple hours for the service," Dan said. "C'mon, Ma. Let's go rest until it's time."

I walked them to the door of my office. A woman with long dark hair held back from her face by a wide black band looked up from her seat in the hall. She stood, clutching a handful of tissues.

She could have been a sister or a cousin, or just a family

friend, but the way Dan's eyes lit when he saw her told me there was nothing else she could be but his.

"Elle," he said. "Hi."

"Hi, honey. Hi, Dotty." Elle gave a small, half smile when Dotty Stewart embraced her.

"My wife," Dan said to me.

She reached for his hand, and he took it. That gesture seemed more intimate than a kiss. The three of them left.

Sam hadn't shown, just as his brother had said he wouldn't.

My office window had a good view of the parking lot. Dan Stewart and his wife stood next to a dark gray Volvo. He leaned into her, his face pressed into her shoulder and his arms around her waist. She stroked her hand down his back while the other cupped the back of his neck.

It felt prurient to watch them, but I couldn't look away. Her hand moved down his back in a pattern of three. Three strokes, pause. Three more, pause. I felt soothed, watching, and I wasn't even upset.

I didn't expect to feel the prick of envy. The way his face had looked when he'd seen her…I'd never deny wishing sometimes someone looked that way at me. But what if it were her dressed in white and laid in that pine box? How much greater would be his grief if he were faced with the loss of the woman he so clearly adored?

His shoulders heaved a little, and she stroked his back again. I could see her murmuring into his ear. He nodded. She squeezed him, and he pulled back a little. They kissed, there in the parking lot, and at last I turned away.

I'd already had a service planned for later that afternoon, but the Stewarts' religious requirements meant they needed to bury Mr. Stewart as soon as possible. I got started on setting up the chapel. The rabbi was bringing the small booklets containing the Hebrew prayers, since I didn't keep them in stock, and compared to some of the other services we had, this one was going to be swift and sparse.

I'd never fumbled so much in arranging the chapel for a service. I dropped the guest register, its crisp white pages bending, and had to get a new one. I scattered pamphlets left over from a recent service all over the floor and had to scramble to scoop them up. Everything took twice as long as it should have, my speed and dexterity thoroughly constipated by my new habit of looking over my shoulder every other minute.

At last I stood and took a deep breath. Sam would be here with his family to honor the passing of his father. Nothing more. Thinking of anything else was ridiculous on my part. In fact, it would be best if I weren't there at all. He didn't need such a distraction, and I didn't need to be at the service. Shelly and Jared could take care of the mourners as they arrived, and the rabbi, who'd just come in to hang up his coat, would handle everything else.

I didn't really need to be there, but there I stood in my pretty suit, feeling like a fool as one by one the family and friends of Morty Stewart entered the chapel and took their places in the comfortable seats I'd had re-covered in soothing shades of green and mauve. One by one, and none of them Sam.

I shouldn't have had time to think about it. Not with getting the cars aligned and fitted with the appropriate purple "funeral" flags. Not with packing up the leftover booklets for the rabbi and making sure all the mourners knew where to go. Not with doing my job.

I rode in the front of the hearse as Jared drove. He had a habit of humming under his breath and tapping his fingers on the steering wheel. I usually didn't mind, but today I finally had to reach over and stop the incessant motion of his fingers. He glanced at me.

"Are you okay?"

I nodded. "Sure. Fine. Don't forget to turn left up there."

Jared hadn't made many trips to the Jewish cemetery, but he was very good at his job. He didn't need me to give him directions. Jared, mild-mannered as he was, didn't comment on my touchiness again and turned left at my gesture.

At the graveside, those who'd come to pay their last respects gathered around the hole in the earth. Men had labored for days in the past to dig graves; now it was done in half an hour with a backhoe. I didn't need to be close to the grave or part of the service, here, either, and I held back from the crowd, listening to the rabbi as he recited Psalm 91 and led the way to the grave.

"It's not fair to bury someone on a day as perfect as this."

I heard the woman say it as she passed, clutching the arm of an older man, who nodded in agreement. I was glad she hadn't said it to me. I'd been to a lot of funerals, and they were always better on the days of perfect weather. Rain, gloom and snow only made everything more miserable.

Many of the headstones had pebbles placed on top of them. I studied the names carved into the stone as I waited for the service to end so I could herd everyone back into their cars and help them on their way. Many of them would be heading back to Mrs. Stewart's house to sit shiva, the seven-day mourning period, and I had directions and an explanation for the funeral attendees in my neat navy blue folder.

A figure in black eased itself into my peripheral vision, but didn't join the rest of the people gathered around the grave. A man. He spoke along with the rabbi. I didn't know what the words meant— *"Yitgadal v'yitkadash sh'mei rabbah,"* but I recognized the murmur of "amen."

I turned. It was Sam. He wore a white shirt open at the throat and unfettered by a tie, and his black suit lacked a formal cut, but he'd shaved and slicked his hair back from his forehead. The diamond in his ear winked in the sunshine. He stared straight ahead, mouth moving along with the prayers.

I didn't speak. He didn't look at me. The service ended and I attended to the business of making sure everyone knew where they were meant to go.

The argument started as the mourners began filing into their cars. I'd collected all the funeral flags and passed out instructions regarding what was meant to happen after the funeral and was about to close the door of the Stewarts' car when Dan boiled out of the driver's seat.

He, unlike his brother, hadn't shaved, and his hair was rumpled. His suit jacket bore a ragged tear on the left breast pocket, part of traditional Jewish mourning custom for a parent. He was followed almost at once by his wife, whose hand he shrugged off.

"Danny, calm down," Sam said from behind me. "I already told Ma I'm taking my car. I'll meet you back at the house."

Caught in the middle, I took two hasty steps back. Dan didn't look at me, but Sam did. So did Dan's wife. She reached for Dan again, this time snagging his sleeve and holding him from moving forward.

"Why bother, man?" Dan swiped a hand through his hair, then flung it out in a gesture of disgust. "Why even bother?"

Sam's lean features settled into icy distance. "Because Ma wants me to."

"Since when do you do what anyone wants you to do?"

Sam looked at his brother without flinching. "Apparently, since Dad died."

"Dan," Elle murmured. "C'mon. He'll meet us back at the house. It's okay."

"It's not okay," Dan said through gritted teeth, but with another glare at his brother he ducked back into the driver's seat of his car.

Elle looked at Sam with an expression I couldn't interpret, and Sam looked back as blankly. Then she got in the car and shut the door, and they pulled away.

Nobody likes to linger in a cemetery. Everyone had gone, and I needed to leave, too. I had other services to oversee. I was already going to be cutting it close. Jared waved at me from his seat behind the wheel and I gave him a nod, but I didn't head for the hearse just yet.

"You'd better get going." Sam jerked his chin toward Jared. "He's waiting."

"Yes. I know."

The distance between us wasn't vast. Might even have

been considered close by someone who didn't know we'd once spent a couple hours fucking each other to oblivion. I couldn't forget that, once, I'd been close enough to count his eyelashes.

"My brother's going to kick my ass," Sam said conversationally.

"I'm sorry. The death of a loved one's always difficult—"

Sam shook his head, and the slicked-back hair feathered forward over his forehead. "That would be a nice excuse, but it's not really about my dad dying."

"So…what are you going to do?"

He smiled. "Apparently, I'm going to get my ass kicked."

"Good luck with that," I told him, and backed up a step.

"Hey." He took one forward. "Grace, about last night—"

I held up a hand. "Like I said. The death of a loved one is always difficult. People do crazy things. Don't worry about it."

"I'm not worried. Well. I'm a little worried, but not because I kissed you." Sam made as though to reach for me, but caught only empty air. It was enough to stop me, though. "Just worried I might not get another chance."

I turned my back then, despite the leap of my heart. Because of it, in fact. "My condolences on the loss of your father, Sam. You'd better get going, and I'm going to be late."

"Grace!"

I didn't turn, just kept walking toward Jared and the hearse. I could see Jared inside, bopping his fingers on the wheel again, mouthing along to some song. He must have turned on the radio. Without a body in the back, we often cranked up the tunes.

"I want to see you again!"

I stopped, then, and turned, grateful the rest of the crowd had already gone. "I don't think that's a good idea."

"Why not?"

I shook my head. "Not a good time for this discussion."

"I'll call you!"

"No, Sam!" I was almost to the hearse when I stopped this time. "No. Don't."

He shook his head to get his hair off his forehead, and the sun again caught his earring. It caught his smile, too, which was twice as shiny as the diamond. "I'm going to call you."

I shook my head again, but said nothing this time. Arguing would be undignified. I went around the front of the hearse and got in the passenger side. Jared looked up as I slid into my seat. He reached to turn down the music, but I stopped him.

"Leave it. I like this song."

Jared gave me a look. "You do?"

Since we'd often teased each other about musical preferences, I knew he could tell I wasn't being truthful, but I just wanted to get out of there. "Sure. Emo is my new favorite flavor."

Jared laughed and cast a curious glance out the window, where Sam was loping away over the grass-covered hill toward the parking lot. "Does that guy know where he's going?"

"Does anybody?"

Jared laughed and revved up the car. "Deep, Grace. Very deep."

I let him think I was being flip, but as I watched out the window for Sam's car to drive away, I wondered the same thing.

I made it through the Stewarts' service and the one later in the afternoon, but then was finished for the day. I needed coffee. Shelly usually made it, not as strong as I liked to drink it but good enough to get me through the midafternoon lag.

The day had seemed interminable, probably because of my lack of sleep and the amount of paperwork I had to do. I was yawning when she poked her head in again, this time with a plate of cookies.

"I baked. Want one?"

"Sure."

She brought the plate to my desk. "Chocolate peanut-butter chip."

"God." I bit into one. "Sooooo good."

Shelly beamed. "I got the recipe from my baking magazine. I think I'm going to try pecan roll next. With cream-cheese filling. What do you think?"

"I think I'm going to have to buy new pants if you keep this up."

She giggled. Shelly was really a sweet girl, even if she was prone to attacks of excitability and easily made to cry. She ate a cookie, too, but looked as though she was analyzing it rather than enjoying it.

"I think next time I'll use white chocolate chips, instead."

I finished my cookie. "These are great. Why mess with perfection?"

Shelly shrugged. "How do you know it's perfection unless you try something else that might be better?"

"The same could be said for more than cookies," I said.

Shelly snagged another cookie and broke it into pieces to eat each one slowly. "Like men?"

I sat back in my chair. Shelly had had the same quiet boyfriend since she started working for me. Duane Emerich had taken over his family's farm and had, according to Shelly, been hinting at marriage. Whether or not Shelly herself wanted to get married I didn't know, but she hadn't shown up with a ring on her finger yet.

"Depends," I answered.

"On what?"

"On the man?" I took another cookie but only nibbled it. Savoring it. "What's up, Shelly?"

She shrugged prettily. "Nothing. Just thinking about living on a farm for the rest of my life, that's all."

The idea held absolutely no appeal for me, but I wasn't going to tell her that. "Thinking about Duane, you mean. He's a good guy."

"Yes." She sighed. "But…"

I waited for her to continue, but she didn't. "But…?"

Shelly looked up at me. "Well, he's…a little…"

Duane was a little of a lot of things, none of which I wanted to give an opinion about. "He's a good guy, Shelly."

"With shit on his shoes," she said.

I don't know which shocked me more, the fact she'd criticized him or the fact she'd cursed. I didn't know what to say and shoved more cookie into my mouth so I wouldn't have to think of something. Shelly sighed again.

"You go out with lots of different guys, don't you, Grace?"

I chewed and swallowed and sipped coffee to clear my mouth. "Not that many."

"I've been going out with Duane since we were sophomores in high school." She looked at me. "He's the only boyfriend I've ever had."

"There's nothing wrong with that, you know."

"I know." Shelly shrugged again. "But he's just so…good."

"Good isn't something to sneeze at," I told her.

"By good I mean boring," Shelly said.

"Boring isn't so good."

We laughed.

"I just don't know what to think. We do the same things all the time. Go to the movies. Eat pizza on Sunday nights. I can tell you exactly what he'll get me for my birthday. I can tell you what color shirt he'll wear on Thursday."

"There's nothing wrong with any of that," I said quietly.

Shelly nodded. "Yeah. I know."

Part of her must have questioned it, though, else she wouldn't have been talking to me about it. Shelly and I weren't close enough for me to offer her advice, if I'd had any to give. So I ate another cookie, and so did she, and in another minute the phone rang and she went to answer it.

Thinking about what she'd said, I spun in my chair while I ate yet another cookie and sipped my coffee and looked out my window to the back parking lot.

I tried to tell myself it was the plateful of cookies that had soured my stomach, but the truth was, I didn't like facing the memory of my earlier envy. I closed down my computer and made sure to grab my phone, then headed out to Shelly's desk.

"I'm going to run some errands. I don't have any appointments today, but if something comes up, give me a call. Jared can handle pretty much anything until I get back."

I was uncertain of where, exactly, I wanted to go, just that I wanted to get away from Frawley and Sons for a while. Traffic decided for me, making it easier to turn right than left. Five minutes' drive took me to my sister's house, the front yard uncharacteristically scattered with toys. I pulled into the driveway but sat in the car for a minute. What would I tell my sister about why I was here?

She didn't give me long enough to figure it out. The front door opened and Hannah peered out through the screen door. Of course she did. This was Annville, after all. I'm sure all her neighbors were peering out, too.

She opened the door as I got out of the car. "Grace?"

I waved. "Hi."

She held the door for me. "What are you doing here?"

"Oh…just thought I'd stop by, if that's okay."

She closed the door behind me. The living room was a minefield of blocks and action figures. Like the front yard, this wasn't the norm for my sister, who'd inherited our mother's neatness genes.

"Where's Simon?" I asked unnecessarily, since from the basement rec room I heard the drone of cartoons.

Hannah pointed. "Downstairs rotting his brain. Come into the kitchen."

It was also a disaster, at least according to the normal

standards. Dishes were piled high in the sink and on the counter, with the remains of lunch on the table. The sliding door that normally imprisoned the washer and drier hung open, two baskets of laundry sprawling in front of them.

"I didn't have time to clean," Hannah said when she noticed me looking.

"I see that."

"Coffee?" She went to the pot and lifted a cup.

"Sure."

I watched her carefully. She didn't usually wear a lot of makeup, but today she wore none but the shadows of sleeplessness. She'd pulled her hair on top of her head in a messy ponytail and wore a pair of velour track pants and an oversize T-shirt that hung to her thighs. I took the cup she handed me.

"Sugar? Milk?" Hannah was already pulling them out and taking them to the table before I could answer.

"Thanks."

We sat, a plate of misshapen cookies between us. My sister took one and broke it in half but ate both in rapid succession. Then she took another.

"Simon wanted to make cookies." She wiped crumbs from her mouth. "Aren't I the best mom ever?"

"You are a good mom," I told my sister.

She laughed briefly. "Yeah, that's why he's downstairs, glued to the TV."

"A little television's not going to kill him. Cookies won't, either."

Hannah and her husband had always been adamant about Simon's and Melanie's consumption of sugar and cartoons. Never having had children, I hadn't ever felt qualified to comment, but though I thought they might be a little too stringent sometimes, they weren't hurting their children with their restrictions, either. If anything, not plopping her kids in front of the electronic babysitter had been harder on my sister than if she'd let them sit there for hours. She'd always been a crafts-and-cookies mom, the sort who made homemade Halloween costumes and never failed to make something for the bake sale.

"I'm just tired," she told me abruptly.

The washer spun to a stop and beeped to indicate the end of the cycle. Hannah stared at it, then took another cookie.

"I'm just so tired of all of it," she said.

I'd never heard her talk that way before. "Of what?"

She gestured. "This. The house. The kids. The husband. I'm tired of picking up other people's crap all day long. I'm tired of never being finished. Not ever."

She put her hand to her face while I stared, not knowing what to say. She shook her head slowly, grimacing. Then she took her hand away and ate another cookie grimly and without joy.

"I'm tired of never having anything that doesn't get broken," she added with a look toward the sunporch.

I followed her gaze. A blue-and-white pot holding a peace lily lay on the tile floor in pieces, dirt and leaves scattered everywhere.

"I don't blame you," I said.

She laughed again and gave me an older sister's semi-scornful look. "Oh, what do you know? You're young and single and go out with a different guy every week. What would you know about it?"

My mouth parted at her attack, but I managed not to retaliate. "The grass isn't always greener, Hannah."

She raised a brow in a gesture I'd often felt on my own face. We didn't look much alike, her with blond and coiffed hair and me with my dark, straight cut, but that expression was one I'd felt many times on my own face. Proof we were sisters.

"You want to trade?" She got up and yanked open the washer and drier doors and began transferring the wet clothes, stopping every now and then to violently snap the wrinkles out of Jerry's dress shirts and hang them to dry. "You want to wash four or five loads of laundry at a time, trying to make sure you find all the stains so you can pre-treat them and remember to hang up the dress shirts because they get wrinkled in the drier? Do you want to have to fold it all, too, only to have more in the hamper before you're even finished?"

"No. But you act like I don't have to do laundry, Hannah."

"You do laundry for yourself!" Her voice snapped as violently as the wet shirts had. "There's a big difference. Everything you do is for yourself!"

I sat, smacked into silence by her vehemence while she slammed the drier shut and stabbed it into its cycle with her fingertip. She went to the table next, grabbing up the barren cookie plate and shoving it into the dishwasher, then starting to do the same with the dishes in the sink.

"You just have to take care of yourself," she repeated, not even rinsing the dishes before she put them in the washer. She'd be sorry later when the dried mac and cheese didn't come all the way off the porcelain, but I wasn't brave enough to point that out.

"Well, yeah," I said, like I was saying "yeah, duh." "I'm not married. I don't have kids."

My sister's laugh sounded like something from a horror movie. "No shit."

Hannah never swore. I sat back in my chair, not bothering to hide my gaping mouth. She turned, defiant, eyes glittering with anger or tears, or maybe both.

"What? I can't say shit? Shit, shit, shit!"

The basement door creaked open and Simon came up, clutching a handful of action figures in one small hand. "Oooh, that's a bad word!"

Silence surrounded us. Hannah turned back to the dishwasher and her assault on the silverware. I gestured to my nephew.

"Hey, buddy. How about we go to McDonald's?"

His face lit up with the sort of joy only a small child can channel, and he flung his arms around my neck. "Auntie Grace, you are the bestest aunt in the whole wide world!"

I looked at the angry hunch of Hannah's shoulders and the way she kept stabbing plates and cups into the dishwasher. "Let me take him out for a while."

I thought she'd protest, especially the part about McDonald's, but she just waved a hand without turning around. "His booster seat's in the van. Make sure he buckles up."

"How about I pick up Melanie from school?" I added with a glance at the clock. My niece would finish in half an hour. "I'll take them both for an early dinner. Bring them home after."

Hannah nodded without turning around, but she stopped loading the dishwasher. She gripped the sink. Even from my place at the table I could see her knuckles had gone white.

"Great," she said, her voice strained. "Thanks."

"Sure." I kept my voice light. Easy. "C'mon, buddy, let's find you some shoes."

With Simon babbling the entire time, I didn't have to speak to my sister, and I didn't. We got his shoes and jacket and the booster seat from the van. We picked up Melanie from school and I was again greeted with the announcement of being the "best aunt in the whole world," a title I wasn't about to argue.

I took them to the dollar store and the pet store to look at the animals, then to the burger place where they got junk food and junk toys.

When we pulled into Hannah's driveway the van was gone but Jerry's car was there, and it was he who opened the door when I knocked. The kids tumbled through the doorway with excited stories about the exotic pets and French fries. The house had been transformed while we were gone, the kitchen cleaned, the laundry gone, the broken pot removed and the dirt swept up.

"Where's Hannah?"

Jerry looked blank. "I don't know."

I wasn't going to touch that with any length of pole. If my sister had gone out without letting her husband know, that was his problem. I'd safely returned their children and had nothing more to do there.

"She didn't leave anything for dinner," Jerry said. Clearly this was befuddling him.

"The kids already ate," I told him. "I told her I'd take them out. You don't need to feed them."

Jerry looked around. "Did she ask you to bring me anything?"

I made my face carefully blank, as hard as it was not to slap a hand to my forehead. "No, Jerry, she didn't."

I liked my brother-in-law. He was a nice guy. He'd never told me offensive jokes or given me bad advice. In fact, mostly he left me alone and didn't bother with me much at all. But right now I wanted to shake some sense into him.

"Huh," he said while his kids ran like hooligans up and down the hall without a glance. "She didn't leave anything for me."

"Good thing there's peanut butter and jelly."

He gave me a blank look. If he'd asked me to make him something, I might have had to smack him, but fortunately for both of us Jerry just nodded. "Yeah. I guess so."

"Are you under control here?" I eyed the kids, now wrestling on the living-room floor.

"Oh, yeah." He nodded.

I didn't quite believe him, but it wasn't like he was going to let them hurt themselves. Woe to him if something else got broken while Hannah was out, but that also wasn't my problem. With another set of hugs and squeezes for my niece and nephew I headed out, back home.

I caught Jared just as he was leaving. "Nothing going on?" He shook his head. "Everything's locked up."

"Oh, good. Thanks."

Jared nodded. "I'm on call tonight, right?"

"You asked for it, remember?"

"I know. I know."

We smiled at each other and he headed off to his battered pickup truck. As I opened the door to go in, a slightly breathless Shelly came out. Her cheeks had flushed faintly pink and a few tendrils of hair had escaped from her French braid to frame her face. She looked as if she'd put on lip gloss.

Jared turned, waving. Shelly dimpled and edged past me with a murmured goodbye. She wasn't looking at me, she was looking at Jared's truck.

"My car's in the shop," she explained half over her shoulder. "Jared's giving me a ride home."

"Okay," I said, as if either of them needed my permission, or I needed an explanation.

Shelly waved. I stood in the doorway until she got into his truck. Shelly sat as close to her door as possible, staring straight ahead. Jared smiled, his mouth moving as he chatted, but all I saw Shelly do in response was nod her head stiffly once or twice as he pulled out of the parking lot.

Interesting.

Chapter 07

$\mathcal{T}$he knock on the door didn't startle me, but I pretended to be surprised when I opened it, anyway. "I didn't order a pizza."

The man standing outside the door wore a blue shirt and matching ball cap, and the box in his hand undoubtedly held a pizza. "Are you sure?"

"I'm sure. I think I'd know if I ordered a pizza or not."

He frowned and made a show of looking at the front of the door. "This is the room they told me. Are you sure?"

I put my hands on my hips, bunching the silk of my nightgown. "Yes! I'm sure!"

The pizza boy looked confused, then annoyed. "Look, this is the third prank pizza delivery I've had to put up with this week, and I'm getting pretty tired of it."

"Are you saying I prank ordered?"

He pushed forward, pizza in hand, and set it on the table. "Someone in this room ordered a pizza. You're the only one here."

My heart thumped. He looked really angry. I looked at

the door, ajar behind him, and he turned to look at it, too. But then he closed it with a swift shove and faced me again.

"Pay up."

"But I don't have any money!" I protested.

I stepped back. He moved forward. Beneath his unbuttoned blue shirt he wore a white T-shirt that clung to him like a second skin. Beneath the ball cap's brim his eyes flashed, brilliant blue. His hair was hard to see but I knew it was dark. His gaze raked me up and down, taking in my black silk nightgown and the glisten of glittery powder across the top swell of my breasts.

"Then I guess we'll have to think of something else." His mouth tilted, half up and half down, and his voice dipped low.

"If you think—" I started, intending but unable to sound angry. My voice shook just a little, and I had to stop to swallow against my dry throat.

"Turn around. Put your hands on the table."

I did, one on each side of the pizza box, still warm and smelling of cheese and sauce. I didn't dare turn, not even to glance over my shoulder. I closed my eyes so I didn't have to watch my fingers clutch against the sleek laminate of the hotel table, and I waited, every muscle tense and atremble, for him to touch me.

He didn't. Not as soon as I'd thought he would, and the waiting became torture. I felt the heat of his body behind me and caught a whiff of something more delicious than cheese and sauce. I heard the rattle and hum of him pulling down his zipper, then the shush of the material sliding over his thighs. I shifted my weight, leaning forward and moving my feet farther apart. The silk rode higher on my bare thighs. And still, he didn't touch me.

The sound of our breathing mingled and grew loud in the silence. I counted seconds like drops of rain on a roof, a steady rising pattern of them. My fingers ached from their grip upon the slick surface, and I relaxed them. I opened my eyes. Started to turn, a question hovering in my mouth.

Then, he touched me.

His hands lightly clasped my ankles and slid up the backs of my calves, then my thighs, both at the same time and in one, swift motion that left me gasping. His hands slid up, over my ass. He cupped my flesh briefly, and in the next moment the whisper of his breath moved over all the places his hands had just touched.

Oh, God. He was on his knees behind me.

He tasted the invisible trail his hands had left, mapping the path of his touch with his tongue. He paused to lick the back of my knee, then moved to bite the back of the other. If the table had not been so stubbornly slick, my fingernails would surely have gouged out runners in the surface, so fiercely did I clutch it. I opened my mouth but immediately bit back the cry as his mouth shifted higher. His tongue flicked the underside of my buttocks, a place nobody had ever kissed, much less licked. It was a good thing the table was in front of me, because his caress had buckled my knees. His tongue slid higher, along the seam of my ass. When it reached the bottom of my spine, that magic, secret spot that made me writhe, I couldn't have held back the cry if I'd tried.

Pain sizzled in my lower lip; I'd bitten it. My hair fell

down over my face, and I closed my eyes again. I didn't want to be staring at a pizza box when this happened to me.

His hand moved between my legs as his mouth moved upward along the line of my spine. His fingers found my clit at the same time his teeth found my shoulder, and at the twin bursts of pleasure rocketing through me, I cried out again.

The softness of his T-shirt brushed my back as he leaned in and the hard, small chill of his buttons pressed my hip. His fingers played upon my clit a moment more, not long enough, but when he withdrew to use that same hand to push my legs wider apart, I could make no protest. I licked away the salty heat of blood from my lip.

His hand found my heat again. His fingers traced the outline of my cunt and parted me, nudging inside just enough to make me tremble again. The chuff of his breath blew hot on my shoulder, left damp from his mouth. His other hand anchored my hip and held me still. I waited again, tense, for him to replace his fingers with the thickness of his cock.

I felt him all over my back. His mouth again found the flesh left bare around the thin straps of my nightgown, and he fastened his lips there with the hard promise of his teeth beneath. The silk of my gown crumpled in his fist and fluttered around my hips.

His hand replaced his mouth on my shoulder, and he pushed me forward. I bent and my hands jittered across the tabletop. I opened my eyes to see the pizza box teeter on the edge, then tumble off. The hand on my hip now guided his cock between my legs.

He found my entrance with unerring efficiency but took

his damn sweet time pushing inside me. He twisted a little, thrust a little, eased out and then in again while his hands kept me from moving.

His low moan moved across the back of my neck as physically as if he'd used his hand to touch me there. For one endless moment we didn't move, both of us still like a frozen river; solid and unmoving on the top and rushing, rushing underneath.

"Please," I said then, in a voice so small and faint with pleasure I wasn't sure he'd hear me.

The first real pull and push caught me unawares even though I'd anticipated it, nearly begged for it, even. He did it all at once, nothing like the cautious way he'd pushed inside me, but fast. Hard. And harder, then, with the second. Hard enough to move me forward on the table, hard enough to move the frigging table itself.

His hand returned to my shoulder. His thumb pressed the place that on angels sprouted wings, but there were no angels here. His fingers gripped me as he pounded inside me in the smooth rhythm he set all on his own without effort from me. I wanted to push back against him, or to lean forward and lift my ass so he could drive into me deeper, but his hands anchored me. Kept me still, no matter how I tried to writhe. His cock slid inside and against me, hitting spots unused to such attention.

I was caught between pleasure and pain, feeling too good to protest though I wondered if I'd regret it later. Rough sex had a price, but at the moment I was too wildly turned on to care. Every thrust, each pinch of his fingertips on my flesh, sent me soaring closer and closer to the orgasm I craved.

My mouth parted and a low moan seeped out. I closed my eyes again, wanting to get lost inside the sensations sweeping over me. The feeling of advance and retreat inside my body. The slap of our bodies against one another sounded louder with my eyes closed, and so did the harsh pant of his breathing. His low moan answering mine. Even the burble of voices from outside the hotel room sounded louder, and I gasped a small laugh at the passing conversation. They were talking about where to go for lunch while inside we were fucking like animals.

I reached between my thighs and pressed my palm flat against my clitoris. I didn't have to rub or stroke; his thrusts did that for me. I simply needed a little extra, just a little...

"I want you to come." This, said in the low, thick voice laced with desire, earned another whispering gasp from me. Something about the words, the way he said them, the command behind them, pumped my hips forward against my palm. His hand tightened on my shoulder. "Grace, I want you to come."

The sound of my name destroyed any final illusion I'd been trying to keep about him, but I didn't care. He wanted me to come, but he didn't say he expected me to answer. I wasn't sure I could form words. I let my body reply, instead, as my cunt bore down on his cock and I spiraled into ecstasy.

Release. It was so good, so strong, so...necessary. So freeing. In that moment I could do nothing but feel. I could think of nothing but pleasure.

I went up, up, and then floated down, sated, the table beneath my cheek still warm from the pizza box. Jack thrust a couple more times and finished with a grunting sigh. His hands relaxed, letting me go, and it wasn't until he was no longer holding me that I really felt how hard he'd been gripping.

For a few moments we stayed still. I moved first with a subtle shift of my hips, and Jack pulled out. I took a second longer to lean against the table we'd so abused, giving myself time to catch my breath and my legs to stop shaking. I turned to rest my butt against the table. The strap of my gown had fallen down my shoulder, so I pushed it back up, and I let the hem fall back down to my thighs. Jack had turned to take care of the condom, and when he turned back to me, he was already tucked away and zipped closed.

We stared at each other in silence.

Then, the smile.

"That," Jack said, "was totally hot."

I laughed. "Mmm, hmm."

He shook himself a little like a puppy coming out of a bath, then bounced up and down a few times. He took off the cap and looked at it, then tossed it to the dresser. His hair fell forward over one eye at once, and impatiently, he brushed it away.

"My buddy Damien would have a cow if he knew what I was doing with his uniform, though." He took the shirt off, too, and laid it with the hat.

"I wondered where you got that." My heart had stopped pounding and my thighs no longer trembled. I was too languid and sated to move, but the table had started biting into the back of my butt. I bent to pick up the fallen pizza box, which had landed on its front. "And you brought a real pizza, too."

Jack laughed. "Well, sure. Of course."

I glanced over my shoulder at him as I set the box, right side up, back on the table. "It was a nice touch."

He looked pleased. "I was afraid I was going to show up at the wrong room by accident and I figured if I had a real pizza, I'd be more convincing."

I lifted the lid. Some of the cheese had glued itself to the top of the box, but most of it was all right. "This looks good. Double cheese?"

"Yeah." He came closer and took the slice I pulled free to hand him. "Thanks."

Without plates or napkins we had to make do with resting the pizza on our hands, but it was cool enough by that time. "I'm starving. Sit down."

He pulled up the chair next to the table and I took the other. "My friend Ricky Scorza's uncle owns this pizza shop, and they make the best frigging pizza."

I bit into my slice and had to agree, it was pretty damn good. Of course, when you're famished, anything tastes good. The sex had left my stomach growling. "Scorza's Pizza Stop?"

"Yeah." Jack chewed and swallowed. "You know it?"

"I've passed it." Scorza's was stuck between a massage-therapy office and an old brownstone divided into apartments on Third Street. I'd driven by it a few times on my way through town, but never stopped.

We ate in companionable silence after that. Jack wolfed down three slices and I put away two, but I was the one who belched behind my hand. He laughed after a moment and followed suit.

"Nice one," I told him with a sigh, and leaned back in the chair to rest my hands on my stomach.

Jack leaned back, too, and crossed his legs at the ankle. "You're not like I thought you'd be."

A statement like that could either be a compliment or an insult, depending on who said it, but from Jack I was going to assume he meant it in a good way. "How'd you think I would be?"

He shrugged and leaned forward to put his elbows on his knees. "The other ladies…aren't…"

I watched his face work as he struggled to find words. I wasn't sure I wanted to hear about his other ladies. I sure wouldn't have been happy to know he spoke to them about me. I got up to wash my hands free of pizza grease in the bathroom sink. In the mirror I could see his reflection as he watched me without knowing I could see.

He was looking at my ass, no mistaking that, in the way men have that's boyish and lascivious all at once. They look at new cars or power tools the same way they assess a woman, sometimes, pulling her apart piece by piece the way they'd lift up the hood of a Lamborghini and coo over the engine. But when I turned and came back into the room, he wasn't looking anymore. At least not so blatantly.

"So much fun," he finished, though I hadn't prompted him.

That surprised me. I'd expected him to say young, maybe. Or even hot, if I wanted to be bold enough to make an assumption. "Fun?" I smiled at that word, an unexpected and therefore more appreciated comment.

"Yeah." He grinned. "The pizza-boy stuff. Nobody else wants to do stuff like that."

"Ah." I found the clothes I'd worn here, stepped into my panties, tugged the nightgown off over my head so I could put on my bra. I felt him watching me, but again when I looked, his eyes were turned away. "Well…everyone has their own ideas of what's fun, Jack."

"Yeah." He stood and stretched, then ambled into the bathroom. Unlike me, he closed the door, and in a minute I heard the toilet flush and the sound of the water running in the sink. By the time he came out, I'd finished dressing.

"I have to run, I have an appointment at three-thirty." I rustled around in my wallet to find some cash. "How much do I owe you for the pizza?"

Silence greeted that question, and I looked up. "Jack?"

"Nothing," he said after a second. "My treat."

Technically, I was supposed to pick up the cost of anything extra, but since the search for cash in my wallet was revealing only a few limp, dog-eared dollars and a coffee-club card from Sheetz, I didn't argue. "Thanks."

"No problem." He slaughtered me once again with his smile, and I didn't want to leave. "It was fun."

"It *was* fun." I paused, frozen, knowing I should just leave. I was going to be late. Yet I stood, captured in place by the tilt of Jack's mouth and the glint in his eye, trapped by the fall of his silky black hair.

He saved me from myself by turning toward the pizza. "Mind if I take this home?"

"Of course not." The moment broken, I slung my purse

over my shoulder and snatched up the key I needed to drop off in the office on my way out. "Don't forget your uniform."

"Hell, no. Damien would beat my ass." Jack laughed and balanced the pizza box in one hand as he grabbed up the shirt and hat with the other.

At the doorway, we collided, bouncing like pinballs until we laughed and he stepped back to let me through. The door closed behind us. Clouds had covered the sun while we dallied inside, and I smelled rain. A breeze flipped Jack's hair back from his face and fluttered the edges of the borrowed shirt he clutched. I spotted his motorcycle parked a few spots away.

"How are you going to drive with that pizza in your hands?"

Jack squinted up at the sky. "I'll be okay. I'll strap the pizza to the back of the bike, no problem."

"Jack." I also squinted up at the sky, which had grown darker even as we stood there. "It's going to rain."

Thunder rumbled.

"See?"

"I'll be okay. I won't melt."

I raised a brow at him. "Your pizza will get soggy."

"You offering me a ride?"

"I hate to think of you riding in the rain, that's all." I'll admit it, I was hoping for another glimpse of the panty-dampening smile.

I got it.

"Uh-huh."

I feigned innocence. "What? You're telling me you'd rather get soaked and have soggy pizza? Fine, forget I offered."

I'd taken only two steps toward the office before he caught up to me and snagged my sleeve. "Wait."

I stopped. To our left, lightning crackled in a bruised sky. Thunder like the beat of drums followed it a moment later.

"You can give me a ride. I'll have one of my buddies drive me over to pick up the bike later. Thanks."

Again we stared at each other, but I was the first to look away. Offering him a ride had been spur-of-the-moment and probably not wise, but it was too late to retract the offer now. Besides, I didn't feel right sending him off in the rain on a motorcycle with a pizza. I had too much personal experience with the aftermath of bad motorcycle accidents. If something happened to Jack that I could've helped prevent, I'd never forgive myself.

I took only a few minutes to drop off the key and check out of the room. Once again the clerk didn't do more than glance at my face, a habit I usually appreciated but that today seemed to make what I'd just done feel illicit in a way I'd stopped feeling quite some time ago. By the time I got to my car, Jack had grabbed his helmet and balanced it on the pizza box with his buddy's shirt draped over one arm and the baseball cap dangling from one finger. He was looking at my car almost the way he'd been ogling my ass earlier.

Behind the wheel, I reached over to unlock the door for him. Jack slid in just as the first fat drops of rain splattered on the hood. He closed his door to the accompaniment of thunder. He twisted to put the pizza and extra clothes on the backseat and buckled himself right away as I started the car.

Betty roared like a lion, though maybe a lion with bronchitis and not one in the peak of health. I let the engine rumble for a minute before I shifted into Reverse and backed out of the parking spot. By the time I pulled to the edge of the lot, the skies had opened and rain poured down so hard the wipers had a hard time keeping the window clear.

"Wow." Jack craned his neck to look out the window. "I'm glad you offered me a ride."

I risked a glance at him, then put my gaze firmly back on the road. "Which way?"

He gave me easy and succinct directions to a section of Harrisburg that wasn't exactly the stomping grounds of the well-to-do. It should've taken about ten minutes to get there, even in heavy traffic, but with the rain we spent closer to twenty. I tried not to keep looking at my watch, but three-thirty was creeping closer and closer and I was still forty-five minutes from home. By the time I pulled up in front of the building Jack directed me to, I had only an hour and a half to get home and get ready for the appointment. I wouldn't be late—I hoped—but I'd spent most of the day away from the office, and God only knew what awaited my return.

I meant only to drop him off and be on my way, but just as I pulled up to the curb, a delivery truck lumbered down the narrow alley toward us. "What the hell? Isn't this street one-way?"

Jack snorted. "Yes. That dude's a moron. This is, like, the third time he's done this."

I looked out my fogged-up back window. Backing up would take driving skill I didn't have, not to mention send me down the street in Reverse and going the wrong way. "I hope he makes it fast. I really need to get going."

"Hold on. I'll check."

Before I could stop him, Jack had hopped out of the car and run through the rain toward the delivery truck, where he pounded on the door until the driver opened it. I saw waving hands and gestures but couldn't hear what they were saying. In moments Jack was back in my car, sliding across the vinyl seat and slamming the door. He was soaked.

"Says it should only take ten minutes."

"Great." I slapped the wheel with the flat of my hand and looked at my watch. "I hope he hurries."

"Are you going to be late?"

"I hope not." I sighed.

"Maybe you can call your office?" He offered helpfully. "Reschedule?"

"Thanks, but I can't, really." The best I could do was call Jared and tell him to start the process with the family, but they hadn't decided to come to Frawley and Sons to have Jared take care of their mother. They'd asked for my business because of me, or more likely because of my dad. I trusted Jared to handle the paperwork, but if I had to miss the appointment with the family, I'd be letting them down.

"I'm sorry," Jack said.

Pulled from my musings, I looked up at him. "For what?"

"You shouldn't have given me a ride. Then you wouldn't be late."

"Oh, Jack. It's okay. Don't worry about that," I told him, even though he was right and I'd been thinking it myself a moment before. "I couldn't let you ride in the rain. Look at it out there. You're still dripping."

I reached into the backseat and grabbed an old sweatshirt emblazoned with my college emblem. "Wipe yourself off."

He dried his face and ran it over his hair, then looked at it. "Your sweatshirt? Thanks."

I laughed. "Don't worry about it. I left it in there months ago and haven't worn it. Or missed it. It can stand a little wetness."

Jack grinned. His damp hair clung to the sides of his cheeks, and on impulse I reached out to smooth away one sleek piece. He turned his face to push his mouth against my hand.

One small, perfect moment.

I don't know how I managed to get onto Jack's lap without impaling myself on the gearshift, but I did it. I straddled him with his face in my hands and his hungry mouth devouring mine. I tasted pizza and rain and felt his wet hair on the backs of my hands. My skirt rode up as his hands slid up my thighs. I wasn't wearing stockings, and his shirt dampened my skin.

Jack's hands cupped my ass, pulling me closer. My crotch ground against his belt buckle, the metal cold through the thin satin of my panties. My nipples rose in taut peaks through the lace of my bra. Jack reached to nudge open the buttons on my blouse and pushed his face against my skin. His lips tightened on one nipple, the heat of his mouth a sharp contrast to the chill of his rain-wet skin.

I was in the middle of a moan when the bleat of the delivery truck startled me so much I hit my head on the roof. I muttered a curse. My breast, bared and no longer shielded by Jack's mouth, popped out from my blouse and I scrambled to cover my bare flesh with the hand not rubbing the top of my head. Fortunately, our heated make-out session had steamed up all the windows so there was no way anybody could possibly have seen anything embarrassing.

I looked down into Jack's face as he looked up into mine. With another bleating honk, the delivery truck rumbled by, leaving the street once more clear. I licked my mouth and tasted Jack. I felt him, too, between my legs and on my ass. On my nipple, still hard beneath my palm.

"I need to go," I whispered.

He nodded. His hands caressed my rear again. His belt buckle had warmed against me and under it I felt the bulge of his erection. A squeak eeped from my throat at the memory of how he felt inside me, but though he leaned up to kiss me again, I didn't let him.

"I really have to go, Jack."

He paused, back arched and mouth parted for the kiss I had denied, then settled back against the seat. His hands left my butt and settled on my thighs. "Okay."

I'd managed to get on his lap without injuring myself, but crawling back to my seat proved to be more awkward, especially as it was done in utter silence. I managed, finally, though my skirt had twisted and the seat was chilly on my bare thighs. I concentrated on fixing it. My shoe had twisted, too, and I reached down to slide the back of it up higher on my heel.

I used the excuse of fixing my clothes to not look at Jack. Not even when he leaned into the backseat to grab up his pizza and his clothes and he was so close to me I could smell myself on his skin. Not when he sat back in his seat again, pizza in his hands, and looked at me.

I kept my eyes on the windshield as I waited for him to say something. Anything, just so I didn't have to. And Jack, bless him, did.

"Thanks for the ride." His voice sounded too formal. He waited while I murmured a response, then got out of the car. The Camaro's doors were heavy and the rain outside fierce, but I wasn't convinced those were the reasons he slammed the door. He didn't turn to wave goodbye, either, just disappeared inside the door to his building.

And what had I expected? We weren't dating. I paid him money to take me places and, on occasion, to fuck me. Expecting anything else was just asking for things I kept telling myself I didn't want.

Chapter 08

*B*y the time I got back to the funeral home, the rain had cleared. I wasn't late, but I didn't have time to do more than use the bathroom, brush my hair and swipe my face with powder and lipstick before my three-thirty appointment was due. Shelly brought in a stack of messages for me, all the pink "While You Were Out" slips stacked neatly and printed in her fine, careful hand.

"Anything important?" I asked as I shrugged out of my damp blouse and into a dry one I'd kept on the back of the door. It didn't quite match my skirt, but with the suit jacket overtop it would be fine. I took the messages but didn't have time to do more than lay them on my desktop blotter.

"The new priest from St. Anne's called. He said he wanted to meet with you about the cemetery regulations."

I fluffed my hair and blotted my lips, then turned to look at her. "Huh?"

Shelly shrugged and rolled her eyes a bit in her own private expression of what she thought about the new priest at St. Anne's. "Something about the cemetery committee had a meeting and they wanted to make some new regulations? Or something?"

"But I have nothing to do with that," I protested, rolling my eyes, too. "When does he want to meet?"

"Tomorrow morning."

I sighed and clicked my computer's mouse to wake the monitor from sleep. I had my calendar up on the screen as always, and a quick glance showed me the morning was as yet unscheduled. "Can you call him and tell him that's fine?"

"Sure. When the Heilmans get here, should I send them in?"

"Sure, Shelly, thanks." I gave her a grateful glance. "I'm a little frazzled."

"I see that." She didn't ask me why, just as she never asked me where I went on the days I left the office in my Camaro and didn't come back for hours. "Want a cup of coffee? And I made pecan sandies."

"Coffee, yes. Cookies, no."

She laughed, ducking out of the office. "Okay, okay!"

"But I bet Jared would like some," I called after her.

It was mean to tease like that, but her embarrassed giggle told me what I'd already guessed. Shelly was crushing on Jared. I couldn't blame her—he was a cutie with his dark, shaggy hair and dry sense of humor. But Shelly had a boyfriend who clearly adored her and wanted to marry her.

It also wasn't any of my business.

I also didn't have any time to think about Shelly or Jared because my appointment finally showed. "Hi, Mrs. Heilman."

Evy Heilman swept through the door with her son, Gordon, in tow. "Grace, honey, it's so good to see you again."

Mrs. Heilman had been in to discuss her funeral arrangements with me three times previously. Her son always attended and sat without speaking while his mother went over the lists of casket and vault choices.

"What do you have that's new for me to look at?" She settled herself into a chair and waved a hand at Gordon. "Honey, go get me a coffee."

Gordon, never married and always dutiful, nodded and did as she said.

Evy turned to me. "Gordon thinks I should stick with the pale pink lining and the white casket with the inlaid roses, but, honey, I just don't know if I want to spend eternity feeling like I'm buried inside Barbie."

I laughed. "I don't blame you. I got a new catalog, if you want to take a look."

Evy Heilman took as much joy from a new casket catalog as some women did from designer shoes. Her eyes alight, she held out her hand. "Ooh, yes!"

By the time Gordon returned with the coffee, his mother had already stabbed a few pages with her finger. She "oohed" and "aahed" over the new items and discussed the merits of each with me while he nibbled on a few of Shelly's cookies and gave an opinion only when asked for it.

I didn't mind that Evy Heilman came in every few months and used an hour or so of my time. She had an excellent point of view on dying and death. She wasn't sick or even elderly, but she often pointed out to me that nobody knew when their time was up.

"And, honey," she said as she scribbled down the number of the new casket and vault combination she'd decided she wanted, "there is no reason not to go out with a bang. Am I right, Gordon?"

Gordon shrugged. "If you say so, Mother."

She laughed. "That's my boy."

With more hugs for me, Evy finished her selections and dragged her son out the door. I watched them go with a bit of a sigh. Evy's visits always left me a little exhausted, even though I enjoyed them.

With only half an hour left in the official work day, I returned to my computer to try to get some accounting done, but Shelly knocked on my door frame. I looked up, expecting her to be offering cookies or coffee, or maybe to ask if I minded if she and Jared sneaked out early. She was giving me a funny look, and alarmed, I half stood.

"What?"

"There's someone here to see you," Shelly said.

"Oh." I sat again. "An appointment?"

She shook her head and bit her lower lip. "He doesn't have an appointment."

"That's okay, I guess. Is it an emergency?"

Another shake. "I don't think so. He said he wanted to see you, that's all."

I couldn't figure her out. "Send him in, I guess."

She nodded and disappeared. Two minutes later, another rap on my door had me lifting my head. My chair wasn't the sort with wheels on it, but when I saw who was waiting for me I felt as if I'd been spun around anyway.

"Sam?"

He smiled and hovered in my doorway. "Hi."

"What—" I stopped myself from saying more. Playing it cool. I lifted my chin a little and brushed back my hair from my shoulders, trying not to act as if I was desperately trying to remember if I needed to refresh my lipstick. "Hi. C'mon in."

He did, as tall as I couldn't forget him being. "I know I should've called first. But I figured you might not take the call."

"Oh…um." I chewed my lower lip for a moment as he slid into the chair in front of my desk. "Sure I would have."

Sam laughed. "Uh-huh."

I had to look away for a minute to stop the sense of spinning. When I looked back at him, he was still grinning. "Do you have a reason for being here?"

"I'm hungry."

I sat back in my chair and ran my hands along the smooth, polished wood of its arms. "And?"

"I figured, seeing as how it's almost dinnertime, you might be hungry, too."

"I don't eat dinner at five, Sam."

He leaned forward a little bit. "We can wait until five-thirty."

I glanced at the clock, thinking fast, trying to decide what I wanted to say. "I don't know."

"What's to know?" He settled back in his chair, one leg crossed over the other. "You, me, food. No biggie. You're acting like I got down on one knee and proposed."

"Pffft." I waved a hand. "No, I'm not."

He pointed at me with one finger. "You are. But relax. I'm only here to eat."

"I don't have any food here," I protested, but feebly.

"Grace?" Shelly knocked on the door again. "There's a delivery for you."

Sam leaped up so fast Shelly looked startled and backed away. "I'll get it."

I was already out of my chair and following. "What did you do?"

"I hope you like Chinese," he said over his shoulder as he eased past Shelly and headed for the back door by her desk. "Hey, man. Thanks."

I watched him take the bags of take-out food and pay the deliveryman, and I ignored the looks Shelly was trying to give me. Sam turned, food in hand. Shelly nudged me with her elbow.

"You can go," I told her. "See you tomorrow."

"Oh, but don't you need—"

"G'wan, get out of here," I told her with a joker's smile on my mouth. "It's late."

It wasn't late, it was just a few minutes past five, but Shelly nodded and gathered her things from her desk. Sam had buried his nose in one of the bags and was sniffing loudly and giving a series of contented sighs.

"See you tomorrow," Shelly said with wide eyes.

Neither Sam nor I looked at her as we both said goodbye at the same time. She left. He stayed. I fidgeted from one foot to the other, flummoxed.

"Your place?" Sam pointed at the ceiling. "Table, chairs, plates?"

"Do you always invite yourself to dinner?" I crossed my arms over my chest.

Sam gave me an unabashedly unashamed grin. "Yep. But c'mon. You're not going to turn me away, are you? Not with a container of General Tso's chicken in my hands."

My favorite. My stomach rumbled, loud enough for him to hear it. I put my hands over it. "Damn you, Sam. Damn you."

He wafted the smell of General Tso toward me. "It's whispering your name, Grace. Can't you hear it? Eaaaaat me."

"So long as it's the food and not you saying it."

Sam stared, then put a hand over his heart. He frowned. "You wound me, Grace, with your unjust accusations of ulterior motives. I'm tempted to take my chopsticks and go home."

I kept my arms crossed. "Uh-huh. Let's see you."

Sam looked around the empty hall, then back to me. "But then my food would get cold. Besides, I have way too much. You don't want me to get fat, do you?"

I looked him up and down. He didn't look like he'd ever carried an extra pound. "Somehow I doubt that's a problem."

He jiggled the bags in my direction again. "Okay, so maybe you can resist me, but how can you resist a free dinner?"

I turned, crooking my finger over my shoulder as I headed for the back stairs to my apartment. "All right. When you put it that way."

He caught up to me at the stairs and we both paused.

The crinkling plastic bags filled the space between us, but I still felt as if he'd pressed up against me. Sam looked down at me until I climbed the first three steps and could look him in the eye.

"Thanks for taking such good care of my dad," he said quietly. "Consider this a thank-you, if you don't want to think of it as anything else."

How could I have resisted him after that?

In my apartment I took out mismatched plates and flatware and cartoon-character glasses from the burger joint's promotion of some summer blockbuster. I set my small table while Sam juggled cartons and packets of sauce.

"This is…cozy," he said from his seat in the chair closest to the kitchen's far wall. He had about two inches of space behind him and the same on the two other sides.

I laughed as I slid into the table's only other chair. It didn't have much more room. "Most of my guests aren't as big as you are."

Sam paused in dripping duck sauce on his plate of rice and gave me a lifted brow. "Uh-huh."

I mirrored his look. "Tall, Sam. I meant tall."

"Sure." He shot me a grin and stretched out his legs to the side. They reached all the way to the kitchen cabinets, and he tapped the wooden doors with the toe of his battered boots. "Big works, too."

There wasn't any way to deny that we'd had sex, and it seemed silly pretending. I stirred my portion of noodles with my chopsticks, thinking of what to say about it that wouldn't sound like a come-on or an insult.

"Look," I said at the same time Sam said, "Grace."

We both stopped. Sam gave a nod, letting me go first. I wanted to look away, but I forced myself to look at him.

"About that night."

He waited. *Still Life with Chopsticks*. The dark arches of his brows were so perfect I wanted to run my fingertips over them. I wanted to kiss him.

"I don't want you to think that I just…do that." Although I had. Although I did.

Sam's mouth curved the tiniest bit at the corners. "I don't want you to think I do, either."

We looked at each other another moment before he shrugged and bent to his food like we'd had an entire discussion and come to a conclusion. I wasn't convinced, but I wasn't sure what else to say about it. I ate, too, and the food was so good I had to sigh.

"I haven't had Chinese in forever," I told him.

"That's like a sacrilege. How can you not, like, eat Chinese at least once a week?" Sam offered me an egg roll.

"Uh, a little thing called money?" I took it and cracked it open to let the steam out and drizzled duck sauce into the shredded cabbagey goodness inside.

"Oh, that," Sam said, scoffing. "Money."

"It's easy to laugh about if you have a lot of it." I crunched into the egg roll's crispy outer layer.

"If I had a lot of money, would that make you like me better, or worse?"

I looked up, thinking he must be joking, but he looked serious. "Neither."

Sam lifted a chunk of chicken with his chopsticks and used it to point at me. "You're sure?"

"Why, Sam? Are you a secret millionaire?" I looked to the side, at his boots. "Because I have to say, if you are, you're really good at keeping it a secret."

He laughed and drew in his legs, bumping the table. "No. I'm pretty poor, actually. Starving artist and all that."

"Really?"

He nodded. "I'm wallpaper."

I took a minute to chew before I let on that I had no clue what he meant by that. "Huh?"

"Wallpaper." He waved around the room. "People go to dinner, they eat and talk. They don't pay attention to the wallpaper. Or to the dude playing 'Killing Me Softly' on the guitar."

"I think if I heard a dude playing 'Killing Me Softly' on the guitar, I'd pay attention." Not to mention if said dude was Sam, who couldn't possibly ever blend into the background.

Sam shook his head and looked mournful. "Not so, I'm afraid. Nobody ever says anything about the fact I change all the words, so I'm positive nobody's ever listening."

I laughed at the mental image of Sam bent over his guitar, crooning different lyrics to songs while all around him people drank wine and flirted with everyone but him. Sam grinned and sat back to tip his beer to his lips. I watched his throat work as he swallowed.

"You play guitar for a living?"

"A living? Arguable. Do I earn money doing it? Yes."

"Wow." I made an impressed face.

Sam laughed. "Yeah. My family's so proud."

The way he said it made me think that wasn't quite true.

"Do you think you'll get a record deal or anything?" Not

being particularly creative myself, it was pretty cool to meet someone who was.

Sam laughed again, this time louder. "Oh…right. Hey, you never know. I'd be satisfied getting paid to play for people who actually listen to me sing, at this point."

"Someday," I said, because it's what you said to people when they shared they had a dream.

"Yeah," Sam answered. "Someday."

We both drank in silence for a moment.

"So, about that night," Sam said, catching me looking. "If you don't really do that, and I don't really do that, how come we both did it?"

I couldn't tell him that I'd thought he was my rentboy. "I don't know."

"Fate?" He drank more beer, this time with an eye on me.

"I don't believe in fate."

"Luck?" He grinned and licked his lips and set the bottle on the table.

"Maybe luck. But, Sam…"

He held up a hand to stop me, and I did. He unfolded himself inch by inch from his chair and gathered up the garbage while he talked. "You don't have to say it. You don't want a boyfriend. You're not into dating. You just want to be friends."

I didn't get up to help him, but he didn't really look as if he needed any. He even found my trash can in its hidden place beneath the sink. "Why would you assume I'd say that?"

Sam washed his hands at the sink and turned. "Were you going to say something different?"

"No." I shook my head and stood, too. "I just didn't like that you assumed you knew what I was going to say."

We smiled at each other. Sam looked at the clock, then back at me. "We can be friends."

"We can?" His answer surprised me. Disappointed me, too, a little, I'll admit.

"Sure." Sam grinned. "Until we can both no longer deny our unquenchable passion for one another."

I laughed. "Is it time for you to leave?"

"Yes." He straightened. "I think it is."

I walked him to the front door, and down the stairs to the back door of the funeral home, where he hesitated on the covered porch and I pretended my heart wasn't jumping into my throat.

"This is kind of a pain," Sam said.

I thought he meant the kiss thing—should he or shouldn't he? I was half voting for should, even though I knew it should be shouldn't. "What?"

"The door. You don't have your own entrance?"

"Oh. I do, but I don't use it. When I started renovating the apartment I blocked off the door with the shelves in the kitchen. It's safer that way."

Sam nodded, solemn. "Yeah, I guess you're right. Well, good night, Grace. Thanks for letting me invite myself to dinner."

"You're welcome," I said, and meant it. "We should do it again."

"Sure. Friends eat dinner together, right?"

I nodded and before I could stop myself, I reached to

run a finger along the line of buttons on the front of his shirt. "Sam?"

"Yeah?" He shifted, just barely, when my finger stopped somewhere in the middle of his chest and I pulled it away.

"About that unquenchable-passion thing…"

He smiled and jumped down the two steps to the sidewalk. "Just think about it."

I sighed and watched him walk away. "I'm thinking about it."

"*Keep* thinking about it!" he called over his shoulder, and I went inside and closed the door.

I thought about it, all right. Too much. It was pretty much all I thought about for the next week, but Sam never called. Not that he'd promised to call. Just that after he'd showed up with dinner, I'd expected him to. Shit. I'd *wanted* him to, and that pissed me off more than the fact he didn't.

I could have tracked him down, but I refused. I didn't need Sam's long legs, his shaggy hair, his big, big hands. I didn't need his smile.

I didn't need Sam, period.

Sunday dinner was neither worse nor better than I'd expected it to be. My niece and nephew romped with my parents' dog, Reba, a purebred hunting spaniel they'd rescued a few years ago. My sister helped my mom in the kitchen while my dad and Jerry lounged in front of the television in the den. I wasn't needed in the kitchen where the two whirling dervishes of domesticity tackled the cleaning of dishes with the precision of an army heading to battle.

This left me with nothing to do but climb the stairs to the room I'd shared with Hannah.

I meant to look for some old photo albums. My best friend Mo was getting married next year and I wanted to give her something different than just a set of wineglasses or a gravy boat. I looked around the room, which had once been papered with posters of rock stars and unicorns but now featured plain green walls hung with prints of flowers. The twin beds were the same, covered now in matching comforters with a battered nightstand between them. This was where the kids slept when they spent the night.

I still had junk here, in the crawlspace. I tugged open the small half door set into the wall. Craig and Hannah had both teased me that "Big Jim" lived in there, and that if I didn't do what they wanted, Big Jim would come out and get me. I'd gotten them back by hiding there one night and making scratching and moaning noises that had scared them both so badly they'd called the police. I was pretty sure Hannah still hadn't forgiven me for that little stunt.

The cubbyhole was frigid in the winter and sweltering in the summer, which made it not the best place to store precious things, especially not in cardboard boxes. I dragged the three with my name on them out into the center of the room. I remembered packing them up before I left for college, labeling the contents of each. I remembered thinking how important it was to save these memories of childhood and high school. Test papers, notes passed in class, a journal in which I'd written the name of my first crush.

They didn't seem so important now, not even the collection of plastic Smurfs that tumbled out of their disintegrating shoe box. I lined them up. Smurfette, Brainy, Handy. My favorite was the little Smurf lifting a beer to his happy grin. Him I tucked into my jeans pocket, but the others I divided into two piles to give to Simon and Melanie.

In another box I found the albums. A long time ago I'd decorated the plain vinyl covers with stickers, most of which had lost their glue and fallen off. The inside pages were the sticky kind with plastic laid overtop, and many of the pictures had faded. I flipped through them, marveling at the fashions and hairstyles we'd once considered so "in," then put them aside. Tucked just inside the top flap of one of the boxes was a newer photo album, the kind with slots for the pictures.

I pulled it out and touched the photos in it. Me and Ben. We looked so young. Happy, too. We had been happy.

I put the album aside. I didn't have time for memories right now. I'd take them with me. Who knew when I might suffer some insane desire to read old notes from old boyfriends at three in the morning?

I carried the boxes downstairs and put them by the back door, then called for my niece and nephew. They left off tormenting the dog and ran to me. I had my hands, cupping the bounty of Smurfs, behind my back.

"Pick one," I told them. They of course both picked the same one. Before a struggle could ensue, I held out the hand holding Smurfette to Melanie and the other to Simon, who furrowed his brow.

"What're these?"

"They're nerfs," said his sister with the utmost scorn.

"Smurfs," I corrected.

Simon laughed and held his up. "They're weird."

Since Simon said everything was weird, I didn't take offense. In the next moment, two pairs of small hands grabbed me for hugs and two small faces beamed as they thanked me.

"Mama! Look what Aunt Grace gave us!" Melanie held out her new treasures.

Hannah looked. "Oh, God. Where'd you get those?"

"Out of the cubbyhole."

My sister made a face. "I hope you washed them first."

Of course I hadn't, and both kids were gleeful to inform her of that. More struggles ensued as the Smurfs were deemed unfit for use until they'd been sanitized. Simon didn't want to give his up until Hannah told him they could pretend the sink was a swimming pool. Then he was more than happy to spend the next twenty minutes dipping the small figures in and out of the soapy water even after his sister lost interest.

"Are you sure you want to give them those?" Hannah asked.

"Sure. Why not?" I lifted the boxes. "Get the door for me, would you?"

She did and followed me out into the carport while I settled them into the trunk of my car. "Well, you might want to keep them. They might be worth money or something."

"I doubt they're worth that much, even on eBay. Besides, the kids will like them." I closed the trunk.

"But you might want to keep them for your kids someday."

I turned to face my sister, who still looked tired. She

hadn't said much during dinner, a slack picked up neatly by my mother, but I'd noticed. "I'm not worried about that, Hannah."

"Are you sure? Because—"

"I'm sure."

We stared at each other. She fidgeted. I recognized the half-defiant look in her eyes, but the reason for it escaped me.

"Well. When you do have kids, we'll give them back."

"Holy hell, Hannah, will you give it a rest? I'm not going to have kids for a long time, if ever!" The words snapped too loudly in the carport.

Hannah frowned. "What do you mean, 'if ever'?"

I tried to shrug away the conversation. "Nothing. I mean, maybe I should get married first, you know? Let me find a guy first."

"You have lots of guys, I thought."

We stared at each other. I couldn't figure her out. Was she disapproving? Was she angling for more information?

"Yeah, but I'm not marrying any of them."

Hannah's jaw set. "Obviously."

"What do you care?" I cried, hands on my hips. "What business is it of yours, anyway?"

"Obviously none!"

"That's right," I told her. "None."

We glared. The back door opened and Jerry stuck his head out. Neither of us turned to look at him.

"You ready to go?" He sounded bored. Then again, he usually did.

Hannah looked, then, and her frown straightened to neutrality. "Sure. Are the kids ready?"

Jerry shrugged. "Dunno."

Every line of her body stiffened. "Could you help them get ready to go, then? Simon needs his socks and they both need to find their shoes."

Jerry didn't move. "Where are they?"

"I don't know," my sister said. "That's why you have to find them."

Jerry didn't move for a moment longer, and with a disgusted sigh Hannah pushed past him. "Never mind. I'll do it."

She disappeared into the house and he followed a moment later. My dad appeared in the doorway no more than a few seconds later. He gestured at my car.

"Your car needs to be inspected."

"I know, Dad. I have an appointment next week."

"Next week? And what are you going to do before then? What if you get pulled over?"

"I'll try not to." I hated defending myself to my dad, especially when he was right. "I wanted to take it to Reager's, and next week was the soonest they could get me in."

"Why not take it to Joe's place?"

"Because Reager's gives me a discount," I told him flatly. "And Joe doesn't."

My dad huffed. "I'll call him."

"No, Dad! You won't." I held up my hand. "I've got it under control."

"You need new tires, too." My dad came down the couple steps from the house into the carport and started circling my car. "When's the last time you checked the oil? You put a lot of miles on this car, Gracie."

I bit my tongue against a smart retort. "It's fine. Okay?"

"Lookit there." My dad reached down to run a finger along the grooves in my right front tire. "You're going bald."

"So are you," I said.

He straightened and patted his head without looking offended. He didn't laugh, either. "You need to take care of stuff like that for yourself. Be responsible."

I gritted my teeth. This was working my very last nerve on several different but interconnected levels. "You mean because I'm not responsible or because I don't have a man to do it for me?"

My dad didn't bother to look ashamed. I'm sure because he wasn't. "Am I wrong?"

"Yes, Dad. You are. Absolutely." I pointed to my car. "My car has a lot of miles on it, yes, but those tires were just rotated two months ago and the guy told me they'd last another few thousand miles."

"Maybe if you spent less money on silly things, you wouldn't have to worry."

He had absolutely no idea where I spent most of my discretionary income, and there was no way I was going to clue him in. "That's my business."

"The home is still my business, too, Grace, and it will be until the day I'm laid out in it."

"Dad!"

God, he was stubborn. My dad just glared, arms crossed. Mine were crossed, too, and though I had no mirror I was sure my face was set into the same expression.

"The home's doing fine. I'm doing fine, too."

"I had a wife and three kids and none of us lacked for

anything when I was running the business," my dad said. "There's no reason you shouldn't be making ends meet."

If real-life conversation was like the Internet, I'd have said OMFG. I settled for, "I am more than making ends meet."

We stared each other down. My dad wanted more details, and I wasn't going to give them. While I might concede that the business was still his business, my money wasn't.

"You see the books," I told him. "You know I'm running in the black, no problem. And I'll do what I have to in order to keep it that way. Renovations and upgrades take money. Keeping on top of things takes money. But we're doing fine, and you know we are. Don't worry about me, Dad."

"I'm your father. It's my job to worry."

"I'm fine. I promise."

My dad didn't look convinced, which made me less inclined to forgive him his fatherly right to be concerned. "You have to trust me, Dad."

He looked again at my tires. "I'll pay for new tires."

"You don't have to do that."

He glared again. "Gracie—"

I tossed up my hands, beaten. "Fine. Fine, okay? You can buy me new tires. Great."

"Happy birthday and Merry Christmas," my dad said.

"Gee, thanks."

He ignored my sarcasm. "You're welcome. Don't forget to say goodbye to your mother," he added as he went back into the house.

OMFG.

•

* * *

Kicking myself because my dad's scrutiny had made me paranoid, I opened up my accounting program as soon as I got home. I had all my accounts listed on my laptop, while downstairs in my office I only listed the business accounts.

Frawley and Sons was indeed running in the black as it had done for nearly every year but a few bad ones here and there. I remembered those as the years of scant Christmases and birthdays. The first year I'd taken over from my dad had threatened to be a bad one, too, but I'd made it work by sacrificing my apartment off grounds and moving into the home and finagling some tax breaks like a "company" car. Having a best friend who was an expert accountant had helped a lot.

My personal bank account wasn't overflowing, but looking at it didn't make me want to scream, either. With no rent and sundries like electricity, Internet and car payments filtered through the business, my monthly living expenses were extremely low. I paid my staff well but not extravagantly, in the midrange of recommended salaries. I paid myself the same, and they knew it. They also knew I'd be the first to take a pay cut should the need arise.

Even with the moderate pay scale, the perks of sharing my expenses with my business meant I had more discretionary income than many of my friends. Yet unlike them I didn't stock up on clothes or expensive toys like TVs or stereos. I didn't go on vacation. I bought my groceries from the Amish-run Bangs, Bumps and Bargains store. I wasn't a big spender…except for my excursions with Mrs. Smith's gentlemen.

I looked over the last year's entries. Even though my dad had hinted I wasn't responsible or organized, I kept careful track of all my income and expenses. I had entries for every date including the cost of my companion's time and the fees covering where we'd gone or what we'd done. The least I'd spend in one month was twenty dollars for an initial meeting over coffee to see if the escort I wanted to hire would suit, to a few hundred for a series of dates with a guy named Armando who was particularly skilled with his hands.

I blinked at the screen and sat back against the couch I'd bought in college from the Salvation Army. Nine hundred and seventy-nine dollars and forty-three cents. We'd gone to dinner, the movies, dancing, the museum. I'd paid for four nights in the Dukum Inn. Four nights in one month. It seemed like nothing if you compared it to how many times a dating couple might make love. I'd seen him once a week, and it had cost me less than if I'd had rent and utilities and a car payment.

That had been the most, and even now I considered it money well spent. I studied the numbers. Women paid what I considered outrageous sums of money for someone to cut their hair, or do their nails, to buy the latest clothes and face creams. Hell, a good massage cost nearly as much as an hour with Jack and with him, at least, I was guaranteed a happy ending of the sort not found in Disney cartoons.

I looked around my bare apartment. It could use some paint and pictures. Some real, grown-up furniture. I looked again at the screen. Framed art and throw pillows didn't have quite the same appeal as being fucked up against a wall until I screamed.

Then again, I thought with a grin as I dialed a now-familiar number, not much did.

Chapter 09

*M*y beeper went off two minutes after Jack buried his face between my thighs. I groaned, reaching for it. He paused and looked up at me as I looked at the number on the screen. My voice mail, the after-hours call line. For the first time ever, I wished I'd put Jared on first call.

Naked, Jack crouched between my legs with one hand on his cock. I sat on the motel's straight-back chair with my skirt hiked up to my hips and my panties in a crumpled pile on the floor.

"Do you need to get that?"

"In a minute." I was so close already, it would take only a few minutes more. Even if I hadn't been already primed by half an hour of dirty talk on the cell phone while I drove to meet him, Jack's tongue would have sent me over the edge pretty fast.

He smiled and kissed my thigh. He jerked himself as he licked me. I touched the top of his head, that silky dark hair that tickled, and watched the motion of his shoulder as he stroked his cock. Fast, then faster as my hips pushed forward and I fisted my fingers into his hair.

We came at the same time. I bit the heel of my hand to muffle my cry, but Jack groaned without holding back. I smelled the musky scent of his come and it urged another small yelp from me. Using condoms was necessary and not negotiable for sex, but he wasn't wearing one now. It had made my own orgasm harder, imagining how it had felt for him to pump his bare flesh without the barrier.

Jack kissed my cunt, surprising me with the tender gesture, and sat back. His prick had softened, lying across his thigh. His hand gleamed, wet. I sat up, head a little woozy, and pulled my skirt down.

"I have to answer this," I told him.

Jack nodded and got up, ambling to the bathroom. I dialed my voice mail. From inside the bathroom I heard the whoosh of the shower turning on. I typed in my password.

By the time I hung up, Jack had emerged from a cloud of steam rapidly dissipating in the bathroom. He wore a towel slung low over his hips and had slicked his hair off his face. He gave me a curious look as I shut my phone.

"I have to go." I stood and shook my skirt down, then grabbed my panties. When I straightened, he was there, still flushed and warm and damp.

"Okay." He held my arm to help me balance as I stood on one foot to pull on my undies.

I gave myself a quick once-over in the mirror over the dresser. He watched over my shoulder. I turned to face him.

"Thanks, Jack."

"You're welcome." His lips curved a little. "So much for cuddling."

I laughed. "Yeah. Another time."

He nodded and followed me to the door, where I paused to pull an envelope from my purse. "You didn't ask for this in advance again."

"Grace," Jack said, taking it. "You told me to be naked and on my knees when you got here. Where would I have put it?"

"Good point." Thinking about it now made my still-damp cunt clench.

"Besides. I trust you."

We looked at each other. Jack's smile teased one from me and for one moment we both leaned in a microscopic amount. I stopped first. Instead of kissing him, I cupped his cheek for a moment, and he turned his face to press his lips to my palm.

"Thanks again."

"No problem," Jack said. "I aim to please."

"Your aim is good."

He laughed. "Your jokes are bad."

I had to go. Had business to take care of. A family to help. Yet, I lingered, and so did he, and though I wasn't naive enough to think it had nothing to do with money, I couldn't help thinking it might have something to do, instead, with me.

And it was that thought that made me push away at last, leaving him in the doorway of a cheap motel wearing nothing but a thin white towel.

* * *

I'd known the Johnsons for years. Though we'd never been close, Beth had been in my class at school. Her older brother, Jim, had been a friend of my brother Craig's. Her parents, Peggy and Ron, had been active participants in the band boosters and had often given me a ride home from school after different activities. Today, though, only Beth, Jim and Peggy were there. Ron had passed away after a long battle with cancer.

Peggy Johnson looked pale and thinner than the last time I'd seen her, but she wore bright lipstick and had fixed her hair. She smiled at me as she came in, and took the hand I offered before pulling me closer for a friendly hug that took me a little by surprise.

"Look at you," she said. "My goodness, Grace, you're so grown up."

Beth frowned. "Mom. We're the same age!"

"I know, I know, but…" Peggy turned to her daughter and tweaked her silky shell top. "You're my baby."

Jim rolled his eyes. "What am I, chopped liver?"

"Of course not. You're my baby, too." Peggy tugged the knot of his tie and turned back to me. The too-bright gleam in her eyes was the only sign of her distress. "So. Let's get to this, okay? I've got guests coming in from out of town and I have to go to the grocery store."

Her children exchanged looks, and as they all took seats in front of my desk, I sat, too. I pulled Ron Johnson's file from the small wire rack on top of my desk, blessing Shelly for remembering to pull it before the Johnsons arrived. Ron had made a lot of the arrangements in advance. All we had to do was go over them.

I set the folder down on top of the sheaf of pink slips Shelly had left on my desk. I'd had this conversation with so many families I didn't need to think much about what to say, but as my eye caught the name written on the top slip, every word in my throat dried to dust.

Sam Stewart.

And on the one beneath it, and the one beneath that, too. Stuttering, I flipped through the stack of messages, trying to count and talk at the same time and not managing to do either successfully. He'd called at least four times.

Four times between the time I'd left this morning and the time I'd returned? The man was a stalker. He was insane.

"Ron, as you know, had already picked out the coffin and vault," I managed to say without sounding too much like an idiot.

I covered up Sam's messages with the folder and looked up at all three Johnsons, who were staring at me expectantly. I really needed to get myself in line. I pulled out the list Ron and I had gone over several months before. I'd gone to his house to make it. He'd been under hospice care and too ill to come to my office. Peggy had served us iced tea and sponge cake while we looked at brochures of caskets and talked about pricing.

I looked up at Beth and Jim. "Would you like to see the casket your dad picked out?"

"That's not necessary." Peggy spoke before her children could, and both of them looked as if they disagreed. Peggy lifted her chin. Her hands were clasped very tightly in her lap. "I've made some changes in the plans."

I put my list back in the folder and linked my fingers on top of it to give her my full attention. "All right."

Now Beth and Jim were doing more than exchanging subtle glances. Using the private language of siblings dumbfounded by their parents, they were mouthing words behind their mother's head. Peggy, if she noticed, acted as if she didn't. She stared me straight in the eyes.

"Forget the coffin he wanted, with those fancy corner pieces."

An avid fly fisherman, Ron had picked out a popular-model casket that featured decorative, customized corners. "Did you have something else in mind?"

Peggy took a deep breath, and her gaze flared though her voice stayed calm and her hands never unclenched from her lap. "I want that plain cherry box you talked about that day. The cheaper one. No fancy lining inside, either. And instead of that pricey vault I want to go with the cheapest one you've got that the cemetery will accept."

Most of the cemeteries I worked with refused to allow burials without a vault around the casket—not, as many people thought, to prevent decomposition, though they did. Vaults prevent graves from settling, which allows for easier maintenance of the grounds. Still, they range from simple concrete boxes to elaborate copper and galvanized steel tombs that will keep out moisture and delay decomposition for years. I hadn't been to any disinterments, but my dad had been to a few where he said the corpse looked the same as it had when put into the ground.

"Mom—" Beth began, but her mother at last allowed one hand to ungrip from the other and she fell silent.

"Hush up," said Peggy.

It wasn't uncommon for people to change their minds about funeral arrangements even though they'd been decided in advance. I'd had everything from families who'd decided grandma really should be buried in the better casket and damn the expense, to those who looked at the amount of money that had been prepaid with dollar signs gleaming in their eyes and who downgraded everything in order to get a refund. Peggy would be entitled to a substantial return just with the changes she'd already requested, and she'd get one. It was a point of pride for Frawley and Sons that we provided exactly what the customer wanted, to the best of our abilities. If that meant returning money, we did it, no arguments. I knew there were other funeral homes in the area that weren't so generous.

Peggy hadn't pulled her gaze from mine. "No guest book. No memorial cards. None of that fancy crap."

"Mom!" Jim, this time, sounding shocked.

Beth's eyes went red and filled with tears as her jaw dropped. And still, her mother didn't turn her gaze from mine. Jim was making disgruntled noises, like he meant to speak, but Peggy stopped him as easily as she'd stopped her daughter previously.

"Hush," she said. "I'm in charge of this. He was my husband."

"He was our dad!" Jim had found his voice.

Peggy blinked, finally. "And I'm the one who had to clean him up when he threw up, or wet the bed. I'm the one who had to listen to him moan for hours on end when the pain got too bad. I'm the one who held his hand and read to him and woke in the night listening to be sure I could still hear his goddamn breath, so I am the one who will decide what happens to him now that he's dead!"

She delivered this speech in nearly one breath, the final crescendo of her voice loud enough to make all of us wince. Beth burst into tears as Jim sat back in his seat, seemingly unable to speak.

"I will decide," Peggy said in a much quieter but unbroken voice. "And I don't want to spend all that money on the shell."

"A shell? What's that supposed to mean?" Beth had found her voice again, and it was indignant.

"It means he's dead, Beth. He's gone. All that's left is a body that's going to rot in the ground and be food for the worms! That's what it means! Your dad's gone, he's just a shell, that's all that's left! And I'm not going to waste our money—my money! I'm not going to waste my money on a fancy package for what amounts to nothing more than a beetle's dinner!"

With a strangled sound, Beth got up from her chair abruptly enough to send it sliding across the carpet. She grabbed up a handful of tissues from the box on my desk, and pressing them to her face, fled the room. Her brother stood too after a hesitation, but though he towered over his mother she didn't even look up. Her gaze had gone to her hands folded so tightly in her lap.

"I'll go see about her," Jim said in a grinding voice. "Since you've got it all under control, Mom."

Peggy nodded. Jim gave me an apologetic look I didn't need but probably made him feel better about this bit of craziness. He left the room, closing the door behind him. I waited for Peggy to speak.

"He left me," she said in a dead, dull voice, and when she looked at me again, her eyes were dead, doll eyes. "He left me."

She didn't dissolve into weeping. I think it might have helped her if she had, but Peggy Johnson kept her despair and pain locked up tight inside her. She drew in a long, shuddering breath and forced a smile to unwilling lips. She let out the breath and shook her head to let her hair fall over her shoulders. She was, I realized, about my mom's age, as Ron had been my dad's. She'd always seemed so old to me, the way my own parents always had and still did, but watching her now I saw the girl she must have been. The one who'd fallen in love with a boy and married him. Had his babies. Had made a life with him, until the end.

When he'd left her.

"I understand," I told her, the words feeling empty though they sounded sincere.

"No. I don't think you can. Seeing it isn't the same as living it, Grace."

"No. I guess it isn't. But I am sorry for your loss, Mrs. Johnson. Mr. Johnson was a nice man. A really nice man."

"Yes." She paused. Her fingers twitched in her lap and her lips thinned into bloodless lines in the mask of her face. "He was."

"I'll be happy to change whatever arrangements you'd like. But…if I might make a suggestion?"

A dry laugh barked from her throat. "Go ahead. It's all

anyone's done since he died. Offer suggestions. Well-meaning crap."

I nodded slowly. "I'm happy to change to the less expensive casket and vault and return your payment. And if you don't want the guest register, that's fine, too. But about the memorial cards…" I paused. She looked at me. "They're not for you. Or for him. I think you would regret not offering them to the other people who'd like to have one."

Her lips parted to release a sigh, and after a few seconds, her shoulders slumped. "Fine. Keep the damn memorial cards. And the viewing, though God knows why anyone wants to see him that way is beyond me."

"I'll do my best for him, Mrs. Johnson. You know that. And it helps people to say goodbye if they can see him one last time."

Her second laugh was only slightly less bitter than the first. "Not me. I want to remember him the way he was before he got sick. Can you make him look that way, Grace? Put that sparkle back in his eyes? Make him smile at me the way he used to when he had a dirty joke to tell me?"

I shook my head. "No."

"Of course you can't," Peggy said. "Because he's dead."

I reached out my hand, palm faceup, across the desk, and she took it. She squeezed it so hard my knuckles cracked, but she still didn't cry. "I'm sorry."

She nodded and released my hand. The conversation turned to the time of the viewing and the graveside service, as well as who'd be riding in the lead car and where the flowers were to be sent afterward. Peggy stood at last, her eyes still dry but the stiffness taken away from her body.

"I'm going to go on a cruise," she said from the doorway. "With the money. Ron always promised we'd go, but then he got sick and we couldn't."

"I think he'd understand," I told her.

Peggy shrugged. "He doesn't have to, does he?"

The click of my door shutting behind her sounded very loud.

I didn't call Sam back right away. I wasn't, in fact, sure I meant to call him back at all until I was curled up on my ugly sofa with my phone pressed to my ear and my photo album in my lap.

"Sam I am."

When had his voice become so familiar? "I got your messages. All of them."

"Your secretary's good."

"She's my office manager," I said. "And yes, she is."

"Uh-oh." Sam made a shuffling noise. "It's a good thing I'm wearing a sweater, cuz I think you're cutting me cold, darlin'."

I didn't say anything.

"Shit," Sam said. "Grace, don't be mad at me."

"Why would I be mad at you?"

"Shit fritters," Sam swore. "When girls ask that question, what they really mean to say is, 'Why wouldn't I be mad at you?'"

I refused to laugh with as much resolve as I'd made not

to call him back, which is to say, not much. I did stifle it behind my hand, though. He must have heard me anyway.

"You want to know why I didn't call you for two weeks?"

"I don't, actually. I don't care."

"Oh, Grace," Sam said. "Don't break my heart."

I thought of Jack's face between my legs. I thought of coming from Jack's tongue. I opened the album and touched a picture of Ben's smile, and I thought of Peggy Johnson's too-bright eyes and the slash of her wrong-shade lipstick.

"What do you want, Sam?"

A beat. "To talk to you."

A pause. "About what?"

"Do I need a topic?"

"Why didn't you call me for two weeks?" I flipped the pages of my album through pictures of the past.

"I had to go back home for a while. Settle some things."

I laughed, but it wasn't a nice sound. "Oh? Where's home?"

"New York."

"They don't have phones in New York?" I sighed. "Forget it, Sam. Just forget it, okay? This whole thing is just stupid."

"Grace," Sam said. "How could you miss me if I didn't go away?"

I actually took the phone away from my ear and stared at it hard before putting it back to my ear. "You didn't call me because you wanted me to miss you?"

"Not a good idea?"

"Not even close," I told him. "Goodbye."

"Wait! Grace, don't hang up. I'm sorry."

I closed my photo album on the face of someone I'd once loved. "Me, too, Sam. Goodbye."

I hung up, and he didn't call back.

"I didn't think you'd call me again so soon." Jack sprawled on the rumpled motel bed, taking up a lot of room and leaving very little for me.

I didn't mind. I curled on my side, my ass touching his thigh and one of his arms brushing the top of my head. If I wanted to roll over and face him, I could put my face directly against the dip of his waist. I didn't move.

"Grace?" His fingers toyed with my hair. "You awake?"

"Yes."

I closed my eyes, thinking I should move but unwilling at the moment to get up. I could take a shower before I left, so I wouldn't have to ride home smelling like sex. I sniffed the inside of my wrist, which smelled so much like Jack I didn't want to wash it just yet, even though the real thing was still there with me.

He rolled toward me and the bed dipped. Our bodies touched. We'd been sweating in the midsummer heat, but now I was glad the room's air-conditioner didn't do more than blow out intermittent puffs of stale, lukewarm air. I liked the way our skin stuck together when he pressed himself against my rear. I felt the tug of his fingers in my hair.

"What are you thinking?"

This question seemed so unlike anything a dude would ever ask that I actually turned halfway to look at him. "Why do you think I'm thinking anything?"

He smiled and shifted our bodies so we aligned more comfortably. "You're just quiet, that's all. And usually you're up and out of here. I figured… Hell, I don't know. I thought I'd ask, that's all."

His sweetness touched me. "I don't have to be up and out of here unless I get a call. Or our time's up."

"Our time's not up. Not unless you want it to be."

I didn't. Not yet. I blamed inertia, but that wasn't quite it. It was nice, lying here with Jack after a session of really rousing sex. It was nice having him twist my hair into small dreadlocks and feel him against my body.

"Do you like this?" I asked. Too late, I realized I hadn't meant to ask it quite that way. "Your work, I mean."

"I like this." Jack shifted again and we adjusted ourselves into a companionable tangle of limbs.

"How'd you get started?" I pushed up on one elbow to look at his face.

He laughed. "Some guy offered me two hundred bucks to sleep with his girlfriend and him."

"Both?"

He laughed again, stretching a little. I admired his body without pretending I didn't, and traced the lines of his tattoos with my fingertip while he answered.

"Us both with her. Not me and him."

"He just asked you, out of the blue?"

Jack grinned. "Yep."

"Hmm. How did you know he wasn't some sort of freaky serial killer or something?"

Jack laughed and shrugged. "I didn't. And he wasn't. It was all good. Two hundred bucks to fuck his old lady, who was a smoking-hot piece of ass, by the way. I figured I could do that again. Asked around. Got hooked up with the agency and here I am."

"Here you are." I slid a hand down his thigh to squeeze the muscles of his calf.

His hand came around to grab my butt and squeeze. "Here we are."

I let my hand drift up and down his leg. "I should go."

Jack rolled us both quickly, surprising me. He pushed my hands above my head, pinning my wrists. "Not yet."

His cock pressed the inside of my thigh. "Again?"

He nodded and dipped his head to mouth my throat. "Again."

He was very, very good. I was more than happy to let him kiss my neck and breasts, and to run his tongue in tickling traces over my belly and hip. We didn't even need a game to play.

"Jackhammer," I murmured, eyes closed, as he ran his hands down my body. "You fuck like a jackhammer."

"You like it that way," he said in a low voice against my thigh. His breath, hot, gusted over my skin. "Sometimes."

I had paid him to know how I liked it, but for a moment, having him be so certain opened my eyes wide. Jack didn't seem to notice. He moved between my legs to nuzzle and lick. I thought for a moment I was going to freeze, that my mind would override my body and keep me from the pleasure I knew very well Jack could provide.

Deep breath. Don't think about it. Don't...

"Holy hell," I whispered. "Where did you learn to do that?"

"Practice," Jack murmured against me, and I imagined I felt the curve of his smile. "Lots and lots of practice."

"Tell me about it," I urged as he moved his hand to take the place of his mouth. "The women."

"What about them?" He slid a finger inside me, then another, while I arched.

"Tell me how you fuck them."

"Every one is different," Jack said. He touched my clitoris, rubbing, then left me for a moment to return with a condom. "The way they smell. Taste."

He ran a hand over my body. "Feel."

"Tell me how you feel."

He knelt between my open legs, his prick in his hand as he rolled a condom down over it. He put his hand on the bed next to my side and nudged my entrance with his cock. I held my breath, waiting for the moment he'd slide inside, but Jack took his time. I'd called him Jackhammer, but he was teasing me now.

"I like to watch the way their skin changes color when they come." He touched the heat on my chest and at the base of my throat before pushing forward, inside me. "I like the sounds you make, and the way your nails feel in my back when I'm fucking you hard. The way you like it."

He was not fucking me hard. He was doing it slow, each thrust in and out smooth and long. Thorough.

"You make them all come," I tried to say, though the words got garbled by a moan.

"Yeah. I make them all come." Jack bent to nibble at my shoulder and throat as he moved inside me. He slid a hand between us to give me the pressure I needed.

"Like me..." I was tipping, fast, and my nails found his back.

Jack hissed and thrust harder. I came, electric. He groaned against me and shivered. I relaxed my fingers and smoothed them over the small ridges I'd left in his skin.

"Not like you," Jack whispered into my ear, but I pretended not to hear.

I'd meant what I told Peggy about her husband. Ron had been a very nice man. The sort who good-naturedly played chauffeur to a gaggle of teenage girls after school dances and never failed to attend every band and chorus concert in which his children performed. He'd always worn a red bow tie. It was what had been provided for us to lay him out in, along with a familiar dark blue suit.

It's hard for some to understand how I can work with the dead, particularly the bodies of those I knew. I think it's because people are frightened of death and embarrassed to be so; or because it's too easy to imagine how it would feel to be laid upon a table, naked, with the hands of strangers cleaning you. Nakedness embarrasses people. To be honest, I'm not the sort to parade around in the locker room of the gym, and exhibitionism leaves me cold—but after death, the body is exactly what Peggy Johnson had called it. A shell. An empty package. We're born naked, and when we die we're put into the ground or even cremated with our clothes on, but the modesty this provides has nothing to do with the feelings of the person who died. It's entirely for those left behind.

For me, preparing a body is a matter of respect and honoring that shell. Of cleaning it, embalming it if necessary, of applying cosmetics or restorative techniques to recreate as closely as possible the living face. I don't see breasts or buttocks. I see a human being who can no longer do this for himself; it's my job to do it.

"Can you hand me that gauze?" I gestured to Jared, who was tossing a soiled sheet into the laundry.

Because he'd been in hospice care, Ron Johnson had few tubes to remove, unlike if he'd been a hospital patient. Still, he'd had a permanent IV drip in one arm and that had to come out. Jared and I busied ourselves with our routine, moving in tandem to the sounds of Death Cab for Cutie coming from my iPod speakers.

We worked mostly in silence, though occasionally Jared would break out singing along with the music. As much as he liked to tease me about my taste in bands, he knew the lyrics to most of the songs. I wasn't much of a singer, though I'd hum once in a while. We both paused in our tasks when the simple acoustic guitar and vocals of a new track came on.

"I Will Follow You Into the Dark."

"What do you think?" Jared asked as we slipped Ron Johnson's arms into the sleeves of his suit coat. "Do you think there's a tunnel of light?"

He was referring to the song's lyrics. "I don't know."

I arranged the red bow tie while Jared brushed off the suit's lapels. Ron Johnson was done, ready to be put into the simple cherry casket his wife had decided would best serve as his final resting place. We finished with him and transferred him to the gurney that we'd push into the chapel, where we'd place him in the casket.

"You've never thought about it?" Jared got behind the gurney while I pushed open the swinging doors to the hall.

"No. Not really." We maneuvered the gurney with ease, and I was grateful for Jared's strength. Illness had whittled away much of the belly Ron Johnson had sported, but he was still a large man.

"Not ever?" Jared sounded astonished.

I was a little more surprised he'd worked with me for so many months without ever asking me what I thought happened after death. "Not really, Jared."

The embalming room was in the basement and the chapel upstairs. Though I'd often vowed that the first set of renovations I'd make to the funeral home would be to add an elevator, I hadn't yet managed it. That meant pushing the gurney up the ramp outside the building and onto the main floor. Several years ago my dad had enclosed it to protect it from the elements so we no longer had to struggle in ice or rain, but the effort required at pushing a corpse up or down it was still substantial. The white-painted walls bore the scuffs and scars of many bumps of the gurney, and the wooden floor was heavily scratched.

In the chapel, we placed Mr. Johnson into the coffin. The final viewing was scheduled for a few hours from now. I carefully arranged his hands and made sure none of the makeup had smudged off. I turned to help take the gurney back, but found Jared staring at me.

"What?"

"I just can't believe you don't think about it." Jared took the gurney so I didn't have to, and I followed him back to the prep room so we could finish cleaning up.

"What's to think about?"

When my dad had taken over the business, there had been far fewer regulations. Now we had to follow rules about bodily fluids and human waste or risk a visit from the Occupational Safety and Health Administration. We were inspected and could be fined for not following them. Regulations were one of the few things Jared wasn't skilled with.

He helped me strip the gurney and toss the linens into the red-lined basket, filling it. "C'mon. You're around death every day. You can't tell me you don't wonder what really happens. Bright light, Pearly Gates, burning flames of hell. You never think of anything like that?"

"What do *you* think about it?" I challenged as I slipped on a pair of latex gloves that covered my wrists and pushed the full laundry cart toward the door leading out. "Do you believe in heaven and hell?"

"I think so," Jared said, following.

"See? You don't know, either!"

"At least I think about it!"

Together we wrestled the heavy cart into the laundry room. This part of the basement wasn't finished beyond concrete walls and floor. Unshaded bulbs hung from bare rafters. It was clean of cobwebs, at least, but still the only "creepy" room in the house.

"I don't think we go anywhere after we die, okay? Is that

what you want to hear? It's not a popular opinion, Jared. Not in this business."

He helped me load the industrial-size washer with the dirty linens. "So you do think about it."

"I guess so." I added the special powdered detergent required by law to clean bodily fluids, and turned the dials. The machine grunted. Jared and I both looked at it. "Did the washing machine just...talk?"

Nothing else happened. I finished setting the cycle. We stared at it again.

"How old is that thing, anyway?" Jared asked as we started out of the room.

"It's probably as old as I am."

From behind us, the machine grunted again, then began the normal, groaning churning it always did when it began to fill with water. Jared took the cart from me, though it was way lighter empty, and I held open the doors for him. From the hall came the faint sounds of the songs still playing in the prep room.

"So...ancient?" Jared gave me a charming smile and I responded with a rude gesture. "Nice one. So ladylike."

I laughed. "That's me. A real princess."

"Who's going nowhere when she dies." Jared shoved the laundry basket back into its place and helped me start spraying and wiping all the surfaces we'd used.

"Why does this concern you so much?" I asked him.

"I'm not concerned, really." Jared shrugged. "I just think it's interesting."

From the laundry room came an unmistakable growl. We both looked. I found it funny that Jared stepped behind me automatically. Since he was taller and broader than I, I wasn't sure what protection he hoped I'd offer.

"What was that?" He had the voice of someone who asks hoping there's a good answer.

"I don't know. Let's go—"

Another growl, followed by a roar and a crash. And then the sound of rushing water.

We ran. Before we got even a few steps out of the prep room, the flood greeted us. Waves of dirty water flowed from under the laundry-room door. They didn't appear to have any intention of stopping.

Jared and I sloshed through it. The sound of growling got louder. By the time we got through the laundry-room doors, the water had risen to our ankles. Jared stopped just inside the door and snagged my arm to stop me, too.

"Watch out!" He pointed to the ancient, straining washer, which was rocking on its base.

I'd have laughed if I could, but nothing came out but a gasp. A moment later he'd proven me right not to laugh, because sparks started shooting out of the back of the washer along with the torrents of water pouring from the wildly flailing black rubber hose that had come disconnected.

I didn't have to be a genius to figure out that water plus electricity equals bad news, so, taking Jared's arm, I turned and ran. Every step through shin-deep water left me cringing, expecting the snap, crackle and pop of electrocution. The fluorescent lights above us flickered and fizzled. If they went out entirely, we'd be up the creek without a paddle, as my dad was fond of saying.

"Shit," panted Jared as we slid in the wet and managed

to fling open the doors to the ramp. "Wouldn't the stairs be easier?"

We both looked across to the stairs, three doors down the hallway. Then at the water, which didn't, thank God, seem to be rising but still gurgled menacingly. And the flickering lights above. A scorched smell had begun wafting down the hall toward us.

"Are you going to put your feet back in that water?" I asked.

"Hell, no."

"Ramp it is, then."

Our wet shoes made the ramp slippery, and I thanked my dad's foresight in laying down the rubberized tread he'd intended to help keep the gurneys from sliding. In moments we were upstairs and bursting through the door.

"Call the fire department!" I shouted this to a startled-looking Shelly who'd come out from behind her desk at the commotion we made hurtling ourselves through the door to the ramp.

Shelly didn't hesitate, just picked up the phone and dialed as, panting, Jared and I flew down the hall. Jared slid on the tile floor of the entryway between where we were and Shelly's desk and wiped out.

"Jared!" Shelly shrieked, and dropped the phone. She ran to him and knelt, even as he groaned, tried to sit. "Are you all right?"

His hand, wet, came up to clutch the pristine white sleeve of her demure button-down blouse. It left a print. "Yeah. I just about busted my ass, but—"

Leaving Shelly to tend her wounded soldier, I grabbed

up the handset she'd dropped and dialed 9-1-1, explaining quickly what we needed before hanging up again. In seconds the ringing of the phone distracted me from the intimate picture before me, and I was glad to have someplace else to look.

"Frawley and Sons, can you hold—"

"Grace?"

"Yes?" I answered automatically, reaching for the pen and message pad to write down the number, for surely I'd need to call him back after I dealt with the fire department. I could still smell smoke, and visions of my house on fire made my fingers clumsy enough to drop the pen.

"Are you all right?"

It was the same thing Shelly had just asked Jared, and I stopped my restless fumbling and went still. "Who's this?"

"It's Sam."

The fire station was no more than a block away, and yet the crew still used the sirens. They were loud enough to make conversation difficult, should I have been able to think of something to say, which I could not.

"Grace? Are those sirens?"

"Sorry," I blurted as I watched through the windows for the truck pulling into the parking lot. "I can't really talk right now."

"Grace, wait! Don't hang up—"

"Sam, my washing machine exploded and I think there's a fire!" I cried. "I can't talk now!"

The fire truck slid into place along the curb and Dave Lentini hopped out along with Bill Stoner and Jeff Cranford. I'd gone to school with Dave and Bill, and Jeff had been a year ahead of us. In their firefighters' outfits they looked exotic and sexier than usual, even though I knew they weren't going to start bumping and grinding and stripping out of them. I yanked open the back door for them and waved them inside.

"The basement," I said. "Be careful, a wire pulled loose and there's water—"

"Got it." Jeff pointed to his heavy rubber-soled boots. He hefted a handheld chemical-fire extinguisher and I felt immediately foolish for not using the almost identical one we kept in the prep room.

"Is he okay?" Bill, not just the local firefighter but also an EMT, jerked a thumb at Jared, who was now sitting up with Shelly's help.

"He slipped."

"I'll take a look."

Dave and Jeff headed toward the basement stairs while Bill gently shooed Shelly away from Jared, whose face had gone pale. In the seconds it took my heart to slow its adrenaline-induced pounding, I realized I still held the phone against my ear. Sam's breathing tickled my ear.

"Sounds like you're having quite the day," he said.

"We've had an accident. I really have to go."

"Grace, wait. Is everything all right? Are the firefighters there?"

"Yes." In fact, Jeff had already reappeared and given me a thumbs-up, situation under control, A-OK. "They're here. I think it's going to be all right."

I waited. My heart started its frantic thumping again.

"I want to take you to dinner."

"I'm busy tonight." It wasn't quite a lie. The mess downstairs would practically guarantee I'd be busy tonight and for a lot of nights in the future.

"Tomorrow night."

"Sam—"

"Why not?" His question sounded reasonable enough to deserve a reasonable answer, or at least a legitimate excuse, but I had none.

"I just can't, okay? I'm sorry, Sam, but I can't do this right now. I've got to go."

Jared was still not on his feet. Worry etched Shelly's pretty face. She'd taken his hand in hers, their fingers linked as Bill felt around Jared's ankle. I listened hard for sounds from downstairs, but Jeff had disappeared again and I heard nothing.

"I can't stop thinking about you."

My thumb, which had been creeping toward the disconnect button, stopped. I pressed the phone momentarily closer against my head, and the back of my earring bit into the softness behind my ear. My lips parted, and a sigh escaped me.

"Just have dinner with me."

I closed my eyes and the world settled into darkness around me, just long enough for me to pull in a breath. Then another. I thought of blue eyes and dark hair, and the taste of him. The way he'd felt inside me.

I didn't believe in white tunnels of light; and I didn't believe in fate.

"I'm sorry. I really have to go."

Before he could say anything more to change my mind, I ended the call and turned my attention to the disaster in front of me.

"What a mess." My dad clucked his tongue and surveyed the laundry room.

"No kidding." I rubbed my forehead. The fire had fortunately been put out before it had time to do more than singe the rafters, but the heavy, electrical smell of the smoke still hung in the damp air. The water from the burst connection had all swirled down the drain in the floor, but a thin film of sludge still clung to everything the water had touched. It was going to take hours of labor to clean.

I hadn't really wanted my dad to come, but once he heard about the fire, there was no keeping him away. He was already pissed off I'd waited until the next morning to call him. My excuse had been that I'd assumed he'd have already heard about it. Annville didn't keep secrets very long, and more than one of my parents' neighbors kept their police scanners on all the time.

"The cleaning service will be here in the morning to take care of it. And Jared's got to stay off his ankle for a day or so." I pressed my middle finger between my eyes to stave off the headache.

My dad shot me a look. "Cleaning service? How much is that going to cost?"

Irritated, I gave him a look right back. "A lot. Of course."

The frown he pulled told me he didn't much care for my attitude, but then I didn't much care for his. "If you got started now—"

"Dad!" For once, he stopped, so I didn't have to talk over him. "I'm not doing this myself. I need the cleaning service to take care of this because it has to be done right, and it's too much for me to do myself. It would take me days and even then, I don't have the equipment. So lay off, okay?"

My dad huffed. "I'm just thinking of the cost, Grace."

"Dad. I've got it covered. Stuff like this happens. We'll be fine."

Sure. If I planned to survive on ramen noodles and bargain-priced mac-n-cheese for a few months. It wouldn't be the first time, but it still sucked. I could deal with the reduced grocery budget, but this also meant my social life was going to be seriously curtailed. That sucked even worse.

My dad sighed and put his hands on his hips. "I can come in. Get a start."

"Dad, no!" I mirrored his stance. "I don't need you to do that."

He looked around again at the mess, then back at me. "With Jared out, you'll need some help around here, won't you?"

"I'll be fine. I won't be going anywhere, anyway." Not without the money to pay for my dates. Sam's phone call rose to the top of my mind like a raisin in champagne, refusing to stay down no matter how I tried to squash it.

"How much is it going to cost?"

I tossed up my hands and left the room, leaving him to contemplate the damage I'd "allowed" to happen to his precious business. Upstairs I found Shelly at the coffeemaker, her hands wrapped around a mug from which she kept taking rapid, nervous sips. Not only wasn't she a champ at brewing it, Shelly didn't drink coffee. She didn't even drink soda or tea.

"Is that decaf?" I pointed to the carafe. She shook her head and gulped another mouthful from her mug. I poured myself a cup and added sweetener and milk from the small fridge. "Shelly?"

She gave me a timid smile. "It's not so bad once you get past the taste."

I nodded solemnly as I sipped. "Uh-huh."

The clock on the wall ticked loudly in our mutual silence.

"How's Jared?" I asked her.

"Oh, he'll be okay. It's just a sprain." Her timid smile faltered. She poured more coffee into her mug, though it wasn't yet empty. "He has to stay off it, that's all."

I pretended to study a pile of brochures in the printer tray as I sipped my own coffee. "Yeah, I know."

Shelly gave a garbled squeak and gulped down more coffee. A sideways glance showed me pink cheeks and bright eyes. She looked tired and hopped up at the same time. Too much caffeine. I recognized the feeling.

"My dad's hanging around," I told her to save her from answering my question. "Just ignore him, okay?"

Shelly put her mug down on the counter. "Your dad?"

I smiled. "Don't let him get to you, Shelly."

Her smile got less timid, and she lifted her chin. "I won't. You're my boss. Not him."

"That's right, and don't you forget it." I gave her a trigger-finger salute and lifted my coffee mug. "Good coffee, by the way."

She beamed. "Thanks."

The phone rang, and she went to answer it while I took my mug and went to my own office to pore over the diminishing balance in my checking account and wonder what I was going to do.

The answer to that was simple enough. Spend less money. I sighed, drinking coffee.

The situation wasn't dire just yet. I lived frugally enough—aside from my dates with Jack. So I'd put off getting a new couch for a while. Not eat lunch out so often for a few months.

It was a matter of priorities, that was all.

Jack met me in the same room we'd used the last time. I knew it not by the verdigris-colored number on the door but by the patch in the wallpaper above the bed and the stain on the bathroom sink where someone had left a cigarette to burn too long.

We didn't say hello. He didn't smile. The door closed behind us and he pushed me up against it with his hands already pulling up my skirt and his mouth already fastening on my throat. He pressed his teeth to my flesh. I reached for his belt. He grunted and wound his fingers in my hair when my hand dived inside his jeans.

Jack pushed me onto the worn carpet that offered no padding for my knees. I might care later, when they sported dark purple bruises the shape of a quarter, but right then the sting of him pulling my hair mattered more.

He freed himself from his jeans with a practiced hand and got himself fully erect in three strokes, up and down.

I could have pulled away, freed myself from his grip, but that wasn't the game we were playing. I let him push my mouth onto his cock, and I took him down as far as I could while my hand crept between my thighs to stroke myself through the thin cotton of my panties.

I hadn't told him on the phone this was what I wanted. I'd only told him what I didn't want. No talking. No coyness. I wanted fast fucking. *Ruthless* was the word I'd used, not sure he'd understand what I meant, but Jack was a champ. He'd gotten better at this, and at that moment it didn't matter if he'd learned it from my tutelage or someone else's with more money to spend. All that mattered was the way he pushed his hips forward to thrust inside my eager mouth.

This was about me. For me, as it always was, but giving pleasure can be better than receiving, if you're in the right frame of mind. I'd knelt this way in front of other men and fucked them with lips and teeth and tongue. Made them come while they muttered and groaned and pulled my hair. Today I was doing it for Jack, who was doing it for me, and somewhere along the way it stopped mattering just who this was supposed to be for.

He shuddered, groaning. The sweet/salt musk of semen flavored the inside of my mouth, but he hadn't yet come. I sucked him softly one moment longer and slid my hand along his wet length to take the place of my tongue.

I'd have finished him with myself just a few seconds behind, but Jack pulled me to my feet and grabbed both my wrists. Breathing hard, he let go of one of my hands to reach for the straight-backed chair beside us and yanked it closer. He moved fast but sure, pulling a condom from his jeans pocket and sitting on the chair without letting go of my wrist.

"Put it on me," he demanded, and pressed the foil package into my palm.

He lifted his ass to shove down his jeans and briefs to his ankles while I ripped open the foil. I slid the latex down his length as he reached beneath my skirt to yank down my panties. Then he put his hands on my hips and turned me, facing away from him, then guided his cock inside me with an expert hand.

I teetered momentarily until I braced my hands on his knees and shifted my feet flat on the floor. Jack didn't move while we settled. This angle, with me sitting on his lap but facing away from him, was different even than if he'd entered me from behind, and I took a second or two to breathe with it.

"Look in the mirror," he told me.

I looked up. I could see myself clearly, my hair tumbled over my shoulders and my face flushed. I looked fully clothed, my skirt pushed up on my thighs but still mostly covering me, and my shirt completely buttoned. Of Jack I saw nothing but his hands anchoring my hips, and when I tried to shift so I could see his face, his fingers bit down against my skirt.

"No."

I stopped.

"Unbutton your shirt. All the way."

With clumsy fingers I started to do as he said, as he began a slow, subtle upward thrust. His thighs flexed be-

Megan Hart

neath my ass. His fingers inched my skirt higher and higher until the first glimpse of my pubic curls peeped from beneath the hem.

Under my shirt I wore a simple cotton bra without lace or frills. My nipples stood out clearly through the thin fabric. Jack's hand slid up and over my stomach to cup one breast, and he pinched my nipple.

"Take off your bra." His voice had gone lower. Deeper. His mouth pressed against my back, and the heat of his breath seeped through my blouse. "Look at your tits."

A crass word, tits. Crude. I licked my lips when he said it, and did what he'd told me. My bra hooked in the front and it took no more than a flick of my thumb to loosen it. The fabric cupping my breasts fell away and my bared skin humped into gooseflesh, then heat when Jack's hand slid across them.

His other hand pulled my skirt even higher.

"Can you see your pussy?"

That word is soft and hard at the same time, crude and innocent all at once. I never think of my breasts as tits, my vagina as a pussy. I use *cunt* if I think of it as anything, *cunt* a word with power.

"Yes." I had to lick my mouth again as I said it. As I watched Jack's hand slide between my thighs and find my clit with his middle finger. As he began to rub me in slow, even circles in time with his slow, shallow thrusts.

He stopped a moment and withdrew his hand. When he returned it, his finger was slick and wet. The thought of him licking it to better slide against me forced a groan from deep in my throat, and my body jerked.

"Do you like that?"

"Yes…" The word became a hiss of pleasure as his circling finger sent warmth throughout my body.

Just as I could have pulled my hair from his grasp, I could have moved on his erection, but there was sweet anticipation in the torture of his slight movements and the slow, slow motion of his finger on my clit.

"Can you see me touching you?"

"Yes."

"Watch."

"I'm watching."

I moaned when he withdrew his finger from my flesh again, and louder when he returned with it even wetter than the first time. He would have tasted me that time, and I groaned and closed my eyes.

"Watch," Jack ordered, and I wondered how he knew I wasn't.

I couldn't see his face in the mirror. Only his hands, one still on my hip and the other working between my legs. I couldn't see his face, but maybe he could see mine, and that thought tore forth another ragged groan. My face, my shining eyes, my mouth slack with pleasure. My tits, nipples tight and red with arousal. The curve of my belly and fluff of dark curls parted by his fingertip.

Jack hadn't been moving inside me very fast or hard, but now he stopped entirely. His finger rested without mercy on my clit, and instead of the slow circles he began a rhythmic pressure, firm and steady, the motion of his hand so slow I couldn't see it.

I could feel it, though. Push. Release. Push. Release. Far

slower than my heart, which beat fast in my wrists and throat and also inside my cunt and beneath the kernel of my clitoris.

The salt of my sweat burned my lips until I licked them, and then it burned my tongue. I watched the pink ribbon of my tongue slide across my mouth and the glimpse of teeth as I bit my lower lip against the low cry easing out of me.

"I can feel you getting hotter." Jack pushed his face against my shoulder blade. "Your clit's getting bigger under my fingers. Watch yourself. Are you watching?"

"Fuck, yes," I managed to say. I wanted to ask Jack if he was watching, but I could only stare at my reflection.

I'd never seen myself come before, not even the reflection of my lover's gaze. I always closed my eyes at the end, as if my ecstasy could be made greater by the colored light-show orgasm created behind my eyelids. But now, myself the only one watching, it seemed important to see.

My body ached for Jack to move and thrust, but he denied me that unvoiced desire. His finger pressed me in its slow pattern, then stopped. Circled me once, twice, until I was on the edge, my thighs quaking with the effort of release, only to stop again. I moved my hips then, desperate for the pressure on my clitoris to send me over. I pushed up with my hands, lifting my body, but Jack's hand tightened on my hip and I stopped. I could have moved, could have taken what I wanted, but I didn't.

His face pressed my back, and his finger started moving again. It went on like that forever, his flesh sliding on mine and teasing me to the edge of climax before easing off. His cock throbbed inside me, my cunt so sensitive, my clit so engorged, that every shift of his breath, the subtle thickening of his penis inside me, was as obvious and arousing as if he'd started to slam in and out of me.

"Are you still watching?" His voice, low and slow, tugged my ear.

"Yes."

I couldn't look away. My cheeks had paled, but the red flush now crept up my chest and along the column of my throat. I couldn't see the motion of Jack's hand, but I could feel it, just as I could feel him throb inside me.

Pleasure engulfed me as my muscles tensed. I had to force my hands to loosen their grip on Jack's knees. My thighs ached with the strain of not moving. Under my butt, Jack's thighs pushed upward, just slightly, and his cock thrust the teensiest bit harder into me. It was enough.

I put my hand over his as I gasped, the small motion of his fingertip on me now too much as my clit beat and my cunt bore down on him. Still, he didn't move or thrust, and still I did not close my eyes.

It was hard, looking at my own face contort with ecstasy, and in the end though I managed to keep my eyes open, I did have to shift the focus of my gaze to a spot on the wall behind me rather than look into my own eyes. I bit down on my lower lip hard enough to break the skin, but miraculously didn't.

I came with a shudder but in silence. My orgasm was too vast for shouts or gasps. It sucked the breath from me and left me panting as the waves of ecstasy washed over me, one after the other. Even when those first few seconds of blinding pleasure had passed, my body didn't subside into satedness. The second I let go of the hand still pressed against my clit, Jack began to fuck me. The motion of his thrusts pushed my still-sensitive clit onto the pad of his palm. I was coming again within moments, not in silence now but with a long, low cry that would have been louder if I'd had the breath to scream.

From behind me, Jack grunted and leaned against the back of the chair, tilting his body and pelvis upward with each thrust. I leaned forward, no longer watching, but opening the passage of my body to take in as much of him as I could. There was no friction, just smooth, smooth strokes as he fucked into me harder and harder. We moved together. I wanted to come again, but a third climax eluded me, the pressure too much or too little and never quite enough.

Jack put both hands on my hips and used his grip to move me as he thrust. It hurt, that slamming, his penis battering inside me, but I didn't care. He shouted, his last thrust lifting my entire body.

Jack's grip loosened. I caught my breath. He softened inside me, and I got up on trembling legs to wobble to the bathroom to splash my face with cold water. Jack followed me after a minute, and I stepped aside to give him room at the sink. He cupped one large hand beneath the water and scooped a drink, then looked up at me with lips glistening.

And the smile.

"Hey," Jack said.

"Hey." I smiled, too.

We had a reflection here also, in the harsh white fluorescent bathroom light, but it didn't have quite the same effect on me. I pulled the cups of my bra around and hooked them, then started on my blouse buttons. The flush was already fading from my throat.

Jack pulled up his briefs and jeans, the condom already gone. He left the belt open, though, his jeans low enough to expose the hint of hair on his belly below the hem of his T-shirt.

"Jesus," I said without thinking too hard about it. "You're so pretty."

Jack, who'd bent to take another drink from the faucet, swallowed and turned off the water. He stood, facing the mirror one way, then the other, checking himself out. He looked at me.

"Pretty?" he said at last, as if he meant to take it as a compliment but wasn't quite sure how.

"Oh, yes." I washed my hands and dried them on the white hand towel folded so neatly on the rack. "Very."

He looked again at his reflection and ran a damp hand through his hair to push it off his forehead. "Huh."

"Nobody's ever told you that before?" I nudged him with my elbow and left the bathroom.

He followed me. "Nope."

I stretched, testing my muscles for soreness. My thighs hurt the most. "Well…you are. Absolutely lovely."

He laughed at this. "Okay. Thanks. You're pretty, too."

It was my turn to laugh then. I found my discarded panties and slid them on. "Thanks."

"No," Jack said. "I mean it."

I looked up then, to look at him. "Thanks, Jack."

"You're welcome."

This time, the cell phone that rang was Jack's, but I checked mine anyway while he looked at his. I had no messages, but I knew he had one. He didn't answer it, though, just glanced at the number and flipped his phone closed.

"I have to get going," I told him. "Thanks for seeing me on such short notice."

He shrugged and shoved his phone down deep into his pocket.

I leaned up to kiss his cheek soundly and grabbed his ass at the same time, then stepped back. "I've got to go. I'll call you."

Jack nodded. "All right."

At home, the dark house greeted me with the powerful odor of the detergent the cleaning crew had used to get rid of the mess in the basement. Jared would be back to work tomorrow, and I had an early appointment.

My cell phone rang as I was halfway up the stairs, and I answered without checking the caller ID. I expected the answering service, but the caller greeted me with my first name only and not "Ms. Frawley."

"Grace." Not a question.

My answer was also not a question. "Sam."

Chapter 11

"*I* bet you're wondering how I got this number."

"I am, actually." I pushed open the door to my apartment and flicked on the light switch. I toed off my shoes and left them scattered on the floor as I padded to the kitchen for a drink and a snack.

"Your office manager took pity on me. I called so many times I convinced her to give me your number."

"How'd you manage to convince her you didn't plan to strangle me and stuff my body in a Dumpster?" I asked without a trace of humor in my voice, even though I was smiling despite myself.

"I don't think I did. Maybe you should pay her better."

I bit down on the laugh, but a giggle escaped me anyway. "I'll have a talk with her."

"Don't be too hard on her. She was just worn down. I can be a real pain in the ass."

I opened the fridge and found a jug of orange juice and a bowl of washed grapes. "You don't say."

"I don't say, actually," Sam replied. "But I've heard it said about me, so I guess it might be true."

I poured juice and tucked a grape between my lips. "It's very late, Sam. I have to go to bed."

"Alone?"

"Yes. Alone."

"That's sad."

I heard shuffling and imagined him stretched out in a bed of his own. "Where are you?"

"In bed. Alone. It's very sad, Grace. The bed has cowboy sheets on it."

This stopped me. "What?"

"Cowboy sheets."

"Why are you in a bed with cowboy sheets?" I nibbled another grape and sipped juice as I headed for the bedroom, where my own bed awaited me with soft flannel sheets.

"I'm at my mom's." More shuffling. "The sheets are actually my brother's. Mine had dinosaurs on them, but I couldn't find them in the linen closet. So I'm stuck with cowboys."

"That is sad." I laughed.

"Not as sad as being alone."

Adept at undressing with one hand holding the phone to my ear, I unzipped my skirt, then unbuttoned my blouse and tossed them in the laundry. "If you go to sleep, you won't notice you're alone."

"I'll dream about being alone, though, and when I wake up, I'll be sad." Sam shuffled again and let out a small groan.

A certain, sudden suspicion struck me. "What are you doing?"

"Nothing." A pause, and I heard a smile in his voice. "What did you think I was doing?"

I wasn't about to tell him I'd imagined him, prick in fist, pumping away while we sallied back and forth with our wits. "You sounded funny."

"Thank you, I'll be here all week. Don't forget to tip your waitress."

"You sounded odd," I amended. I needed a shower before bed, but it was a toss-up as to whether or not I'd take one. I looked into the bathroom, then at the bed, then the phone in my hand. It was late, I was tired, and I had to be up early. "I've got to go."

Sam groaned again. "Odd? I liked funny, better."

I should've disconnected, but...I didn't. I took my empty bowl and glass out to the sink, and once back in my bedroom pulled on pj bottoms and a T-shirt and climbed into bed. "It's late, and I really need to go to sleep."

"Are you in bed now?"

"Yes."

He made an indescribable noise that lifted the hairs on the back of my neck. "What are you wearing?"

"Pajamas."

"Silk?"

"Sorry to disappoint you, but, no. Flannel."

"I'm not disappointed," Sam said. "I love flannel pajamas."

I laughed. "Good night, Sam."

Another slight groan and the creak of a mattress. "At least tell me I can call you again."

My smile faded. I listened to the sound of his breathing, interrupted in a moment by another shuffle and a sharp intake of breath. The vision of him jerking off to this conversation no longer seemed so implausible.

"Sam, what the hell are you doing? Why do you keep groaning? What's the matter with you?"

"My brother," he said, "beat the ever-loving shit out of me. I'm having a hard time getting comfortable. I'd blame the cowboy sheets except I know it's the black eye and the sore ribs."

Shock dropped my jaw. "Your brother Dan?"

"I only have the one."

"He…" I remembered the look on Dan's face at the cemetery, and how his wife had pulled him away. "He really beat you up?"

"Yeah, but I gave as good as I got, so don't you fret about me, Grace. Unless—" his voice dipped low "—you want to come on over and nurse me back to health."

My mouth snapped shut. "I most certainly do not! Good night!"

"So I can call you again?"

"I don't think so." I switched off the light, half hoping he'd ask again. I couldn't be blamed for giving in to such a pain in the ass, could I? If he simply wore me down?

"That's not a no."

There was a long silence. I looked up through darkness at the ceiling I knew was there, though I couldn't see it. "No, I don't suppose it is."

"What are you thinking about?"

"Do you like horror movies?"

"That depends," Sam said.

"On?"

"If you're asking me to go see one."

I tucked my blankets beneath my chin. "More than one. Horrorfeast. I was going to go alone, but you can come with me. If you want."

"For you? Yes."

"Okay. Saturday, then?"

We exchanged details of when and where, and I told him good-night.

"Sleep tight," Sam said, and to my surprise and some disappointment, he hung up, leaving me to stare at something I knew was there although I couldn't see it.

Jared came back to work only slightly worse for the wear, joking as much as usual and only walking a little slower. He surveyed the basement rooms and looked impressed. "Nice washer."

"It better be, for the price." I'd replaced the washer and the drier with heavy-duty new ones that weren't quite industrial-size, but close to it. "And what do you know, looky here, you can be the first to use it."

Jared looked at the full laundry cart and rolled his eyes. "Gee, thanks."

I clapped him on the shoulder. "No problem, big guy. How's the ankle?"

He shrugged and reached for the fresh box of latex gloves I'd put on the brand-new shelves by the washer. He saw regulations, I saw dollar signs flying up into the sky. I put it out of my mind. That was part of the risk of owning your own business. Expenses.

"Hurts," he told me. "But I'm okay."

"Uh-huh." I watched him without offering to help. I had an appointment in twenty minutes, and digging into the soiled laundry while wearing my crisp, clean suit didn't appeal. "It's a good thing you didn't whack your head."

Jared loaded the washer and studied the dials without looking at me. "Yeah."

A small sound from the doorway made us both turn toward Shelly, who'd caught our attention by demurely clearing her throat. She always dressed neatly, usually in knee-length skirts and buttoned blouses with cardigan sweaters if the weather called for it, but today she was even more buttoned up than usual. She'd skinned her hair back into an unflatteringly tight bun. Even her lipstick was paler than normal.

"Phone for you, Grace," she said.

"Thanks." I looked at Jared, who was studiously emptying the laundry cart, then back at Shelly, who was studying the handset in her palm like it was ringing out in Morse code. I took the phone from her, and she backed away, going upstairs as I followed.

The call was from my dad, who wanted to know how the cleanup had gone. By the time I got upstairs to my office, he'd already run through the entire list of usual complaints and admonishments. I listened with half an ear while I checked through the stack of pink message slips on my desk. None from Sam.

"Grace, are you listening to me?"

"Sure, Dad. Of course." I pushed aside the slips and reminded myself I didn't care.

"I said I thought I should come over, take another look at the books. See where you can tighten your belt."

I moved my mouse to wake my computer monitor from sleep, but it stayed black. I turned the mouse over to make sure the red light on the bottom was lit, and it was. The batteries hadn't run low. "Dammit."

"Excuse me?" It wasn't hard to hear the thunder in my dad's voice.

"Not you. The computer. Well, a little bit you, Dad."

He harrumphed. "I know you don't want me noodling around in your business."

"That's right. I don't." The computer screen finally, slowly, came to life, but almost immediately showed an error message telling me I had to restart. I pressed the button on the back of the hard drive.

"Too bad," my dad said.

"Haven't we had this argument before?"

I sighed and waited for my computer to boot back up. It had been acting a little funny since the washer incident, and I was afraid the power surge had broken it. The desktop appeared, but none of my applications wanted to open. The icons bounced merrily in the dock, but that was all. Then the spinning wheel of death showed up, and I powered the machine down again.

"It's not an argument, Gracie. I just want to help."

I sighed again as my computer struggled vainly to boot up. "Dad, I have to go. I think my computer's broken."

I was sure I didn't imagine the small note of triumph in his voice when he said, "I never needed a computer to run my business."

"Yeah, okay, Mr. Quest for Fire, thanks." I watched the screen go black, then the error screen came up again.

"I don't know what Quest for Fire means, but I don't like your tone." He didn't quite say "young lady," but it was implied.

"Dad!" I cried, then lowered my voice. "You're driving me up a wall! If you want to come to check out my books, fine, do it. But I'm telling you, it's all fine! I'm not going to starve, and I'm not going to lose the business, either!"

Once more Shelly's discreet cough alerted me to her presence in the doorway. She did some sort of nifty sign language to tell me my appointment had arrived. "Dad, I have to go."

"I'm just trying to help," my dad said, tone affronted.

I caved. "I know. Come on over this afternoon. If I can get the computer up and running, you can do whatever you want with the books, okay?"

Placated but not appeased, my dad agreed and hung up as I stood to greet the couple who'd come to me to talk about arrangements for a maiden aunt. The rest of the day flew by in a haze of appointments, services and death calls. Feast or famine, my dad had always been fond of saying. The funeral business wasn't predictable. By the time I pulled into the parking lot after our third service of the day, my feet hurt even though I'd worn sensible heels, and my stomach growled.

Shelly had waited for me to come back, though I was much later than usual. She'd tidied her desk in sharp contrast to the mess I knew awaited me on mine. Jared hadn't gone to the final service with me, and I hadn't seen his car in the lot when I pulled in, which meant he wasn't giving her a ride.

"It's late." I hung the keys to the hearse back on their peg. "You should go on home."

"I know." She smiled at me, just a little. "I wanted to make sure you got back all right."

Funny how Shelly's mother-henning me didn't annoy me as much as when it came from my family. "Go on. You don't need to hang around here for me. Is Duane picking you up?"

"No. I drove myself."

I watched her do an unneeded, last-minute tidy of her desk surface as she stood and grabbed her cardigan from the back of the chair. "I thought Jared usually drove you home."

Her swift fingers buttoned her sweater up to her neck, though the weather was mild. She grabbed her purse and began rustling inside it. "Not anymore."

"Shelly?"

She looked up at me.

"Do you want to talk about it?"

It was simultaneously the right and wrong thing to say. Shelly burst into braying sobs and sank back into her chair, then buried her face in her arms on top of the desk. It wasn't exactly what I'd bargained for, though I should've known it was a possibility. I shrugged out of my suit jacket and hung it on the coatrack, then reached for the box of tissues and started handing her one after the other.

"Oh…Graaaaaace," Shelly wailed from the hollow her arms had created to hide her face. "Oh…I'm so…so… So!"

I settled my butt on the edge of her desk and patted her shoulder. "So what?"

"Confused!" More wailing.

Shelly had always been prone to crying under stress, but it was usually a little more restrained. She blotted her face with a handful of tissues, but they did little to stop the torrent of tears streaming down her cheeks.

"About Jared?"

"No!"

"About Duane?" I asked as gently as I could.

"No. Yes. Both." She looked up at me. "What was I thinking?"

I handed her another tissue. "I don't know, Shelly. That you like him? That he likes you?"

"Yes, but… Oh, bugger." She sat up and wiped her face. With her face cleaned of the minimal makeup she wore, she looked even younger. "I'm so confused."

She'd said that already, but I couldn't blame her for saying it again. "Let me ask you something."

She looked up at me, her hopeful face pressuring me to make this all okay. "Sure."

"Are you…happy?"

If someone had asked me that question, I wasn't sure how I'd have answered, but Shelly just shook her head. "No!"

"Well, doesn't that tell you something?"

"It tells me a lot," she said, and burst into more tears.

I really needed a shower and a change of clothes. And also, a beer. Or two. "Shelly, come upstairs with me, okay? I need to eat something. Not cookies," I said before she could offer. "Come upstairs. We'll talk about this."

In my apartment, she sobbed on my couch while I heated a frozen pizza and cracked open two bottles of

Tröegs Pale Ale. I handed her one and changed into jeans and a T-shirt in my bedroom. Once again, my shower would have to wait. By the time I came out, Shelly had chugged down half her beer and managed to stop crying long enough to set my table with paper plates and napkins.

The oven dinged just then, and I pulled out the pizza and cut it into slices. Shelly took one but didn't eat it, while I wolfed down mine and grabbed another. With the emptiness in my stomach subsiding, I drank some beer and sat back in my chair with a sigh.

"He's a good guy, Shelly." I didn't indicate which one. It didn't really matter. They were both good guys; I liked Jared a lot more, but then I was biased.

"Yes." Shelly nodded and pressed a hand to her tear-swollen eyes. "I know."

"Look, without getting into the details—"

"I had sex with him!" Shelly cried. Her chin lifted, her mouth trembling, but her voice was strong. "I couldn't stand it anymore, and I just…did it!"

I swigged beer quickly to cover up the fact I'd gone briefly trout-mouthed. It went down the wrong pipe, sending me into a coughing fit. Shelly blinked rapidly and swiped at her eyes, but staved off more tears by slugging back her own beer.

"I'm—"

"Surprised?" she interrupted. "Why, that he'd do it with me?"

"No, of course not—"

Shelly thumped the table with the flat of her hand. "Guys will screw anything, Grace, and besides, I told him he'd be doing me a favor!"

"I didn't think he wouldn't want to…sleep with you, Shelly." Somehow the f-bomb just didn't seem like the right word to use with my pretty little office manager. "Wait…favor?"

Her chin went higher and her mouth thinned. "Yes. I told him it would be a favor. How am I supposed to know if I want to spend my life with Duane if I've never had sex with any other man? How am I supposed to tell if Duane's any good in bed if I have nothing to compare him to?"

"So…the night he hurt his ankle, you…"

"I did." Shelly looked hesitantly proud.

I finished my beer while she eyed me anxiously. "And how was it?"

A couple more tears squirted out of her eyes but she slapped them away. "Wonderful."

I understood very well where she was coming from. Bad enough that she'd cheated on her almost-fiancé. Worse that the sex had been so great. "You can write off bad sex. Good sex is harder to forget. Great sex? Almost impossible."

"I thought I'd just get it over with. Then I could stop thinking about him all the time," she said. "That if we did it, I'd prove something to myself. And I did. But the wrong thing!"

I bit into my pizza, chewing while I thought of how to answer her. "So what are you going to do now?"

"What should I do?"

"When did I become an expert on relationships?" I got up to put my plate in the cranky dishwasher. "In case you hadn't noticed, I don't have one boyfriend, much less two."

"Jared's not my boyfriend," Shelly answered, but it

sounded automatic and not sincere. "And I'm not stupid, you know."

I turned to look at her. "I never thought you were."

She looked at me. "You can't tell me you don't have a boyfriend or someone hidden away somewhere. Do you think I haven't figured out where you go those days you leave the office? What about Sam?"

"Shelly, you really don't know."

She sniffled. "You're not going to play bingo. I know that much."

"No," I admitted. "But I'm not going to meet a boyfriend."

"You're going to meet someone," she said with that same stubborn, anxiously hopeful look.

"Yes." That was it, no further explanation, no matter how hopefully she looked at me. When exactly had I become a mentor?

"Grace, please," Shelly said. "I really could use some advice."

I sat back down across from her. "Do you love Duane?"

Shelly nodded, but slowly. "I used to think so."

Shit. "Do you love Jared?"

She shook her head far too fast. "No. Of course not."

"Why of course not? Jared's cute, he's funny. He's smart. And he's a nice guy. You say 'of course not' like he rings church bells for a living."

This prompted the hoped-for smile from her. "He is cute."

"Shelly, I wish I had an answer for you, I really do. But the fact is…if I was going to give you some advice…" She waited. I faltered.

"Yes?"

"You're asking the wrong person," I said finally, when the clock's ticking had filled the space between us for too long. "I don't ever want to get married or even have a boyfriend, a real boyfriend, so I'm really not the person to be giving you advice."

"I've made such a mess of things," she said. "I can't tell Duane. It would hurt him, and he'd break up with me."

"Probably. But maybe that's what you want?" I suggested.

If Shelly started crying again, I was prepared to break out the vodka, but she just sniffled again and hid her face in her hands for a minute. Then she got up from the table with a sigh.

"I should get home."

"Are you okay to drive?"

"I know I look like a Girl Scout, but half a beer isn't enough to make me too drunk to drive."

I'd meant her mental state, not the beer, but I laughed anyway. "I'm just checking."

"Do you need help cleaning any of this up?" She waved a hand at the table.

"No. You go on home. I'll see you tomorrow."

She nodded and smiled, and when I got up to walk her to the door, she surprised me with a hug. "Thanks, Grace."

I hadn't done anything, really, but watch her cry. Protesting it would only be awkward, so I hugged her in return. "Sure. Anytime."

She was already at the top of the stairs and I was closing my door when her voice stopped me. "Oh, I forgot to tell you. Your dad came by when you were out."

I sighed, slouching in the door frame. "And?"

"I told him you hadn't had time to fix your office computer. He came up and took your laptop."

Fury isn't always hot. Sometimes it's a frigid icicle slammed down your spine. "What?"

"I didn't think you'd want him to," Shelly said hastily. "But your dad—"

My face must have frightened her, because she ended with a squeak. "My dad. I know."

"I told him you wouldn't like it," she added, backing toward the stairs. "I'm sorry."

"It's not your fault," I said through numb lips, though the truth was, I wanted to strangle her. I had suddenly way less sympathy for Shelly and her romantic problems. "I'll talk to him."

"Thanks," she said, and disappeared, wisely, before I had time to come after her.

My laptop. Where I did keep records of the business expenses, all right, but also kept accounting of my own. Which included things I'd really rather not share with my father.

Fuck.

There wasn't anything to be done now but clean my neglected apartment, and I set to it with a vengeance until the dust flew. The shrill bleat of my cell phone tore me from my mad mopping and had me diving toward it, ready to confront my father with "I can't believe you!"

Too late, I realized it was too late an hour for the call to be from my dad, who made a point of being in bed by nine so he could be up by six.

"Who is this?" I demanded finally when the caller said nothing.

"Keanu Reeves."

"Sure. Right. Well, hi there, Kiki. What's up?"

"Not much. Just got finished riding my motorcycle around the world."

The ice of my fury was melting. Just a little. "How was that?"

"Crossing the ocean was a little tough, but good thing for me, I can hold my breath a really long time."

"Hello, Sam," I said. "Why are you pretending to be Keanu Reeves?"

"You said you couldn't believe me before I'd even said a word. I figured if you didn't want to go out with me, Kiki might have a better shot."

"Oh. I thought you were my dad calling." A second too late, I remembered that he'd just lost his own father. I hoped the mention of mine in a less than glowing tone wouldn't upset him.

"Nope. Just me."

I looked at the clock. Just past 10:00 p.m. "Let me guess. The cowboy sheets are keeping you awake?"

He laughed, and ice of a different sort tiptoed up and down my spine. "I'm not in bed. Yet. Should I get in bed?"

"Are you tired?" I was suddenly very wide-awake.

He laughed again. "Not really."

"Don't you have to be up for work or something in the morning?" I moved around my apartment as I talked, putting away dishes and wiping down counters.

"Me? Hell no." Sam's soft snort sounded amused. "According to my brother I'm a lazy-ass son of a bitch."

"Huh. Are you?" I wrung out the dishcloth and hung it

over the faucet of the sink to dry, then turned to lean against the counter.

"Nope." Sam sounded unapologetic, though I detected a hint of tension in the answer. "Personally, I think he's an overworked son of a bitch. But what do I know?"

"Nothing?"

He laughed. "Tell me something. Do you think I'm an annoying pain in the ass, or charmingly persistent?"

"Well, there's a loaded question." In the dark I made my way without fumbling into my bedroom and turned on the bedside lamp. It was in the shape of a doll, the shade her overlarge hat. I'd had the lamp since childhood, and it cast a warm glow around the room and let me ignore its flaws.

"I'm serious."

He sounded serious, so I gave him a serious answer. "Why do you keep calling me?"

"Because I want to see you again, and showing up on your doorstep seemed to freak you out. I have to tell you, though, I might resort to standing outside your window with a boom box pretty soon."

"That desperate, huh?" I sank lower onto the pillows, crushing them beneath my head and wriggling until I'd made a nest for myself.

"Yes."

That simple answer forced a sigh from my lips, and I didn't bother trying to joke with him. "Oh, Sam. Why?"

"I think that should be obvious," Sam said.

I rubbed a hand across my forehead and stared up at the shadows on my ceiling. "You're unbelievable!"

"I do think," Sam said loftily, "that's where we began this conversation, isn't it?"

I rolled onto my side to look at my alarm clock. "Might be a good place to end it, too. I have to go to sleep."

"Grace." Sam's voice went scratchy and seductive, and my body responded instantly. "I can't wait to see you again."

"You only have to wait until tomorrow."

"I don't want to wait."

"It's not good to want something so much. You know that, right? You'll only be disappointed."

"I'm a big boy."

As if I could forget. "Good night, Sam."

He sighed. "Won't even throw me a bone?"

"I can't do that. I'm sorry."

"Don't worry. I've got one, anyway." And laughing evilly, giving me a mental image again of him naked and erect, he hung up.

Dammit.

Chapter 12

$\mathcal{H}$orrorfeast had described itself as "Eight movies too terrifying for the general public," but we'd only get to see three. I hoped they weren't too terrible instead of too terrifying.

"Hi." Sam waved at me from the sidewalk. "I already bought the tickets."

"You didn't have to do that. I invited you."

"I wanted to make sure we got them. There was a long line." He bounced a little.

I looked around and saw no line, but with Sam giving me that grin I wasn't going to argue. "You look like…"

"Like my brother beat the crap out of me?" He grinned again.

I looked at the fading shiner on his eye, the slightly puffed lip. "Yeah. You really got into a fistfight with your brother?"

He laughed and looked a little ashamed. "He started it."

"Yeah. I bet." I couldn't stop myself from reaching to touch the bruise on his cheek, just lightly. "Does it hurt?"

"Nah. Not so much anymore." Sam shrugged. "C'mon. Let's go in."

Inside, he insisted on paying for the popcorn and drinks, which came in outrageously sized cartons and were, the clerk ensured us enthusiastically, "refillable."

"Refillable, God." I looked at the nearly gallon-size cup. "I'll float away."

"Hey, six hours of movies means a lot of popcorn and drinks." Sam winked with his good eye.

It was nice, actually, this dating business with him picking up the tab, even though it felt a little odd. We settled into seats in one of the multiplex's smaller theaters. So far the crowd hadn't filled in many of the seats. We got a primo location in the center in front of the open row where wheelchairs could park—we could put our feet on the railing and Sam did at once. He tossed popcorn into the air and caught it neatly in his mouth, a trick I wanted to emulate but couldn't manage.

"Good thing it's refillable," I said after my fourth attempt sent popcorn into my hair but not between my lips.

Sam chuckled. "Yeah. Here."

He offered me a kernel, which I took from his hand after only a moment's hesitation.

"So what are we seeing, anyway?" He rustled open the plastic wrapper on the ridiculously large box of nonpareils that was only half-full.

I checked the flyer I'd picked up at the desk. *"Dead Spot, Maternal Instinct* and *SlipKnot."*

"Never heard of any of them."

I handed him the paper, but he waved it away. "Nah. Doesn't matter, does it? This way, I won't be spoiled."

The theater filled slowly. The atmosphere was rowdier than a normal showing, but I guessed a lot of the people were also here for more than one film, the way we were. Lots of people had huge vats of soda and popcorn, too.

When the lights dimmed and the first preview began, Sam leaned over to me. "Grace?"

"Yes?"

"Can I hold your hand?"

I turned to look at him. "Why, do you think I'm going to be scared?"

That smile. Fuck, that smile! "No. But I might be."

I offered my hand. "Okay. If you insist."

Sam took it and settled down lower in his seat with a smug look. I squeezed his fingers hard, and he looked over at me and winked. Halfway into the first movie, I figured out Sam hadn't been trying to be winsome. Though the film was a predictable slash-and-gash about teenagers lost in the woods and hunted by the standard-issue homicidal maniac, Sam jumped at every scare. He sunk lower and lower in his seat, his fingers gripping mine.

"Do you want to leave?" I whispered when he'd leaped so high he'd scattered popcorn.

He looked surprised. "No, do you?"

"I thought maybe—"

He shook his head. "No."

Maybe he was being manly and brave. Maybe he had a masochistic streak. Whatever it was, watching Sam was more entertaining than watching the movie. When the credits rolled and the lights went up, he let go of my hand and stretched.

"Did you like it?" I sounded amused, and he heard it.

"Yeah. It was okay. You?"

"I thought there were some pretty big plot holes." Dissecting the movies was a big part of the appeal, but I wasn't sure Sam was up to being the Ebert to my Siskel.

"Yeah. But you have to admit, they tied it all up at the end. You knew that some of them were going to die, but did you think it was going to be that first dude?"

I hadn't. That had been a surprise, killing off the character that had been set up to seem like the hero. "That was good, you're right."

With half an hour between each showing we had plenty of time to talk about the film, and we did. Sam might have watched parts of it from behind the shield of his hand, but he hadn't missed anything important.

"But did you like it?" I asked again as the lights went down for the start of the next feature. "I don't want you to sit through something you hate."

Sam reached for my hand again. "These movies scare the crap out of me, but I like hanging out with you."

It didn't seem as if we'd spent close to eight hours in the theater, but the empty popcorn and cups proved we had. So did my aching bladder, which protested the abuse of being made to contain so much liquid. The ladies' room, typically, was full and it took awhile for me to get out. By the time I did, Sam had gone outside to wait.

He smiled as soon as he saw me. "Hey. Thought maybe you'd drowned."

"Long lines." We'd entered the theater in the light, but

it seemed somehow fitting after a day of scares to exit in darkness.

He turned to me. "So."

"So." I cocked my head to look at him.

"Did you have a good time?"

"I did." We started walking toward my car, and this time I couldn't have said who was leading and who following. "How about you?"

"Stellar." Sam took a deep breath and looked up at the night sky. "I'm going to have to sleep with the light on, but it was great. Thanks for asking me."

"The look on your face when that guy jumped out of the closet with the meat hook was worth it."

Sam palmed his face. Below his hand I caught a glimpse of another of his lovely smiles. "Man. You must think I'm some kind of dork."

"No. It was sort of cute." I didn't tell him how much I'd liked the fact he could discuss the movies with me, unpeel them like layers. He'd picked out visual effects I'd have missed. He had a good eye for detail.

He moved a little closer. "Great. Cute. That's like saying I have a good personality."

I had to laugh. "Well, you have that, too."

Sam groaned. "Grrrrrrreat."

I laughed harder as we walked toward Betty. "This is me."

"This is your car?" Sam ran a hand over Betty's hood.

I unlocked the door. "Yep."

Shaking his head, Sam laughed and pointed a few spaces down. "That's mine."

I stared. He stared. His car was a Camaro, too. His was in much better shape.

He'd taken up my hand before I could pull away.

"Fate," Sam murmured. "Or luck. Whatever."

I let him move closer to me. Heat from his body surrounded me, though I hadn't been cold. He didn't touch me with his hands, but the caress from his gaze was enough to make me swallow hard against a dry throat.

"Do you want to go someplace?"

"Oh, yes," I said. "Definitely."

He took me to the Pancake Palace.

It wasn't exactly what I'd had in mind, but what do you say to a man when you think he's taking you to a by-the-hour motel and instead he leads the way to an all-night breakfast joint?

"I'll have coffee."

The waitress smiled at us both as Sam ordered their huge breakfast platter, "minus the pig."

Then he sat back in the garish orange booth and smiled at me. I ordered chocolate-chip French toast and a side of hash browns.

"And some more coffee," Sam said. "Keep it coming. We'll be here for a while."

"Will we?" I asked when the waitress left the table.

He nodded and stripped the paper from a straw. He twirled it into a knot and offered me one side. "Pull."

I pulled. He got the knot.

"Someone's thinking about me," he said, and tossed the paper to the side. "Is it you?"

"I'm sitting with you, Sam, I guess I might be."

"Something good, or something bad?"

I laughed. "You know what? I honestly don't know."

We talked about the movies until the waitress brought us steaming platters of food and set them down, refilled our mugs and asked us if we wanted anything else. Sam hadn't looked away from me. Not once.

"We're good," he said. "For now."

I picked up my fork and stabbed into the stack of French toast. I felt him staring, but concentrated on cutting my food. When I looked up, he was still looking.

"Aren't we?" he asked.

I didn't know the answer to that, either. I chewed a bite of syrup-soaked bread while I thought. Then I drank some coffee. Sam had dug into his own breakfast, chewing and swallowing and not pressuring me to reply.

When my phone began to sing to me from my purse, Sam stopped with a fork halfway to his mouth. "'Don't Fear the Reaper'?"

I pulled out my cell and gave him a smile. "I got tired of Deep Purple."

Sam put a hand over his heart and pretended he was staggering back in his seat while I answered. It was the answering service, of course, and I took down the number in the small notepad I carried with me for just that reason. Sam watched me write. I clicked my pen as I hung up.

"Are you always on call?" he asked.

"Mostly, yes. I have an intern, Jared, but..." I shrugged.

Sam studied me. "He's not good?"

"Oh, he's great. Really good. I just like making sure,

you know…things are…done." I faltered uncharacteristically, I thought.

"Do you have to go?" he asked.

"I might. I have to answer this call first. Maybe not."

He nodded. I dialed and spoke to a weary-voiced man whose father-in-law had passed away in a nursing home. We made arrangements to meet the next morning, and I called the nursing home to schedule the pickup of the body. I ate in between phone calls and drank as much coffee as the waitress brought.

"You're never going to be able to sleep tonight," Sam commented when I finally finished all my calls.

I looked at my watch. "By the time I get home, I'll be fine."

Sam had finished his breakfast and settled back with his mug. "I'm impressed."

"By my caffeine intake?" I stirred sugar into another mug and lifted it to sip.

"No. By the way you talked to those people. You're good at what you do, Grace."

"Thanks, Sam. Thank you."

"I mean it."

Later, when we walked to our nearly identical cars sitting side by side in the parking lot, I'd stopped expecting a kiss. Of course, that was when he decided to swoop in for one, but instead of putting his lips to mine, Sam kissed my cheek.

I put a hand over the spot where his lips had left their heat when he pulled away. "What was that for?"

"I didn't want you to think I didn't like you." Sam winked.

I unlocked my door and opened it, but stared right at him when I said, "Do you?"

Sam had put enough distance between us to make asking the question easier, but I'd have asked it even if he'd been close enough to touch. I was out of practice at having to guess a man's intentions.

Sam opened his car door and tossed his keys in his palm before curling his fingers over them. "Yep."

Nothing more. I waited, then shook my head and got behind the wheel. I watched him pull away and waved when he waved. By the time I got to the highway, I'd decided not to stress about it. My phone hummed "Don't Fear the Reaper" and I answered it.

"A lot," Sam said.

And though he hung up immediately after that, the call so brief I might have imagined it, I smiled all the way home.

I'd expected the world to end when my dad opened my files and discovered my personal expenses were going to pay for my sexcapades, but so far I hadn't heard a peep. The problem was, I had severe laptop withdrawal and needed my personal computer back from my dad. With my desktop acting up, that became my first priority. After my morning appointments I spent an hour and a half trying to get my iMac up and running again without interruption from him, from Shelly, who was unusually silent, or from Jared, who was downstairs avoiding us both. Fortunately, despite the problems, my Mac was a workhorse that didn't lose any data, and once I'd figured out exactly how to go through and repair my disc permissions and a whole bunch of stuff I had no clue about, the computer powered up again without an issue. I backed up all my data onto disc, just in case, and pushed my chair back from my desk feeling like nothing short of a genius.

Sam hadn't called me in three days, but I wasn't surprised. That seemed to be his M.O. Each day that passed without hearing his voice reminded me all the more of the reasons I didn't want to deal with dating. He liked me, he didn't. I liked him, I didn't. I was plucking an entire field of mental daisies and coming up with no good answer.

When at last he called, it was again on my cell and not the office phone. I knew it was him before I answered. Who else would call my cell during business hours?

"How are you?" he asked.

"I'm fine, Sam. How are you?" I heard the rush of liquid and his swallow, and I thought of watching the smooth skin of his throat work.

"Good, good. Great, actually. I got a pretty permanent gig at the Firehouse. It won't affect my teaching, either."

He'd said it as if I should know what he was talking about. "Teaching?"

"Yeah. I got a job at Martin's Music. I didn't tell you? I'm giving guitar and piano lessons. Oh. And selling cellos and violins to elementary-school students on commission. I don't suppose you've ever yearned to play the cello?"

"I can't say that I have, no." Through my office door I caught a glimpse of Shelly and Jared talking. He leaned close, his hand on the wall by her head. Interesting.

"Too bad. I could get you a good deal. But what do you say? Come see me play. We can have a few drinks. Hang out. Then if we both want to have some mind-blowing sex, we can talk about it."

"On your cowboy sheets? So sexy," I told him.

There is a frisson, a tension, when men and women talk about sex. Face-to-face it can be too much. Ridiculous, even. But over the phone, with nothing but the sound of each other's voices and imagination, the ridiculous seems practical.

"Of course not. We'd have to go to your place. I can't bring you back to my mom's."

"I don't bring men to my place."

"Well, that would cause a problem then." Sam chuckled. "I do notice, though, that you didn't tell me mind-blowing sex was completely out of the question."

No matter how many times you eat, your body still eventually hungers. Fucking is the same way. No matter how many times you come, eventually you want to do it again.

"I didn't want to deflate your...ego."

Sam guffawed. "Okay. I get it. You have a boyfriend? Bring him along."

Again, he'd twisted me into surprise. "What?"

"Bring him. I don't care."

I had no idea how to respond to this. Had I been reading him wrong? Frustration whirled its gears in my gut and I tapped the top of my desk with my pen. "You don't care if I have a boyfriend?"

"Nope." I could hear the grin in his voice and could imagine it all too well.

"So if I showed up with a boyfriend, that wouldn't bother you at all."

"Not a bit."

Why not? I wanted to ask, but bit back the question. "It might bother the boyfriend, don't you think?"

"Somehow I doubt that if you had a boyfriend, you'd tell him that you wanted to have mind-blowing sex with me."

I snorted. "Wouldn't want you getting another beating, would we?"

"Cold, Grace. So cold. Does that mean you're coming?" He sounded immensely pleased with himself.

"Maybe."

He laughed. "I'll see you there."

I disconnected and stared at my phone for a minute. I plucked a few more imaginary daisies before I started printing out my business register. I didn't exactly want to face my dad, but I wanted my computer. Being able to watch TV from bed while I instant messaged and surfed the Net had become too convenient.

I called my parents' house, only to have my mother tell me my dad wasn't there. He'd gone fishing, of all things.

"Dad? Fishing?"

"Him and Stan Leary. Stan's got a boat." My mom said this as if it was no big deal, but in all the time I'd known my dad, which was my entire life, I couldn't recall him ever going fishing. Or doing much of anything besides work, as a matter of fact.

"When will he be back?"

My mom had no idea, but she didn't seem to care that I'd be stopping by to exchange my printout for my laptop. I told Shelly where I'd be and made sure my phone was on, and hopped into the Frawley and Sons van. It took only ten minutes from the time I hung up with my mom until I was pulling into her driveway, but though I called out as I entered the kitchen, nobody answered me.

"Mom?"

Nothing. I looked down the back hall, in her bedroom and the small spare bedroom where the kids stayed when they slept over. Both empty. I opened the door to the finished basement but heard nothing from down there, either.

Finally I found her in the backyard, sitting in a lounge chair with a glass of tea in her hand. Melanie sprawled on a fashion-doll towel and colored in a book with the same theme. Simon pushed a dump truck back and forth in the grass and made revving noises. When he saw me, he leaped up with joy and threw his arms around my waist, squeezing.

"Hey, monkeybutt."

"Auntie Grace! What did you bring me?"

"Nothing," I told him. "Do I always have to bring you something?"

Simon seemed to ponder this. "I like it better when you do."

"I bet. Hey, Mom." I held up my sheaf of clipped papers. "Where should I put these?"

"Oh. I guess on your dad's desk. I don't know what he's going to want to do with them."

Simon had gone back to his truck.

"Where's Hannah?"

My mom shrugged. "I guess she had an appointment or something."

"Nanny's gonna let me watch *Frankie's Teddy*," said Simon, like we shared a secret.

"Again?" I gave my mom a look, and she laughed and shrugged. "So, Dad's fishing, huh?"

My mom nodded. "Yes, he is."

"Wow." I snagged a handful of graham-cracker bears from the bowl next to my niece.

My mom laughed. "Honey, I told your dad if he didn't find himself a hobby, I was going to make him go back to work."

My dad had always worked a lot. Nights, weekends. We'd learned not to hold dinner, or wait to blow out the birthday candles or open the gifts. My dad had always been there when we needed him, but he hadn't been there for much else.

"I thought you'd like him being home more." I crunched the head off a teddy.

My mom gave me a look. "We're talking about your dad, Grace. He wants to reorganize my cabinets or give me hints on my knitting. I love your dad dearly, but sometimes it's easier to appreciate someone when they're not breathing down your neck all the time."

I laughed. "Right. I get it. Well, have fun. I have to get back."

I kissed my nephew, niece and mom, and went into the house to drop off the papers. My dad's office was the house's third bedroom, slightly larger than the spare room but not by much. It was the one room in the house my mother didn't touch, and not because she didn't want to. My dad had banned her from it, and it showed.

It looked as if someone had set loose a Tasmanian devil inside the room. Bookshelves lining one wall held hardcover texts on military history and other nonfiction subjects in which I had zero interest, while others showcased half-finished models of Civil War soldiers and weapons. The desk, a simple plank of wood laid across two saw-horses, disappeared beneath the weight of dozens of news-papers and magazines, everything from the *New York Times* to *People*. Since his "retirement" my dad had taken up reading in a big way. I shifted a handful of paper to clear a space and put down my printout, then started looking for my computer. It wasn't on the desk, but since it was only a twelve-inch, it wasn't large enough to stand out amongst the chaos.

It wasn't on the desk, or on the armchair in the corner beneath a reading lamp. It wasn't on the sideboard that was also covered with a mass of slippery, shifting papers that fell onto the floor when I tried to lift them. I looked around the room and could find no evidence of my little laptop anywhere.

Dammit.

I didn't have time to go searching for it, either, because my phone rang, with Shelly telling me there'd been a death call and I needed to retrieve a body. I didn't recognize the name of the family. I told Shelly to have Jared finish up whatever he was doing and meet me in the parking lot in ten minutes.

She squeaked at that.

"Is there a problem with that, Shelly?"

"No, it's just...I mean..."

At this rate, I'd be there before she got up the nerve to speak to him. "Just intercom the prep room and tell him to come up, Shelly. You've done it a thousand times."

She squeaked again. By this time I'd pulled out onto the street and was only a few minutes from the funeral home.

"Shelly! C'mon! Tell him to get out here. We've got a call!"

And wouldn't you know it, she stuttered with me, too, making me feel bad. "Can't you call his cell?"

I turned on the side street and pulled into the semicircle driveway beneath the portico. "Don't be ridiculous. I'm here."

"He's not talking to me," she whispered, suddenly fierce. "He's ignoring me. He's really mad, Grace."

I had a hard time imagining mild-mannered Jared angry, but I could guess at his reasons. "I'm sorry to hear that, but I need him to go on this call for me, and you need to get him out here."

"He's really mad at me," she repeated.

Somewhere inside me I found the patience to be kind. "Just talk to him, Shelly. Like you've done a hundred times. Nothing's different about that."

She made a sort of sniffling snort, but I heard the crackle of the intercom system and after a second she stuttered his name. "J-J-Jared?"

His reply was less clear, filtered by the intercom, distance and my phone, and I rolled my eyes at her for not hanging up with me to talk to him. He showed up a couple minutes later, but not through the door from the lobby. He'd come around out of the back, which could have been for the convenience of leaving from the door closest to where he'd been working, or because he was avoiding Shelly. He slid into the passenger seat and buckled his belt without a word.

He stared out the window during the entire drive, and I didn't break the silence with even the radio. At the family's house we took care of their grandma as quickly as we could, though she'd passed away in an upstairs bedroom with a doorway too narrow for our gurney to fit through. In fact, Grandma was nearly too wide to fit through that door, a problem that caused Jared and I a few minutes of careful manipulation that left us both sweating. Lifting bodies is an activity more suited for sweatpants, but we never went to a death call at a house in anything less formal than a suit. We owed the family that measure of respect, even if it made our jobs that much more difficult.

Jared took the body to the van while I spoke briefly with the family, who agreed to come to the funeral home later that day to make the arrangements. I offered my condolences and met Jared, already behind the wheel of the van.

"Jared."

His shoulders slumped a bit. He pulled the keys from his pocket and shoved them in the ignition. "Yeah."

The situation with him and Shelly wasn't my concern except in how it affected my business, and so far I couldn't see that his behavior was. He'd been polite and personable to the family, and helpful to me. Yet there was no mistaking the fact Jared wasn't acting like himself.

We didn't have a terribly long drive back to the funeral home, but I wanted to talk about this before we got there. There's something about conversations in the car that make some things easier to say. Concentrating on the road meant he didn't have to look at me.

I asked him the same thing I'd asked Shelly. "Want to talk about it?"

"I think you and Shelly talked about it enough." He signaled for the turn, but traffic going in both directions meant he couldn't pull onto the main street.

So I hadn't been imagining that he was avoiding me, too. "She was upset. I asked her what was wrong. Look, you kids—"

"I'm not a kid, Grace. Neither is she."

I'd only meant to tease. Both of them were only a few years younger than I. "I know that."

Jared's fingers tapped rapidly on the wheel, and he stared straight ahead while I stared at his profile. It wasn't hard for me to see why Shelly liked him. He had a good face, not classically handsome but appealing.

More cars passed in front of us, and I watched Jared watch them as he waited for his chance to pull into traffic. He'd set his mouth into a thin, grim line that didn't suit him.

"I didn't come on to her." He bit out the words. "I know she's got Duane. I'm not the one who started it."

At last there was a break in the traffic and Jared pulled onto the main street, his driving still careful despite his agitation. It didn't make much of a difference in our position on the road. We were on the main street, but it was still a two-lane, backcountry road that twisted and turned and only needed one slow driver to back up traffic for a mile.

"She told me what happened."

"Yeah." He bit out a laugh along with the word. "The favor. Doing her a favor."

Traffic crept along, but the source of the delay was too

far ahead and behind the curve to know the cause. "She told me, Jared."

He shook his head as if he couldn't believe it. "She asked me to do her a favor, like I was some sort of gigolo. And I did it! God, Grace! I did it!"

"Don't be so hard on yourself," I offered, but the bricks had already started tumbling.

"Why? Because I'm a guy?" Jared's hands tightened on the steering wheel, but he kept his eyes straight ahead as the cars in front of us sped up and he followed. "It's okay because I'm a guy, and everyone knows we all think with our dicks, right?"

"I didn't say that."

"No. *She* did." He shook his head again as the van picked up speed around a turn. "Or something like it, anyway. About how we should just forget about what happened because it didn't mean anything."

I gripped the padded door handle as he took the turn too fast. "Jared—"

"It meant something," he snapped. "At least it did to me."

We whipped around the turn and caught up to the long line of cars once more stopped behind the construction that had closed one side of the road. I gasped and braced myself on instinct, but Jared eased the brakes swiftly and with such skill the van didn't even rock as he stopped.

He turned to look at me, one hand still gripping the wheel but the other resting on the edge of his seat. "She told me you're the one who said it shouldn't mean anything. Thanks a lot."

My mind raced as I tried to recall what, exactly, I'd told

Shelly. I was pretty sure that wasn't it. "Jared, I never told her to sleep with you."

"You did. Even if you didn't say it, she took you as an example."

That slapped me, hard, into anger. "What's that supposed to mean?"

The construction crew flipped the sign from Stop to Slow, and we began inching forward again, the cars ahead of us picking up speed that hadn't yet made it to the end of the line. Jared half turned to the front, easing off the brakes but not yet using both hands on the wheel again.

That's when some moron with a fire in his pants came flying around the turn behind us, didn't bother to check the fact that though traffic was moving, we and the four cars in front of us were not, and rammed into the back of the van.

It was a helluva way to get out of an uncomfortable conversation.

Chapter 13

*M*y seat belt cut into my shoulder and the air bag deployed, making the world go white in front of my eyes. I heard Jared shout but could make no such noise myself. I could think it though, over and over.

Oh, shit. Shit, shit, shit and double-damn shit on seven kinds of shit-covered bricks.

Then, silence.

I was vaguely aware of Jared asking me if I was all right, but I was already fumbling with my seat belt and pushed open my door to stumble out of the van. I fell on some loose gravel, skinning both my knees and ruining my last good pair of panty hose. I got up and went around to the back of the van, sending up a prayer to any deity that would listen that there hadn't been too much damage.

The driver of the other car was getting out more slowly. I caught a glimpse of gray hair and polyester and bit back another curse. Someone's grandma had rear-ended us in her big old boat of a car and pretty much crunched us all to hell.

"What were you doing?" she shouted with the self-righteous fury of the wronged. "Why were you stopped in the middle of the road?"

We had an audience. I hadn't noticed until that moment that our van had leaped forward to hit the back of the car in front of us. We couldn't have slammed it that hard, but it was enough to crumple the bumper. The driver of that car was out, too, staring at the damage with Jared, and the road crew on our side had put down their signs to run toward us.

Feeling suddenly woozy, I put a hand on the van. More important than my vehicle was its cargo, and I was almost too afraid to look. I forced myself forward to push in the button to release the hatch. Though the bumper below it was mangled and crunched, the hatch opened, albeit slowly and with much protesting.

The gurney had shifted askew, the body upon it uncovered now with one hand knocked free to trail on the carpeted floor, but she looked otherwise unharmed.

"Oh, God!" This cry came from the formerly indignant driver of the car that had hit us. "Oh, I've killed her!"

The screaming wasn't funny, as none of this was, but I had to hide my face in my hands to stifle my sudden, inappropriate laughter. I couldn't even explain to the now-hysterical woman in the purple polyester tracksuit that she had not, in fact, actually killed anything but my van. She screamed. The audience grew. And I, my face hidden by my fingers, laughed until my shoulders shook.

Jared put his arm around my shoulders. "Hey. Grace. You okay?"

"Do you know how much this is going to cost?"

That's what I meant to say, anyway, but since my face

was buried against Jared's chest, I'm not sure he heard me. He understood, though, and put his hand on the back of my head briefly before hugging me.

"It's okay," Jared said. "It'll be okay."

"No, it won't! This after the washer? And…" I shook my head, taking a deep breath. "This is just…bad. It's bad."

"I'll help you take care of it," Jared said. "I'll help you. Don't worry. You don't have to do it all by yourself, okay?"

No wonder Shelly had fallen in love with him.

By the time we got everything figured out with the police and the other drivers, it was too late to make it back to the funeral home to meet the family of the woman in the back of the van. I had Shelly call them to tell them there'd been an unexpected delay, but I knew that wasn't going to satisfy them for long. I mean, who wants to hear that their beloved grandma was in a car accident on her way to the funeral home?

We'd been able to avoid going to the hospital, at least, though my neck was growing increasingly stiff and Jared had somehow ended up with some bruised ribs to go along with his sprained ankle. The driver of the car that had rear-ended us had started suffering heart palpitations and had been taken away in an ambulance. I could only hope I wouldn't end up having to go pick her up.

The van, though battered, was drivable and we made it back to the funeral home where Jared unloaded our charge and I went to talk to Shelly about the afternoon schedule. The family had called four times, the last time only a minute or two before we got back. Frankly, while I understood their concern and didn't mean to be unsympathetic since they didn't know we'd been in an accident, I was more than a little irritated with their persistence.

Still, I called them back from my office phone as I stripped out of my ruined panty hose and sank into my desk chair to scramble in my desk drawer for some ibuprofen. "Mrs. Parker, I'm sorry about the delay in getting back to you—"

Mrs. Parker, who this morning had seemed a reasonable enough woman, had apparently been taken over by a raging demon. Without allowing me to get a word in edgewise, she reamed me up one side and down the other, cast aspersions on my professionalism, criticized my clothing and told me I'd better give them a discount on the best casket I had.

All because I was late?

"Mrs. Parker, I know you're upset, and I'm sorry. Something unexpected came up, and that's why I was unable to meet you at one o'clock. But rest assured, your mother-in-law is being taken care of, and I have cleared my schedule for the rest of the day. I can meet you—"

"Well, *we* can't meet *you!*" She shouted through the phone. "We have plans for dinner!"

Since she'd just spent five full minutes ranting and screaming in my ear about how important it was for all of this to be taken care of as soon as possible, I couldn't respond to her for another full minute.

Sixty seconds of silence can feel like an hour.

"I apologize," I told her finally. "I'll be happy to meet you whenever it's convenient for you."

There was a moment or two of muffled conversation before she came back on the line. "Seven o'clock tonight. And it had better take no more than an hour. My show's on tonight."

I've had to bite my tongue plenty of times, but this time my jaw was too sore to contain my snark. "It will take as long as you feel is necessary to adequately decide how best to take care of your mother-in-law, Mrs. Parker."

The silence this time was no less loud, but it was much shorter, because she hung up on me.

What a bitch.

I sank my head into my hands, willing the ibuprofen I'd swallowed dry to unstick itself from my throat and start working on the growing aches and pains.

"Grace?"

I looked up to see Shelly in the doorway with a mug of coffee and a plate of those damn cookies. "Are you okay?"

Anger, like lice, can jump amazing distances from one person to another.

"Do I look okay?"

She stiffened at my tone and brought my coffee to me. "Should I call the insurance company?"

I made no move to take the coffee. "That would be a good idea. Can you manage it?"

Oh, that was mean.

Shelly stiffened further, drawing herself up and clutching the front of her sweater. "Yes. Of course."

"Then do it, please." I added the please, but it didn't do much to soften my tone.

Without saying anything, Shelly left my office. I should

have felt worse, but I was tired, aching and pissed off at the world. It wasn't a good excuse, but it was the only one I had. I got up to close the door she'd left open, probably on purpose to spite me, and heard Shelly and Jared in the entryway by her desk.

"I'm busy," Shelly snapped at his request to help him find the new box of cleaning fluid that was supposed to have been delivered. "Find it yourself."

"Fine," snapped Jared. "Excuse me for asking you for a *favor*."

Ouch.

I'd seen Shelly cry and blush and even be annoyed, but I have to say that until that moment I'd never seen her angry. She whirled on him so fast I wouldn't have been surprised if she'd displaced enough air with her motion to make a tornado. She didn't quite bare her teeth. Not quite.

"What did you say to me?"

A sane man would have backed away, but Jared, who towered over Shelly by almost a foot, leaned in even closer. "I said," he told her through gritted jaws, "excuse me for asking you for a favor."

"You are such a jerk!"

"And you're a coldhearted bitch!"

Shelly hauled off and slapped him across the face hard enough to rock his entire body.

Fucking World War Three was breaking out in my funeral home, and all I could do was stare.

For a minute I thought Jared was going to hit her back, but all he did was grip her by the upper arms to keep her from hitting him again. He shook her just a little, then let her go and threw up his hands like he didn't want to dirty his grip. Shelly let out a small, stunned cry as he stepped away from her.

Turning, he saw me, and following his gaze, she did, too.

"Pissflaps," I said aloud. "What the hell do you two think you're doing?"

Shelly started talking and Jared gave me a sullen, silent glare, but I held up my hand to stop her.

"This is my business," I hissed. "Not a playground! What if there were clients here! What the hell are you two doing?"

I was repeating myself, my voice pitching higher and hoarser. I thought my head might explode from the pressure inside it, and I realized I was about to burst into tears again.

"BEHAVE YOURSELVES!" I screamed louder than I've ever yelled in my life. Louder even than I've ever hollered at my sister, even during one of our worst fights.

Both of them stared at me, their jaws dropping, and I stepped back into my office and slammed the door so hard I knocked a glass-framed photo off the wall. The picture hit the carpet facedown, and when I picked it up, the glass had cracked. I couldn't decide whether I should laugh or cry, and so I did both.

Hysterics were new to me, but I'm not ashamed to admit I gave in to them behind the safety of my closed door. I used up an entire box of tissues in about fifteen minutes, but at the end of it I felt better. I needed a drink, and lukewarm coffee wasn't going to do. I wiped my face and yanked open my door to come face-to-face with both Shelly and Jared.

"How long have you been standing there?" I demanded.

The guilty looks they gave each other were answer enough. I put my hands on my hips and glared. Jared cut his gaze from mine and shuffled his feet as red tinged his ears and cheeks, but Shelly didn't look away.

"There's mail for you. Why don't you read it while I go get you a cup of coffee." She handed me a pile of envelopes. "Go on. We've got it covered out here."

Her concern and spot-on deduction about what I needed was nice, but I wasn't ready to forget the scene the two of them had made. "Thanks."

"I'll start on Mrs. Parker," Jared said. "And the laundry, too."

"Fine. Good."

I took the mail and stepped back into my office as Shelly and Jared gave each other a few more guilty glances and headed off to their respective tasks. None of this had been resolved, but I didn't have the energy for it now. Taking the mail, I went back to my desk and put my feet up to sort through it while I waited for Shelly to bring my drink.

Bill. Bill. Solicitation for a charity I didn't and had never supported. Another bill. My Funeral Directors Association magazine, which I put aside to read later. And finally, a business-size envelope, addressed to me by hand and bearing the postmark from Lebanon, two towns over from us.

I slit open the envelope and pulled out a trifolded sheet of white paper, blank on one side. The other featured a line drawing of a man with a guitar, and typed text showing the date, time and location of a show.

SAM STEWART.
Tonight—9:00 p.m.

I stared at the flyer for a long time, closing it only when Shelly brought my drink and opening it again as soon as she left. The drawing had captured so much of him there was no question who it had been meant to represent. His long, long legs, the big hands, the swoop of his hair along the back of his neck. The face was turned so only the profile had been sketched, but there was enough there to remind me all too fiercely of the way his mouth curved.

This was dangerous ground. Wanting this. Him. I couldn't forget how Sam had been a stranger to me, or how easily he could stop being one, if I let him.

I wanted to see him again, there was no question of that, but if I went to watch him play, he'd know I wanted to. Or he'd think he knew, and I suspected just thinking would be enough incentive for Sam. His interest and attention were flattering, I wasn't going to deny that. And part of me believed that if he got what he wanted, he might not want it anymore, because that was sort of the way those things work. That same part refused to admit I didn't want him to stop wanting me, even as I refused to admit it.

Yeah. I was conflicted. I was also weak of will, unable to go watch him play on my own and see what happened and unable to convince myself not to go.

I shoved away the sound of my bank account squealing like a pig as I picked up my phone and dialed a familiar number. A few hours of Jack's company would cost me more than I could afford, but would save me from a much greater price in the end.

"You look pretty." Jack walked around me to admire my outfit.

I still wore my suit from work. Blessing Mrs. Parker's addiction to reality TV, I'd hurried through the arrangements just as she'd wanted and not even bothered to change before heading out. I'd run a comb through my hair and brushed my teeth, swiped my cheeks with powder and my lips with gloss, but hadn't even put on new panty hose.

"Thanks. So do you."

"You like it?" Jack buffed his nails on the front of his blue button-down shirt, which he wore open over a white T-shirt tucked into faded jeans. A thick black leather belt completed the outfit and matched his black motorcycle boots. He looked more appropriately dressed for a night in a club than I did.

"You look scrumptious," I told him. "I'm glad you were free."

He gave me that grin, and God, how could I have ever thought I was going to pay only for his conversation? "I had to juggle a few things, but that's okay."

I'd met him in the parking garage, as we planned to walk together to the club to see Sam play, and I grabbed Jack's arm to steady me as we crossed an uneven block of pavement. "Did you?"

"Yep." He held out his elbow for me to take a better grip, his hand stuck into his jeans pocket. I didn't let go even once we'd passed the bumpy sidewalk. "Just for you."

"Oh, Jack." I laughed. "Stop it."

He looked over at me. "I mean it, Grace."

We stopped in front of the Sandwich Man. "You canceled other appointments to take mine?"

"Yep." The smile.

There was no earthly way any woman could look at that face and not return the grin. "How flattering."

He shrugged as we started walking again. "I like you."

"I like you, too." He walked slower so I wouldn't stumble on another ragged section of pavement.

"Good." He looked over at me again.

It's a compliment when your hired fuck tells you he'd rather be with you than another client, but it's also rather disconcerting if the reason you hire men for sex is because you're trying to avoid relationships.

"Jack." I stopped again, this time just inside a small alley. "Look–"

Jack leaned in close, surprising me with the brush of his mouth along my ear. "Don't freak. It's still business."

Which of course made me happy and a little disappointed at the same time.

"Where are we going?" he asked in the next second, saving me from having to react.

"The Firehouse."

"Mmm. Dinner?" Jack put his arm around me as we walked, a position that felt less formal than my hand on his elbow but no less comfortable.

"Depends. Are you hungry?"

"I could eat." He patted his stomach. "I can always eat."

"Bastard." I patted his lean hip. "Must be nice."

"It's all the exercise."

Jack's leer sent me into laughter, and everything was all right. "Uh-huh. Well, I'm on a very tight budget, but I think I can spring for an appetizer."

Jack glanced at me. "Don't worry about it."

I did worry about it, of course, because this wasn't a date, it was an appointment. I wasn't obligated to buy him dinner, but I liked Jack. "I'm hungry, too. It's okay."

"Grace, seriously." Jack's fingers tightened on my shoulder. "I could've had dinner tonight. That's not why I'm out with you."

I didn't want to ask what he was out with me for, because the swift flutter of my inner muscles already knew. By that time we'd reached the three-story brick building that had actually once been a real fire station. I did have cash for the cover charge, but the guy at the door recognized Jack and they did the whole clapping on each other's shoulders and posturing so typical of men, and it turned out he knew Jack from working together at the Slaughtered Lamb, and we ended up getting in for free.

"Nice work," I told him as we wove our way through the front dining room toward the stairs to the second level. "Thanks."

Jack laughed. "I think Kent has the hots for me, that's all."

At the top of the stairs I paused to scan the room. While I could see a small stage set with a chair along the back wall, it was empty. Tables and chairs filled the rest of the space, most already taken, but at Jack's words I paused in scanning the room to stare.

"You think so?"

He shrugged and gave me a smug smile. "He offered to give me a blow job once or twice."

I blinked. "And did you let him?"

Jack laughed again and put his arm around my shoulder to pull me close so he could murmur into my ear, "That depends."

"On what?" I turned my head to murmur into his ear, the gesture automatic.

"If saying yes would get you hot."

The flicker of his tongue sent a shiver racing down my spine and peaked my nipples beneath my plain silk blouse. We were blocking the stairs, but since nobody was trying to go up or down, I didn't care. I tried to answer but could only lick my mouth.

Jack nuzzled my neck briefly, his breath hot, but he didn't answer my question with a yes or no, and I wasn't sure what I wanted him to say.

He led me to one of the last empty tables, the one farthest from the stage and tucked into a corner by the swinging doors to the kitchen. The group next to us had taken two of the chairs for their own table, turning a four into a six, and while Jack and I only needed two, the way they'd seated themselves meant one of us had to be wedged along the back wall with little room to move. The other chair had been pushed into the path of the servers, and Jack insisted I take the seat that didn't end up getting bashed by a door every other minute.

The perky waitress who came to take our drink orders informed us the kitchen was closed for dinner, but the bar was serving food, and that was good enough for me. I ordered an appetizer plate that was still expensive enough to dent my wallet but wasn't going to break me, and we both ordered beers.

"I like that you drink beer." Jack shifted his chair a little closer to mine, so our thighs touched. "That's cool."

"Is it?" From my seat I had a good, unobstructed view of the stage, but if I had to get up for any reason, I was in trouble. A single spotlight illuminated the still-empty stage, and I began to wonder if I'd read the flyer wrong. I looked at Jack, who nodded.

"Yes. Girls who drink beer rock." He played an air guitar, and I laughed.

"It's cheaper than something fancy, but I like the taste, so that's okay."

He nodded. "And you look fucking sexy as hell sucking on the bottle."

I blinked again. "My, my, my, Jack my dear. Haven't you been practicing the lines?"

"You told me to be myself," he said, and pointed at his chest. "This is me."

If that was him, I wasn't surprised he'd been getting a lot of business. "I'm glad I could help."

"You did." He nodded and took a long pull on his own beer. "A lot. I don't have to work at the bar anymore, and I'm going to start full-time school in the fall. Graphic arts."

"That's great!" I said sincerely. "Good for you."

He shrugged, but looked pleased. "Thanks."

Our conversation was significant only in how simple it was, and how easy. It seemed obvious to me that Jack felt far more comfortable in his role than he had before. Confidence is sexy on anyone, and on Jack it only accentuated his natural hottitude.

As the waitress brought our platter of food, Sam took the stage. I paused with an onion ring halfway to my lips as he made a shadow across the chair, then took a seat with his guitar cradled on his lap. The light winked on his earring and in the brilliance of his smile as he looked out into the audience.

He waited for the brief spattering of applause to fade before he spoke. "Hey. I'm Sam."

More applause and a few good-natured hoots and comments made him laugh. "Thanks. Yeah. If you're here to hear Green Eggs, you're out of luck."

His mention of another local music favorite earned him more applause and commentary, and he shaded his eyes to look out at the crowd as he replied. My heart skipped when his gaze swept over the room, but it was silly to think he could've seen me, tucked away in the darkness. Nevertheless I imagined his eyes met mine, and that his smile was for me.

Hearing him play before hadn't prepared me at all for hearing him perform. Sam had a low, easy voice reminiscent of Simon and Garfunkel. His fingers moved easily on the guitar's strings and urged forth songs that sounded simple only if you weren't paying attention. He covered classic hits and sang a few I had to assume were original because I didn't recognize them.

The crowd loved him, probably more for the sly, self-deprecating anecdotes he fed them between songs. He sipped occasionally from a bottle of water, nothing stronger, and it was too soon when he finished, saying he would take another break and be back in fifteen minutes for his last set.

"Grace?"

Jack had been talking, but my mind was wandering until he pulled me back with the sound of my name. "Hmm?"

"You want another drink?"

"Yes." My bladder screamed. "Just a soda, please."

I fished for money in my wallet, but Jack waved away my hand. I watched him head up to the bar. Heads turned as he passed, women and men, and I thought of what he'd said about the bouncer at the door.

As much as I might have wanted to fantasize about Jack and some other cute boy in a lip-lock, there was no way my bladder was going to let me last that long. I inched my way from behind the table and headed for the glowing arrow pointing to the bathrooms. I'd expected a line, but whoever'd remodeled the fire station had done a good job. There were several stalls and women moved in and out of them in record time.

Sam had come back to the stage, though he wasn't on it, just by it. He wasn't alone, either. Sam had a groupie. I wish I could've thought something mean about her, but other than the bright golden hair and tight-fitting T-shirt, she didn't look trashy enough to get my hackles up. Nope, what got my lip curling was the fact Sam was snuzzling with her. There was no other way to put it. They weren't kissing…exactly. And they weren't hugging. Not exactly. He was simply leaning in super close, as if he needed to hear what she was saying, except closer than that.

Body language says a lot.

I said his name before I knew I was going to, and he turned away from the blonde with stars in her eyes to stare at me for a full five seconds before he smiled.

"Grace. Hi! You made it!"

"I made it."

The blonde's smile wilted at the corners, but the stars managed to still twinkle. It would have been a cliché if she'd thrown daggers at me with her eyes, though I was sort of prepared for it. She merely gave me an inquisitive look and turned her adoration back toward Sam.

"Marnie, this is Grace." Sam gestured.

"Hi," I said.

We didn't shake hands.

Women know how to cut each other down in ways men never see, and Marnie was very good at it. She'd even added the subtle touch to his shoulder to get him to turn his head toward her as she spoke. "So, Sam. I loved your song 'Captain Backyards.'"

"Captain…oh." Sam laughed.

The song had been "Cap On Backwards." I knew because not only had I been listening, but watching his mouth, too. Marnie gave him a quizzical look at the laugh as Sam scratched his ear self-consciously.

I caught sight of Jack, his head bent to listen to something from the girl next to him. I'd seen her earlier. With her blue- and purple-streaked hair, she was hard to miss. Jack was smiling, though, so maybe she wasn't an angry ex-girlfriend.

I looked back at Sam. His gaze had followed mine, but when I half turned toward him, he looked at me. "I've got to get back up there."

He sounded apologetic, but I waved a hand. "Of course."

"But I'll see you after, right? You'll stick around?" I looked over my shoulder toward Jack, just a quick glance, and before I could answer, Sam was shaking his head. "Don't say no."

"It's late." It was a well-worn excuse. "I have to be up early."

"I'll be here," Marnie said, and earned a smile from Sam.

Ah. Here came the daggers. I smiled at her, but blandly. Funny how easy it is to defuse someone when you're not willing to fight them for what they want.

"Bye, Sam."

He snagged my arm as I turned to go. "Wait a minute."

I watched Jack laugh at something the girl with the blue hair was saying and looked at the time. One way or another, my date was winding down. I'd only paid for four hours. The girl with Jack punched him on the arm as she moved away, and he rubbed the spot. He gave her the smile.

Wow.

I looked back at Sam. "I've really go to go."

He turned to look toward Jack, who'd grabbed up the drinks and was heading toward us. "Yeah. Okay."

Sam let me go. I pushed past Marnie and met Jack before he could reach us. He handed me my glass of soda and put an arm around my shoulder.

"Hey. You okay?"

"Fine. Just a little tired. I should get going." I smiled and drank my soda, and Jack gave a curious glance past me toward Sam, now taking the stage again.

"Do you know him?"

"Not really. A little. C'mon, let's go."

The crowd hushed as Sam took the stage again and the spotlight hit him, just so. I didn't have to be looking at him to see that. I just knew the light would love him.

I put my soda down, half finished. "Jack, let's go."

He took another long pull on his beer but set the bottle down quickly when I told him to. He didn't question my sudden haste, just moved alongside me to put his arm around my shoulder as we pushed through the crowd. From behind us came the first few chords of a song.

"This is something new I've been working on." The whole audience heard him, but his words were mine. "It's called 'Grace on the Stairway.'"

We were almost to the stairs when he said it, but I stopped so fast Jack kept going for a few steps. I didn't turn to look toward the stage as Sam began to sing.

"Hey," said Jack. "Grace on the Stairway."

He was laughing, but I wasn't. "C'mon, let's go."

Jack didn't protest, though he did look over his shoulder again as we left. Outside, the August night had turned cool. Gooseflesh humped my arms, and I rubbed them briskly as we walked toward the parking garage.

"Thanks for coming with me tonight," I said as he backed me up against the smooth, cold metal of my car. "It was—"

His hungry mouth stopped me. His breath, redolent of beer and onion rings, seeped between my lips until I opened for him. His tongue stroked mine as the hand not holding his helmet and jacket gripped my waist.

"Don't go yet," he said against my mouth. "It's not that late."

"I can't pay for a hotel room," I told him honestly.

"Come to my place."

I pulled away to look at him. "Jack."

It was proof of how well he knew me by that point, because he used the smile on me without any show of remorse. "Come on. I'm horny as hell."

His drifting hand slid to my back and pulled me harder against him. I wanted to laugh, but the press of his belt buckle on my stomach turned my nervous giggle into a gasp. Suddenly, I was horny as hell, too.

Jack kissed me again, then pulled away to look at my face. "Our date ended half an hour ago."

"I know it did." I tipped my head a little, my lips parted and yet my tongue still tasted him.

Jack took my hand and put it on his crotch, where under the faded denim his cock had grown. "Consider it my tip."

I did laugh, then. "Fucking me is your tip?"

He grinned and rubbed my hand in a slow circle on his denim-caged dick. "Yep."

I didn't think it was such a good idea, me going to his place. Fucking him for free. It was a little dangerous, actually, but I simply didn't have the cash to insist on the wall that money allowed me to keep between us.

And I didn't want to be thinking about Sam.

"If you're that horny, I'm sure you could find someone to go home with." It was a last, feeble attempt, and Jack didn't buy it.

"I'm not a slut," he whispered in my ear and added a lick to my neck that sent a shard of pure pleasure straight down to my already slicking cunt.

I really had no more excuses after that, but as I followed his motorcycle in my car down Harrisburg's dark streets, I almost chickened out. Three times. Jack pulled up onto the sidewalk and parked the bike, and I found a spot for Betty between a beat-up Metro and a garish green Accord. I got out and locked my doors, then looked up at the brick building.

"C'mon in." Jack held out his hand, and I took it.

Chapter 14

$\mathcal{H}$e lived on the third floor, and though the place didn't look like much from the outside, his apartment was clean. Almost stark. Plain white walls and bare wooden floors in one main room with a small bathroom and bedroom tucked off to the back. His furniture looked battered, but his sink, unlike my own, wasn't piled high with dishes and his garbage pail didn't overflow with trash.

Jack hung his jacket and helmet on a set of large metal pegs drilled into the wall and tossed his keys into a glass dish on a small table by the door. He gestured. "This is my place."

"It's nice." I looked around, noting the art on the walls. "Did you draw those?"

"Some of them. Yeah." He ran a hand through his hair. "Some are from friends."

I was no expert, but even I could see he had talent. "You're good."

He put his arms around me from behind, pulling me back against him. "Yeah, I think you told me that before."

I mock elbowed him. "I meant your pictures."

He turned me in his arms and pulled me flush against him. "I know."

It was different without the money between us, in a subtle way I couldn't put my finger on and didn't want to think about. Jack didn't seem to have any trouble. He slid his hand under my hair to cup the back of my neck and bent to kiss me as he backed me toward the bedroom.

We'd done a lot of role playing, but this time there was no pizza delivery boy, no naughty schoolboy. No bored housewife or demanding boss. No more lessons, as a matter of fact, because he'd learned them all very, very well.

He undressed me carefully, using his hands and mouth to map the curves he revealed. His mouth lingered at the swell of my breasts above my lacy bra while his fingers skimmed the edge of my matching panties and slid beneath my ass. He took his time but didn't do it slowly, and his careful haste, his eagerness to reach my nakedness, thrilled me.

Still kissing me, he tugged open his belt, undid the zip, pushed the jeans over his lean hips and to the floor. He took his mouth from my flesh only long enough to pull off his long-sleeved T-shirt. I stopped him when he put his hands on the waistband of his boxers.

"Wait."

He gave me a curious look.

"Let me."

Standing at the edge of the bed, Jack lifted his hands in acquiescence as I scooted forward. Sitting on the edge of the bed, I curled my fingers into the soft fabric of his boxers and pulled it down.

We'd spent a lot of time on making me happy. It was what I paid for, after all. To be pleased. Jack had learned my body far better than I'd learned his.

I also took my time, but didn't hesitate in revealing his body to me. I'd seen it many times before, and yet tonight it felt different to trace with my tongue the outline of the stylized sun on his lower belly. He kept his pubic hair trimmed short, and I nuzzled his skin as I breathed in his scent, purely male. His cock brushed my cheek and my hair tangled over it as I mouthed his tattoo. I gripped his ass and held him still as I licked and sucked and bit his stomach, hip and thigh, but I let him go and looked up at him without taking his erection into my mouth.

"Tell me what *you* want." It was the first time I'd ever asked.

Jack passed a hand over my hair and down to caress my cheek briefly. He stroked his erection slowly a few times with my hair still wrapped around it in places. "Use your mouth on me. Please."

It wasn't an unreasonable request, considering the times he'd done the same for me, but I liked the way he asked. I lifted a hand to smooth my hair off him, but didn't take him into my mouth right away. I looked first. Really looked. I'd spent hours with him inside me, but had never really seen his prick up close.

I studied the smooth, thin skin beneath which his blood pulsed. I slid my hand slowly down his length and cupped his balls, then moved up again and gripped his cock just below the head. Jack put his hand on my hair, but didn't push me. His breathing got heavier, but he waited.

I liked that, too.

"Tell me something. Did you used to have...something?"

He smoothed his hand over my hair. "Something like what?"

"A...thing? Here?"

"A Prince Albert?" Jack laughed, low. "Yeah. Got tired of it. Took it out. Why, do you like that?"

"I don't think so." I studied his cock and saw something that might have been a small scar. "No. I like you the way you are now."

"Good."

When at last I dipped my head to close my lips around his cock, Jack groaned. Such a simple, basic noise of pleasure, but something tightened low in my gut. I closed my eyes when he murmured my name and I thought of Sam.

I thought of Sam's eyes and mouth and hands, of Sam's impossibly long legs and the glint of his earring. Of his shaggy hair that begged for the taming of scissors and comb. I had another man's cock in my mouth and my own hand between my legs, but it was Sam's face that filled my mind. His voice, and the strum of his guitar as he sang a song that could only have been meant for me. I took Jack inside my mouth, and I knew something he didn't.

This would be the last time we fucked.

I couldn't afford this anymore. This was costing me too much, and not in dollars.

He pushed forward into my mouth and I put a hand at the base of his cock to control his thrusting. Using hand and mouth in tandem, I sucked and stroked until his fingers tightened in my hair hard enough to hurt.

I left his prick covered in the wetness from my mouth and looked up at him. Jack's eyes had glazed and his mouth was lax from pleasure, but he smiled when he saw me looking.

He didn't ruin it with talking, just leaned in to kiss me. His tongue dived into my mouth. We ended up on the bed, flesh on flesh and limbs tangled. His hands roamed over me, dipping between my legs. I was already wet from my own touch, and he slipped one finger inside me, then up and over my clit.

Sensation leaped through me, and Jack swallowed my gasp. His hand moved against me. I was almost there already, but he knew me well enough to know when to ease off. To tease.

I let him lead us, to decide when we'd stop kissing and stroking and licking and actually start fucking. We kissed for a long, long time. Longer than we ever had when I was in charge. I couldn't remember the last time I'd spent so long kissing and stroking without moving right into sex. High school, probably. We kissed for so long I thought I might come from the pressure of his tongue on mine alone, or the skid of his fingertips along my belly. He'd slid a leg between mine, my cunt pressed to his thigh, and I thought I might come from that, too.

I didn't look at the clock. I didn't care about the time, though hours were passing. This was the last time, and I wanted to remember every moment of it. I wanted to make this as good for Jack as he'd been for me.

In the midst of our foreplay we'd moved all over the bed. I don't know when or from where Jack got the condom, but when he finally pressed it into my hand my hands shook too badly for me to put it on him. Desire and anticipation made me clumsy. So did another, deeper emotion, something like sad tenderness or tender sadness, or something not like that at all but indefinable.

He took the packet from me and tore it open, kissing me as he put it on. Kissing me when he pushed me onto my back and parted my legs with one of his. Still kissing as he slid inside me with one, smooth thrust.

My orgasm stuttered, struggling, and my body arched to meet his without my conscious effort. I'd reached incoherency, my thoughts reduced to flashes of raw need. Want. Thrust. Clench. Pull, push, fuck. Come.

My body strained as Jack moved inside me. I pulled my mouth from his, the distraction of his lips and tongue too much. He buried his face in the curve of my shoulder. He bit, harder than he ever had, and the pain was so sweet I cried out.

It wasn't the first time we'd come together, but it was the last, and I held on to it all the more tightly for knowing it.

After, sweat glued us together until he rolled off me with a sigh. I stared at his ceiling and listened to the sound of his breathing as it slowed. Jack kissed my shoulder and got out of bed, used the bathroom and came back. I hadn't moved. He crawled into bed next to me, our shoulders and hips touching, and he linked his hands on his chest with another sigh.

"Damn," he said after a while.

I smiled. "Mmm, hmm."

He turned to look at me. "You can stay if you want."

I turned to my side to look at him, and reached to touch his face. "Thanks, but I've really got to get home. It's late."

"Yeah. And you have to work in the morning," he said with a wry grin.

I had nothing scheduled, actually a rare Saturday in which I had no obligations. The thought of falling asleep here wasn't tempting enough to make me do it, not compared to what I imagined waking up here would feel like.

Jack looked to the ceiling and yawned. "Did you know that guy?"

I didn't bother feigning ignorance. "Yes."

"That song was about you, huh?"

"I think so. I guess so." I sat and swung my legs over the bed, thinking of a hot shower and my own warm bed. Of the phone call I knew would come.

Jack was silent while I used the bathroom. When I came out, he'd pulled on his boxers and lit a cigarette. The ashtray rested on his belly.

"You shouldn't smoke in bed, you know." I hunted for and found my clothes and started dressing.

"Yeah, yeah." He blew a smoke ring. "You like him a lot, huh?"

I tried not to pause, but my hands wouldn't keep buttoning. "Oh, Jack."

"Grace, why do you do this?"

I jammed my shirt into my skirt without finishing the buttons. "Because I owed you a tip and I had no money."

It wasn't a kind or honest answer, but Jack didn't appear to hold it against me. "C'mon."

I looked at him. "Because I prefer it."

"Why?" He shook his head. "I don't get it. You don't need to pay to get laid. Plenty of guys would go out with you. You're pretty. And fun."

"I don't do it because I can't find someone to go out with. Okay? I do it because I want to."

Jack smoked and looked thoughtful. "That guy likes you."

"Gee, Jack. What makes you say that? The fact he wrote a song about me?" Ah, sarcasm, defense of the defenseless.

"Hey, I'm just saying."

"Well...don't." I shoved my feet into my boots. "I don't pay you for commentary."

Jack snorted. "You're not paying me right now."

"Well, what about you?" I whirled, hands on my hips. "Don't think I didn't see how that girl was looking at you!"

"Girls always look at me." He blew another smoke ring and wooed me with his smile.

"You were looking at her, too. I saw it." I finger-combed my hair and shuddered at the sight of the hour on the clock. "God, I've got to go."

Jack sat up higher and stubbed out his cigarette, then put the ashtray on the nightstand to get out of bed. "Her name's Sarah, and yeah. I like her."

"And yet you brought me home," I pointed out.

Jack stretched. "She can't afford me."

"I can barely afford you."

He smiled. I raised an eyebrow until he shrugged again. "You answer my question and I'll answer yours."

"I don't want to get hooked up to someone only to have it end. Okay?" The words shot out of me.

"Whoa." Jack raised his hands.

"Yeah. Whoa."

"What makes you so sure it would have to end?" My face must have looked scary, because he amended himself quickly. "I mean, that's just such a downer way to look at it, that's all."

"Everything ends, Jack. Everything. One way or the other."

He studied me. "Someone hurt you?"

My laugh tasted more bitter than it sounded. "No. Not really."

Jack looked bemused. "It's just that you're—"

"Pretty and fun," I cut in. "I know, Jack. You told me that already."

Now, finally, I'd wounded him, but I could take no pleasure in seeing the way his expression closed against me. "Sorry."

I softened and touched his shoulder. "It's okay. But I think maybe this was a mistake."

I patted his shoulder and moved toward the front door, grabbing my purse along the way. He came after me, not content to let his voice stop me. His touch wasn't rough, but I turned at it with a look that made him drop his hand.

"It wasn't a mistake," he said.

"Good night, Jack."

"Grace, wait."

I waited, but he said nothing, though I could see his mind working. I sighed, a headache starting. If I got to sleep in tomorrow, it would hardly count.

"You'll call me again, right?"

An easy lie rose to my lips but was kicked back by the truth. "No. I don't think so."

"Because of him?"

"No, Jack." I touched his arm, the bare skin warm beneath my fingers. "Because of you."

"Because...you don't like me?"

I shook my head and backed toward the door. He followed, brows knitting and mouth gone grim. His arms were longer, and he reached over my shoulder to slam the door shut as I tried to open it. He caged me with his arms.

"Why, then?" he demanded. "I didn't give you your money's worth?"

"Stop it!"

"Then why? I want to hear you say it!"

"Just the fact you're asking me should be the answer!" Our voices had risen, and I wondered briefly about neighbors, but I wouldn't have to answer to them.

"Well, it's not!" Jack leaned in close, but I turned my face. "You stink of smoke."

"Don't worry," he said. "I'm not planning on kissing you."

That stung, and I put a hand on his chest to push him away. "You're being an asshole."

He shrugged and grabbed up a pack of cigarettes and a lighter from the table where he'd put his keys. He lit up and took a few steps back, leaving me free to go. "So go."

I didn't want to go like this. Messy. Emotional. "You see what I mean? Everything ends."

"It doesn't have to end." He pointed at me with his cigarette.

"Yes. It does."

"Why? Because of the money? I think it's pretty obvious I don't mind fucking you for free."

Tears swelled in my throat and behind my eyes, burning. "Stop it."

Jack said nothing.

"I like you," I told him, each word sharp like glass. "Okay? I like you a lot."

"But not enough? What?"

"This is supposed to be a business arrangement. I pay you to give me what I want, which is uncomplicated, no-strings sex. That's it."

His shoulders hunched momentarily before he straightened them. "Yeah. Well. I guess it got a little complicated."

"Yes. And I don't want that."

"I don't blame you," he said. "Because it fucking sucks."

I wanted to touch him but didn't. "Maybe this isn't the right line of work for you."

Jack laughed around a mouthful of smoke. "No shit. Being a fucking lapdog for rich old bitches who can't be bothered to learn my name? Being arm candy for uptight career chicks who just need a date to impress their uptight career-chick friends? Being a cover for lesbians who don't want their families to know they're dykes?"

It was a tirade, and a surprising one. "It's a job."

"Yeah. And I get paid really fucking well to be a whore." He spat out a crumb of tobacco and stubbed out his cigarette on a plate on the table. "But it was different with you."

"No," I told him gently. "It really wasn't."

He sneered and looked away. "It was. You're the only one who ever took the time to talk to me like I was a real person."

"You are a real person."

I could see the quirk of his mouth even though his face was turned away from me. "But you'd rather pay me to take you out than just hang out with me."

"You should ask her out," I told him. "Sarah."

He looked at me then. "And you should ask him out. That guy. Sam."

We stared at each other in silence until he shivered and grabbed a sweatshirt from the back of a kitchen chair. I put my hand on the knob and opened the door, and this time, Jack didn't try to make me stay.

"You really are perfect," I told him.

Jack looked at me. "Yeah. Maybe in the morning I'll cross-stitch that on a sampler and hang it on my wall."

"It's already tomorrow morning."

He smiled, finally, and the tightness eased inside my chest. "I'd better get stitching, huh?"

"Goodbye, Jack."

He nodded and lifted a hand, but made no move toward me. I ducked out the door and closed it behind me, and drew a shaky breath.

Everything ends.

Light was breaking in the sky by the time I crawled, bleary-eyed, into my bed without even washing my face or brushing my teeth. No sooner had I closed my eyes than my cell phone jangled from my purse, which I'd tossed onto the chair in my bedroom.

I had to answer it.

It rang again, but I couldn't move.

I had to answer it. It could be a death call. At this hour, what else would it be?

"Dammit, Sam," I breathed into the mouthpiece when I answered it as it rang again. "Don't you know what time it is?"

"Sure. I thought you'd be up by now."

"You must be joking. It's the ass crack of dawn."

"Just getting in then?"

My eyes snapped open. "Seriously. Are you stalking me?"

"No. I'm just guessing that if you didn't just get up, you're just getting in. Because I know you don't take men to your place."

"You are so fucking annoying."

"And you're delightfully charming when you're exhausted."

I rubbed the sand gritting into my eyeballs. "What do you want!"

"To talk to you."

"Talk to me in a few hours," I mumbled, burying my face against my pillow.

"Grace."

I waited, but he said nothing else. I groaned. "What?"

"Remember what I said about me not caring if you had a boyfriend?"

It was my turn to be silent. "Yes."

"I'm ashamed to tell you, I lied."

"He wasn't my boyfriend." I paused, and went for it, with only exhaustion and emotion as my excuse. "He's just someone I fuck on occasion."

Sam made a small noise. "Uh-huh."

"How about that?" I challenged. "Do you care about that?"

"I'd be lying if I said I didn't."

The night had been an up-and-down roller coaster, and the ride wasn't over yet, even though my stomach had gone sick with the loop-dee-loops. "Goddammit, Sam!"

"Do you love him?"

"No!"

"Does he love you?"

I sighed. "I hope not."

"Good."

I wanted to scream at the smile I heard in his voice, but I bit it back. "I'm hanging up now."

"I'll call later."

"Oh. My. God." I writhed in my bed in an agony of frustration. "Why? Why would you do that?"

"Because I want to talk to you," came his mild answer. "Maybe take you to lunch. What do you say?"

"I say I still stink from sex with another man!" I shouted into the phone. "What in the fucking holy seven layers of hell do you want to take me to lunch for?"

"I thought a sandwich, maybe a bowl of soup—"

I burst into laughter that sounded suspiciously like tears. "You are insane."

"Not insane. Crazy, maybe."

"Sam…" I trailed off. "This attention is flattering, if not a little creepy…"

"Only a little though, right? Mostly flattering."

"You're crazy," I whispered, and yawned. "What kind of man says things like that for serious?"

"A patient one."

"Patience implies waiting for something."

Sam laughed. "Don't forget. I remember exactly what I'm waiting for."

He hadn't said it seductively, but somehow that made it sexier. "I told you I don't do that regularly."

"Yet you do have men you fuck on occasion. Why can't I be one of them?"

"If that's all you want," I told him, "why bother with lunch?"

"Because I also like to eat. I figured I could kill two birds with one stone, as the saying goes."

"You…you are…" My mind refused to provide my tongue with what, exactly, I thought Sam was.

"Yeah. I know."

"I have to go to sleep, Sam. I really do."

"Me, too."

I paused on the brink of unconsciousness, my finger poised over the disconnect button. "Tell me you stayed up all night."

"Oh, yeah. I just got home a little while ago."

This shook me into wakefulness. "You did?"

"You're not the only one who fucks on occasion, Grace."

This was not what I wanted to hear, though I had absolutely no right to complain. "The blonde."

"Was she blond? I don't remember."

"Are you messing with me?" I asked, suspicious.

"Does it matter to you if I am?" Sam said. "Ask yourself why."

I grunted. "You are not only crazy, you are a pain in the ass."

"Oh, my aim is much better than that."

Dammit. He made me laugh again, though it quickly trailed into a whine. "Sam, c'mon, I have to get some sleep."

"Lunch with me later?"

"You're taking advantage of my exhaustion. You know that, right?"

"I'm shameless that way."

"I'll call you," I said finally, the words slurring. "Don't call me. If you wake me up, I'll seriously kill you."

"You'll call me," he said. "Promise?"

"Yes, you annoying pain, yes. I promise."

"I'll wait."

My chest got tight again. "Oh, Sam. Don't wait too long."

"Oh, Grace," he mimicked. "I have nothing better to do."

"Fine. I'll call."

"Jesus doesn't like liars, Grace."

"Jesus—" I coughed. "I thought you were Jewish."

"You're not, though."

"I'm not particularly religious at all."

"Okay, fine. Kiki doesn't like liars."

"Kiki?" It took me a few seconds for the sleep syrup in my brain to drain long enough for me to get it. "Oh, God."

"Go to sleep, Grace. And call me later. You promised."

"I promised," I muttered, thumbing off the phone and falling asleep without another word.

I didn't sleep long enough, but the next time the phone rang it was the answering service and not Sam. I fought my way out of dreams to grab it up, listened to the message and fell back onto my pillow wishing this was a nightmare. That, at least, wouldn't be real.

I didn't know the man who'd called me, but I knew the waver in his voice well enough. I didn't have to say much, or lead him. He had all the information I needed. I was grateful for that, at least. It didn't make it easier, but it made it faster.

I showered fast and dressed, then took the van to the Hershey Med Center alone. I wouldn't need Jared with me for this. I didn't need help lifting the body of a child.

They met me in the hospital lobby. A young couple, both about my age. Grief had stolen the color from their faces and left them pale, but the man's handshake was firm when he greeted me. They wanted to know if they could meet with me right away to plan the service for their son. They didn't want to wait, he said, his wife silent but nodding beside him. They had no family to come in from out of town and wanted to bury him as soon as they could.

"It's for my wife," he said when she excused herself to use the bathroom. "It's killing her, you see? We didn't even know he was sick until two days ago. We need to…"

He choked on the word *bury*, but though his gaze flared bright with tears, he didn't weep.

"I understand." I rubbed his shoulder through the fleece of his pullover jacket and he put his face in his hands for a moment before pulling it together.

"I have to be strong for her," he muttered.

He spoke to me, but the words were meant for himself.

When his wife returned, it took only half an hour and a few phone calls to arrange for the service and burial the next day. The chief of the cemetery crew wasn't happy about coming in on a Sunday. When I explained the need, he went silent on the phone for a moment before he agreed.

The wife gave me a paper grocery sack filled with clothes. I left the couple, neither of them crying, in the lobby and picked up my young charge in the morgue. I've made hundreds of similar journeys and will admit to having gained a certain degree of callousness about my silent passengers, but not this time.

I had never taken care of a child before. A few teenagers, a few young adults. But never a child.

He was four years old when he died, victim of a sudden and inexplicable fever caused by a particularly virulent strain of summer flu.

My nephew, Simon, was four years old.

In the hospital the boy had been placed into a body bag, but when I took him to the funeral home I had to lay him, naked, on my table and prepare him for burial.

The parents had chosen to lay their small son to rest in his footy pajamas with his blankie and teddy beside him. I had to pad his cheeks with cotton to keep them pudgy, and my hands shook when I did it. I wept as I dressed him carefully and tucked the soft blue blanket under his arm, and harder when I brushed the soft curls over his cold forehead.

Though I have often felt empathy and sorrow for the families who entrust me with their loved ones, it's never been my own sorrow. Even when the dead person was someone I knew, a part of me larger than sadness understood grief is for the living. The dead are gone and can't care anymore. Grief is for the ones left behind, and though I understand it, I'd never felt it for myself the way my clients did.

But for that small boy whose eyes had closed too soon, I wept. When his parents came to see him, a woman and a man driven apart by the awfulness of their relentless pain, I wanted them to see him as he'd been, not how he was. I didn't want them to know about the cotton in his cheeks, or how beneath his pj's crept a line of stitches like railroad tracks from where the doctors had cut him open trying to save his life. I wept as I placed him in the smallest casket I had. A nicer one than they could afford...but I wouldn't tell them that. I wept in silence, with hot tears slipping down my face and pooling salt in the corners of my lips as I worked. I wept, too, as I called Jared to let him know he'd need to come in the next day to help me.

I wanted them to see him as he'd been, to offer them that small comfort and save them from further pain. I wanted to tell them he was safe and in a better place where he couldn't hurt any longer, but I didn't believe that. I knew he was gone. Just gone.

I told them that anyway, an easy lie because I knew it was expected and would layer over them with the hundred other whispers of something better beyond. Because it would help, if not then but later, when they looked at his photos and told each other not to forget the sound of his sweet, small laughter even as they already had begun to.

I couldn't make myself believe it, so I did what I could, instead, which was help them, too.

Night had fallen by the time I was done, and I went to bed still weeping, and woke with my pillow damp from tears. I'd arranged for a 9:00 a.m. viewing, and at the families' request a 10:00 a.m. burial.

At nine forty-five, ten minutes after we needed to leave for the cemetery, people were still arriving to say goodbye. The husband and wife seemed overwhelmed by this show of support, some of the mourners strangers who'd known the parents as someone to say hello to on the street. Every chair in the chapel was filled.

I didn't cry during the service. It wouldn't have been appropriate, and they didn't need my tears. They needed me to make sure the hearse had gas in it and the driver knew where to go. They needed me to fill out the forms making their son's death official, as if they needed ink on paper to make their loss true. They needed me to greet the other mourners and direct them to the chapel, to point them to the restrooms and the guest book, to make sure everyone sat when they were supposed to and got to where they needed to be. That man and woman whose world had torn itself to pieces needed me to help them hold it together for just a few hours, and I did the best I could.

They'd planned no eulogy; after all, what four-year-old had accomplishments to brag on? But as the room filled to overflowing, the boy's father looked around and asked me if it would be all right if he said a few words before we left to go to the cemetery.

He got up in front of the crowd in an ill-fitting navy suit that looked borrowed. If he'd wept at all, his face showed no signs of tears, though his eyes burned as bright as they had in the hospital lobby. He cleared his throat once, then again, and all of us waited, silent in our respect for what he would say.

"He never did learn to put away his blocks," the man

said. His grief welled up, then, in great shining waves that spilled out of his eyes and down his face to wet his lips.

I knew what that tasted like.

A single sob broke free from his wife and she stifled it with her fist. She was not the only one crying. Her husband cleared his throat again but made no attempt to wipe his face. Tears glistened and dripped off his chin.

"He was my son. And I loved him. And I don't know what we're going to do without him."

He looked around the room and nodded once, as though satisfied, then reached for his wife. They wept together then, but they weren't alone with it. Not the way they'd been in the hospital, or the way I think they believed they'd been.

When we were done at the cemetery and the line of cars with their lights on and the purple "funeral" flags stuck with magnets to the hoods had gone, I went home. I closed the door and went to my apartment. My cell phone hadn't rung all day. No message blinked on my answering machine. I hadn't eaten enough. Hadn't slept enough. I teetered on the edge of exhaustion, my nerves raw and my world tipped upside down.

I sank onto the couch and put my face in my hands, and I wept again, this time forcing tears that didn't want to come so I could put it away.

I had to put it away.

My fingers fumbled the number twice before I managed to finish dialing, and the phone rang a long time without being answered. So long I feared I would get nothing but static or a voice mail, and I couldn't leave a message. I counted the rings, thinking I would hang up after three. Four. Another, just one more.

And finally, at last, he answered, his voice not questioning who was calling, because it sounded as if he already knew.

"Sam," I said. "I need you."

Chapter 15

*H*e brought me matzo-ball soup in a plastic container and did everything but feed it to me. Then he ran the shower for me, hot, and put me under the water while I cried again. He pulled a T-shirt over my head and helped me into pajama bottoms, and he tucked me into bed where he spooned me.

I was sort of delirious at that point, wrung out from emotion and exhaustion, and I know I rambled on and on about death, life, fate, the lack of white tunnels. The unfairness of a god that would take a child so young. The undeservedness of grief.

Sam was silent for the most part, his body tucked up against mine and his arm cradling me. The bed was rocking like a boat on the sea, and Sam my anchor, keeping me still. His breath touched the back of my neck.

"If there's no sorrow," he murmured, "how can anyone appreciate the joy?"

He was right. Of course he was. But there was no comfort in that for me that day. And though I knew this shattering grief wasn't even mine, that time would pass and I would get over that child's death faster than those who'd loved him, that did nothing but make me rage all the more.

At some point, I slept, unable to stay awake any longer. The body wins out over the mind, always. I don't remember what I dreamed, only that when I woke to the sound of Sam's soft snores, I didn't want to run away.

I woke him with gentle kisses down the side of his neck and his bare chest—when had he changed? Further exploration below the covers revealed that at some point he'd stripped to boxer briefs, the front of which bulged a bit more and more as my mouth moved over his skin.

There must be sorrow to truly appreciate joy. I knew it. He was right. But I was right, too, when I said that everything ends. Correct in my belief that grief is for the living, the ones left behind, and I hadn't stopped being afraid of that. If anything, watching that man and woman put their child into the ground and seeing how they clung to each other for support had only stiffened my convictions.

"Miz Grace," Sam drawled. "Are yew tryin' to seduce me?"

About two minutes too late I realized I must look like the Elephant Man. "It's not working?"

"I didn't say that." He smiled at me.

Mindful now of the fact I was sure to have awful morning breath, I didn't move to kiss his mouth, though I did give in to the urge to nibble his chest again. Sam touched my hair, softly.

"What time do you have to go downstairs?"

"Shit." I looked at the clock. "Half an hour ago. But I didn't have any appointments this morning, so it's okay."

He touched my hair again, just as softly. "I'd say after the day you had yesterday, you deserve to sleep in a little bit. I, on the other hand…"

"Lessons today?" I sat up and chained my knees to my chest with my arms. They made a nice resting spot for my chin.

Sam grinned and stretched and looked utterly delicious. "You know it."

He sat up and ran a hand through his hair until it stood on end. It's really not fair how men can roll out of bed and face the day and even the least appearance-conscious woman still needs at least a shower.

Here I was in bed with him, after months of flirting, and he wasn't even trying to kiss me. I must look worse than I thought. I surreptitiously touched my eyes to check for puffiness.

Sam, on the other hand, swung those long legs out of bed and started dressing. I noticed he'd folded his clothes neatly on the chair. I hadn't even noticed him getting out of bed the night before.

"I must've been really out of it last night."

Sam's head appeared from the neck hole of his plain blue T-shirt. "You were."

I was suddenly, uncomfortably aware that strangers we had met and strangers we still were. Mostly. Sam seemed utterly at ease as he pulled on his jeans and shrugged into a button-down shirt he left untucked. He was acting as if we'd spent a thousand nights together already, but he hadn't even tried to fuck me.

I watched without saying anything as he finished dressing and helped himself to my bathroom. I heard him gargling and sat up straight. Was he using my toothbrush? Sharing saliva was one thing, but not on my toothbrush! He appeared a moment later and I smelled mouthwash on his breath when he leaned to kiss...my cheek.

Again.

"I'll call you later," Sam said. "Let's go to dinner."

He chucked me under the chin—yes, an actual chuck, like I was some cute, tomboy cousin with a crush! If my life had a sound track and a Foley crew, just then you'd have heard the sound of spring being sprung and a bell being rung. Sproing-oing-oing, ding!

"No?" He gained points for interpreting my expression, at least.

I shut my mouth so hard my teeth clicked. "Dinner would be fine."

Sam rolled up his sleeves to his elbows. "The look on your face says dinner isn't fine."

"No." I shook my head and got out of bed, conscious that with him dressed and mouthwashed, he had the emotional advantage, even if it was purely imaginary on my part. In the bathroom I scrubbed my teeth quickly and spoke through foam. "Dinner's good!"

Sam looked taller than ever in the slightly skewed doorway to the bathroom. His spiked hair actually brushed the top doorjamb. "What's the matter?"

What could I say that wouldn't make me sound like a complete idiot? That after sleeping with him once and putting him off for weeks, I'd finally decided that something with Sam wasn't something I could deny I wanted any longer? That while I would forever appreciate the comfort he'd offered me last night, morning had come and I wanted to do the same?

Which, idiotic sounding or not, was exactly what I said.

"And apparently, you're not interested!" I finished, slightly out of breath, and crossed my arms over my chest.

Sam had listened to my words with a faint smile, but now he leaned forward to say into my ear, "I'm interested."

I wasn't totally mollified. "So...?"

"So, this way," Sam murmured with an added flick of his tongue on my earlobe that sent a shiver along my every nerve, "you'll be thinking about me. All. Day. Long."

Oh.

Was that perhaps the longest day I've ever spent? With each minute seeming to last an hour, I'd say so. I kept myself busy with updating our Web site and ordering new brochures and forms, but it didn't help much.

"More coffee?" I asked Shelly, who sat reading a tabloid magazine at her desk.

She looked up from the lurid tales of celebrity divorces. "More? Grace, you're going to overdose."

I lifted my mug. "So, is that a no?"

Shelly smiled. "No. Are you okay?"

"Sure. Fine. Why wouldn't I be?"

"Well...because this is the fourth time you've asked me if I wanted more coffee." She looked as if she meant to say more, but the phone rang and she answered it, while I tensed.

Death call? Would I have to miss my dinner date with

Sam? My coffee sloshed over my fingers, burning them, and I grabbed a tissue from the box on her desk to wipe them. She didn't gesture to me, and I relaxed.

There are days in the funeral business that begin before sunrise and don't end until night falls, with death calls and services and deliveries. There are also days when I sit at my desk and file my nails while I play game after game of solitaire on the computer. Today was shaping up to be one of those days.

It gave me too much time to think about my date with Sam. Date.

I winced as I filed too hard and brought blood to a cuticle and looked up at the knock on my door. My dad, my laptop in hand. My stomach did a flip-flop and skidded down to my toes before rocketing up to my throat.

I got up. "Hey, Dad."

"I brought back your computer. Heard you got the other one up and running."

My dad held out my PowerBook, which I promptly cradled like the baby I never intended to have. "Yes. I did. Did you…get everything you needed from this one?"

My dad shrugged. "I printed out the register, but your mom's been keeping me so busy I haven't had much of a chance to look it over. I figured if you were having real trouble, you'd let me know."

It was the closest I'd get to him backing off, and we both knew it. "Yes. I would."

He nodded again without looking at me or coming farther into the office. Since usually he charged right in and made himself at home, to see him lingering there in the doorway seemed odd. I stepped back, giving him room to enter if he wanted, but my dad didn't come closer.

"I've got to get going," he said. "Me and Stan are going fishing tomorrow and I want to get to the sporting-goods store to check out a new rod."

"Again?"

I'd been a little worried about the way he was acting, but the look he shot me confirmed it was, indeed, my father standing in my doorway and not a pod-person. "Aren't I entitled to a little relaxation?"

"Of course you are, Dad."

My dad made a familiar, half-disgruntled snorting sound and waved as he backed out of my office, leaving me to stare after him in confusion. I didn't have time to ponder his odd behavior because the phone on my desk rang, which meant Shelly had switched the call through to me…which meant she knew it was from someone I'd want to talk to. Which meant I grabbed it up and tried not to sound too eager as I expected Sam to be on the other end.

"Grace? Are you all right?"

My sister.

Everyone kept asking me that. "Yes. Fine. What's up?"

"I know it's last minute, but I was hoping you could come over after work to watch the kids until Jerry gets home. I have to go someplace."

"I can't. I've got plans for dinner."

The dead silence that followed my answer told me Hannah had been expecting me to say yes. "Oh."

"Yeah…sorry."

My sister must have heard the lack of sorrow in my

voice, because she sniffed. "Can you maybe go later? I just need you until Jerry gets home."

Since Jerry had a history of never being on time, I wasn't convinced today would be any different. In fact, he'd probably be even later than normal just because I really needed him to be home on time. "I can't. I have…a date."

More silence, so long I wasn't sure if my sister had hung up until she said, "Oh, really?"

"Yes. Really."

"Great." Just as I hadn't sounded sorry, she didn't sound happy. "Well, good for you. I guess."

Annoyed, I looked at the clock. An hour to get ready before Sam would be by to pick me up, and I still wanted to shower and change. "I'm sorry I can't watch the kids, Hannah, but maybe Mom can."

"She can't. I already asked."

"Sorry."

Hannah sighed, sounding incredibly put out. "Never mind. I'll just have to wait until Jerry gets home."

She'd always been good at making me feel guilty about things that weren't my fault. Though sort of, this time, it was my fault—inasmuch as I wasn't saying no, as I'd done in the past, because I had to work, but because I had social plans. I thought back quickly. I'd never told my sister no in favor of my own social plans, which had always generally been set to my own convenience.

Clearly, Hannah didn't think that ought to change.

"Sorry," I repeated, sounding less so than I had earlier.

"Have fun on *your* date," my sister said, and hung up.

Her emphasis on "your" had seemed out of place, but

time had ticked by while we talked, and since Shelly hadn't appeared in the doorway with a message slip saying I needed to return a family's call, I wanted to take advantage of the timing to run upstairs and spend the extra twenty minutes plucking and tweezing and shaving myself into presentability.

I shut down my computer and tidied the papers on my desk into one neat pile then went out to tell Shelly to lock up behind herself when she was done. I found Jared leaning on her desk, his face intent and hers unreadable. Neither looked up when I came out, until I spoke, and then only Shelly turned to me. Jared just walked away, his back stiff and straight, as if someone had whacked him someplace tender.

"I'm going to head upstairs. Can you lock up before you go?"

Shelly nodded, then blinked, and I caught a sheen of tears. "Sure."

"Do you have a ride home?"

Another nod, and this time she bit her lower lip. "Jared's taking me home."

Oh, how much I wanted to comment on that, but I didn't. "Good. See you tomorrow."

She nodded and busied herself with tidying her papers and shutting down her computer, looking for all the world like any other busy office manager. But I saw the way her gaze kept cutting down the hall I couldn't see, the hall down which Jared had stalked only moments before.

"Good night." Shelly answered half a minute after I'd already walked away, and as I glanced over my shoulder, she was looking down the hall again.

* * *

Sam scared the living bejesus out of me by knocking on my apartment's never-used outside-access door. I'd been pacing the kitchen, wishing I had a bad habit like smoking to keep me occupied while I waited for him to show up, and the rap on the door startled me so fiercely I knocked over my can of cola and watched the puddle spread along the kitchen table and start dripping onto the floor before I could wrassle my mind into grabbing a cloth to toss down on top of the mess. By that time, Sam had rapped again, and I'd determined the noise was coming from the door behind the set of steel shelves I'd set up to give myself some more storage.

"Just a minute!" It didn't take much muscle to move the shelves, laden with disorganized cookbooks, pots and pans and several boxes of whole-wheat pasta I'd forgotten about until they fell off. It didn't leave much room to get the door open, though, which was sort of the point.

"Hey." Sam slid in between the narrow space between the counter and the shelves and let the door close behind him. He pulled his hand out from behind his back.

"Flowers?"

He grinned. "Just for you."

They looked a bit worse for the wear after being slightly mangled in their precarious journey, but I lifted them to my face and breathed in. "Wow, Sam. Thank you."

Sam opened his arms. "That's all I get? A thank-you?"

I hesitated, the flowers in my hand making me abnormally shy. Sam saved me by turning his cheek and tapping it with one finger. Laughing, I moved in to kiss him there, but at the last moment he turned his face. My kiss landed on his lips, instead, and his arms closed around me to hold me close.

Neither of us noticed we were crushing the flowers.

"Now, that's what I call a thank-you," he murmured against my mouth. His hands pressed my back for a moment before he let me go and I stepped back with heated cheeks and parted lips.

"You scared the hell out of me," I accused, turning to find a vase and using that as a good excuse to hide my hot face. "Nobody ever uses that door."

"Yeah, I noticed that." Without asking, Sam reached to lock the door and pull the shelves back in front of it, losing only a pot and a wire whisk in the process. Both fell with a clatter but missed his feet, and he picked them up to put them away while he grinned at me. "I thought it would be better than ringing the bell downstairs. More dramatic."

"It was dramatic, all right." I fluffed the velvety petals and leaned in again to sniff them. "You'd think I'd hate the smell of lilies, since we have so many of them around here."

Sam leaned forward to sniff, too, before sneezing loudly. "I figured if you liked it in your froufrou bath stuff, you'd like the flowers, too."

I didn't ask him when he'd noticed my bath products. His sneeze had made his eyes wet and nose a little red, and he looked incredibly adorable. So much that I turned away to feign fussing with the flowers some more.

I knew this feeling. The skip-jump-pitter-pat of my heart. The flush of my cheeks.

Holy shit, I was back in junior high, crushing on the senior captain of the football team.

"Ready to go?"

I looked up. "Yes. Is what I'm wearing okay?"

He hadn't told me where we were going. I'd figured a slim black skirt and hot-pink blouse were dressy enough to go anywhere but still casual enough to be comfortable. The look on Sam's face made me think again, though. He circled me, shaking his head and frowning.

"No?" I said.

"I'm going to have the damnedest time keeping my hands to myself." He looked up.

"Well," I said with a hand on my hip, "who says you have to?"

"We don't want to shock my brother, do we?" Sam reached for my hand. "He's already going to have a cow that we're late."

"We're going to dinner with your brother?" I grabbed up my purse and lightweight jacket as he led me to the front door. "We're late?"

"I'm never on time for him," Sam said as I locked the door to the apartment and we headed down the stairs. "He'd have a heart attack."

I personally didn't like being late for anything. "I thought you and your brother didn't get along."

Sam waited as I locked the main door behind me. "Why? Because he beat the crap out of me?"

"Well...yeah." His car waited next to Betty, proving again what a little love and work could do for my poor old car.

"Nah." He opened the door for me and waited until I'd slid all the way in before closing it for me.

"So you've worked things out?" I glanced at him as he slid into the driver's seat, and he gave me a grin.

"Sure." The Camaro roared to life with a rumble I felt in the pit of my stomach. Then again, maybe it was the way Sam reached over to slide his hand along my thigh. "For now."

Dan Stewart lived in Harrisburg, but though I'd made the drive up Route 322 through Hershey many times by myself, it went much faster with Sam in the car. He sang along with the radio, changing the lyrics and challenging me to do the same. My voice wasn't as good, but I was better at coming up with off-the-cuff rhymes, and more than once he high-fived me.

He was a good driver, though, rarely taking his eyes off the road. That meant I could stare at him as much as I wanted. I wanted to quite a bit. He caught me though, when he pulled up in front of a nice little house in an older neighborhood. The worst part was, he didn't seem surprised. Like he'd known all along I was watching him.

"This is it." He made no move to get out of the car.

I peered out the window at the neatly trimmed grass and hedges. The house was small, but this neighborhood was one of the nicest in the city, with well-kept homes and nice vehicles parked in front of them. Sam's car, as well as it had been refurbished, looked out of place at the curb between the Mercedes and the Jaguar.

"My brother's a lawyer and his lady's some sort of fancy number cruncher," Sam explained. He leaned over me to look out my window. "Pretty soon they'll start pumping out little nerdlings. Ain't that cute?"

Something in his tone turned my face toward him, and

he turned toward me. We were at kissing distance, though we weren't kissing. He blinked, his mouth thin, and I gave in to my impulse to cradle his face in my hands and kiss him back into a grin.

"Whoa. What was that for?"

"Do I need a reason?" I stroked my thumb along his lower lip, gently teasing open his mouth.

"No. I guess you don't." Sam leaned in to kiss me again, but we both caught sight of the front door to Dan's house opening and he sighed. "Hold that thought for later, okay?"

As if I could forget about it. It was all I'd been thinking about all day long, just as he'd promised I would. I used the minute it took him to open my door to swipe my nose and cheeks with powder and freshen the gloss on my lips.

I was a little overdressed for dinner at someone's house, but I shouldn't have worried. Dan's wife wore an even more formal outfit, probably what she'd worn to work, though instead of matching pumps she wore a pair of ridiculously large, fuzzy slippers.

"Nice kicks," Sam told her, kissing her on the cheek. "Elle, you remember Grace, don't you?"

"Of course." She shook my hand and smiled. "It's nice to meet you under different circumstances. Dan! Sam's here!"

"Tell that bastard he's late!" came the answering shout from down the hall.

Sam and Elle shared a look, and she put on an even bigger smile. "Your brother's making spaghetti."

Sam rolled his eyes. "Don't you mean pasta à la Dan?"

Elle covered a laugh with her hand. "Shh, Sam, he's actually made his own sauce."

She looked at me. "C'mon, Grace. Let's get you some wine and let those two wallow in their own testosterone."

I wasn't going to turn down the drink. As Sam headed down the hall, Elle took me down the two steps to the sunken living room, where she poured me a glass of good red wine and showed me around.

"How long have you lived here?" I admired their floor-to-ceiling bookcases and the casually elegant furniture. I'd never be able to throw together something like this, even if I did have a much higher cash flow.

"A little over a year. I had a town house down by the Broad Street Market and Dan had his own place, but this place needed a lot less work than either of ours. And... well, it's more practical for a family."

"It's beautiful," I told her sincerely, and her face lit.

"Elle!"

She looked toward the sound of the shout, then back to me. "I'm being paged. C'mon."

In the kitchen, Sam sat on top of the counter, his long legs dangling and a beer cradled in one hand. His brother stirred a pot on the stove from which steam wafted. I smelled rich, tomatoey goodness and garlic bread...and smoke.

"Grab the bread, Elle, would you?" Dan jerked a thumb toward Sam. "Sammy's claiming oven phobia again."

Elle laughed and set her wineglass on the table to open up the oven and pull out the tray of garlic bread. "Sammy, move your ass. I want to set this there."

Sam hopped down at once and came to stand next to me. "See how my brother has corrupted her? It's Sam, Elle. Sam."

Elle gave him a glance over her shoulder that didn't look

as if he'd convinced her, and she leaned over to taste the sauce on the spoon Dan was offering. "Fine. Sam. Move your ass, Sam, and set the table."

He gave me a look. "See how I'm abused?"

I laughed and poked him. "Poor boy."

Together we set the dining-room table. As he had in my house, Sam seemed to have made himself at home, searching through drawers or hollering for directions on where to find a tablecloth, napkins and silverware. I wasn't sure Dan and Elle had meant to serve dinner on such finery, but I couldn't stop laughing as Sam pulled out the ugliest pair of silver candelabra I'd ever seen and settled them with a flourish in the table's center.

"Voilà." He kissed his fingertips. "She is complete."

"What the—" Dan stopped in the doorway with a full platter of steaming pasta in his hands. "Jesus, Sammy. Where the hell did you find those?"

Elle peeked over Dan's shoulder and started laughing. "Oh, God. My mother gave me those as a wedding gift. Sam, put them away."

Sam shook his head. "What? They're…chic."

Dan put down the platter. "Dude."

"Dude!" Sam said, hands spread.

Elle shouldered her way between them and plunked a set of fat white candles into the holders and lit them. "Sit down and eat. Grace, ignore them."

None of them seemed to have given a second thought to my being here, or to making me a part of what was clearly, despite the beatings, a close family. I wondered what Sam had told them about me. I wasn't getting a vibe about being surreptitiously checked out or approved of. Or not.

Dinner was nice, too, with good food and increasingly rowdy conversation. Sam and Dan circled each other with words, taking jabs whenever possible, and though I detected an undercurrent of tension between them it was good-natured for the most part. Elle was quiet, but with the sort of dry humor I always admired and never quite managed, myself, but she kept the pair of them in line with her subtly snarky comments when all I could do was laugh at Sam's put-upon expressions and Dan's grandiose hand gestures. Nobody treated me like Sam's girlfriend, which led me to believe that was what he'd told them I was.

Seated across from me, Sam wasn't close enough to touch me. Not with his hands, anyway. His gaze, however, managed to caress me with no problem, and I felt that touch all over my body.

"So, Sammy's got another few gigs lined up around here." Dan held up his glass for Elle to refill. "Have you heard him play, Grace?"

"Yes, I have." I waved away the offer of a refill for me. Even though I'd finally let Jared take first call, I didn't want to get drunk. Plus, I'd been watching Sam put away beers with barely a pause between them.

"Bastard's not half-bad, huh?" Dan grinned as Sam flipped him off with both hands.

Elle got up to clear the table and I rose, too, and she waved away Dan when he tried to get up, too. "Play with your brother."

In the kitchen, she opened the dishwasher. "The last

time we had dinner together, they ended up having a sponge battle in the kitchen. I'd rather clean up, myself, than have to spend the whole night mopping."

"I don't blame you." From the dining room came a flurry of insults. When I looked back at her, she was smiling.

"I don't think they're going to punch each other. Not tonight, anyway." Together we cleared the table and tidied the kitchen while Dan and Sam watched some shoot-em-up movie on the big-screen TV in the den.

I was definitely the girlfriend.

Elle pulled out a thick chocolate cake from the fridge and put it on the table. "The fudge icing on this is thick enough to make me gain ten pounds just from looking at it. Let's eat it before they get a chance at it. If I know Sam, it'll be gone before we get more than a nibble."

"He's got a sweet tooth." I laughed as she put out clean plates and forks. The first bite of cake was good enough to make me groan.

"Yeah." Elle sighed and licked the tines of her fork as she leaned against the counter. "Heaven, huh? Coffee'll be ready in a minute. We'll call them in when it's done."

She wasn't much of a talker and didn't fill the silence between us with lots of happy chatter the way many women would've, but with the cake to occupy my mouth I was glad not have to come up with small talk.

"So," she did say after a minute filled with the clank of our forks on the plates and our chocolate-sated sighs. "Sam."

I looked at her and wiped my mouth carefully with a napkin. "Is this where I get some speech about not hurting him?"

Elle looked surprised. "No. Did you expect that?"

I put my plate in the dishwasher so I wouldn't be tempted to have another slice. "I didn't know what to expect, actually. My relationship with Sam is—"

"Complicated?"

"That's a good way to put it."

Elle helped herself to another forkful of cake and sighed happily. "Good cake. Well, Grace, I'm not Sam's mother, so it's not really my place to protect him, is it?"

I laughed. "I don't think you need to protect him from me, anyway."

Elle brought down cups and saucers, then sugar and cream from the fridge. The coffeepot hissed and the good, strong scent of caffeine filled the air. "Sam's a good guy. I don't know him that well. I mean, I've only really had the chance to spend time with him since Morty died. Not the best time to make a judgment on someone, would you say?"

"No." I helped her put out spoons, but didn't shy away from meeting her frank gaze. "Listen, did Sam tell you something about me?"

"No. But I think he told Dan some things. They had a fight about it. Dan seems to think Sam's got his head up his ass a lot of the time." She smiled and looked toward the den, where a shout had arisen over something on television. "Dan's had a hard time with his dad's death. And I think he's upset that it hasn't been harder for Sammy."

I'd never have guessed Dan had a problem with Sam dating me by his treatment of me, and I told her so.

"It's not you," she said as she poured coffee. "It's about Sam and Dan. I stay out of it. But I did want to tell you something, Grace. Something I do know that I think neither one of them do…or would admit to, maybe."

I waited.

"Sam's having a harder time about his dad dying than he's letting on. Harder than Dan, I think. Dan had issues with his dad, but he got to work out a lot of them before Morty passed away. Sam didn't. And as much as Dan wants to share his misery with his brother, and as much as he won't admit he's jealous that his baby brother seems to be getting away scot free yet again, I think he's glad to be the only one suffering. Gives him a reason to be angry at Sammy for a lot of things but blame it all on that one. You know?"

She said all of this calmly and slowly. She sounded as if she'd spent a good deal of time thinking about this situation. Elle impressed me as the sort of woman who thought a lot about a lot of things.

"I know. Death affects everyone differently." I stirred sugar and cream into my coffee.

She nodded and might have said more, but the room was suddenly a lot smaller with the addition of the two men. Sam slapped the back of Dan's head as they came through the doorway, and Dan turned without a pause and punched Sam in the arm hard enough to make a loud noise. It was like watching a tumbling pair of puppies scrambling for the alpha spot.

I looked at Elle, who stared at her husband as though she'd never seen him before. "That's my Dan," she murmured with a slight roll of her eyes.

Dan straightened, brushing back the hair Sam had tousled, went to her and dipped her down for a kiss. She didn't protest too heartily. Sam, apparently thinking this was a good idea, went for me with a warm, beery kiss. He kept me dipped a few seconds too long for comfort and nearly stumbled when pulling me up.

"Get some coffee in him," Dan suggested, rubbing his hands in glee at the sight of the cake. "Sober him up."

I eyed Sam as he poured himself coffee and cut a huge slab of cake. He'd had a few beers, but I hadn't thought he was drunk. He looked up to see me watching and shot me a grin.

"Don't pay attention to my brother. He can't hold his liquor." Sam forked a huge bite of cake between his lips.

Dan and Elle exchanged looks I couldn't interpret. Sam didn't notice or ignored them, but I did and it left me feeling awkward enough to say, "Sam, it's getting late."

He didn't even look at the clock, just nodded and put his plate in the sink. He kissed Elle's cheek loudly and punched his brother's arm, then turned to me. "I'm ready."

I thanked them for dinner and offered to help clean up the rest, but Dan waved me away. "No. You're right, it is late. Get going. Nice meeting you, Grace. Again."

I echoed the sentiment, but we were out the door and down the sidewalk in minutes. I stopped Sam at the car, though. "I'll drive."

He stopped, keys in hand, at unlocking my door. He straightened. "Don't let what my brother said worry you."

"I had one glass of wine. You had a few beers. There's no point in taking chances. Cops hang out up here, Sam. You don't want to get pulled over."

I watched a series of emotions flit across his face. He wasn't a stranger anymore, but I couldn't read him. He handed me the keys without further protest, though, and I was glad. Some men got belligerent.

Sam didn't. Sam sang all the way home, loudly and in tune. Sam opened the window and stuck his face into the breeze. Sam told dirty jokes that made me laugh even as I cried, "Ew!"

When I pulled into the parking lot behind the funeral home, easing Sam's car into the space next to Betty, he'd toned himself down a little. The wind had rumpled his hair, but that was a good look on him.

"Are you going to invite me up?"

I pulled the keys from the ignition and handed them to him. "What do you think?"

"I think yes." A small smile tugged the corners of his mouth.

I'd expected a grin. Honestly, after the months of pursuit, I'd sort of expected not to make it into the house at all. And suddenly, I was as nervous as Sam looked.

No longer singing and telling jokes, he followed me inside and up the stairs. I fumbled with my keys in the lock, and he waited patiently until at last I got the door open. Inside, he stood, hands in his pockets, while I hung up my coat and purse and tossed my keys into the dish by the door.

I'd imagined hands groping, mouths meeting, bodies slamming up against walls. Yet neither of us moved toward the other. I asked him if he wanted something to drink, and he asked for water. I poured us both glasses and we sat at opposite sides of my small table and stared at each other.

"Dinner was nice," I said.

"My brother's an okay cook. You can't do much to ruin pasta."

"Yeah."

Silence. We stared at the floor, the table, our glasses. Anywhere but at each other.

"Sam?"

"Yes?"

"Do you think…do you think that if we do it, we'll still be friends?"

Sam smiled. "Grace, we already did it."

"I know. But that was before." I pushed my glass back and forth along the tabletop.

"It didn't make a difference then. Why would it now?" Sam leaned back in his chair and beneath the table his leg pressed mine.

"I'd just hate if it did, that's all." I pressed back.

"Nothing's going to change except where you let me kiss you." Sam hooked his foot on the back of my calf and moved it up and down.

I rolled my eyes even as an image of Sam's dark head between my thighs filled my head. "Promises, promises."

Sam leaned across the table to kiss me. "I meant, in the kitchen or the car or in front of other people. You've got a dirty mind, Grace."

"Maybe I'm just optimistic," I whispered against his mouth.

"Maybe just realistic," Sam whispered in reply. "Grace. Can I make love to you now? I've been waiting an awfully long time."

My answer slid out on top of a sigh. "Yes, Sam. Please."

Chapter 16

I took him by the hand and led him to my bedroom where he tried undressing me and I fumbled with his belt before I took his hands away from my buttons and held them still.

"Wait."

"I don't think I can," Sam said in a hoarse voice.

"Sit down. You're too tall." My earlier nervousness had retreated. I knew what I was doing. I pushed Sam to sit on the edge of the bed. With his face at my chest level, I didn't have to crane my neck to kiss him, but we both had easy access to the other's clothes.

His hands shook a little when he eased open the fabric of my blouse. Sam leaned back to study my breasts, now revealed, and the black lace bra containing them. It was one of my favorites, and it plumped my size Bs into a pretty good imitation of Cs. The lace dipped low, just above the slightly darker pink of the flesh around my nipples. Sam teased the satin rosebud in the center with a fingertip, then ran his finger down my belly to the hem of my skirt. He looked up at me, his eyes bright.

"Take this off."

I reached behind me to unhook it and let the fabric slide down my arms. Sam replaced the soft lace with his palms. Each of his hands was big enough to cover a breast, and I shivered, my nipples tightening against the calluses on his fingers.

I'd managed to get his shirt mostly open, and I reached to slide my fingers along the collar, opening it. "Take *this* off."

"Then I'd have to let go of you." Sam shifted his hands to run his thumbs over the sensitive flesh of my nipples.

"Hmm. Tough decision. How about if I promised you I have other places you can touch?"

Sam laughed and leaned to kiss the soft curves of my cleavage before he sat back and shrugged out of his shirt. At first it seemed funny to see a chest and arms undecorated with hardware or ink, and I blinked with a small laugh.

"What?" Sam looked at himself, then flexed. "Not as buff as you recall?"

"That's not it." I traced the line of his collarbone with my finger, then found the sweet circle of his nipple and rolled it between my fingers. His small jump satisfied me, and I leaned in to kiss his jaw and throat as his hands came up to hold my waist.

I straddled him on the bed, a leg on each side of his hips. He pushed up my skirt as we kissed, but Sam took his mouth from mine when he reached the lacy straps of my garters and the tops of my stockings.

"Fuck," he breathed. "The first time I ever jerked off was to a picture in a catalog of something like this."

The image of a teenage Sam, prick in his fist, gave me tingles. "Garters?"

"Uh-huh." He slid an experimental hand along the bare skin of my thigh, and the back of it brushed the edge of my panties.

I put a hand on his shoulder to keep myself straight as he pushed my skirt around my hips. "You like these?"

"Yes." Sam put a finger underneath one and plucked it like a guitar string. "Did you wear them just for me?"

"I did."

His hand moved higher, brushing my panties again, before he reached around to unzip the back of my skirt. We spent the next few minutes wrestling our way out of our clothes and figuring out how to untangle ourselves without actually letting go of each other. True to my promise, Sam found several places he could touch, and he was touching one or more of them at all times until at last we were both naked.

There's always a moment of insecurity about undressing in front of someone, even someone you've known for a while. Maybe more when it's someone you've known for a while, when going skin on skin can change it all. Naked, Sam looked younger. Longer. I'd forgotten how he'd looked to me that first time, when I saw only a stranger. I looked at him with new eyes now, noting the places on his hands where the guitar strings had built calluses and the white lines of old scars on funny places like his knees and the inside of an elbow. At the way the line of hair on his belly thickened around his cock, already hard, and how much longer his penis seemed with my hand upon it.

"Did you think about me all day long?"

I nodded as I stroked him and he arched into my touch. "Yes, Sam. I did."

"That's good."

I couldn't tell if he meant my stroking or my thoughts. His eyes closed and his tongue swiped out across his mouth. His hands moved over my body. He remembered, even months later, the way I liked to be touched. Maybe he was just that good. Either way, his caresses sent shivers through me.

Heat swelled between my legs. Sam touched me there with gentle fingers, using just the tip of one finger to find my clit and make small circles on it. He stroked my folds, opening me so he could slide a finger inside and draw it back to smooth his strokes. I still straddled him, his erection in my hand, and I reached up with the other to tug the barrette I'd been using to hold back my chin-length bangs.

There's something so incredibly sexy about my hair falling forward over my face. The strands tickle my lips and cheeks and cover my eyes. The only time I wear it down that way is when I'm sleeping or fucking. I like the way it moves when I move, and how I can use it to shield my expression when I don't want my lover to see my eyes.

Sam wasn't having any of that, though. He reached to push my hair back from my face, then cupped the back of my neck and pulled me down for a kiss. It went on for a long time like that, us kissing and stroking each other, until at last he started thrusting into the circle of my fingers.

He closed his fingers over mine to stop me from moving. He took his hand from between my legs.

"Condoms are in the bedside stand." Everything about me seemed hot and wet, and still I had to swallow hard before I could speak. Sam could reach from where we were, and I admired the lean lines of his body as he stretched. "How tall are you, anyway?"

"Six-five." He snagged open my drawer and felt around inside.

Too late I remembered that the condoms weren't the only things inside that drawer. When Sam pulled back with something small and pink, I laughed, embarrassed, and tried to grab it away from him. He didn't let me. He held up the latex cock ring with the vibrating bullet tucked into it and stared at it with confusion.

I hadn't actually ever used it with a partner. I'd bought it from a sex-toy party at a friend's house because it had been the cheapest bullet vibe available, and I liked the steady, constant buzz along with the triple, flickering "tongues." Vibrators with flashing lights and multiple speeds intimidated me. I didn't want to land aircraft in my vagina; I just wanted to get off.

"Let me show you." I took the cock ring and mimed sliding it down over his erection, then showed him how the small latex tendrils fluttered.

Sam's cock twitched. "Do you want to use it?"

I looked at it, then at him. "Do you?"

He got up on his elbows. "If it will make you feel good. Sure."

"I've never really used it with someone," I told him.

He grinned. "All the better. Put it on me."

I did. We both stared. The ring disappeared into the fluff of black curls at the base of his prick, but the bullet sat just right. It would hit my clit every time he thrust, and the vibrations would work against me. Just the way it was meant to.

I slid a condom down him and then eased myself onto his cock. I bit my lip. He groaned. I made the small, subtle adjustments necessary to get everything to fit the way it was supposed to, then reached between us to push the base of the bullet.

"Oh, God." The instant I turned it on the vibe started buzzing, fluttering the small latex ribbons against my already swollen clit. But not hard, not constant. Just enough to tantalize and tease and get me close to the edge without sending me over.

I put my hands on Sam's shoulders and leaned forward with another muttered exclamation. I couldn't even think about moving yet. The vibe was taking up all my attention. Not that I cared. It was too fucking good to complain about. Already I felt a surge of orgasm building in the pit of my stomach.

I pushed on my knees to lift my ass a little, giving Sam the room he needed to fuck into me. "Fuck. That's good."

He grunted. His hands gripped my hips, moving me. Every thrust hit me deep inside and every time he filled me, the vibe buzzed my clit. It was different than using it by itself. Better, with Sam's thickness inside me, stretching. I wanted him to fuck me harder and faster, but he kept the pace steady and slow.

"Can you feel it?" I asked him. My hair had fallen into my eyes again, but this time he didn't push it back.

"Yeah." Sam licked his mouth, his eyes closed. "Feels good."

The sex was less frantic than it had been the first time, and that was fine. We moved together, and my first orgasm rocketed through me like a whip cracking. Only then did Sam speed the pace, pushing into me faster and harder the way I'd wanted him to. I got off again without much effort, the vibe a help but not the only reason. It was Sam. It was thinking about him all day, and smelling and tasting him, and watching the way his mouth grew thin with concentration. I came watching Sam come.

After, our bodies sticky and aligned, he put his hand on my belly and turned to face me. I only had one pillow, so neither of our heads rested all the way on it, and he used his hand to prop his head where the pillow ended. "Do you always come more than once?"

I yawned, already edging toward sleep. "Yes. Usually."

"Three times?"

I cracked open an eye. "Usually only two."

"Okay." Seemingly satisfied, he lay back on the bed, looking at the ceiling.

"Why do you want to know?" I yawned again.

Sam laughed. "I wondered if it was the cock ring. Or me. Or if you were just lucky."

"I don't think luck has anything to do with a woman's orgasm." I reached to my nightstand for a ponytail holder to pull my hair back again for sleep. "I know how to make myself come, but that didn't happen by luck. It took practice."

This perked him up. "How much practice?"

I pulled the covers up over both of us and wriggled down into my pillow. "I've been masturbating since I was in junior high. You figure it out."

Sam looked at me. "I've never been with a woman who admitted she jerked off."

"Sam. Women don't jerk off."

"Rub off. Whatever."

"Well, then you've either been with a lot of liars or some very uptight chicks." Yawning again, I reached to turn out the light.

In darkness it took my eyes a few moments to adjust before the faint light from the street lamp began illuminating the room. The light didn't shine directly in my window, so nothing was clear. Just bumps and lumps. The same old room, yet different with Sam beside me.

"I haven't been with a lot of women at all." Sam shifted onto his side. He kissed my shoulder and rested his hand on my belly as he drew his legs up, touching my calves with surprisingly icy toes.

I yelped. He laughed. I wiggled around until we could both be comfortable, which put us in a sort of complicated tangle of limbs and blankets. After a few minutes of silence, I asked, "Is that true?"

"About the women?"

I murmured an assent. Next to me, Sam took up a lot of room in my bed. His breath tickled the side of my neck.

"Yes. It's true."

"How come?"

"Are you sure you don't want to ask how many?"

"No." I looked at the ceiling, lit with a stripe of silver. "I don't care how many."

"But you want to know why there weren't more?"

I waited a beat before answering. "Sure."

Sam chuckled again. "It might surprise you to learn that not all women succumb to my persistence, Grace. Only the crazy ones."

I laughed. "Gee, thanks."

"Don't mention it." Sam sighed and shifted his arm, then a leg. "So, you don't care if I sleep here?"

"Do you want to?" I had been thinking of it, actually. How it would be for him to come downstairs in the morning, dressed in rumpled clothes from the day before. "Won't your mom worry?"

"I am a grown-up," he said. "But if you don't want me to, I'll go."

"No." It seemed bitchy not to let him sleep with me after he'd slept with me. "Unless you want to go."

Silence, but for the sound of Sam's breathing. "Maybe I should go."

I sat up and turned on the light. I deliberately avoided looking at the clock, as if not knowing how many hours I had left to sleep would make it feel like more. "Sam…"

"Grace." He sat up against the headboard, the covers pulled low around his hips. "What's up?"

"I'm a little freaked." Until the words blurted out of me, I hadn't known how freaked I was.

A frown furrowed his brow. "Because of me?"

I nodded. He held out his arm and I pillowed my face on his chest. "I'm sorry. It's not you. It's me."

"Uh-oh." Sam pushed me gently so he could look at my face. "This sounds like a three-in-the-morning argument waiting to happen."

"No. I don't want to argue." I shook my head and sighed, then sat next to him with our backs against the headboard. "I think I just have to warn you."

"Oh, boy." Sam scooted over a bit. "When I told you that only the crazy chicks dig me, I wasn't kidding. Are you going to tell me something weird? I mean, weirder than the fact you live in a funeral home?"

He had such a knack of making me laugh, even when my stomach was churning and my eyes felt as if they'd been filled with sand. I didn't want to know if it was really three in the morning, not when I had to be up by seven. "I just think we need to talk about what this is."

"Ah." He returned to my side. "It's *that* sort of three-in-the-morning conversation."

"I don't want you to think I'm some sort of clingy, desperate woman. And I'm not saying this has to be anything. But…I think it is." I'd admitted it. "And I'm not used to that."

He looked at me. "You don't do the boyfriend thing. I got it."

"I don't. I haven't, not for a long time."

His tilting grin tempted me to return it. "But you think you might want to now?"

I bit my lower lip to hold back that return smile but lost out. "I'm just saying that I want us to be up front with each other. That's all. If you're just interested in being fuck-friends, I'm not saying that's out of the question—"

"Hey!" Sam frowned again, turning. "Don't say that!"

I stopped, confused. "Don't say fuck?"

"Fuck," Sam said, and ran a hand through his hair. "No. I mean, don't say that all I want is to be your friend with benefits."

I waited a second or two before continuing. "Well, what do you want?"

Sam got out of bed and I was certain I'd lost him. Why, exactly, I didn't know. I watched him grab up his boxer briefs and put them on, and after a minute I did the same with my pj's. I'd pissed him off somehow, but I couldn't be too surprised. Conversations about what "this" was usually had an element of angst in them.

Sam put his hands on my shoulders to get me to look at him. "What I want," he said slowly, "is to keep doing what we've been doing for the past few months, only with a helluva lot more of what we did for the past few hours."

My heart dropped as my stomach jumped, and both met someplace in the middle with a nearly audible *thunk*. "Okay."

"No." He shook his head. "Not just okay. Okay?"

"O...kay?" I laughed. "Sam, it's very late. We're both tired."

Sam didn't laugh. He pulled me close and kissed me. "I like you a lot, Grace. I like spending time with you, hanging out. I like kissing you. I like touching you."

"I like all those things, too," I told him, half melted already.

"I don't want to be just some guy you sleep with. I don't want to be just some boy toy."

Oh, the irony of that. "Of course not."

Sam nodded, as if my answer had satisfied him. "Good. It's settled."

Nothing seemed settled to me other than my insides had become a tumbled, jumbled mess and I couldn't quite think straight. "It is?"

"Us. This." He waved a hand around the room.

I stared at him. "Us. We're an us?"

Sam got on one knee, my hand clasped in his. "Cuz you're my lady!" he sang. Loud. The next line, too, and the one after that, while I laughed and tried to pull away.

"No! All right! All right, anything you want, just stop singing that song!"

He got up, and up, and up. Long, tall Sam. He kissed me again. "Admit it. You're crazy about me."

"I think I'm just crazy."

Sam scooped me up with a hand beneath my knees and the other behind my shoulders and laughed when I yelped. "That would be par for the course. Bed. Now. You and me."

He tossed me onto the bed and followed after with a leap. Onto my ancient, hand-me-down bed. The footboard promptly cracked in half and the mattress hit the floor.

"Well, then," said Sam. "I think that bodes well, doesn't it?"

All I could do was laugh.

I had on a few occasions in college gone to work without enough sleep, but never since graduating had I gone to work with no sleep at all. After breaking my bed, Sam and I had decided breakfast might be in order. Over eggs and toast we'd talked until dawn lit the sky. The conversation was serious but punctuated with laughter and joking as we talked about ourselves. About us.

Sam didn't delve into why I'd avoided boyfriends or ask me about my sexual history, and I avoided asking him the same. We concentrated on a subtle negotiation some people would have found extremely unromantic but I liked because it laid it all out on the table for both of us.

No, we wouldn't see other people. Yes, he could sleep over as long as he brought his own toothbrush. No, we didn't have to see each other every day, but yes, we could if we wanted to.

Sam understood the nature of my job and warned me his wasn't much more predictable. The lessons he gave during the day sometimes got rescheduled and if the opportunity for a gig came up, he needed to be able to take it.

By the time I had to get ready for work I'd passed exhaustion and had started operating on caffeine and determination. When he kissed me goodbye to head off to his mother's house to get ready for his own day, Sam smiled.

"See you later," he told me, and I had no doubt I would.

Unfortunately, that was when all hell decided to break loose.

It wasn't that I'd never had all hell break loose before. Let's face it, when you work in the funeral-home business, all kinds of things can go crazy in a day.

"Shelly? Have you seen... Shelly?"

No Shelly.

No Shelly at her desk, or in the bathroom, or in the small lounge where families waited for me. No Shelly in the parking lot or the chapel, either. I called her name again. I'd seen both her and Jared earlier, each going about their separate tasks. Jared had gone to the basement to work on unpacking some boxes of supplies, but that had been a few hours ago.

I called both their names again. I needed that paperwork before I could get started on Mrs. Grenady, waiting for me in the embalming room. Her family wouldn't be happy if it came time for the service and she wasn't ready.

"Jared? Shelly!"

I heard a soft hum of music from the embalming room, but neither of them were in there. Only Mrs. Grenady, and she wasn't able to tell me if she'd seen my office manager and my intern. The music, though, was something Jared would have chosen. I turned it off to listen.

The room where I'd heard Sam playing his guitar was just down the hall, and the door to it was closed. I knocked, but nobody answered. I didn't have anyone scheduled to be waiting in it, but I suspected it wasn't empty.

"Shelly?"

I opened the door and closed it again just as quickly, my eyes shut and face burning.

Oh. God.

That was a sight that would linger, and not in a good way. Seeing Jared and Shelly in flagrante delicto was sort of like catching my brother beating off to *Hot Juggz* magazine. Embarrassing and more than a little disturbing.

I was at the end of the hall when the door opened and Jared came out. Fully dressed, thank heavens, though his hair and shirt both could've used a good brushing. He'd misbuttoned but managed to tuck it into his belt. He had forgotten, though, to zip up his fly.

"Grace, I– We–"

I held up a hand. "Not interested."

"But wait!"

His pleading tone gave me pause, though I didn't turn. I had no desire to catch another glimpse of Jared's junk. "Think carefully about what you say, Jared. I'm not in the mood to be generous."

"I know. But it wasn't what you think. And it's not Shelly's fault."

"That's not true!"

I almost turned at Shelly's voice, but at the last minute kept myself staring at the door to the embalming room. I had even less desire to see Shelly's goods. "Both of you get dressed. Fully dressed! And come upstairs."

Silence met my proclamation and I imagined them exchanging looks. Dammit, I hated playing the Gorgon, but for the love of all that was holy…in the funeral home? At work? I'd had sex in some risqué places, but never at my job!

Though I had had some screaming-hot loving in the funeral home, I thought with a grin as I left them to prepare themselves. The grin had faded by the time they got up to my office. Jared looked sheepish, but Shelly had that stubborn tilt to her chin.

I'd found the paperwork by then, but that didn't make me inclined to be forgiving. Their behavior was out of control, and I was beyond tired. I gave them each a glare. Jared cut his eyes from mine, but Shelly took that time to take his hand. She linked their fingers, and he looked down at their hands with a grateful expression.

"I told you before not to let this thing get in the way of work or to affect my business." I stared at Shelly.

She tipped her chin up a bit farther. "It wasn't getting in the way of work."

Jared was smart enough not to make excuses. "I'm sorry. It won't happen again. But it wasn't Shelly's fault."

"Stop saying that!" she snapped, and dropped his hand. She looked at me. "Don't listen to him."

"So, it was your fault?" I was careful not to yawn in front of them, though my mouth desperately wanted to stretch open.

"That's not what I meant. I meant, there's no fault."

"Shelly, are you seriously telling me that fucking Jared in the basement of my funeral home while you're both supposed to be working is appropriate?"

We stared each other down, and damned if she didn't give me even more attitude.

"We got a little carried away, but we weren't…doing what you said!" There came the blush, painting twin circles high on her cheeks.

"You would've been if I hadn't walked in just then."

"If you hadn't walked in just then," Shelly snapped, "you'd never have known!"

Jared and I both gaped at her. I recovered first. "Oh, no, you did *not* just try and make this somehow my fault."

Shelly crossed her arms and said nothing. What had happened to the shy girl who baked me cookies and cried when my dad looked at her the wrong way? I eyed Jared. He must have a magic wand in his pants, and not one for making good spells. He'd turned Shelly into a witch.

He didn't seem to have expected the change in her, either. "Shelly!"

Then the waterworks started, and Shelly fled my office, slamming the door behind her. Jared and I stared at each other until he sat in one of the chairs in front of my desk. He rubbed his face with a sigh.

"I'm sorry," he said again. "It just got out of control."

"Jared, I can't have this sort of thing going on. You know that." I sighed, too. I wanted a cup of coffee. A vodka. A nap.

"I know. But she told me she broke up with Duane, and I kissed her, and it just went on from there." He looked up at me. "Were you ever doing something that you knew was going to get you into trouble even when you were doing it, but you couldn't stop yourself?"

"Um…yes. I have. But not," I said sternly, "at work!"

Jared gave me a small smile. "It won't happen again."

"It better not. And you're lucky I'm too tired and desperate for help around here, or I'd fire you both."

He smiled again as if he knew I didn't mean it and got up. "Thanks, Grace. I'd better go check on her."

"Tell Miss Attitude she'd better get back to work pronto." I was too tired to put much force behind the threat. "And we need to take care of Mrs. Grenady, so be back in five minutes or I'll kick your butt."

Jared saluted. "Yes, ma'am."

God. I was *so* not a ma'am, but whatever. "Go!"

We spent the next few hours actually working. Jared was bubbling with enthusiasm about music, about the upcoming weekend, about what he was going to have for dinner. He was so caught up in his own little love bubble he shouldn't have noticed mine, but he must've caught sight of my own secret smiles because he pinned me like a wrestler on the Friday-night smackdown.

"So, who is he?" Jared ran water in the sink and started tidying the equipment we'd used in Mrs. Grenady's preparation.

"Don't forget we need to order some more of that cleaning fluid." I wasn't pretending I didn't hear him. I was deliberately not answering.

"Yes, boss. But c'mon. You've got a grin on your face and you otherwise look like crap." Jared stepped in front of me so I had to look up at him. "Hey, I don't think we have any secrets from each other anymore."

I raised a brow. "I hardly think what I saw this morning puts you on a 'need-to-know' basis about my private life."

Jared grinned. "Come on."

I grinned, too, giddy from lack of sleep and the sheer emotional roller-coaster ride I was on. "It's Sam."

It was Jared's turn to raise a brow. "Sam Stewart? Dude with the earring?"

"Yes."

"The one who brought Chinese?"

"Same Sam."

Jared let out a low whistle. "Same guy whose dad we took care of?"

"Yes, Jared. Is that a problem?" I glared, again without strength. "I need some coffee."

Together we transported Mrs. Grenady up to the chapel to await the service with her family later that afternoon. Jared didn't continue poking me about Sam, but when I'd poured us both coffee and given him a mug, he grinned again. I ignored him this time and told Shelly to order more cleaning fluid. She, apparently, wasn't speaking to me, but she sniffed and flipped open the supply catalog.

"Sam Stewart," Jared said. "Wow."

"What's wrong with Sam?" I snapped.

Shelly looked up. "Grace is going out with Sam?"

"None of your business!"

"She is," Jared said.

"You'd think she'd be a little more understanding then," Shelly muttered.

I chose to ignore her. I didn't really want to fire her. Who'd make me cookies?

"I think it's about time." Jared nodded. Suddenly an expert.

"Are you two finished with the commentary?" I glared at them both.

Shelly shrugged and picked up the phone to take an order. Jared laughed and said he had to finish cleaning up the embalming room. I was taking my coffee to sit in my office and maybe steal a power nap, when the back door opened and Hannah came in with the kids in tow.

Hannah never came here. It was something of a tradition, if not a joke, that my sister never came to the funeral home where she'd lived until she was four. Now she hustled in, a hand wrapped firmly around each of her children's wrists.

"I need you to watch the kids for half an hour until Mom can get here to pick them up." Hannah didn't waste any time.

Two small bodies buffeted me with jostling hugs.

"Bother!" Melanie said in a high-pitched voice, imitating an Internet cartoon I'd shown them once while baby-sitting. "Bother, bother!"

I unstuck my niece and nephew and told them to go into my office and find the candy jar, a command they followed willingly and at once. I looked at my sister.

Hannah wore a pair of neat black slacks and a sky-blue, button-down blouse. She wore makeup and had done her hair. There wasn't anything showy or flashy about her. There never was. Nevertheless, I could tell she'd made more of an effort than seemed normal.

"Where are you going?" I asked, suspicious.

"I have an appointment. Mom will come for them in half an hour. I have to go."

"Hannah, wait!"

She did, just barely. Her shoulders hunched and she turned, every line of her body so tense she appeared to be hovering. "I'm going to be late, Grace! C'mon, can't you just do this for me?"

The way she said it, as if I never agreed to watch them, set my teeth on edge. "This isn't a preschool! It's my business! I have to work."

"The kids don't mind it here. Let them watch TV or something." Hannah stared right at me, neither to one side or the other, as if she was afraid she might accidentally catch sight of a corpse. "Half an hour."

With that, before I could protest, she ducked out the door, leaving me to stare after her with my mouth open.

"You catching flies?" Jared had just come up from the basement.

I closed my mouth and mumbled something as I went

to my office to make sure Melanie and Simon hadn't added it to the path of their worldwide destruction. I could entertain them for half an hour, no problem. I'd stick them in front of the cartoon channel if I had to. The more concerning question in my mind was, what was so important to my sister that she'd come to the funeral home to drop them off? What sort of appointment would be so important?

It hit me like a snow shovel to the back of the head. So obvious I couldn't believe I hadn't noticed it before. So preposterous it had to be true.

Hannah was having an affair.

Chapter
17

$\mathcal{I}$ wasn't sure what to do about Hannah, so I didn't do anything. My mom came to pick them up in an hour instead of thirty minutes, but the kids had occupied themselves with cartoons and candy and I wasn't called away to pick up a body or oversee any burials. I didn't mention my concern to my mom. After all, what would I have said? I thought about it, though, as the days passed.

Contrary to what our Puritan heritage teaches us, I'm not convinced monogamy is the natural resting state of human sexuality. I don't think people are wired to attach themselves to one another forever and ever, amen. I think it can be done successfully, sure, and I understand the appeal of being secure in your emotional connections, knowing your partner isn't expending his or her emotional limit on someone else. I even think it's better for most people to convince themselves monogamy is what they prefer, that there's something to be said about a little self-delusion now and again. But I don't think monogamy is easy or natural, and I think most people spend too much time worried about their spouse or partner cheating on them.

I'd sort of always looked at my sister's life as one more example why I was glad to stay single, but since meeting Sam my mind had begun changing. It seemed like overnight I'd ended up with a guy who wasn't a hired companion or a one-night stand. A boyfriend. Like a late-night B movie, the thought of Sam Stewart being my boyfriend alternately thrilled and chilled me. One minute I couldn't stop grinning. The next I broke out in a cold sweat, wondering what the hell I'd gotten myself into.

Sam made it so easy. I'd watched my friends and listened to them complain for years about boys who didn't give a hint about how they felt. I never had to doubt with Sam. Not that he declared his undying love. We didn't use that word. For months we'd been building a friendship, though, and now we'd added the sex—or returned to the sex, as Sam was sometimes fond of pointing out—Sam wasn't shy about showing affection. He kissed and hugged me no matter who was around and held my hand whenever it was feasible. He brought me flowers and left me notes on the mornings he spent the night with me and left to go to his teaching.

Those mornings were becoming more and more frequent. Sleeping over at his place was out of the question. I'd met his mom, a woman so tiny it was hard to believe she'd birthed such a gargantuan son. Dotty Stewart was a sweetheart. She'd embraced Elle as if she were her own daughter, so I wasn't particularly worried that she didn't like me. We didn't see much of her, though. Dotty grieved by keeping herself busy with friends and her sisters. She usually wasn't home the few times I'd stopped by to see Sam.

Though Sam had met Jared and Shelly and a few of my friends whom we'd bumped into at the movies or restaurants, he hadn't met my family. Not that he was a secret. A town like Annville doesn't really allow them. Not when Mrs. Zook who lives next door notices the same "strange" car parked overnight in the lot more than once or twice a week. The days of the party line are gone, but now we have e-mail and instant messaging, and people still gossip when they meet up with each other at the grocery store.

I wasn't quite creating a scandal, but Sam was definitely not a secret.

I'm sure it bugged the hell out of my dad that I didn't talk about it, but he'd stopped just "dropping by" the funeral home to check up on me. That was fine with me. I missed the way he sometimes took me to lunch unexpectedly and always treated, but I didn't miss his constant poking into my business, both personal and professional. And I won't deny that I was a bit miffed at the fact that for the first time since I'd taken over full-time from my dad, despite the recent spate of hard luck, the business was growing faster than ever and I couldn't even brag about it to him.

I was going to be able to hire Jared full-time when his internship ended, if I wanted to. I could even afford to take on another intern. Hell, I could have afforded to pay for dates every week instead of once or twice a month, if I wasn't getting all the hot monkey sex I wanted for free.

It was great that business was good, that my marketing efforts were paying off, that the town had started accepting me in my dad's place. It was good to know I was providing a necessary and vital service to people who needed it, and that I was more than decent at it. I was good.

Everything, in fact, was good.

I had a great job, good friends. And finally, surprisingly, a boyfriend who brought me flowers and played love songs for me on his guitar. With the money I was saving by not paying Mrs. Smith's gentlemen, I was even starting to think about finishing the renovations on my apartment.

"But I like it this way," Sam said when I told him. "It's got a certain lackluster chic."

I smacked his arm and reached for the bowl of popcorn he'd been hoarding. With my feet propped comfortably on his lap and my head on the pillows, I had the best of both worlds—a great view of the television and a free foot massage.

"Need I point out to you that at least I have my own place? And my own sheets?" It was sort of a running joke between us. Sam had made no plans to move from his mother's house. He said it was because she needed him there, now that his dad was gone, but I suspected laziness on his part.

"Hey. I had my own place. And I still have my own sheets. They're in storage in New York, that's all."

"For what you're paying to store them in New York, Sammy, you could rent an entire house in Annville."

Sam curled his lip. "I've had my own place, *Gracie*. Let me tell you how much nicer it is living with my mom."

"Why?" I tossed a kernel of popcorn at him. "Because she cooks and cleans up after you?"

He caught the popcorn in his mouth. Talented boy. "You got it."

I liked most everything about Sam except that attitude. I didn't know if he was serious about his reasons for still living with his mother. Maybe he was afraid to leave her alone, despite how well she seemed to have adjusted. Or maybe he couldn't afford to live on his own and was too embarrassed to admit it. It just seemed so at odds with the rest of him, the man I'd come to know who didn't have to be told to wash a dish or put the seat down or even to make the bed; the same one who treated me to dinner without making me feel as if he were buying my company and yet had no problem with me picking up the tab when I offered. It seemed hard for me to believe that he was still squatting in his childhood home because he didn't want to live on his own.

So, typically, I pried.

"Didn't your mom say she was thinking of going on a cruise with your aunt?"

"Yep." Sam crunched more popcorn, his eyes glued to the TV. "Next month."

"How will you manage?" I teased. "Who will do your laundry and pack your lunches?"

The corner of his mouth twitched upward. "Someone who loves me?"

I nudged him with my foot to cover up my reaction. "Your brother?"

Sam looked at me with big puppy-dog eyes. He even fluttered his eyelashes. He pouted, too.

"Don't look at me," I said. "I don't pack lunches."

The lower lip pooched out farther as he leaned over to tickle me. "No? Not even for me?"

"No fair!" I tried to get away, but my desire for the

arches of my feet to be rubbed was my downfall. He'd trapped me effectively with one arm while the other hand meandered around my most sensitive spots and sent me into breathless hysterics. The popcorn was the victim of our wrestling, the bowl tipping off Sam's lap and overturning onto the floor as he pinned me.

God, he was huge.

One hand easily gripped both my wrists above my head as he straddled me, the cushions of my battered couch sinking under our combined weight and his knees trapping my thighs. He played a chord on my ribs and the insanely ticklish spot just above my hipbone, and no matter how wildly I tried to buck him off, I couldn't.

He was breathing hard and I was sipping in gasp after gasp of giggle-infused air. Sam leaned down to put his mouth a breath from mine. Salt and butter painted his lips. It took me a minute to notice he'd stopped tickling, because his kiss left me just as breathless.

Sam was big, but he knew how to cover me without crushing me. How to move down my body with his as he held his weight on an elbow, a knee, a palm. Now he let go of my wrists and tipped my head back with his nose so he could get at my throat and neck. His mouth skimmed the scooped neck of my T-shirt. When his tongue darted out to lick the hollow of my throat, my back arched all on its own. My nipples hardened at once. The spot between my legs began its subtle, familiar pulse.

He returned to my mouth. Sam's kisses were like his songs, different every time he sang them even though the words and the melodies were the same. He had a certain trick he did with his tongue and teeth, a sort of nibbling lick. He used it only once in a while, and each time it was an unexpected change of key in a song you thought you knew. Like John Mayer covering Marilyn Manson. It drove me crazy.

He did it then, and my hips pumped up. My crotch connected with his belt buckle, and I wasn't going to turn that down. I grabbed his ass with both hands and tucked my heels around the backs of his thighs to hold him in place. He only had to move a little bit to give me the delicious pressure I craved.

He knew what I was doing, and smiled through his kisses. He pushed forward, giving me what I wanted though the position had to feel awkward for him. Sam slid his hand beneath my shirt and deftly unhooked my bra. He covered my breast immediately, kneading gently before lightly pinching my nipple to its peak. He did the same to the other, then pushed up on his hand and tugged my T-shirt to my waistband. The thin fabric pulled tight over my breasts and outlined my upright nipples.

"God, I love it when you look like that. I wish you never wore a bra."

The visible evidence of my own arousal turned me on more, too. "I'm sure that would go over well. Here, let me give you a remembrance card and oh, while I'm at it, let me poke out your eyes."

Sam rubbed his hand over the curves and bumps outlined by my shirt. With the fabric barrier, his muffled touch became a tease. "I'd love it. At least don't wear one when we're alone. Wear tight T-shirts and no bra, just for me."

"For you?" I pretended to think, though with his mouth and hands and belt pressing against me in all sorts of delicious places, my mind had become nothing but a swirl of pleasure. "You might be able to convince me."

"Yeah? How?" Sam's lips tugged a cloth-covered nipple.

I reached between us to cup him through his jeans. "Give me this whenever I want it."

Heat hit my fingers even through the denim. Sam pushed his erection into my palm. "Deal. What do I have to do to get you to pack my lunch?"

I laughed. "Forget it."

"How about one day for every orgasm?"

"Orgasms are not bargaining chips, Sam." Yet I was smiling as I said it, because he'd begun working his way down my body to the hem of my shirt and pulling it up with his teeth to get to the soft flesh beneath.

"What's the most number of times you've ever come?"

"With someone else?"

He stopped and got up on his hands to look at me. "You're killing me, here. Yes, with someone else. I know you can go off like a rocket ship a hundred times in a row when it's you and your bullet. Stop giving me a complex."

"Sorry."

"You don't sound sorry. You sound smug."

I'm sure I meant to protest, but just then Sam unbuttoned my jeans with his teeth and I lost my train of thought. He slid his hands under my ass to lift me up enough that he could slide off my jeans. My panties came down, too, everything tangling with my socks around my ankles. I helped him tug them off and laughed at the face he made as he tried to figure out the tangle of material.

"Why are women's clothes so complicated?" he grumbled from his place at my feet. He didn't wait for an answer before tossing my clothes to the floor.

I was bare from the waist down and he was fully dressed. Unacceptable. "Take yours off."

Sam stood and watched as I lifted my shirt off over my head and threw it to add to the pile on the floor. Beneath my skin, the couch cushions were nubbled rough. I shifted, crooking my finger. "C'mon, Sammy. Naked."

"It's Sam," he protested, but his fingers had already worked open the buttons on his shirt.

Sam shrugged out of his shirt and undid his belt and the zipper. His jeans gaped open but the hem of his T-shirt hung down too far. He bent and pulled off his socks, one at a time, and I knew he was deliberately teasing me. A sexy bump-and-grind striptease would have made me giggle. Sam's deliberately slow removal of each layer of his clothes was made more erotic by its pure masculinity and normality. I wasn't watching some rentboy tantalize with glimpses of flesh. I was watching Sam strip down to all his naked glory as if it was the most natural thing in the world for him to do in front of me.

"God bless denim," I murmured, watching the way his belly tightened when he pulled his T-shirt off over his head. "Where do you find jeans that long, anyway?"

"Big and Tall." Sam grinned and tucked a thumb into the waistband, dipping it just low enough for me to see the sleek dark tuft of his pubic hair.

An incoherent noise slipped from my throat. He pushed his jeans a little lower, and the briefs he wore beneath slid, too. Down, down, down each long leg the material moved until at last he stood and kicked off the jeans. Naked at last, a hand on his cock as it grew.

"Are you going to fuck me on my couch?" I scooted back onto the pillows.

"Nope." Sam's penis was getting harder as I watched.

"No?" Confused, I swung my legs around to put my feet on the floor.

Sam stopped me before I could stand. "No. I'm not going to fuck you on the couch. I'm going to go down on you on the couch. Sit back."

I did, voiceless. Sam kissed my mouth as his hand went between my legs, priming me. He didn't waste time kissing down my body or lingering on my thighs. He went straight from my mouth to between my legs, parting me with his thumbs to suck gently on my clit.

The electric, sudden shock of it forced another inarticulate noise from me. I arched instinctively before I could force myself to still, but I'd already wrapped my fingers in Sam's thick, dark hair. I wanted to look down, to see him there between my legs, but pleasure forced my eyes to close as it parted my mouth in a silent sigh.

Sam paused with a shuddering sigh to murmur something sweet, something sexy, something like, "Oh, fuck, you taste good." Something that said in the context of anything but sex would sound fake, but I didn't doubt he meant it.

He pushed my legs open wider and used the flat of his tongue in smooth, even strokes. The pressure, the heat, the wetness of his mouth were perfect. He didn't pinpoint the sensitive bead of my clit or drill me with his tongue. Instead he kept the pressure steady and constant, just above my clit, using my own shifting flesh to further arouse me. White-hot pleasure balled in my gut and burst.

I came the first time.

Sam withdrew, but not far. His breath still caressed me, but now he slid a finger inside me before I had time to do more than gasp and shudder with my orgasm. He curved it and found the small, sensitive spot just behind my pubic bone. I'd experimented with my G-spot before and never found it particularly exciting. Too often it distracted me from climax, or worse, made me feel like I had to pee. But Sam didn't rub me there, just pressed gently in time to the small, pointed flutters of his tongue.

Oh, fuck, he did the nibbling-lick thing. I'd thought it was good on my mouth. On my cunt it was utopia. He licked, nibbled and pressed.

I came again, hard on the heels of the first time. I drew in a deep breath, hard, and opened my eyes. He wasn't looking at me. He was still kissing my cunt, clenching tight around his finger. I blinked, streamers of red dancing in my vision and fading as the waves of my orgasm abated.

"God," I said. "Sam—"

"Shh…"

He didn't lick me. Didn't nibble, or push, or press inside me. Sam put his mouth on me, not even kissing. Just touching me with his lips and breath. His finger was still inside me, but he wasn't moving it.

"I like to feel the way you move when you come," he said, his lips forming the words the only motion he made. "I can still feel it. You're still beating."

I was, no longer in the rapid-fire burst of contractions my body made during climax, but an occasional slow throb. The spaces between each stretched out. I got my breath back. Sam didn't move. I thought about shifting, but was too sated for the moment to do anything but recover. After a second he licked me again. Different this time. Softer, but not hesitant. His finger moved, too, twisting.

"Sam, I can't." My protest was weak, and I didn't try too hard to move away. From him.

He said nothing, just continued what he was doing. I knew my body well enough. Its limits. Yes, I'd made myself come three times in a row and once a memorable four, but I'd been watching a Justin Ross marathon and had been at the point in my cycle when everything turned me on. Even then it had been hard work, the final climax more like an afterthought than a real orgasm.

"Sam—"

"Shh."

I didn't protest again. What he was doing felt good, even if he wasn't going to get me off doing it, and if it made him happy, who was I to complain? I'd have been happy to return the favor or even finish by making love to him without trying to come myself, but I'd also learned not to struggle too hard against Sam's persistence.

I thought for sure he'd get tired, or too horny to wait, but he kept going. Long after I'd have given up, Sam licked and kissed and stroked me. He used his mouth and hands, but he used his words, too. Sam was a talker. The things he said should've sounded ridiculous, but coupled with the gentle seduction of his lips and tongue they only sounded beautiful.

I love the way you taste. I love the way you sound. I love the way you move. I love the way you say my name, just like that.

Sam.

I love you.

And I, selfishly caught up in the ecstasy he was giving me, didn't have to say anything. I only had to burst apart.

Sometime after that I took him to my bed and made love to him for too short a time. I wanted it to last, but didn't have the heart to torture him after he'd been so generous. He closed his eyes when he came and I watched his face and marveled at how this had all happened.

Later, in the dark, Sam turned his back to me and said so quietly I almost didn't hear, "It's because it's easier to pretend."

"What is, baby?" My voice sounded as sleepy as his had, but my eyes had flown open wide and my heart pounded.

"Staying at my mom's. At night, in that room, it's easy to pretend I'm a kid again and my dad's still alive."

I didn't know what to say to that, so I did what I could. I spooned myself along his back, my arm around his waist a comfort I wasn't sure he wanted. His shoulder beneath my lips rose and fell with his sigh.

I spend my life helping people mourn, and yet I don't believe I've seen grief in all its forms. Sorrow, like songs, is never the same.

"He never saw me play," Sam said. "He told me if I went to New York to try and make it, I'd fail. We fought about it. I didn't come home for a long time, and when I did, he never asked me how I was doing. Not one fucking time, Grace. I sent the write-ups I got in the indie papers. Not one fucking time."

The muscles of his arm tensed, bunched. He drew his legs up and trapped my arm between his knees and belly. He curled over himself, a big man making himself small.

"And then he died, the fucker." Sam's voice broke. "And I was still the bad son, the one who didn't come to see him. But it wasn't because I was still mad, Grace."

Sometimes people don't need you to answer them. They only need you to help them say what they need to say.

"Why, then?"

"I didn't want him to still think I was a failure. I didn't want my dad to die thinking I was a failure. But you know what? He did anyway. He fucking died, and I fucked up again. Now my mom thinks I suck. So does my brother. So do I. Fuck. Fuck!"

His body jerked, his voice muffling into the pillow. His shoulders twitched rhythmically, and my throat got tight in sympathy.

"Sam."

He saved me from trying to find the right words by turning and burying his face against me. Hot tears wet my skin as he clutched me. I stroked his hair over and over as he gritted back sobs, his entire body tense and tight. When at last he relaxed, long limbs going slack and breathing slow and even, I kissed the top of his head.

"You're going to be okay."

I'd thought he was asleep, but his arms tightened around me at once. "Am I?"

"Yes, Sam. You are."

He'd said he loved me, and I hadn't. I sort of thought that would change things, but it didn't. Not outwardly. Inside I continued to marvel at how easy it had become to imagine a life spent with Sam. How I could see him with gray in his hair and lines around his eyes. How I could envision children with his dark hair and my light eyes.

I didn't share this with anyone, of course. I barely wanted to think about it myself, the old fears easily resurfacing every time I had to face a grief-stricken widow who moaned she didn't know how she'd be able to go on. Yet it was easier now to see the women and men who spoke with joy-tinged voices about the good times. The memories. Of how much richer their lives had been for having loved. How loss couldn't take away any of those memories, and how they regretted nothing.

Shelly had started speaking to me again, though not in the same chatty way she'd used to. She'd changed her hair. Her clothes, too. She spoke with more confidence to the clients. Before, she'd have had to ask me several times about tasks she knew how to perform, simply for the assurance she was doing them right. Now she didn't ask. It was a relief, sort of, not to have to babysit her so much. It freed up a lot of my time. But since I knew it was because she was refusing to talk to me and not solely because of some personal epiphany for her, I couldn't quite enjoy the changes as much.

Nearing the end of his internship, Jared had received job offers from a couple other funeral homes in the area. It surprised me that he'd told me about them. He told me he was thinking about it, and we left it at that. I wanted to beg him to stay, the luxury of having help not one I wanted to relinquish, but I wouldn't have blamed him for taking a job with someone who could pay him more and give him better hours.

Jared's possible departure prompted me to revisit my budget, though. I wouldn't have admitted it to him, but I actually missed my dad's head for finances. I had more money in my personal account than ever and could have used some advice on how to invest it. Looking back over my accounts, I couldn't believe how much I'd spent on Mrs. Smith's gentlemen…yet I didn't regret a cent.

A rap on the door pulled my attention from my fond remembrance of the way I'd burned through five hundred dollars on a night filled with feathers and chocolate body paint. I looked up. "Shelly?"

She came into the office without waiting for me to gesture, and shut the door behind her. My brows lifted as she took a seat. On her lap she had a folder, and my heart sunk. She was going to give her notice. I knew it.

"Grace, I want to talk to you about Jared."

I closed my accounts and gave Shelly my full attention. "What about him?"

Shelly cleared her throat and I caught a glimpse of the girl who'd first come to work for me. "I love him."

"Good for you. For you both." I wasn't sure what Shelly wanted me to say. Her declaration wasn't exactly news.

"We want to get married."

"Congratulations." I offered my kudos with caution. "That's good news."

A small smile cracked Shelly's aloof facade. "I'm so happy!"

"Uh-huh. How'd Duane take it?"

A pained look crossed Shelly's face. "He won't believe me."

This floored me for a second. "What do you mean, he won't believe you?"

"He says he doesn't believe I won't come back to him when I'm tired of Jared."

"Huh." Frankly, I didn't see what was so fantastically bright and shiny about Shelly that would make Duane want to hang on to her after she'd cheated on him, but I was willing to admit my opinion of her was slightly colored by her recent spate of bitchiness toward me. "I guess he'll figure it out eventually."

"I guess. But that's not what I want to talk to you about." Shelly held up a folder. "These are the other offers Jared's been getting. One from Rohrbach. One from Kindt and Spencer."

My biggest rivals, if you could say there was such a thing. I'd gone to mortuary school with Steve Rohrbach, who'd taken over the business from an uncle. Kindt had bought the former Spencer Brothers about five years ago in an attempt to expand his family's business. Both operated in towns next to mine.

"Jared told me he'd gotten a few other offers. It's time he started making decisions. Especially if he wants to get married."

Jared, married to Shelly. A few months ago I'd have laughed at the thought. Now it only made me feel sort of moodily envious and annoyed I felt that way.

"Yes." She nodded. "Well, I want him to stay here. With you."

"You do?" I sat back in my chair. "I'd have thought you'd be encouraging him to go someplace else."

Shelly looked faintly ashamed. "I want to stay here, too. He can get more money some other place, but you need him more. And you're going to make this place a success. I know it."

"I thought I already was a success."

She shook her head. "No. I mean…you're going to really be a success. People like you. I hear people talking about how nice it is here. Especially now that Miss Grace Frawley looks like she's going to settle down."

"Oh, is that so? Who's saying that?" I tapped my fingers on the desk rapidly.

Shelly shrugged with a small smile. "You know how people are. Never happy unless they can tell tales."

"Shelly, are you spreading rumors about me?" I demanded, leaning forward.

Shelly's smile grew. "Is it a rumor if it's true?"

I frowned. "Where exactly are you going with this? Because right now I'm not all that thrilled with you blabbing my business to the world."

Shelly nodded again, hastily. "Frawley and Sons is doing so well, and I know it's going to keep doing well. I like it here. I like how you run things. Jared does, too. We want to stay here."

"I told Jared what I could offer him. He knows I'd love for him to stay on, Shelly. But I can't give him more money right now."

"I know. But I'd like to propose something else."

My head throbbed. "Would you please get to the point? Are you going to keep me in cookies for life, or what?"

"I thought you didn't like cookies."

"Shelly!"

"I want you to make Jared a partner."

"Oh, Shelly." I sighed. "What?"

She outlined quickly her plan, that Jared would become a partner in the business in return for bonuses based on business performance.

"How much would it take?"

I named an exorbitant sum, just to watch her cringe. She didn't.

"Would you take it from our paychecks?"

"You're insane! Why would I want to take Jared on as a partner instead of as an employee? This business has been in my family for a long time."

"Do you plan on having kids?"

That set me back since I'd been musing on it earlier that morning. "I don't know. What does that have to do with anything?"

"If you don't plan on having any kids, who's going to take over the business when you die?"

"Melanie or Simon."

Shelly snorted. "What happens if neither of them want it?"

"You're making my head hurt."

She smiled. "If you did want to have kids, you know, it

wouldn't be hard to make arrangements for them to take over the partnership."

"Geez, Shelly. You're a shark." I had to admire her, just a little bit. "What does Jared have to say about all this?"

I'd caught her. "I haven't actually asked him."

"Shelly, Shelly, Shelly." I leaned back in my chair and tossed my hands in the air. "Then why come to me?"

"I had to know if you would consider the idea before I brought it up to him. I wouldn't want to get him all pumped up only to have you shoot him down."

I stared at her. "Damn, you've changed."

She simpered. "Is that a good thing?"

"I don't know," I answered honestly. "Part of me misses the sweet, naive Shelly who wore Peter Pan collars and didn't screw her boyfriend in my lounge."

She snorted delicately. "Part of me misses the Grace who left the office whenever she had the chance and didn't pay so much attention to my business."

I snorted far less delicately. "I'll think about it, okay? That's not something I can decide all at once."

"Fair enough." She stood and held up the folder. "I can leave this if you want."

"I don't need it. If I'm going to offer him a partnership, it won't be based on what someone else thinks he's worth."

Shelly stared a moment, then nodded. "Good. Because Jared's worth a lot."

"I know he is, Shelly."

She paused in the doorway to stick her head back in. "Not that you care what I think, but so's Sam."

I knew that, too.

I tossed around the idea of making Jared a partner, but the idea was too overwhelming to think about all at once. I'd worked hard to build up my business and make improvements. A partner would mean I'd have help to share the burdens, but would also have to share the decisions.

I was just getting used to the idea of having a romantic partner. I wasn't sure I was ready to take on a business partner, too, no matter how much I liked and respected Jared. The only person I could really count on to help me decide was my dad, and I was pretty sure he'd blow a gasket at the mere suggestion.

It was almost enough to make me offer Jared the partnership right away.

Chapter 18

$\mathscr{S}$am greeted me with a kiss that made the whole day better, and it hadn't been so bad to start. "How's tricks?"

I filled him in on the whole story as he set up the stage the way he liked it. He'd been the regular "wallpaper" on Thursday nights at the Firehouse now for a couple months, and the owner liked him enough to offer him an open-ended contract. I didn't make it to hear him play every Thursday, but I went as often as I could.

"Can you grab me a beer?" Sam adjusted his chair the way he liked it, just under the single spotlight. He was an acoustic player and didn't need to do much preparation, but he had an almost obsessive ritual about how to set everything up.

Including beer. I brought him one, though, and one for myself. I didn't ask him how many he'd already had, though his kiss had tasted of hops and barley. He finished the one I'd brought in record time and gestured at the bartender for another.

"You're going to drink your entire paycheck." I meant

to tease, but Sam shot me a look that hovered on the edge
of being a glare.

"It's part of my paycheck," he said.

"Sorry." The apology tasted bad. I don't have a problem saying I'm sorry when I should, but it rankles when I
didn't do anything wrong.

Sam shrugged and went back to adjusting the height of
his microphone. The doors would open for dinner in
about half an hour and he was scheduled to play for the
night, starting at eight. We had an hour and a half to spend
together before he had to work. I thought we might wan-
der down to one of the other places along Second Street
and grab something to eat, but Sam had other plans.

"Come in the backroom with me." He wiggled his eyebrows.

I glanced at the backroom, which stored extra tables and
chairs and various restaurant junk. "Uh-huh. I don't think so."

"C'mon." He took my hand and kissed the palm. "It'll
be quick."

"Yeah, that's what I'm afraid of." I tugged my hand
away and looked around, certain the bartender was eaves-
dropping. "Quick is good for you. Not so much for me."

"What are you talking about?" He leaned in to nibble
on my ear. "You're like a bottle rocket."

I laughed, ducking away from his tickling touch. "I'm
not a machine."

"So, you don't want to do it because you're afraid you
won't get off?" He was frowning again. "Fine. Forget it."

This was unlike the persistent but charming Sam I knew.
"Sam, this isn't the place, you know? Later."

He shrugged, the line of his shoulders angry as he gave me his back. "Sure. Whatever."

Oh, no, he was *not* giving me attitude because I wouldn't fuck him in the backroom of a public place. "Hey."

Still frowning, he turned. "Let me finish this up and we'll go do what you want to do."

"What's with the bitchface?" I asked, hands on my hips. "C'mon, Sam, if you're mad, just tell me."

We stared at each other for a minute until he softened and pulled me closer for a kiss. "I'm not mad. Just a little nervous."

"About what? Playing?" Mollified, I looked at the stage. "You've done it a thousand times."

"Yeah. And I get nervous every time." Sam shrugged and kissed me again, then finished off his beer. He took the empties to the bar and brought back another. "Did you want one?"

"No." I watched him sip at his. "Are you really nervous?"

He shrugged without looking at me. I sat next to him on the stage as we both drank our bottles. He finished his third as I drained my first and then stood and offered me a hand up.

"C'mon. Let's hit the Sandwich Man or something," he said. "Unless you want to eat here."

I liked the food at the Firehouse, but not so much the prices. "A sandwich is fine."

At the Sandwich Man, Sam dug into a steak sandwich and I had a tuna sub. He seemed in a better mood than he had earlier, but I couldn't stop thinking it had very nearly been our first fight. A milestone, one I wasn't really that jazzed about reaching, but one that seemed significant nevertheless. I made sure to hold his hand extra tight on the walk back to the Firehouse, and to kiss him with extra passion before we went inside.

"What was that for?" Sam asked, eyes bright.

"So you won't be nervous."

He smiled and kissed me. "Thanks, honey."

The endearment gave me giddy shivers up and down. "You're going to be great tonight."

Sam waggled his brows and touched the tip of my nose with his finger. "I'll do my best."

"I meant inside." I swatted him.

"There, too."

He hugged me tight. With my face pressed against the front of his coat, a button scratching and the smell of him filling my senses, I wanted to cry from a rush of sudden emotion. I loved him. I loved this man, Sam, who played the guitar and had Seven League legs and who made me laugh.

Sam kissed the top of my head. "Gotta go in. Clap for me."

"I always do."

Together, we went upstairs where Sam took the stage to a lot of clapping that didn't come from me. Not wanting to take up an entire table to myself, I found a place at the bar where I nursed a beer. Sam had another, I saw, from which he sipped from time to time.

About half an hour after he'd started playing, someone tapped my shoulder. The crowd had grown and I'd had eyes only for Sam, so I hadn't noticed anyone standing so close to me. The tap startled me, but when I saw who'd done it, I broke into a grin.

"Jack!"

I got off my stool to hug him and step back to look him over. He looked good, but then, could Jack ever look bad? A few seconds too late, I noticed he wasn't alone, but the girl with him wasn't glaring at me. She held out her hand, instead, and we shook.

"Sarah," she introduced herself.

I recognized her, of course. The blue hair and the metal in her face weren't hard to forget. She was the girl who'd been talking to Jack the time we'd been here together. I gave him a look, and he responded by putting his arm around her shoulders. Sarah beamed, her hand going into Jack's back pocket.

"I started school," Jack said. "Full-time."

"Good for you," I said sincerely.

I heard Sam saying something onstage, and laughter, but I'd missed most of it.

"See? She is ignoring me."

I heard that and turned to see most of the audience looking at me. Embarrassed, I gave a little wave and did my best to send Sam a mental vibe to stop talking about me. He must have got it, because he started plucking a new song, leaving me to wonder what exactly I'd missed that had made everyone look at me.

Sarah invited me to join her and Jack at their table, and though I hesitated, she insisted. There didn't seem a graceful way to refuse, so I ended up sitting with them. Jack left to use the restroom, and I waited for awkwardness to fall over us.

Sarah wasn't awkward. "I think it's great you're cool with talking to him," she said cheerfully, if a bit out of left field.

"Why wouldn't I be?"

She laughed. "Well, you'd think someone who'd had a dude's dick in her mouth wouldn't be all freaked about saying hi to him in a bar, but you'd be surprised. And they sort of act like 'how dare he be here' when hey, here's a free country and it's not his fault they're embarrassed by what they did."

The stream of words left little room for a reply, but I laughed. "Um…"

Sarah laughed, too. "It's cool. I just thought it was nice you seemed happy to see him."

"I was happy to see him. I like Jack very much." I drank some beer.

Sarah nodded. "Yeah. Me, too."

We smiled at each other.

"He told me you told him to ask me out," she said after a second. "So…thanks."

"You're welcome." The conversation was a little surreal, and not because of the alcohol.

Sarah lifted both hands to give me devil horns with her fingers. "Also, thanks for, like, teaching him manners and stuff. I've known Jack a long time and he's positively suave now. It's awesome. You rock."

"It was my pleasure, really."

Sarah tipped her head back in raucous laughter. "Oh, I believe that!"

We laughed together until Jack came back to the table and we tried to stop, but a look at each other sent us into gales of giggles again. Jack just shook his head and sat between us.

Sam's singing sounded a little hoarse, but that didn't stop the crowd from loving him. He played some covers and a few originals, all songs I'd heard him play half a dozen times. It wasn't that I was ignoring him. It was just that…well…talking with Jack and Sarah was fun, and Sam's music was in the background.

Before I knew it, though, he was finishing up and it was time to go. Jack and Sarah both hugged me goodbye at the same time, making a sandwich until I shooed them both off, laughing. They left, and I waited for Sam to finish putting away his guitar.

I was sitting at the bar again when he came over to me. He gestured for a beer, but I put out a hand to keep him from taking the bottle. "You have to drive."

Sam lifted my fingers from his wrist and took up the bottle. "I'm fine. Let me finish this last one and we'll go. It's late."

It was late, and the sort of night I suspected would end in me getting a death call in the wee hours simply because I hadn't gone to bed at a normal time. That was often the way it worked. Still, Sam's attitude concerned me.

"I think you shouldn't, Sam."

"Well," Sam said. "Too bad you're not me."

I blinked and took my hand away. Took my entire body away, as a matter of fact, creating a physical gap between us on the bar stools. Sam hunched with his elbows on the bar and lifted his beer to his mouth.

"How many have you had?"

He didn't look at me. He didn't answer, either. I waited, but he said nothing, ignoring me. A dozen responses to his silence filtered through my mind, but none of them seemed worth the scene. Instead, I got up and put some money on the bar to cover my bill and a tip, and I walked away.

Sam caught up to me on the sidewalk outside. I'd pulled up the collar of my coat against a brisk late-September breeze, but Sam had no coat. He shivered and bumped my leg with his guitar case. It didn't hurt, but I stepped aside with a pointed look.

"Am I coming over?" he asked.

"I don't know," I answered coolly. "Are you?"

"If you want me to."

"You can if you want." I started walking toward the parking garage, my stomach a knot of toads and my throat tight.

We were going to have a fight, and there wasn't anything I could do to stop it. I felt it as surely as anything. Tension hung between us like a sagging laundry line hung with clothes the soap didn't quite clean.

Yet once again, Sam backed off. He kissed my cheek and hugged me with one arm. "I'll meet you there."

I nodded stiffly. "I'll be in bed. I'll leave the door unlocked. Lock it when you come up."

"Yeah. Okay." Sam hesitated, kissed me again and headed off in the opposite direction toward his car. He'd parked on State Street.

My anxiety eased on the ride home. Every couple had disagreements. It was part of being a couple. Even when you loved someone, you could be angry with them. There wasn't anything to worry about. It was, in fact, a good thing. It showed we were comfortable enough with each other to express our opinions and emotions.

Fuck. I didn't want to fight with Sam. I didn't want to lose the fresh and new feeling of this. I didn't want us to become just another couple. Not yet.

Hell, not ever.

I showered and got into bed, but without Sam there I couldn't sleep. I tried not to look at the clock, but each time I did the minutes had ticked by. The drive from Harrisburg took forty minutes, and even if he'd left a few minutes behind me, he should've been there already.

I tried counting the number of beers he'd had, but couldn't be sure if it was four or five. He hadn't acted drunk, but he could've been pulled over. He could've been in an accident.

I shot straight up in bed, a hand clapped over my mouth to hold back a sudden wave of nausea.

Oh, God. He could be dead.

I got out of bed to pace, wishing again I smoked or knitted or liked to do sit-ups. Anything to take my mind away from a vision of blood on the asphalt and a windshield starred and broken.

When the doorknob of my apartment door turned I gasped aloud and jerked open the door before Sam could finish opening it. "Sam!"

He blinked at me. "Last time I checked, yeah."

My eyes watered at the stink of beer on his breath. "Where the hell have you been?"

"I had to make a stop." Sam lifted a six-pack missing all but one of its members.

Anger replaced my anxiety, so harsh my legs shook with it. My teeth chattered until I slammed my jaws together. I slammed the door behind him.

"I was worried sick, Sam! Are you drunk?"

Sam held up a hand, seesawing.

"Fuck you," I told him, and turned on my heel. "Sleep on the goddamn couch."

I slammed the door to my bedroom, too, so hard a picture fell off the wall. Breathing hard, my stomach pitching, I paced at the foot of my bed. I knew he liked to drink, but this...

Instant doubt assailed me. Was I right to be pissed off? Sam was an adult. I didn't own him.

But he was my boyfriend, didn't that give me the right to expect certain things from him?

Fuck.

I didn't want to be the sort of girlfriend who ruled her boyfriend. I liked Sam the way he was. I didn't want to change him, or own him or tell him what to do.

Then again, since we got together he'd pretty much done everything I wanted him to do, so how did I know anything different.

"Pissflaps," I muttered, and sank onto the foot of my bed.

Sam hadn't even knocked. Maybe he'd left. Maybe he was, even now, driving drunk down the road and into the path of a tractor-trailer—

"Sam!"

I flung the door open to stare at an empty room, and my heart leaped into my throat again. Until I heard the snoring and my gaze followed the sound to where a pair of long legs dangled over the edge of the couch.

He was asleep in his clothes. His mouth parted with each breath. Anger and anxiety tumbled around in my guts, refusing to quell themselves until I took a few swigs of pink bismuth liquid.

I sat in the chair opposite the couch and watched Sam sleep. What if he puked in his sleep and choked on it? What if he'd drunk so much he had alcohol poisoning?

What if he got cancer? Pneumonia? Tuberculosis? The flu? Leprosy? The plague?

Oh, God, what if Sam, my Sam, died and left me? What if I had to be one of those women who had to choose what casket he should be put into the ground in, the suit he'd wear, what to say on his memorial card?

But I'd have no rights to make any of those choices because I wasn't Sam's wife but just a girlfriend. If Sam died, I might be the one who missed him most, but I wouldn't be the one who got to mourn him the loudest. I'd fallen in love and there didn't seem to be much hope of falling out of it.

My sobs must have woken him. A shadow loomed over me, and big hands pulled me onto a lap with plenty of space for me to curl up. I sobbed into Sam's chest with the smell of beer and his cologne surrounding me, and I breathed in, over and over, forcing my exhausted brain to hold on to that smell. To remember him, his smell and the feeling of his hands, the texture of his hair. The length and breadth and width and girth of him.

Of Sam, whom I could not bear to lose.

It had sort of been aborted, but was our first fight anyway. It made a difference between us for a couple days, in which Sam seemed to try extra hard to make me laugh and I tried extra hard to let him, but soon enough we were back to the way it had been before that night. At least almost.

My heart still clutched at odd moments when I thought of all the things that could happen to Sam. Every person I took care of, each heart attack or, God forbid, suicide, even the peaceful face of Mr. Rombaugh who'd passed away in his sleep, wore Sam's face for a minute or two while I prepared them.

"I'll be glad when I finally get my license," Jared said as we went through the embalming procedure on Mr. Rombaugh. "Then I can do this without supervision."

I looked up, grateful for the conversation to take my mind away from its melancholy. "Have you thought about my job offer?"

Jared nodded. "Yeah. I've been thinking a lot about it, Grace. A lot."

I didn't want to pressure him. "Your internship's over at the end of the month. You know I'd love to have you come back when you've passed your test."

He nodded again. "I know."

"I know you've had other offers. And I understand you have to do what you think is best, Jared. I won't be mad or anything."

He looked up with a small grin. "I know. I know, okay? And I want to take the job. I'm just worried about the test, that's all."

"You'll pass. You're good at this."

Together we finished with Mr. Rombaugh. I was looking forward to Jared getting his license, too, if it meant I might get a break once in a while. The emotional ups and downs of the only job I'd ever considered were as upsetting to me as the reasons I was having them.

Jared shrugged. "I hope so."

"Listen, Jared…about the partnership thing. I haven't really had time to think about it. I didn't want you to think I wasn't considering it."

I'd turned to the sink to wash my hands after stripping off my latex gloves, but Jared didn't answer. I thought maybe the sound of the water had garbled my words, but when I turned to repeat myself, his expression stopped me.

"Huh?"

Shit.

"I thought Shelly would have mentioned it to you by now…" I trailed off. It's hard to speak with a foot in your mouth.

"About a partnership?" Jared looked momentarily pleased before his brow furrowed. "Shelly talked to you about making me a partner?"

Double shit.

"Um…yeah. She did. Last week. I told her I'd have to think about it. And I have," I added hastily. "But I haven't made a decision yet."

Jared shook his head, his jaw setting. He finished up what he'd been doing and stripped off the apron he'd used to cover his clothes. "Don't worry about it. I can't believe she'd talk to you about something like that and not tell me."

"I'm sorry I said anything."

He shook his head again, harder. "No. I'm glad you told me. Are we done here?"

"I can finish up."

Jared looked upward, his gaze probably shifting through the ceiling to find the bottom of Shelly's desk just above us. "Would you mind if I took Shelly out for a long lunch?"

Instead of having them battle it out here? "Sure. Go ahead. It's been pretty quiet. I'll page you if I need you."

He nodded and left the room without another word.

One more reminder of just how complicated relationships could be.

The perfect occasion for Sam to meet my family arose in early October when my brother, Craig, came home to celebrate my mom's birthday. Because he came home so rarely it was more of a party for him than for my mom, but we were going to have dinner and cake and presents. Hannah had planned just about everything and given me a list of tasks to complete, which I was more than happy to do, since it took most of the pressure off me.

"And you're bringing your friend, right?" This came over the phone.

I hadn't seen my sister much since the day she'd dropped off her kids with me. She'd always been too busy to have lunch with me. I thought I understood, even if I didn't want to dwell too long on what she was doing with her time.

"Yes. My boyfriend." I paused for her reaction, but while admitting what Sam was to me meant a lot to me, it didn't seem to register so much with her. "Sam."

"Sam. Right." I heard the scratching of a pen on paper.

"Hannah, are you making place cards? Please tell me you're not making place cards."

"Relax," Hannah said. "I'm just making a grocery list. Geez, Grace, since when did you get so uptight?"

"Pot, have you met kettle? I think you have a lot in common."

My sister, to my vast surprise, laughed. "Ha, ha. Very clever. Did you read that off a gum wrapper?"

"You're in a very good mood," I told her. Unusual for being in the midst of planning a party.

"Let's just say I'm learning to let a lot of things go."

Hmm. I wasn't sure I wanted to touch that one. "Well, good. E-mail me what you want me to pick up."

"I'll drop it off on my way to the library with the kids for story time."

"Here?" Again?

"Yes. There. It's easier for me than e-mailing. Not everyone lives their life online, Grace."

"Okay by me." I wasn't going to tell her I was surprised.

"Oh, make sure Sam wears a suit and tie."

"Hannah!"

"Just kidding," my sister said, and hung up with a laugh.

When I broached the subject of the family party with Sam, it was in the shower while he soaped my back. And my front. He didn't miss my sides, either. In fact, Sam was being so thorough in his attentions, I had to repeat myself because he hadn't been paying attention to my words.

"Sam." I put my hand over his. "You're not listening."

He tore his gaze away from my suds-covered breasts and looked into my eyes. "I was listening. You want me to go to a party with you at your parents' house."

"Yes. Will you?"

"Of course." He shrugged. Water splatted down between us, wetting my hair but only reaching Sam's chest. "If you want me to."

"Why would you think I didn't want you to?" I grabbed up the net sponge and the body wash and made him turn around so I could scrub his back.

Sam looked over his shoulder at me. "Because we've been together for a couple months now and you've never introduced me to your family. I thought maybe you were ashamed of me, or something."

"Oh, Sam." I poked his side. "Stop it."

He laughed and leaned forward to put a hand on the glass brick wall. "That feels good. Not the poking. The washing."

I scrubbed a little harder. "Like this?"

"Yes. Oh, yes," he said in a thick pirate accent. "Purr, purr. That be nice."

I moved lower, from behind, slipping a hand between his legs to fondle him. "How's that?"

"Purr, purr, that be nice, too." He hummed and shifted his feet wider apart, but a moment later his entire body jerked. "Shit! What the hell?"

I dropped the sponge and stepped back before he could slug me in the face with his elbow. Sam turned, holding out his hand. A deep white slice welling with crimson crisscrossed his palm. He held it out under the shower spray and blood spattered under the force of the water.

"Hold it under the water for a minute while I get a towel." I reached to grab one from the hook near the shower and brought it in as I turned off the water. Sam held out his hand for me to wrap in the absorbent fabric, but blood had dripped onto the shower floor. It dotted his legs and stomach, too. I pressed the material hard onto the wound and together we eased out of the shower and onto the floor mat.

"Sit down." I pushed him to sit on the toilet while I rifled through my medicine cabinet for some gauze pads. "The same thing happened to me a few months ago. It must be a crack in the glass."

He hissed when I pulled away the towel, but the cut had mostly stopped bleeding. I cleaned it with peroxide and bit back my laughter when he yelped. I blew on the wound to ease the sting, then bandaged it.

I kissed it gently. "There. All better."

Sam took up a lot of space in my small bathroom. With him sitting on my toilet, his knees nearly hit the opposite wall. His shoulders almost filled the small toilet alcove from side to side. Naked and wet, his skin humped with gooseflesh and his wounded hand laid out faceup on his knee as if he was afraid to touch it, he looked as if he belonged there.

"I would never be ashamed of you, Sam. I hope you know that."

He touched my cheek with his unhurt hand. "Give it time."

Chapter 19

I laughed off what he'd said, though it lingered with me. I'd never been ashamed of Sam, just wary about introducing him to the people I cared about in case things didn't work out. Like most things, it had been all about me.

In front of my parents' house we sat in Sam's car with the engine running. He wore a shirt I'd never seen before, tucked into khaki cargo pants instead of his familiar jeans. He looked presentable and teacherly, even with the glinting earring and feathery spiked hair. I missed his big, clunky brogans and his layered shirts and the worn black leather belt. Still, it was obvious he'd made an effort, and I leaned over to kiss his cheek.

"Are you ready?"

He smiled. "You act like your family's a pack of cannibals or something."

"No. They're not that bad." I laughed and ruffled a hand over his hair. "They're just not used to me bringing anyone home. You're probably going to get a lot of attention from my niece and nephew."

"That's okay. So long as your dad doesn't ask me to go for a walk out back to where he keeps his guns or anything."

"Oh, Sam." I punched his upper arm lightly and rolled my eyes. "My dad doesn't have any guns."

Sam grinned and kissed me. "Cattle prod?"

"C'mon, let's go in before they wonder what we're doing out here." I sighed. "Because you know they're all peeking out the windows."

He peered around me to look up at the house. "Can I ask you something before we go in?"

I'd already put my hand on the door handle, but I stopped before opening it. "Sure."

"Why didn't you ever bring anyone home before?"

That was a heavy question with no simple answer, and one I didn't think we had time to really discuss at the moment. "I guess I haven't met anyone in a long time who I wanted to keep around long enough to bother introducing to my family."

Sam's grin tickled my insides. "Didn't I tell you that you wouldn't regret giving me a chance?"

"I think you mentioned it once or twice." I ran my fingers through the soft fringes of hair over his ear.

"Are you glad?" Sam looked sincere, not joking, so I didn't tease.

"Yes, Sam. I'm glad."

He gave a half nod. "Me, too. Let's go."

Just to prove I wasn't ashamed, I held his hand as we went into the house and I introduced him to my parents, to Craig, to Hannah and Jerry, and finally, Melanie and

Simon. The kids looked up, up, up, eyes wide in little faces and mouths agape.

"Are you a giant?" asked Simon.

Sam laughed and squatted to bring himself eye to eye with my nephew. "Yo, ho, ho. But, nope. I can do magic, though."

Simon's eyes lit. "Like Criss Angel?"

Sam shot me a look. "Maybe not quite like him."

He pulled a quarter from his pocket and did a passable sleight-of-hand trick to pull it from behind Simon's ear. He then had to repeat the trick for Melanie. When the kids each took him by a hand and pulled him into the den to look at the fort they'd built with cushions, I knew he'd made two small friends.

My sister bustled in my mom's kitchen, setting up the sandwich tray and rolls. "Grace, put out the mayo and pickles, would you?"

"You cut your hair."

Hannah stopped and turned, one hand going to the new, shorter cut. She'd worn her hair long and pulled back for as long as I could remember. Now it swept her shoulders in a sleek bob with amber highlights. She'd changed her lipstick, too, to something brighter.

"Do you like it?" She patted her hair a little fretfully.

"It's great."

She smiled. "Thanks. I thought it was time for a change."

I got out the mayo and pickles from the fridge. "Been making a lot of changes lately?"

When I reappeared from out of the fridge, my sister was staring. "What's that supposed to mean?"

I shrugged. "Just asking."

Something flashed across her face so fast I couldn't quite discern the expression. "Don't forget the mustard."

Lunch was, predictably, chaotic. The kids jabbered at Sam who fully won them over by answering every knock-knock joke with a game "Who's there?" and laughing even when they made no sense. Craig, Jerry and my dad earnestly discussed finances and the market, both topics I knew I should pay attention to but couldn't follow. Hannah and my mom discussed the town's business, calling for my input now and again, though I usually had none to share. I had stories aplenty, but like a doctor I kept them confidential.

We finished lunch and the traditional Frawley women cleared the table while the men wandered into the den to admire my dad's new big-screen television. I squeezed Sam's hand before he followed them, and kissed him, too, for fortitude. I hurried through the cleanup as I fended off my sister's casually probing questions and my mom's fussing over whether or not Sam had had enough to eat.

"A big boy like that," she said. "He's got to have a big appetite."

"Mom, he's fine. Seriously." I filled the dishwasher with soap and turned it on to run. "Don't worry about it."

"Well, if you're sure…"

Hannah and I exchanged looks and smiles, a rare instance when we were united against my mom instead of them against me. "Mom, let Grace go rescue Sam from Dad and Craig."

My mom nodded. "Good point. Go, Grace. Before they pin him down and start interrogating him. Oh, heavens,

Hannah, remember when you brought Jerry home for the first time?"

"Shit," I said, ignoring my mom's tut-tut. "I'd better get in there."

Yet when I found them all, Craig and Sam were talking about New York City, and my dad and Jerry had zoned out in front of the television. The kids had been booted out of their fort and were arguing over an ancient game of Clue.

"Hey." I sat on the edge of Sam's chair and he put an arm around my waist. I kissed the top of his head. "Is my brother bragging again?"

Sam laughed. "He lives around the corner from the deli where I worked when I first went to the city."

"Biggest city in the world and we both go to the same dry cleaner." Craig shook his head. "Small world. Do you think you'll go back, Sam?"

Sam didn't look at me when he answered. "I haven't decided."

His answer twisted my stomach. I'd teased him plenty about going back to New York, but I didn't really expect him to go. He wouldn't now, would he? Not now that we were together.

The conversation moved on to different things. The kids finagled Sam into playing Clue with them, and me too. We had cake and watched my mom open her presents, all of which she claimed to love and not deserve.

I couldn't stop from looking at Sam amongst my family. Like the way he fit on my couch and in my bathroom and in my bed, he looked at home between my niece and nephew. When he got up to help my sister gather the discarded wrapping paper she even let him help her with the garbage bag, and for my sister to relinquish any sort of domestic task without specific instructions on how to complete it was something like a miracle.

I hadn't been anxious about introducing him to my family, just a little wary, and it was a relief that everything had gone so well. Only my dad hung back from the conversations, and more than once I caught him looking at me but turning his eyes away when he saw me looking. The party hadn't ended when we decided to leave. As usual, I had a service to oversee in the morning.

"No rest for the wicked," I joked as I made the rounds of hugs and kisses goodbye.

My mom patted my back. "I remember that. It's so nice to have your dad home on the weekends now."

My dad snorted. "Is that why you keep telling me to get a hobby so I'm out of your hair?"

"During the week," my mom said. "It's nice to have you home on the weekends. And not having phone calls at all hours of the night, too. I don't miss that."

"Yeah, that's pretty bad," Sam said. "It's like sleeping with a doctor. Always on call."

I don't imagine it was a big secret to my family that Sam and I were sleeping together. I'm sure the gossip line had filtered to my parents about his car being there overnight. But put out there like that, it left a huge gap of silence in the conversation.

"Sam, do you sleep with my aunt Grace?" asked Simon innocently.

More silence.

"They probably don't do much sleeping," muttered Jerry, the comedian. Hannah slapped his arm, hard.

"And on that note," I said brightly as I took Sam's hand, "I think we're out of here."

More kissing, more hugging, though I'd probably see all of them again in the next few days. My mom even hugged and kissed Sam, insisting he come back again when she could feed him more. By the time we made it through the gauntlet of affection, I was more than ready to head home, put on a pair of sweatpants and collapse in front of the TV.

My dad caught up to us in the carport. "Grace, wait a minute."

Sam and I stopped, but after a significant look from my dad, Sam excused himself and went to wait for me in the car. I waited until he'd disappeared around the corner before I turned to my dad. He pulled an envelope from his pocket, but I didn't reach for it.

"What's that?"

"Take it," my dad said.

I did and found money inside. A lot of money. I looked up. "What's this for?"

"Because I think you need it." My dad held up his hands in refusal when I tried to press the envelope back into them.

"I don't want your money, Dad. I'm okay. Really."

"Grace, take it." My dad's stern voice cast me back to days of curfews and allowances. "I know you have… expenses."

"The business is fine," I insisted, stubborn.

"Personal expenses," my dad said, for once looking uncomfortable. "Hourly expenses."

If I hadn't picked it up by then, the way he jerked his chin toward the street would have clued me in. My fingers convulsed on the envelope, crumpling it. I tried to laugh, but the noise came out sounding strangled.

"Sam's my—"

My dad held up a hand and looked pained. "Please, Grace. I don't want to know any more than I already do."

"You looked at my personal accounts, Dad. Why would you do that? They have nothing to do with the business."

"There were discrepancies," my dad said. "I wanted to make sure you weren't in trouble, that's all. And then when I saw the e-mails—"

"You read my e-mail?" My laugh might have been choked, but I had no such issue now. My voice rang through the carport loud enough to hurt my ears. My dad winced.

"Grace, I'm your father."

"Yeah? Well, I'm not a kid anymore, Dad! Okay? You had no right to take my computer without asking, no right to look at my personal accounts and absolutely, positively *no* right to read my e-mail!"

"I wanted to make sure you weren't in trouble!" my dad roared, but I was past being threatened by the growling.

"You wanted to check up on me!" I shouted back, stepping toward him with the envelope still clutched in my hand. "You just wanted to know my private business!"

"Yes, I did!" he shouted. "So what? I'm your dad, Grace, it's my prerogative to keep tabs on what you're doing! Especially when you're making mistakes!"

I saw red. Literally. Crimson ribbons flashed in front of my eyes, and I thought the top of my head might explode.

I threw the envelope at my dad's feet. Money scattered. Neither of us bent for it.

"It's a little late to start 'being there' for me, Dad." I took several shallow, rapid breaths to ward off the rage, but it still twisted barbs inside me. "I don't need your money. And I don't need your advice."

My tone made it obvious what I thought of his advice.

"Don't you talk to me like that."

"Don't you talk to *me* like that," I said through clenched teeth. "You gave me the business because I was the only one who wanted it. And sure, it's been tough, but I'm pulling it together. People like me. They like what I'm doing with the place. So tell me something, what really pisses you off? The fact I'm using my own money for something you don't approve of, or the fact that I'm not failing without you there to tell me what to do and how to do it?"

My dad sputtered, his face getting red, but I didn't wait for him to reply.

"I thought so," I said. "I'm sorry that you're disappointed in me, Dad, I really am. But what I do with my money is my business. And what I do with my business is my business."

He called after me, but I didn't look back.

I was silent and seething on the car ride back to my place, where I slammed out of Sam's car and stomped up the stairs to my apartment. Sam followed a few moments later and helped himself to a beer from the fridge. I thought about having one, too, but my stomach had knotted so tightly I thought I might puke if I tried to drink it.

Sam watched me stalk around the living room, punching pillows into place and sweeping the scattered magazines into neat piles. I even rearranged the remote caddy. I needed something to do with my hands so I wouldn't punch something.

"I'm sorry," Sam said at last. "I wasn't thinking."

I stopped and looked at him from across the room. He leaned against the kitchen counter. He was on his second beer.

"What?" I asked stupidly, so consumed with my own private fury I couldn't even think of what he might have meant.

"About saying that thing about sleeping with you in front of your mom. That was stupid."

"Oh, Sam." I said that a lot lately. "I don't care about that. If my parents want to pretend I'm a virgin, that's their problem."

The irony of that hit me. Obviously my dad knew I was having sex. Shit. He'd assumed worse than that of me. He'd thought I'd actually brought a paid-for boyfriend to my family party. Brought a casual fuck-buddy around my niece and nephew. The more I thought about it, the angrier I got.

"Goddammit!" I threw a sofa pillow across the room, where it hit the wall harmlessly.

"What's the matter?" Sam asked.

I wanted him to come over to me and enfold me the way he did so well, but he didn't move. He tipped the beer back and set it down on the counter. He crossed his arms over his chest and watched me.

"It's my dad," I said. "He's a nosy son of a bitch."

"Huh." Sam's face made me sorry I'd said anything. Dads were a sore subject with him. "What did he do?"

"He tried to give me money."

Sam raised a brow. "And that's bad because…?"

I sighed. "He thinks I need it."

"Not following you."

"He thinks I'm ruining his business, but I'm not."

Sam nodded as if that made sense. "He's your dad, Grace. I'm sure he's just worried about you."

I snorted indelicately. "He read my private e-mails. He dug into my personal bank accounts. He totally crossed the line this time."

"I'm sure you'll get over it," Sam said.

Oh, he did *not* just tell me I'd get over it.

"Excuse me," I told him. "But I don't exactly think you're the dude to be giving me advice about getting along with my father."

Sam said nothing, and instant regret flooded me. We stared at each other across the room. I hadn't stopped wanting him to put his arms around me and make me feel better.

He cracked open the fridge and pulled out another beer. It was my turn to make a bitchface. There was no way he could've missed it. I felt the frown on my mouth and the corners of my eyes.

"Get off my back," Sam warned, though I hadn't said anything. Defiantly he unscrewed the bottle top and drank. "Your dad wanted to give you money. I don't see what the big deal is."

"The big deal is," I said, "that he was giving it to me to pay for you."

Sam's bottle paused at his mouth. "Come again?"

"My dad thinks I hired you."

"For what?" Sam put the bottle down, finally.

I sighed and crossed to him. "Because he found some stuff on my computer that made him think you were a gigolo."

Sam laughed. "Why would your dad think I was a gigolo?"

"Because," I said with another sigh, "I spent a lot of money on rentboys and he found out, and he assumed you were one."

Sam's smile looked strained. "You spent a lot of money on rentboys."

"Yes."

Sam went back to drinking his beer. I leaned against the kitchen table, directly across from him. He moved his legs so we didn't touch.

"What does that mean, exactly?" he said at last.

"It means that I used to hire men to go on dates with me."

Sam took a long, silent pull on his bottle and put it down. Another dead soldier. He wiped the back of his mouth. "Just for dates?"

"Sometimes." I put my hands flat on my stomach, wishing I didn't feel so much like I might vomit. Or scream. Or cry.

"And sometimes…?"

"Why don't you just ask me what you want to know, Sam."

"Grace," Sam said. "Why don't you just tell me."

"Yes. I fucked them sometimes, too. More than just sometimes. A lot of times."

Sam pulled another beer from my fridge. The last one, I thought. He rolled it in his palms before opening it. I really hoped he wouldn't, but he did after a minute.

"That guy you were with at the Firehouse?"

"Jack. Yes."

"Fucking hell." Sam looked sick. He hadn't started on the beer, at least. "For how long?"

"A few months."

I could see him turning the idea over in his mind. He drank silently. I pulled a cola from the fridge to drink myself, hoping it would settle my stomach.

"Jesus," he said after some long minutes of silence. "You've been fucking him since we met?"

"Since after we met. Before him it was a few others. But Sam," I said, pleading, "not since we've been together."

He pulled his arm away when I tried to touch him. "You just said you started with him after we met."

"But we weren't together—"

"We were together the first night we met!" he shouted.

Sam is big. Angry Sam was bigger. He loomed over me, and I shrank back instinctively though I wasn't afraid he was going to hurt me.

Sam was also smart. "That night. I didn't just get lucky."

"No. I was there to meet an escort. A stranger."

He muttered something in disgust and pulled away from me, turning. "Fucking hell, Grace. What the fuck? Why?"

"Because it was safer!" I shouted. "Safer than picking up a real stranger!"

"Safer than having a real boyfriend?" he retorted.

I'd been quivering with rage earlier, but now I shook with a combination of anger and dismay. "Yes."

"So what happened?" Sam challenged. "Why pay for the milk when you can fuck the cow for free?"

"It wasn't like that!"

He shrugged and drank, and I wanted to slap the bottle from his hand. "I'm a lot cheaper."

"Stop it, Sam."

He finished the last beer and put the bottle in the sink. "So tell me, then, why?"

"You kept calling me." It sounded lame. "And I liked talking to you."

"So it was easier for you? I get it now."

"No! You're not listening. Or maybe you're too drunk," I added.

Sam bristled. "You don't think it was fate that brought me to you? The fact we met in a bar and had sex, then you turned out to be the person burying my dad? You don't think that was some sort of...destiny?"

"I don't believe in fate, Sam."

"No," he said slowly. "I guess you don't."

He went for the door and I watched him get there before I found my voice. "Where are you going?"

"Out."

"Sam, don't go. Please." I tried to snag his shirtsleeve, but once again he pulled away from me.

"I can't believe you thought I was a whore," he said. "I can't believe you never told me."

"It wasn't any of your business." I knew at once it was the wrong thing to say.

Sam spoke without turning. "For months I called you. You knew I wanted to take you out."

"But you didn't, did you!" It was my turn to shout. "You'd call and flirt and then I wouldn't hear from you for a week! You're acting like we had this great thing going, Sam, but the fact is, I never knew what the hell was going on with you!"

"For months, Grace. And all that time you were paying some punk to get you off. All that time and you were fucking some other guy!"

"It's not like I was cheating on you!" I cried.

"Well, that's how it feels!" His hand turned the knob.

"You didn't even know me, Sam."

He turned to look at me at last as he opened the door. "I don't think I know you now."

I would not beg him to stay, so he didn't. He left without closing the door behind him, and I watched him without following. I muttered a curse to an empty room and closed the door.

I tried calling Sam on his cell and at his mother's, but nobody answered at either number. For three days I tried before I stopped. On the fourth day, he called me.

"I'm at the police station."

I'd just changed into my pajamas and popped some corn. I was going to indulge in a sappy chick-flick fest. It was already past 8:00 pm.

"What happened? Are you all right?"

"DUI," Sam said after a pause. "Can you come pick me up? And post bail?"

I spilled my popcorn. "Yes. Of course. Oh, Sam—"

"Don't. Please. Just come."

Sam had been there for me once, when I needed him, and had come without question. I heard the same desperation in his voice. I was already looking for a pair of jeans and a T-shirt.

"Of course. Tell me what I need to do."

He named a sum high enough to make my checkbook scream and gave me the address. I could make it in half an hour, and I prayed I wouldn't get a death call.

Sam looked like hell and smelled worse. Dark circles shadowed his eyes and he looked as if he hadn't shaved in a few days. His hair was matted and rumpled and not in the sexy, just-rolled-out-of-bed way I liked so well. They let me take him after I'd signed away practically my whole life and the lives of my unborn children.

He was quiet in the car and sat hunched in his seat, arms crossed and shirt collar pulled up high around his throat.

"Want me to turn up the heat?"

He shook his head. A few more miles down the road he asked me to pull over, and he got out of the car to be sick on the side of the road. The sound of retching made me gag, too. I didn't get out to help him.

I didn't take him back to my place, but rather to his mom's. The dark house showed no signs of occupancy, and I remembered Dotty Stewart had gone on a cruise with her sister.

He didn't ask me to come inside, just stumbled out of my car and into the house, but I followed. He went straight upstairs and into the shower. He was in there for a long time. When he came down to the kitchen, I'd made coffee. For myself, mostly, but he took some and sipped it as if he thought it might escape his stomach if he drank it too fast.

"They pulled me over on the way to the Firehouse," he

said, though I hadn't asked. "Gave me a field sobriety test, which I passed, by the way."

He put his face in his hands, the heels of his palms making cradles for his eyes. "Then they gave me a Breathalyzer. Which I didn't."

I held on to the edge of the table, tight, to keep myself from tumbling into the huge abyss that had suddenly yawned between us. "Why, Sam?"

Sam's laugh hurt my ears. "Because I was drunk."

"That's not what I meant."

He looked up then, into my eyes. "Because."

"You couldn't just talk to me?" My voice cracked. I was on my feet without realizing I'd stood, but I still gripped the table.

He didn't nod or shake his head. He just looked away. "I lost my apartment in New York because I couldn't make the rent. I had to ask my dad for money. He told me to come home if I had to. I didn't come home until he was dying. When it was too late."

I put my hand on his shoulder, and he didn't pull away. Beneath my fingers his bones poked, sharp. The edges of his hair brushed the back of my hand.

"You can't blame yourself."

He looked up at me with an awful smile. "Yes, I can."

I said his name like calling on a talisman, but this time it didn't work. Sam got up from the table and poured his coffee down the sink. His shoulders hunched as he gripped the counter, facing away from me.

"I fucked up. I never got to show him I could make it, Grace. I never told him I was sorry for disappointing him. Nothing."

I had known some of his regrets about his dad, but not how deep they went, or how he'd been trying to relieve them. "Maybe you need to talk to someone about this."

Sam's laugh broke in the middle. "Why? It won't bring him back."

"It might make you feel better than drinking does."

"And it won't get my ass tossed in jail, right?" He turned. "Won't make me fuck up yet again, right?"

I didn't answer that. I didn't want to fight with him again. "I know how hard this must be for you."

"Right. Because you see it all the time? Because it's your job to make people feel better about death?"

"Because I care about you, Sam."

He shook his head. "I can't do this right now. Go home."

"No."

"Go home," Sam said. "I don't want to see you anymore."

Of all the things I'd imagined might happen, that wasn't one. "Why not?"

"Because it's too hard," Sam said without a trace of mockery or irony in his voice. "It's too hard to disappoint you."

"Why would you want to?" I cried, hating the tears in my voice.

"Because I'm really fucking good at it!" Sam turned again.

"Sam. Don't do this. I love you."

It was the first time I'd said it to him, and even I knew it was too late.

He shook his head, not turning. "You don't really know me, either."

"Why did you call me instead of Dan?"

"How do you know I didn't try him first?"

I scowled. "Because even though your brother gives you a hard time, I know he would've helped you out. Why'd you call me, instead?"

"Because if my brother came for me, I'd have to pay him back. If you bailed me out, I figured I could work off the debt. Isn't that how you like your men? Bought and paid for?"

"Fuck you, Sam," I answered evenly.

"Did you cut the coupon out of the Sunday paper? I'm running a special."

I crossed my arms over my chest. "That's not funny or clever."

"Damn," Sam said. "There goes my career in stand-up."

"Would it make you feel better if I'd fucked them for free?"

"Yes," he replied. "I don't know why, dammit, but yes."

"I'm sorry it upsets you so much." I sighed, exasperated.

"But not sorry you did it."

"No, Sam. I'm not sorry I did it."

He sighed, too, and bent to splash a few handfuls of cold water on his face. Dripping, he blew out water in a fine spray and hung over the sink for a minute. Then he cupped his hand to drink some water before turning off the faucet. He looked at me with water streaming down his face.

"Why did you do it? Why pay for it?"

"Because I've watched too many people crying, Sam. Because I didn't want that to be me."

"Good, then. You can go back to it now. Hell, I need some cash. Maybe I can get a job. Use you as a reference."

His words hurt, but I tried not to show it.

"Why did you spend all that time?" I didn't really want

an answer but asked anyway. "Why bother with me? Was it a challenge or something? Why did you keep coming back all that time if you're just going to throw it all away now?"

"I thought it would be worth it," Sam said.

I had to swallow hard before I could answer. "And now you don't? Because of decisions I made before I even met you?"

There was more to it, I was sure. More about his dad. His music. My sweet Sam was a bundle of issues he didn't want to share.

"Look at it this way," he said at last. "I'm giving you what you wanted. Now you don't have to worry about crying."

"It's too late, Sam. I already am."

For a minute, I thought he'd take me in his arms. That everything would be all right. I thought we'd work through this and come out stronger for it.

"Just pretend I'm still a stranger," he said, and that was when I left.

Chapter 20

*I*t would be dramatic to say the earth stopped turning for me, or the sun stopped shining. I could say I plunged into a deep depression and couldn't get out of bed, but that would be a lie. I didn't have time not to function. Jared's internship had ended and he'd passed his license test. He'd accepted the job I'd offered him and would start after a month's vacation. Good for him, bad for me. I still hadn't decided about offering him a partnership.

Shelly, however, had quit. She and Jared had fought horrifically about the whole partnership thing, and she'd broken up with him. I hadn't heard if she'd gone back to a smug and formerly forsaken Duane, but I was sure to find out sooner or later.

I stopped hoping each phone call I answered would be Sam after the second week, not because I didn't want him to call, but because I had to force away the sadness and concentrate on my life. I cried, sometimes, but even the urge to do that faded every day.

With Jared gone and a temporary office manager who

didn't know the routine, I was trying to juggle eggs without making omelets. I could handle the services and burials. I could even handle the embalmings and preparations. I didn't sleep much, but that was okay because it meant when I did that I didn't dream of Sam.

What I prayed wouldn't happen was a home-death call. Most of the calls we got came from hospitals and nursing homes, and I kept my fingers crossed that nothing else would happen until I could get Jared back on the job.

No such luck.

The call came in the early afternoon from a family who'd been in a month before to make arrangements. The wife was dying of pancreatic cancer and had hospice service at home. They'd expected her to pass away much sooner, but she'd held on.

I assured them I'd be there to take care of her as soon as the doctor signed the papers, and then I hung up the phone and buried my face in my hands.

"Ms. Frawley?"

I looked up. No matter how many times I'd told Susie to call me Grace, she hadn't quite mastered it. And she still closed her eyes at the sight of a corpse. "Yes?"

"You have a couple messages."

I thanked her and took them, sorting through them and finding nothing from Sam. No message from Jared telling me he'd be back earlier than planned, either.

Dammit. What was I going to do? I couldn't go alone. I couldn't tell the family I wasn't able to take care of their wife and mother.

I did the only thing I could do. I called my dad.

Things had been strained between us since the day of my mom's party, but he didn't refuse to help me. I knew he wouldn't. No matter what he might think about me, my dad wouldn't let down a client.

I'd worked with my dad often enough to know his style. The words he used to offer comfort to the family, the way he preferred to cover the bodies and tuck in the edges, all of that. But watching him this time I seemed to see it all with fresh eyes. I saw myself in my dad, in subtle ways, like which straps on the gurney I buckled first or how I folded the body's hands.

At the funeral home he helped me get everything settled and started, but instead of telling me what to do or correcting me when I did something differently, he followed my lead.

"Things have changed," was his only comment.

I'd been thinking a lot about the partnership idea. Jared was a good worker, and taking on a partner would mean more freedom for me in many ways. Making this business a corporation would change things but also make them better, I thought. I thought my dad might growl when I brought the subject up, but I had to ask someone and I respected his opinion.

We talked about it for a long time, as we worked and later, in my apartment over coffee and doughnuts. He had a lot of good points, but more importantly, he listened to what I had to say and didn't try to tell me what to do. He offered advice without orders.

I got up to hand him another doughnut when he sideswiped me.

"We haven't seen you in a while. Why don't you come over for dinner on Sunday. Bring Sam."

I put the plate back on the coffee table. "I don't see Sam anymore, Dad. We broke up."

My dad didn't have to say anything. He just held out his arm and made a place for me to cradle my face against his shoulder when I started to cry.

"It hurts, doesn't it," he said, patting my back. "I know."

That was all he said, but it was enough. Later, when I'd stopped crying, he offered me the ever-present white hankie from his pocket. I declined with a grimace, and we laughed.

"I'm sorry I wasn't there enough when you were younger," my dad said. "I know you think I don't have the right to tell you what to do now."

"And I know you're just trying to help. I do. But...it's better if you let me ask you. Okay?"

He nodded with a sigh. "Yeah. For what it's worth, Gracie, I'm sorry about your fella."

"Me, too, Dad."

"I think it's a good idea. Offering Jared the partnership. The home's too much work for one person. I had your uncle Chuck and it was still a lot of work. I missed things I shouldn't have. It's good to have time for your family, too. Your kids."

I gave a soft snort. "I don't have kids."

"Someday," my dad said.

I'd thought I was done crying, but I was wrong.

The service had been simple but well attended. Mrs. Hoover had been loved by many. I'd hung back to make sure the chapel was empty before I drove the hearse to the cemetery, and found Mr. Hoover still sitting in the seat in front of the poster-size photo of his late wife.

"Mr. Hoover, it's time to go."

He looked up with a smile. "I know. I just wanted to sit here for a few minutes. I'm tired. I haven't been sleeping well. The bed's just not the same without her in it."

"I understand," I told him, and I did.

"Of course, she hasn't been in our bed for months, but I guess while she was still in the house I could imagine that one day she might be."

I nodded. Time was ticking, but I didn't even glance at my watch. I sat beside him, instead, and we both looked at the picture of Mrs. Hoover.

"That was her graduation picture," he said. "I already knew then that I wanted to marry her, but she wouldn't say yes. I'd asked her twice by the time we graduated from high school, but she said she wanted to wait until after she'd gone to nursing school."

"She was lovely."

"And headstrong. Mercy, but that woman was bossy."

I handed him a tissue, but he waved it away and took out a white hankie to wipe his eyes. I patted his hand. We both looked a bit longer at the picture.

"If you'd known back then that someday you'd be sitting here like this, getting ready to bury her," I asked him, "would you still have married her? Even knowing one day you'd have to live without her?"

"Oh, heavens yes," Mr. Hoover said with a sigh.

"Even though it hurts so much?" I heard the quaver in my voice and fought to hold it back.

"Of course." Mr. Hoover patted my hand now. "Because my life's been so much richer for having had her in it, you see. And I know I'll see her again. I believe I will. I wouldn't trade one minute of what we had together even if it meant I'd never have to feel this way."

He patted my hand again and stood. "I believe my son's waving at me from the doorway, there."

I looked and sure enough, young Mr. Hoover was waiting for his dad and me. "I'll be right there."

I looked a moment more at the picture of that bossy, headstrong woman who'd made his life so much richer, and then I went to help them finish saying goodbye.

When my phone rang in the middle of the night, I always answered it, even if I wasn't on call. With Jared now a full-time partner and the paperwork under way to turn Frawley and Sons into Frawley and Shanholtz, I wasn't always the one on call, but I always answered my phone in the middle of the night.

"Were you sleeping?"

I refused to even crack an eye to check the time. "Well, I wasn't in a coma."

Soft laughter. "How are you?"

"I'm tired, Sammy. How are you?"

"I'm a little drunk, Grace."

"No kidding."

"No." He laughed again.

"Did you have a reason for waking me?"

"I was thinking about you, that's all."

"I'm thinking about hanging up."

"Don't. Please," Sam said, and I sighed but didn't.

I listened to the sound of his breathing. I closed my eyes and wished I could make myself believe he was breathing beside me, in my bed, but no amount of imagining would convince me. The plastic of my cell phone pressed too hard against my ear and though I could hear his breath, I didn't feel it on my face.

"I got a call from Phil. My agent," he said. "He says if I can get to New York, he'll get me some studio time. Book me a few shows. See if he can get me on the radio or something."

The way he said it, like it didn't matter, meant it did. Very much. "Good for you."

"I'm going next week."

"I'm happy for you, Sam." With my eyes closed, it didn't matter if my vision blurred with tears.

"Can I come over, Grace?" A crackle of static would have stolen his words, spoken in a tone so low, but the connection was clear and without interruption.

"Yes. You can. But will you?"

His breathing shifted. He was drinking or weeping, and I didn't want to imagine him doing either. "No. I guess not. It's late."

"Send me a copy of your album when it's finished."

"Don't cry," Sam said. "Please don't cry."

"I don't understand," I told him. I buried my face into the pillow and bit down hard, to force away tears. "I don't understand you, Sam. I let you in, and you don't want to be in. Why?"

Misery painted his words, but I had little sympathy for his sorrow. "I'm sorry. I know you hate me."

"Goddammit, Sam! I don't hate you! That's the problem!" I punched the pillow this time. "I wish I did."

"I wish you did, too."

I smiled into the softness of my poor abused pillow. "You sneaked in under the radar, you know that?"

Sam's soft chuckle tickled up and down my spine the way it always had. "You didn't want a boyfriend."

"Yeah." I sighed, thinking of what Mr. Hoover had said to me. How he regretted nothing, not even the pain of losing the one he loved so much, because his life had been made so much richer for knowing her. Knowing Sam had made my life richer.

"I should have left you alone," Sam said. "You wanted me to."

I opened my eyes, finally, to the light of dawn creeping through my window. "No. I took a chance on you because I wanted to, Sam. And I don't regret a minute of it, because knowing you has made my life better. And maybe next time I won't let being afraid of what I might lose keep from appreciating what I have."

"Next time?" His voice sounded thick, but he didn't clear his throat.

"I used to think I wanted to spend my life alone, but not anymore."

"But–" He stopped. Breathed. Sighed. "No more rent-boys?"

"Maybe one or two."

"You're killing me, Grace. You know that."

"They have phones in New York, don't they?" I asked him. "Call me."

And then I hung up.

Sam did not call me from New York.

I'd only half expected him to. I'd only half wanted him to. As each passing day put more time between us, I could step back further and further from my thoughts of him. We'd spent less time as a couple than we had together. Love had sneaked up on me out of the blue. I'd watch out for it better, next time.

There didn't seem to be a next time now that I was open to the idea. I met men here and there, when I went out with friends. At the gym I'd started frequenting, now that Jared could oversee more of the business without my supervision. Even, heaven forbid, on a few blind dates set up by my mother with sons or nephews or grandsons of her friends. The world had become a wonderland of possibilities, and though I had fun and met a lot of nice guys, I couldn't picture any of them making the sort of difference Sam had.

Jared and I began switching our on-call weekends and taking time off during the week to compensate. It was the best arrangement for both of us. Though we jokingly referred to each other as "work spouses," and we had more than one knowing smile sent our way from people who assumed we were dating, nothing awkward reared its ugly head between us. Though sharing my business with him had its ups and downs, I didn't regret asking Jared to be my partner. Jared, with his sense of humor and steady commitment to making Frawley and Shanholtz a success, had made my life better, too.

Despite what I'd told Sam, I didn't go back to hiring any of Mrs. Smith's gentlemen. Playacting had lost its appeal when held up against the memory of something real. I had Sam to thank and curse for that, and some days I did both.

He didn't call me, but I looked him up on the Internet now and again. I read reviews of his shows and of the CD he'd made. Both got good press, even if it was only in the small independent bar magazines. He didn't seem to be making it big, but he was making something, anyway.

I hoped he was happy, and as the time passed, I tried to be happy, too.

My job meant I wasn't the most reliable babysitter, but I was free, which made me a better choice than the teenager who lived down the street. Besides, my sister had said, she trusted me with her kids. Perhaps more importantly, she could leave them with me without a long list of instructions. Leaving them with me, she said, was being able to get dressed and walk out the door without worrying. It was worth it, she said, even if sometimes she and Jerry had to come home early because I got a call.

So far, so good this afternoon, though. Melanie and Simon had been ecstatic to learn I was taking them to Mocha Madness, a coffee-and-sandwich shop with an indoor playground in it. The idea was that the kids could run themselves ragged on kid-safe climbing walls, tube mazes and other play equipment, while the adults sat and soothed themselves with coffee and pastries and read the newspaper. With its one-way-in and one-way-out entrance to the playground, monitors and clean restrooms, it was well worth the twenty-minute drive and the five bucks each it cost to let them loose for a few hours.

"Auntie Grace, you are the bestest aunt ever!" Simon clung to my legs as I settled my jacket and bag on the back of a chair positioned so I could watch them play.

His sister joined him on my other side, her arms going tight around my waist. "We love you!"

"Oh, you kids, I love you, too," I said, imitating the popular Internet cartoon called Potter Puppet Pals they loved to watch over and over. "Now get off me."

Giggling, they did and left me to my refillable mug of coffee and the latest romance I'd had on my to-be-read pile forever. I'd been getting a lot of reading done in the past few months.

Simon, cheeks flushed, came to the table a while later to drink from his plastic cup of lemonade. "Auntie Grace, your cheeks are pink."

"So are yours, buddy." I stuck a finger inside my book to hold my place as I pushed his sweaty hair off his forehead. "Are you having fun?"

He nodded and squirmed away from my touch. "Yeah. That boy over there. He's my friend."

My gaze followed his pointing finger toward a little boy wearing a stuffed steering wheel attached around his waist and running around a racetrack laid out on the floor. "Oh, yeah? What's his name?"

"I don't know." Simon shrugged, unconcerned, and headed back to the playground.

I watched him leap right into the game with a friend whose name didn't matter, and I tried to remember what it was like to instantly trust every stranger who came along. I scanned the crowd of gamboling children, found Melanie and, satisfied, turned back to my book.

The story engrossed me, but my need for coffee raised my head. Only a glance, but my attention tore from the book and I let it close without the benefit of my finger to keep my place this time. Across the room, sitting at a tiny table meant for two, a man stared back at me.

Sam.

He saw me. I knew he did, because he'd been staring at me, but as soon as our eyes met he looked away. A moment later, a young woman with blond hair joined him. With her back toward me, I couldn't see her face, but the low-riding jeans and tight T-shirt told me enough. She handed him a large cup and set one down in front of her. She spoke to him, and he answered, his eyes moving once more over her shoulder to meet mine.

That time, I looked away, back to the book on which I could no longer concentrate. I was more upset by the fact I couldn't focus on the story than by the fact Sam was obviously not going to greet me. That, I understood.

It didn't hurt my feelings.

It didn't make me feel.

Oh, but it did, the fact we'd stared each other in the face, both knowing the other, and had said nothing. Not even a casual lift of our fingers, the sort of gesture you'd give to an acquaintance whose face you recalled while their name escaped you. He didn't acknowledge me. I didn't acknowledge him. We pretended we'd never known each other at all, even as we stared and looked away like just looking at each other would burn.

We had danced together, eaten together, gone to the movies. We'd been naked and sweating with each other. I knew the taste of his skin and the way his face looked when he came inside me, and how his hand felt smoothing through my fuck-tangled hair.

We knew all that and still we looked and looked away.

I tried hard to focus on the book, but the words had been spoiled for me. I couldn't read about lovers finding their way into each other's arms. I blinked hard, and the tiny black letters swam viciously on the sea of their white pages, refusing to settle into words I could read.

Melanie came to the table next to drink from her bottled water. She chattered and I answered with a nod and a tight smile. She wriggled on her seat, telling me about the puppet show she was putting on with another girl.

"I have to go to the bathroom. You and Simon stay in the playground. Don't go anywhere." I kept my voice from sounding strangled, though I wasn't sure how.

"Okay," came her cheerful answer, and she headed back into the playground.

In the garish, jungle-painted bathroom, I splashed water on my cheeks again and again, not caring that I washed away my lipstick. I blotted my face with paper towels and stared at my face in the mirror. My cheeks still blushed pink. My eyes were too bright, the gaze bordering on frenzied, and I blinked again and again until I forced my expression into blandness. I wasn't ready to leave the bathroom, but I couldn't forget my responsibility to my niece and nephew, so I pushed through the swinging door into the corridor outside.

He was there.

At the end of the hall I could see the play area, teeming with kids, two of them belonging to me. I saw my table, my book propped unceremoniously against the napkin holder. And, through the plate-glass windows at the front of Mocha Madness, a thin and lovely blond woman holding a little boy by one hand while she stepped off the curb into the parking lot.

For one heavy second we looked at each other before something in me kicked to life and I forced a shiny-bright smile that made my face ache. "Hi."

"Grace. Hi." Sam looked hesitant, but this time he kept his eyes on my face. "How've you been?"

"Fine. Good. You?" The hallway in front of the bathrooms was not the best place for a reunion, but it was the only place we had.

"Good. Great." He nodded.

I had thought pretending we were strangers had been bad, but making each other into nothing was worse. Because even if I was nothing to him, he wasn't nothing to me. My smile melted into a frown, and Sam frowned, too.

"Hey–"

I waved a hand. "Shh."

We stood and stared in the narrow hall stinking of chemicals with the sounds of hyper children echoing all around us. He only had to take one step to put his arm around me in a half hug that brought my face to his shoulder. My body stiff, my eyes closed.

It's the same, I thought as I drew in a deep, deep breath, smelling him. *It's the same as it always was.*

He smelled the same. I felt the same, this close to him, the trickle of his breath caressing my ear and his hand a weight on my back. His knee bumped mine. It was all the same. Everything and nothing. So much to say. So much that couldn't be said, all packaged into the casual bump of a knee against knee and the smell of cologne.

I was the one who pulled away. The embrace had lasted no more than a few seconds, not even long enough for his touch to leave any lasting warmth. I stepped back and sidled past him, toward the main room. He stared after me.

"It was good seeing you," I said. "I've got to get back. Simon and Melanie…"

"Yes. Right, sure. Right." Sam nodded and followed me.

At my table he hesitated again, but I was already settling into my seat and picking up my novel. I looked up at him with a brief, tight smile and then back to the book in my hands, and though he paused for a few moments longer than was necessary, Sam didn't try to get me to look up.

"Good seeing you, Grace."

"Goodbye, Sam."

I didn't look up to watch him go, but I knew when he'd gone all the same.

At my sister's house, Melanie and Simon ran off to the basement to battle each other with the crude plastic swords they'd used their prize tickets for. My sister offered me coffee. I don't know who was more surprised when I burst into tears.

She poured us both cups while I sobbed out the entire story. Sam with the bimbo. How he'd smelled. How it had felt the same as it always had, that brief moment, and how much more I wanted to hate him now, and still couldn't.

She listened without saying anything. The lack of advice was what finally dried my tears. I wiped my face and drank half a mug of now-cold coffee.

"Nothing?" I said.

Hannah shook her head. "Love stinks?"

"Not helpful." I rested my chin in my hand. "I thought I was over it."

She laughed. "You've been moping around for months. If you thought you were over it, you were fooling yourself."

"But...I'm not sad all the time," I protested. "I don't even cry about it anymore! At least, I didn't until today."

"You don't have to be sad to miss someone and wish they were still in your life."

When the kids pounded up the stairs, each bearing a handful of stuffing from a pillow they'd dismembered, I braced myself for a Hannah explosion. Instead, my sister sighed and rolled her eyes, took the stuffing and gave them both pudding cups to take back downstairs. Chocolate pudding cups.

I stared at her until she raised an eyebrow. "What?"

I took a plunge. "He's been good for you."

"Who?" I'd caught her, but she wasn't going to admit it.

"Him. Whoever he is." I poured more coffee from the pot and warmed my hands on the cup, but didn't drink. "I don't judge you, by the way."

My sister laughed. "For what?"

"For what you're doing. I understand. Just be careful, that's all."

Hannah blew out a long breath that ended in another laugh. "You think I'm having an affair."

We both drank coffee while she laughed and I felt stupid. "You're not?"

"No, Grace. God, no." She laughed again and made a face. "I've been going to therapy."

Many replies to this tried to burst out of my mouth, but I held them all back while my sister watched and looked amused.

"Go ahead, say it," she told me. "It's about time?"

"I wasn't going to say that." I'd been thinking it, though.

"It's okay," my sister said. "It's true."

"Does Jerry know?" I studied her again, this time without the assumption that lust had changed her. She still looked different. My perception of her reasons for changing were different, but that was all.

Hannah shrugged. "He does now. He didn't at first. It's made a big difference, though."

"I can tell." I watched her tidy the sugar packets in their small basket on the table. She hadn't been replaced by a pod person, after all.

"Maybe you should call him, Grace."

I blinked in surprise. "Your therapist?"

"No, dork. Sam."

"Right. Sam."

"Just call him," my sister said.

But I couldn't. Turns out, I didn't have to. Sam called me at his usual time of half-past ass-crack o'thirty. I swam up from sleep with a thick tongue that stumbled on the syllables of "hello."

"Grace?"

"Timezit?" The bright blue screen of my phone pierced my eyelids but faded after ten seconds and put me back into darkness.

"You don't want me to tell you."

"No, I don't. Hi, Sam."

"Are you going to hang up on me?"

I thought for a second. "I don't think so."

Sleep was fading. I couldn't decide if I wanted to cling to it, or just face the fact this was going to be another one of those nights. I pulled the covers up higher on my neck.

"Good."

"Are you drunk?" I asked.

"No. Not at all. Do I have to be drunk to call you at–"

I coughed. "Ah, ah. Don't tell me."

"I'm not drunk. I promise. I haven't been in more than a month."

I believed him. "I miss you, Sam."

"If I knocked, would you open the door?"

My eyes had started fluttering open, but when he said that, I sat straight up in bed. My heart pounded. I almost dropped the cell phone but juggled it back against my ear as I swung my legs over the side of the bed.

"Why don't you try and find out?"

Five steps took me out of the bedroom. Another six to the kitchen. I waited, sleep gone, my insides bouncing.

He knocked.

I tossed the cell phone to the kitchen table and yanked aside the shelving. Boxes of pasta and some pots clattered to the floor, but I ignored them. I fumbled with the locks and cursed, but in another minute had the door open.

Sam.

"I didn't want to scare you," he said into the phone still held at his ear, though he was looking right at me.

"Come here," I ordered, but didn't wait for him to obey before I went to him.

His mouth tasted the same. So did his skin. He felt the same, too, under my palms as I slid them up his chest to take his face in my hands. When he put his arms around me, I was ready to jump, and he caught me.

Long legs, smoothly bunching muscles, a hint of stubble. His stubborn belt buckle and the layers of his shirts. Sleek, dark, feathery spiked hair. These were not new to me, either. Time hadn't made him once again a stranger.

He carried me to the bedroom, where we fell onto my bed. I waited, breathless, for it to break, but the old wood creaked in greeting as Sam covered me with his body and his kisses.

Naked, we couldn't get enough of each other. He kissed me from the arches of my feet to my earlobes, and when it was my turn, I paid extra attention to the places I'd missed most. The backs of his knees and insides of his elbows. The dip next to each hipbone. The bulge of his shoulder blades.

When Sam finally slid inside me, we both sighed. No fancy tricks this time. No kinky positions, no toys. Nothing but him and me.

We made love slowly, each thrust building the pressure until I came saying his name. A moment later, Sam murmured mine into my ear and shuddered. His hair tickled my cheeks when he buried his face into my shoulder. I stroked my hands down his back until he rolled off me, and then I pulled the blankets up over us both.

"Do I get a discount for repeat business?" I asked him sleepily.

"Fuck you, Grace," Sam said fondly.

"So soon?" I tweaked one of his nipples, and he wiggled satisfactorily.

"Don't we have to talk about stuff?" he asked.

"Talking's your thing, dude," I murmured, already dozing. "Save it for the morning, 'kay?"

Sam turned to spoon against me from behind. "I still love you."

"I know you do." I smiled. "You'll love me in the morning, too. Go to sleep."

But Sam wouldn't sleep. "I'm sorry."

I turned to face him. I loved the way he looked with moonlight painting the stubble on his cheeks. "Have you come back to me, or are you just here for an old-time's-sake fuck?"

He kissed me so hard my lips bruised. "I'm back. Don't ask about the music now. I'll tell you later."

"Okay." I stroked his hair, then his face, and breathed in the warm, male scent of him. My knee nudged up between his and even though we'd only finished making love a short time before, he stirred against me.

"Do you still not want a boyfriend?"

"Depends on who he is, Sam." I kissed the little divot in his throat.

"Me, Grace. I'm asking if you want me."

"You're really determined to talk about this now."

Even my yawn didn't deter him. "Yes."

"Oh, Sam," I said. "Yes. I do. Can we go to sleep now?"

He gave me another five minutes, just long enough for me to doze again, before he spoke. "Do you forgive me?"

"I never blamed you," I said. "Things happen. You taught me something."

"It wasn't that trick you do with your tongue," Sam said. "You already knew that when I met you."

I laughed. "Not that. I learned that I didn't want to live without you, but that I could."

"I'm not so sure that's a good thing." Sam kissed me again.

"It's a good thing. A very good thing. Because before you, I was so afraid of being unable to live without someone, I could never live with someone."

At three in the morning, things are easier to say and understand even when they don't make as much sense. Sam knew this because he was a master at middle-of-the-night philosophy. His arms pulled me tighter against him, and for once, he was silent.

"Go to sleep," I told him, and I think he did.

There'd be time later for talking. For listening. Time to negotiate. When daylight came, I might even be angry with him again, but that would be all right, too, because no matter what happened, I knew I wouldn't regret this moment, now. Sam had told me, *One must have sorrow to truly appreciate joy.*

For the first time ever, it seemed like a fair trade.

* * * * *

ABOUT THE AUTHOR

Megan Hart is the acclaimed author of over thirty erotic novels and novellas, including *Dirty, Broken,* and the best-selling *Tempted.* Megan lives in the deep dark woods of Pennsylvania with her husband and two children, and is currently working on her next novel for Spice.

You can contact Megan through her Web site at: www.meganhart.com.

ACKNOWLEDGEMENTS

Special thanks to Steve Kreamer of Kreamer Funeral Home in Annville, Pennsylvania, for coming in to my high school class and making me think about the funeral director business as a career. And thanks as well for the time spent years later helping me understand just what it's really like. Anything I got right is because of him—anything I got wrong I messed up all on my own.

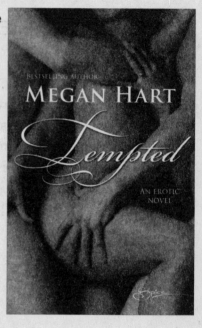

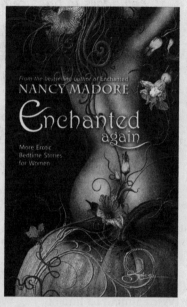

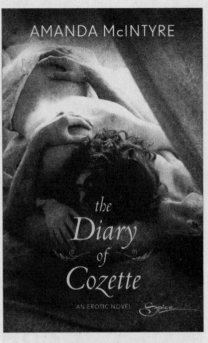